GRAMERCY PARK

GRAMERCY PARK

PAULA COHEN

St. Martin's Press

New York

www.stmartins.com

ISBN 0-312-27552-8

First Edition: February 2002

10 9 8 7 6 5 4 3 2 1

For my mother,
EDNA RAE GOLDMAN;
always loving, always loved, always with me

Acknowledgments

I owe many thanks to Donald T. Rave, Esq., for his invaluable assistance in the matter of wills and trusts, and to my dear friend Susan E. B. Dahlinger, for her knowledge of matters Catholic. Any mistakes that may be found in this book on either topic are the result of my misunderstanding their very excellent information.

Thanks are also due to Elizabeth Ayres, an extraordinary poet, teacher, and confidence builder, who read the manuscript in its early infancy and gave me my first jolt of hope. She also introduced me to an audience to read it to, chapter by chapter, over the years. That audience is, of course, my writing group: still going strong, still an inspiration. I never could have done it without all of you.

I will be forever grateful to Meredith Bernstein, my agent, and Jennifer Enderlin, my editor at St. Martin's Press. They took a chance on a first-timer and made a dream come unbelievably true. I wish every writer such staunch and knowledgeable advisers and allies.

A special thank you goes to Ava Pennington—friend, alter ego, number-one fan, kindred spirit, and reality check—who always understood what I was trying to say, always asked the right questions, and always made success seem real and possible, long before it was either. She knows that faith can move mountains; hers in me is a very great part of why she can hold this book in her hand today.

Last on the page but first in my life . . . thanks to my husband, Roger Cohen, best friend and absolute center of my world, for having patience with a wife living in two centuries at once. His great love of books, his intelligence and clear thinking, his gift for calm, honest, and fair criticism, and his unwavering encouragement have been priceless to me. But most of all . . . he makes me laugh.

BOOK I

Mario

Prologue

DEATH IS A GOOD TOPIC for conversation. The fascination with it seems ingrained in human beings, and there are few acts performed during the lives of most people that are so endlessly discussed, so lovingly dissected, as the act of leaving it. A natural modesty seals the lips of even the most talkative when procreation or birth are mentioned, and the intimate details of marriage, child-rearing, and family life are, at best, confided to one's closest friends.

But death is different. The last, lingering illness and all of its symptoms are picked over with morbid glee; and the greater the suffering, the longer the illness, the uglier the end, the more the head-wagging preoccupation with it.

The passing, therefore, of an elderly gentleman, dying quietly in his bed, would normally elicit little discussion. It is a fact, however, that there is one topic upon which people love to dwell even more than death. That topic is money. Should the elderly gentleman have been rich, therefore, the heads would wag with no less vigor, but the solemn preoccupation would be with the size of the fortune, the way in which it was amassed, and (most important of all) how—and to whom—it would be bequeathed.

Such was the case in the passing of Henry Ogden Slade—financier, philanthropist, pillar of the community—in the late winter of 1894. Sixty-six at the time of his death, Slade had been known in many circles of New York society as an upright and God-fearing, though slightly peculiar, man. That he was upright was proved by the exemplary lack of scandal surrounding his business dealings, all of which were large, lucrative, and accomplished with unusual ease and goodwill. That he was God-fearing was proved by his success. That he was peculiar was attested to by the presence in his house of a ward—a young woman taken in by Slade at the age of fifteen, and reared and educated, for the four years until his death, as his own daughter.

What made this rather ordinary situation unusual enough to earn Slade a reputation for peculiarity were three facts. Fact one: Henry Ogden Slade was a bachelor who had lived alone for more than forty years. Fact two: Clara (for that was the young ward's name) was neither related to Slade nor the orphaned, penniless child of friends of his youth. Fact three: her father, reputedly still living and quite prosperous, was a German immigrant who was, also reputedly, of the Hebrew faith.

All this, of course, was enough to fuel sporadic fires of conversation for years within New York society, for yet another example of the man's eccentricity was the extreme secrecy with which he shrouded his domestic affairs. Few people had ever actually met Clara, as Slade kept her carefully cloistered within his house at Gramercy Park; and those who had, mainly elderly men like himself, come to discuss weighty matters of business over dinner, were frankly unable to say much about the girl, other than that she was tiny, pretty (in a rather Semitic way—dark, and all eyes, with an air of melancholy), and had a positive genius for vanishing silently at the tread of strangers' feet, and the sound of strangers' voices.

Slade's reasons for taking her in, therefore, remained a mystery. All that was definitely known was that he and the girl's father, one Reuben Adler, had had financial dealings, and that in the summer of eighty-nine they had met at Adler's home on the south Jersey shore, to discuss business away from the stupefying city heat. There he had been introduced to Clara. Three months later, shortly after her fifteenth birthday, Clara had moved permanently into Slade's home.

Perhaps it was felt that the young Miss Adler would benefit from being in the great metropolis, where she could regularly attend the opera, ballet, concerts, and the theatre, and where she would have the opportunity to meet people from a wide spectrum of acceptable society. Perhaps Slade, who should have known better, neglected to tell both the girl and her family the brutal fact that her ancestry would bar her from the company of that acceptable society, regardless of the identity of her sponsor. Or perhaps he did tell her, at some later date, for society was never once disturbed by having to refuse the discreetly dropped suggestion that Slade's ward desired an invitation to tea, or wished to pay a call. Instead, Clara had spent the four years with Slade in nearly total seclusion, and her appearances at the ballet or opera were memorable simply because they were so rare.

Like Halley's comet, vast stretches of time seemed to pass between her being seen; unlike that heavenly apparition, however, Clara's appearances followed no fixed schedule. It was their very unpredictability, in fact—and her forever downcast eyes, and the way she would cling to Slade's arm as if terrified of being swept away and drowned in the glittering crowds—that caused the performances on the stage to be all but forgotten in the endless, whispered speculation about her.

"Out of sight, out of mind," however, has become a proverb precisely because it is true. During those long stretches in which Slade's box at the opera house sat empty, New York turned its collective mind to other, more immediate—if less exotic—matters, and the mystery of Miss Adler, and her reasons for being where she was, lay dormant.

Until that terrible night in February of 1894.

According to the information gleaned from the servants, Miss Adler had been awakened, in the small hours of the morning, by cries from the dying Slade's room. She had rushed across the passageway and arrived just in time to see his eyes glaze over. Her screams had awakened the rest of the household, and a footman had been dispatched to summon the doctor.

One horror had followed another. The worst blizzard of a bad winter had delayed the doctor; and when he finally arrived, breathless and soaking wet, Slade had already been dead for close to an hour. There was nothing to be done for the deceased but to close his eyes, fold his arms, and pull the sheet up over his face. The girl, however, had not left the dead man's side since entering his room, but had sat holding his hand in her own. That hand had been warm when she had taken it; by the time the doctor pried it from her frantic fingers, it was growing cold and beginning to stiffen.

The combined strength of the doctor and the girl's maid were needed to get her back to her own room. She had fought them wildly in her efforts to stay with her guardian, seemingly unwilling, or unable, to believe that he was truly dead. Even after they forced her to lie down, and a sedative had been administered, she continued to cry. What had been most terrible, however, and a sure sign that her mind had become unbalanced, were the fits of laughter that had alternated with her tears. The doctor, being a prudent man, had stayed with her until she fell asleep, and had kept her heavily sedated for the next few days. He had also refused to allow her to attend the funeral.

Thus was New York cheated of seeing, up close and lacking the shield of her guardian's protective arm, the little Jewess who was expected to inherit all of her guardian's very great fortune.

So affected was she, in fact, by Slade's passing, that the reading of the will had to be postponed for a full month, there being genuine concern about her health. It was not until late March, therefore, on a gray and chilly morning, that the lawyers, led by one Thaddeus Chadwick, Esq., the late Mr. Slade's personal attorney and oldest friend, had appeared in Mr. Slade's library to unseal and read his final intentions, and to announce to the waiting ears of New York the advent of an heiress—the city's newest, and possibly one of the richest, if rumors about the size of the Slade estate were to be believed.

Clara entered the room last of all. Still six months shy of her twentieth birthday, she was not yet fully recovered from the shock of her guardian's death, and her skin had an unhealthy, chalk-white pallor made even whiter by the severity of her black dress and dark hair. That within minutes she might be one of the world's wealthiest women seemed incongruous, at best; there was simply nothing about her that could serve to explain Slade's interest in her. Certainly, there was nothing evident that morning, as she slipped quietly into her chair. She looked as plain and as ordinary as a shop girl, with her small, pinched face and nervous, nail-bitten hands. Only her enormous eyes, bright with unshed tears, lifted her from the realm of the commonplace.

Immediately after her arrival, the library doors were closed, shutting off the proceedings from the eyes of the servants who lingered nearby, finding more to do in the vicinity than could possibly be accounted for by their usual round of morning duties. For twenty minutes the only sound to reach their ears was the dry hum of Chadwick's voice from behind the huge ebony doors. Then, suddenly, in the expectant hush there was another sound; a sound so out of place, so inappropriate in that house of mourning, that the hovering servants stared at one another, shocked, and one Irish housemaid, more devout than the rest, made the sign of the cross.

Laughter. Girlish laughter, which did not remain girlish long. Low at first, and musical, it rose swiftly, becoming high and strident: peal after sobbing peal of mirthless, helpless, hysterical laughter.

The heavy doors banged back; Chadwick and his colleagues, ashen-faced, hurried from the room. Within the library, tiny, shy, quiet Clara Adler sat and rocked, tears streaming down her face, laughing the laugh of a demented thing.

Once more a servant was sent flying for the doctor; once more the sedatives were administered. The lawyers went away shaking their heads, and the servants scattered to their separate duties, to whisper what they had seen and heard into the ears of fellow servants in other houses. By the next day all of New York knew that Slade's ward had been struck down, and knew, too, what had caused it.

What many could not understand, however, was the laughter. Tears, perhaps, but never laughter. Clara Adler, taken in by Henry Ogden Slade at the tender age of fifteen, and reared and educated as his daughter for the four years until his death, had been dispossessed, utterly and completely. Her name had not even been mentioned in his will. It was as if she had never existed.

Still, there was nothing funny—nothing funny at all—about losing thirty million dollars.

. . .

DEATH IS A GOOD TOPIC for conversation, and never better than when money is involved. The last, lingering illness, and all of it torments, are picked over with morbid glee; and the greater the suffering—the younger the victim—the more the head-wagging preoccupation with it.

The passing, therefore, of a young and innocent girl would elicit much discussion, in voices hushed and solemn, about life's vicissitudes and the sudden, inexplicable workings of Fate. Should the girl be one about whom hung an air of mystery, and who had not even the consolation of the Christian faith to sustain her in her final hours, the pious platitudes would rain thick and fast, reminding all that even in the midst of life we are in death.

So New York listened for word of the end of Clara Adler, struck down by brain fever at the age of nineteen, in the spring of 1894, the fever brought on by the twin shocks of the loss of her guardian and his estate. The hysteria with which she had greeted the news of the latter had been the onset of her illness. She was not expected to recover.

It was all very sad—and very satisfactory—and the city settled in, with melancholy anticipation, to await her passing. It was no more than what any truly well bred young woman would have done in her place; and certainly there was nothing else for her, with propriety, to do. The only problem, as the days became weeks and the weeks became months, was that she did not do it . . .

Chapter One

From Fifth Avenue, with its gleaming carriages and fine, new mansions, and its smell of money only lately won and not yet fully grasped by the minds of its makers, it is merely a healthy stretch of the leg to Gramercy Park.

There, enclosed on four sides by a high, iron fence, a small oasis beckons the passerby: a graceful green rectangle of shady paths and wide, low benches scattered beneath trees thick with years. It is an odd sight: nature penned in amid a forest of brick and stone, and the innocent stranger might be tempted to pass through the black-barred gate, to spend a quiet hour in contemplation of such a wonder. But the gate is locked, and only the privileged few who live on the borders of the little park possess the key that will open it.

Life appears to be sweet for these keepers of the keys of this tiny Eden, and drudgery is evidently not their daily portion. On warm summer afternoons, one can see nursemaids wheeling the infant lords and ladies of the great Republic along the dappled paths, and spy daintily clad children at play beneath the gaze of vigilant nannies.

But the vulgarly obvious wealth of Fifth Avenue is missing here; these houses, for the most part, are vestiges of an earlier day. Red brick and white stone, they stand side by side with not even a handbreadth of space between them, forming a solid square of dignity, and those who dwell within them have no need of pomp to proclaim their worth to casual passersby. Like their houses, their wealth and power were built in bygone days, and possessing them has become a part of the natural order of things, occasioning no more thought than, say, breathing or sleeping. *They* know what they have, and that is all that matters.

Near the southeastern corner of this demiparadise stands one house different from the rest. Built of drab red brick in a dull, square shape, its front door is the only one which does not face the park, but opens, instead, onto one of the small, cobbled streets that radiate from the green like the spokes of an angular wheel, as if to declare itself even less guilty of ostentation than its neighbors by virtue of its refusal to acknowledge the center of their common universe.

Somber and self-contained, with windows too narrow for the expanse of wall between them, it is a house which does not welcome: a massive, reclusive, indifferent pile of stone, which holds what it has within it, and takes no notice of anything else.

Of the two men approaching it from the direction of Fifth Avenue on this particular afternoon in late May, the house is wholly oblivious, although the many people enjoying the brilliant spring sunshine in and about the little park do not share this disregard.

The men present an interesting contrast in types, for one of them, a pale man of medium build and middle age, is outstanding only in that he is so very ordinary. His companion, however, seems to be the focus of every eye as he passes—women, particularly, seem to find him of uncommon interest—and this fascination could be laid to his height, which is well over six feet, or the exceptional breadth of his chest and shoulders, or even to the cut of his impeccable clothing. About forty years of age, black-eyed and swarthy, he is clean-shaven and well made, and he draws eyes like a magnet, seeming not so much unaware of the glances cast his way as accustomed to receiving them; a man very much at ease beneath the gaze of others.

"I am grateful for your time, Signor Alfieri," the nondescript man says to his dark companion as they draw near to their destination. "I will waste none of it, for I know that you must have a great deal to do."

"On the contrary, Mr. Upton"—Signor Alfieri's heavily accented English fully corroborates his foreign looks and name—"for the first time in years I am completely free and have absolutely nothing to do, at least until the middle of July. Until then, my time is my own."

"And will you be in New York until then?"

"Until then and after then. I must be in Philadelphia from mid-July to early October. After that I will return here."

"For the opera season."

"For the opera season," the signore agrees, smiling.

"And you have been staying at the Fifth Avenue Hotel since your arrival?"

"A week ago, yes. Originally, I had thought to make the hotel my home while in New York."

"A year is a long time to live in a hotel, signore."

"Ah, you see, Mr. Upton? Mr. Grau agrees with you, which is why he sent you to me. And because it would not be right for me to refuse the kind suggestion of the general manager of the Metropolitan Opera House, I am here with you. Also, both Mr. Grau and I feel that my continued presence at the hotel might disturb the other guests—"

"Your consideration does you credit, signore."

"—and I am absolutely confident that before long the other guests certainly would disturb me." His smile is amiable. "That has a miserably ungrateful sound, does it not? Nevertheless, you can have no idea of what it is to be pursued everywhere by admirers who have heard you perform. I am afraid, Mr. Upton, that privacy has become a necessity for me."

Being a house agent, Mr. Upton is both sympathetic and quick to take professional advantage of this opening. "You needn't fear being disturbed here, sir, I assure you," he says. "And as for disturbing others, such a thing would be quite impossible. The late Mr. Slade's house is admirably well built and wonderfully spacious, with absolutely every-thing Mr. Grau said you would require. Most important, of course, is the music room, which contains a superb grand piano, and even a small eighteenth-century pipe organ, which Mr. Slade had brought over from Germany and built into the walls.

"In addition," he says, counting on his gloved fingers, "there are a reception room, two drawing rooms, a library, a picture gallery, a ballroom, a conservatory, and a billiards room. The dining room seats twenty comfortably. And, of course, there are the ten bedrooms. The late Mr. Slade lived on quite a lavish scale in his younger days."

Alfieri smiles. "So I see, Mr. Upton. But," he says, gazing up at the long rows of curtained windows, "perhaps this house is somewhat . . . too spacious for my needs? Along with everything else Mr. Grau told you, he must also have told you that I am only an unmarried man, after all, traveling with only one servant. What on earth am I to do with two drawing rooms, a dining room that seats twenty—comfortably or not— and a ballroom?"

"Ah, but you must remember, signore, it was Mr. Grau who suggested that I show you this house. He feels that the music room will appeal to you particularly. And as for its being too spacious, the late Mr. Slade was unmarried too . . . although, quite frankly," he adds confidentially, "I cannot ever recall hearing that he made much use of the public rooms in his later years."

"Or of the ten bedrooms."

"Or of the ten bedrooms," Upton agrees. "Much of the house was shut up a great deal of the time," he says, fitting the key into the lock and struggling with the stiff mechanism, "which accounts for the marvelous condition in which everything has been left."

"Indeed. Was Mr. Slade a recluse, Mr. Upton?"

"I'm sure I couldn't say, signore. I never had the honor of meeting him. It is known, however, that he kept more and more to himself as he grew older."

"Indeed," Alfieri says again. "Perhaps he, too, found people disturbing."

"Perhaps, sir. Anything is possible." Upton pulls the key from the lock, reads the paper label pasted on it, smiles apologetically, returns it to the lock and continues his efforts.

"And just when did Mr. Slade die, Mr. Upton?"

"Just this past winter, signore, very suddenly."

"Had he no heirs? Was there no one to inherit this admirable house?"

The house agent is momentarily silent as he searches for the right words. "Mr. Slade died a bachelor, signore, and left no heirs." He hesitates slightly. "He grew somewhat eccentric in his last years. There were a number of bequests, of course, most of them to charitable organizations, but the great bulk of his personal fortune, and this house, were left to his estate. His attorneys wish to keep the house intact and furnished as it was during his occupancy until such time as they see fit to sell it, which they are in no hurry do to. That is why it is available for lease. According to the executors, to keep a staff on to maintain an empty house would be a drain on Mr. Slade's estate."

"Really? Did he die impoverished?"

"Oh, very far from it, signore. But the executors, who have retained me to show the house, feel that it is not their place to spend Mr. Slade's money if it can be avoided, even if it is for the upkeep of his own house. However, if they *lease* the house, the rental income will defray the cost of keeping it up."

"That is very sensible, Mr. Upton. Now if only we can get in, so that I may see with my own eyes this house with ten bedrooms that one man inhabited." The signore smiles. "You know, Mr. Upton, I fear you will never make a successful burglar."

As if in answer to his words, there is a sudden click, and the key turns in the house agent's hand. "Ah! That does it! Not a burglar!" he laughs. "That's very good! Come in, Signor Alfieri, come in."

The two men step through a vestibule into a cavernous entrance hall. Upton shuts the door behind them, leaving them momentarily blinded. What light there is comes from distant rooms, and is filtered through drawn curtains. Yet, even to eyes not adjusted to the sudden dark, the floor, walls, and ceiling, marble all, glisten in the dimness. Huge archways, flanked by onyx pillars, lead off left and right, and on the far side of a gleaming expanse of floor an alabaster staircase soars palely up, to disappear into the twilight.

Upton slides his hand along the wall until his fingers come into contact with a recessed button, which he pushes. The sound of a click in the darkness is the only response.

"Mr. Slade was one of the first to install an electrical system in his house," he says, "but it has evidently been turned off for safety's sake. Shall we move on? We can open the curtains in the other rooms."

The house agent's voice is low, out of respect for whatever lurks just beyond the borders of hearing in silent, shut-up houses, but even so it fills the air with rustling echoes. Alfieri follows him through the doorway on the left, into the first of the house's two drawing rooms, a chamber so vast that its far end is barely visible in the half-light. The furniture, in muslin shrouds, looks humped and unnatural; what can be seen of it is in a style current twenty years ago. Upton pulls aside the heavy drapery, and colors—ivory woodwork limned in gold, dadoes and friezes of Pompeian red—leap from the walls, only to retreat again into shades of gray as the curtain falls back into place.

Two massive sliding doors lead from there into the library and the adjacent picture gallery. Upton pulls aside a crimson plush curtain, revealing walls covered in gold and green silk above ebony bookcases filled with rare volumes. A pair of slender marble columns frames the entrance to the picture gallery. The works of art are gone from their places; they rest, instead, on the floor, carefully swathed in muslin and ranged against the sides of the chamber. Lighter patches on the silk walls show where they were accustomed to hang.

"Would you care to see more, signore?"

The signore does not answer. He stands in the center of the darkened room, a vaguely distracted expression on his face, as if trying to recall something that remains just out of reach of his memory.

"Signore?"

Alfieri rouses. "Yes, I would care to see more, Mr. Upton, but some light to see it by would be most welcome."

"Then allow me to leave you for a few moments to find the footman—I know he must be around somewhere. There is a private generator, and if he can turn it on we shall have the whole place as bright as day. Don't wait for me, signore. Feel free to explore more of the house while I'm gone, if you'd like. I'll find you, never fear."

But fear is not what Alfieri feels. The great house holds no terrors for him, despite the darkness; there is a sense, instead, of something almost remembered, like an old, familiar melody, just beyond hearing, that he cannot place.

With Upton gone in search of the generator, Alfieri retraces his steps to the front hall. The music room has been on his mind since Upton's first mention of it, and he is understandably eager to see it. Florentine by birth, the son of a physician, his great gift had become evident at the age of four, when, seating himself at the piano, he had played, flawlessly, three exercises from *The Well-tempered Clavier*, learned solely from listening to the efforts of his mother, a talented amateur who was accustomed to practice the piano while her little son amused himself with his toys in the corner of the parlor. His lessons had begun immediately, and, when he was old enough, singing in his church choir had augmented his other musical studies.

When he was fourteen his voice changed.

For no reason which, in later years, he is ever able to explain, except that this is the right way, he climbs the alabaster stairs to the floor above. The darkness here is almost total, for the walls are no longer pale marble, reflecting whatever faint light may exist, but smooth wood, or so his fingers tell him; and all the doors on either side of the broad landing are shut.

He has never been in this house before today. For that matter, until one week ago he has never been in this city, or on this continent. And yet he gropes his way directly to the second door on the left, and enters. This room, too, is enormous and very dim, its drapes drawn against the glory of the spring noon. But after the oppressive darkness he has just left, his eyes easily take in his surroundings.

The music room.

Here, again, the ubiquitous muslin shrouds the furniture, and the many-armed and -globed chandelier, swathed in netting, blooms downward from the high, coved ceiling like a monstrous wasps' nest. The pale Aubusson carpet, however, still covers the floor, and deadens his footsteps as he crosses to the grand piano between the windows, dropping his hat on a table as he goes. He seats himself at the instrument, raises the cover of the keyboard, and plays a few exploratory chords. The piano's keys are stiff, at first, and the sound tentative, as a voice would be that had not been used in a great while, but it mellows and grows full and sonorous as he continues to play.

After a few minutes, he begins to sing. *"Una furtiva lagrima negl'occhi suoi spuntò . . ."* Sweet and beautiful: Donizetti's Nemorino, telling of his beloved, and the secret tear that spills from her eye . . .

Downstairs, at the back of the house, Upton stands by the generator, listening to the distant music, and he gapes, just a little. He is a house agent, not a poet, and not particularly gifted with words. He would not be able to describe the sound of the voice he is hearing if someone were to ask him. But others have described it for him.

It is honey, and cream, and gold. It is dark velvet and sunlight. It is incomparable. For as long as it lasts, Upton stands immobile, forgetting time, forgetting his work, forgetting everything but the sound of that voice. When it stops, finally, he stands dazed, and sighs as the everyday world settles around him once more; and as he bends to help the footman, there are tears in his eyes.

Chapter Two

Alfieri knows nothing of Upton's tears, nor would he care greatly if he did. Twenty years of singing before audiences all across Europe have accustomed him to that phenomenon, and left him largely indifferent to the power he has to make men weep. Audiences themselves are of negligible importance; they provide an excuse for him to sing, and enable him to spend his life doing what he desires by rewarding him prodigiously well for it, but they are not the reason he sings.

They are, however, the reason he is here. Paris has named him "Le Rossignol," the nightingale; London knows him as "the Lord of Song"; to all of Italy he is "Maestro Orfeo." His fame has become such that walking unmolested in the street—any street, in any city in Europe which boasts an opera house, and in many which do not—has become a near impossibility for him. He has left Europe to regain, for a while at least, his own soul; and Upton's tears, did he but know of them, would be of infinitely less moment to him than what he will have for dinner.

Rising at last from the piano, more satisfied with the sound of his voice than he has been in months, he flings the curtains wide, noting with approval that the room faces onto Gramercy Park itself. The trees dance in the May wind, beckoning and abundantly green, and he unfastens the latch on one of the tall French windows and pushes the double panes outward. The fresh air, rushing into the long shut-up room, smells the color of the leaves, and all but sparkles in its clarity.

He breathes it in deeply, hands resting on either side of the window, idly watching a couple walk arm in arm in the park while two small girls chase each other in and out of the trees, and he suddenly realizes that he is happy—truly happy—with the sheer, effervescent happiness of youth; happier, in this house, than he has been in years. The very walls seem to greet him kindly, and to embrace him, as if they have been waiting for him for a long, long time.

No one lies in wait for him here, just outside the door. No one clamors for him, clutches at him, prays to him, leaves gifts for him, or flowers, or notes. If he must be lonely—God!—then let him be alone. He has not known such relief as this, such lightness of heart, for twenty years. He can be solitary in this house, and happy, the vast walls around him forming an impenetrable shell. Until he returns to Europe, he will revel in this solitude, wallow in it, free of hangers-on, of the endless crush of people that surrounds him always: smiling, weeping, fawning; ready to sell themselves at a moment's notice, to trade their husbands or wives, sons or daughters for the slightest hint of stature, power, influence, fame . . . eager to suck the very breath from his lungs, or the soul from his body if he will only let them . . .

The breeze blows, cooling his face again, carrying music with it from the other side of the park . . . the raucous, lighthearted sound of a hurdy-gurdy, drifting on the air. He listens . . . *"Libiam',"* it pulses, *"ne' dolci fremiti, che suscita l'amore . . ."* the brilliant *brindisi* in waltz time from *La Traviata.* "Let's drink to love's sweet tremors," it says, "to those eyes that pierce the heart . . ."

Verdi, wafting in from a New York street . . . the melody a reply to his own music at the piano. He is not one to ignore omens: the welcoming house and its grateful solitude, the sense of remembering what he cannot possibly know, his discovery of the music room, the arias, statement and answer: it all means a successful stay in America. He needs to see no more . . . he and the house have clearly chosen each other, and his possession of it will begin, appropriately, here. With both hands he seizes the sheet which drapes the piano, snatches it off and tosses it to the floor, then moves on, stripping the cover from each chair and table in his progress around the room.

The open window does not illumine the farthest corners, which remain lost in shadow, but Alfieri does not even notice; his mind is too full of his newfound elation, and his own momentum carries him along with no slackening of pace until, turning to wrest the cover from an armchair backed against a distant wall, he stops with a quick intake of breath.

Something—someone—is curled within it.

Except for Upton, somewhere in the bowels of the house, he should be completely alone, and so for several heartbeats he only stares in disbelieving silence. The figure does not vanish from beneath his gaze; it merely huddles deeper into the cushions, moving Alfieri to confirm the evidence of his eyes. As he stretches out his hand to touch what he knows cannot be there, the figure puts its hand out to ward off his, and Alfieri finds himself grasping the fingers of . . .

A child. A little, pale, sad-eyed child clothed in black, more like the ghost of a child than a living one . . . except that its fingers are real, small and very cold, and the nails are ragged and bitten. The child raises its head—her head—and meets his eyes for one moment only, then looks away.

It is long enough.

Her face glimmers white in the gloom, and he can see the marks of illness plain upon it. A hint of freckles once dusted her cheeks; they have faded now, with the rest of her, and the blue hollows beneath her eyes look like old, old bruises. The eyes themselves, gray-green and very clear, are even older: windows onto some ancient, bottomless grief; haunting, in the face of a child.

His own joy of a moment ago is dwarfed by the magnitude of this pain. He covers her hand with his own, speechless in the presence of such sorrow, and raises it to his lips.

The shadowy room, the silent house, the young girl with her old eyes: there is a dreamlike quality to them all, as if Alfieri has stepped out of the stream of time into a moment which has been there always, waiting for him, and which he has always known would come. He will never entirely leave it again; for the rest of his life a part of him will be there still, in the dusky room, at the instant she raises her eyes, with his lips against her hand.

The moment passes; the child lowers her eyes, her hand slips from his; the spell is broken. Time takes up where it had left off: the wind stirs the curtains, the sound of a passing carriage rises from the street below. Nothing has happened at all, except that Alfieri's life has changed forever, and that he knows it.

"Who are you?" he says, when he can speak again. "How did you come here?"

"I live here." She speaks with her head down, and directs her words to the fingers clenched in her lap.

"Here? But this is an empty house."

"It's not empty. I live here."

"With the furniture all covered over and no light? How do you live in this place? Are you alone?"

"Two of the servants have stayed on. There are candles for the evening." Her words, almost inaudible, are disjointed and utterly incomprehensible to him. "Don't look at me, please. Just let me go away again. This is the closed part of the house, and I mustn't be found here. I was walking for my exercise, but I became tired and fell asleep. The music woke me."

"You are not one of the servants. That is not possible."

The wan cheeks flush an imperceptible pink as she draws herself up in the depths of the chair and lifts her chin for the first time. "This is my guardian's house."

"Truly? I was told that the owner of this house had died."

The momentary bravado fades; she droops again and her small voice falters. "He did. But he was still my guardian."

He looks at her bowed head. "My dear, I am so sorry. I was not thinking . . ." She does not move.

"What is your name?" he says gently.

"Clara. Clara Adler," is the whispered reply.

"Then, Miss Adler, as there is no one to introduce us properly, please allow me to introduce myself. I am Mario Alfieri."

"How do you do, Mr. Alfieri."

"Well, thank you. Very well. And how do you do, Miss Adler?"

"Better," she says. "I am better, now. I have been ill." Her own words suddenly recall her to herself. "Oh, but you mustn't look at me," she says, shrinking further into her chair.

"Why?"

"My hair . . ." At her words he realizes, with a small jolt, that it has been cut pitifully close, like a boy's. Unable to hide the disgrace of her shorn head with her hands, she covers her face, instead. "Please don't look at me."

"And if I told you," he says, "that until this very minute, when you brought it to my attention, I had not noticed your hair, would you believe me?" He touches her sleeve. "I promise you it is true."

"How can that be?" she says through her hands. "I am so ugly."

"Not ugly. Never ugly. Only recovering from an illness. Your hair will grow back."

"Not for years."

He laughs. "Do you wish to know why I did not notice your hair? I was looking too much at your lovely eyes."

She lowers her hands. Those eyes are spilling slow tears, which she wipes with the handkerchief he offers her. "I am sorry," she says. "Please don't think badly of me."

"Badly? Of you?" He shakes his head. "You are still weak and you have had a shock, which is my fault. I do not wonder at those tears. Are you strong enough to return to . . . where do you live in this great house?"

"My rooms are on the next floor. I will be all right. I am stronger than I look."

"The stairs will not be too much for you? Let me help you."

He takes her hand again and helps her to rise. Her head, with its ragged, dark curls, reaches no higher than the middle of his chest.

"You needn't," she says. "I can get there by myself."

"No gentleman," he replies, "would ever permit a lady of his acquaintance to return home unescorted. Now that we have been introduced, I must see you safely home."

They climb the stairs together, stopping every four or five steps to allow her to catch her breath and rest.

"You are so kind," she says. "I hope it didn't frighten you too much to find me there."

"Oh, after the initial shock I bore up quite well. I must admit that, at the very first instant, I did think that I had stumbled upon a ghost—which would have been most interesting, for I do not believe in them—and for a few moments I thought that I would have to rethink all my most deeply held philosophies. But it is you who are truly brave. To wake and find a total stranger in your house, tearing the covers from the furniture? How I must have frightened you!"

"No," she says. "I heard you singing. I knew you wouldn't hurt me."

When they reach their destination, Alfieri opens the door for her and stands aside to let her pass.

She hesitates, not knowing what etiquette might demand in such a situation. To remain alone with a stranger cannot be proper; but he has been so kind that, surely, it would be terribly rude simply to send him away. "Would you like to come in?" she says shyly. "Perhaps you would like a cup of tea?"

Alfieri loathes tea. A true son of his country, his beverage is coffee: thick, strong, and taken black.

"I would love a cup of tea," he says.

Home" consists of two rooms, a bedroom and a sitting room, facing south and east over the garden at the back of the huge house. The sitting room is a pleasant, airy chamber, with sunlight falling like water through curtains of lace, and its bright comforts seem touched with some kindly magic, permitting it alone to escape the dark spell which has plunged the rest of the house into profound sleep. Adding to the feeling of enchantment is a table before one window, set with covered dishes, a cup and saucer, a round blue teapot, and a small kettle which steams cheerfully above a spirit lamp, as if invisible hands had been there only moments before. While Clara busies herself with the tea things, taking for her own use a glass tumbler fetched from the table beside her bed, Alfieri examines his surroundings.

His eyes travel from the soft rugs on the floor to the books piled on the tables, to the hoop of half-finished embroidery lying on the window seat, to the mantelpiece, which is white marble carved with swags of roses. Upon it sits a vase filled with tulips and anemones, a fountain of bright reds, blues, and yellows; on the wall above hangs a portrait of a girl with long chestnut hair tumbling about her shoulders, looking like a flower herself in a pale blue gown. The artist, with masterly hand and eye, had captured his subject at a magical time—no longer a child, not quite a woman—and Alfieri stares at it, once more feeling something that he cannot explain . . . the tilt of the head, the slant of the eyes, the oddly knowing expression, smiling and infinitely sad . . . all achingly familiar—and then he is back, and realizing that the wan little creature now pouring out tea is the faded shadow of the portrait's original.

"My guardian had me sit for it, two years ago," Clara says, following his gaze. "I was very young then."

"So I see. How young, if I might be permitted to ask?"

"Seventeen."

"Why then you are very old now," he says gravely, and is rewarded by one of her rare smiles.

"Sometimes I feel very old. I tire so quickly."

"You must give it time."

"It's taking so long."

"I know. But you will grow well and strong. If you do not believe me, I will show you." He takes the teacup she has handed him and quickly drinks off its contents, leaving a small amount in the bottom. Swirling the remaining liquid around, he pours it out into his saucer and holds the empty cup out for her inspection.

She peers into it. "Do you read tea leaves?"

"I am famous for it. In my family I am the only one permitted to read them. It is a rule."

"Whom do you read them for?"

"My brothers and sisters and their children."

"Does what you read always come true?"

"Always."

"What do you see there?"

He holds the cup to the light and rotates it between his hands. "I see a very beautiful young lady—radiant with health, and with long, chestnut hair—in a park. Not a little park, like the one outside here, but a big one, like the Bois de Boulogne, in Paris. See this?" He points to a smudge of tea leaves inside the cup.

"What is it?"

"A ship. And here are waves and seabirds."

"What does it mean?"

"It means that you will grow well and strong, and travel across the sea."

"You are very kind," she says, looking away. "But I think not. Not I."

"Miss Adler, do you doubt me? You do me an injustice. I have predicted it, and, as my family will tell you, my predictions are never wrong."

"But . . ." She stops, puzzled by a new thought. "Mr. Alfieri, forgive me, but I fear you've made a mistake."

"Never. Not with tea leaves. It cannot be done."

"But that is *your* teacup. You would need to read my glass to tell my fortune, wouldn't you? That was your own fortune you just read."

Alfieri smiles gently and puts down the cup.

Chapter Three

Like Juno on Mount Olympus, Mrs. William Backhouse Astor stands at the pinnacle of New York society. From her exalted vantage point, with its commanding views, Mrs. Astor single-handedly metes out the fate of those would-be immortals who everlastingly strive for a place on the holy mount. The self-appointed arbiter of worth in her rarefied universe, Mrs. Astor admits only the most deserving to the ranks of the blessed. In all such matters her power is absolute, and her word, law.

In consequence of such toilsome efforts to organize society into a finely measured hierarchy, and to elevate it to ever new levels of distinction, Mrs. Astor's life had been measured not in days or weeks or months, but in cotillions and balls and levées. For twenty years, newcomers worthy of a foothold on the lower rungs of the celestial ladder might have been invited to an afternoon reception, one of the lesser observances in Mrs. Astor's ritual; only for those in the preeminent ranks of the pantheon would there have been an invitation to one of her weekly dinner parties.

But alas for New York! The goddess's consort is two years dead. While Mr. Astor lived, Mrs. Astor's year would begin in the autumn, when the elite, after the summer's diaspora, were gathered once more in the city; would build momentum through the fall and early winter with patriarchs' balls, assembly balls, family circle dancing classes, Monday nights at the opera, and a hundred exquisite suppers at Delmonico's; would whirl past Christmas and the New Year; and would achieve its culmination at her annual ball, held on the third Monday of each January—the single most sacred occasion of the social year. Since Mr. Astor's translation to an even higher sphere, however, his widow has ceased to entertain. For two years, no events have breathed life into the great crimson and gold ballroom in Mrs. Astor's Fifth Avenue mansion.

Until tonight.

Tonight is a supreme occasion, in every respect worthy of bringing society's queen out of mourning: not merely an amusement, but a portent of glories to come . . . a ball to welcome Maestro Mario Alfieri, *primo tenore assoluto,* to New York. Moreover, it is a radical departure for the fastidious Mrs. Astor, an anomaly that in itself would be enough to bring society snapping to attention. Mrs. Astor has long held that artists of any ilk—painters, authors, actors, and the like—merit no recognition unless safely dead, and that meeting them risks both needless mental fatigue and the possibility of social contamination.

But Mario Alfieri is no ordinary artist. The reigning god of Europe's opera stages for as long as Mrs. Astor has been the reigning goddess of New York society, he is still bettering his art, going from strength to strength, and triumph to triumph. What is more, he is said to be able to trace his ancestry back, in an unbroken line, for five hundred years, a feat that dazzles in a country where four generations of known ancestry constitute an aristocracy. Lastly, and providing the absolute gilding on the lily, is the fact that he dines regularly with the Prince of Wales. Alfieri is notorious, in fact, for having certain tastes in common with His Royal Highness that cannot be mentioned in polite society, and it is widely rumored that the two have been known, on numerous occasions, to cap their dinners with visits to certain private establishments where exquisite young women use astonishing skills to gratify quite other kinds of appetites.

True or not, it makes no difference. The entire Continent lies at the tenor's feet, and those American aristocrats who have seen and heard him during seasons in London, Paris, and Milan have, for several years, been feverishly negotiating for the honor of humbling themselves before the tenor on their own soil.

And success is theirs at last. On the nineteenth of November, a little less than six months from tonight, Maestro Alfieri will make his debut at the Metropolitan Opera House and begin his conquest of yet another continent. To have ample time to prepare for this momentous occasion, he arrived here a week ago; and the reverence in which New York holds him can best be appreciated by realizing that Mrs. Astor had arranged to call upon him—*in her own person*—on the very next day, bearing an invitation to tonight's gala.

Alfieri had been reluctant to attend at first, pleading the fatigue of his travels, but Mrs. Astor had, of course, carried the day . . . with the result that he is here, now, looking like a prince of darkness with a familiar in mauve and purple—which is Mrs. Astor herself—appended to his arm.

Magnificently arrayed, formidable in her majesty, Mrs. Astor stands in her traditional place beneath the celebrated life-sized portrait of herself by Carolus-Duran, bidding welcome to the long line of lesser divinities as they approach. Pearls and diamonds glitter, thick as the stars of heaven, across her antique lace bodice and down her long velvet train, and crowning her black pompadour is the fabulous diamond and amethyst starburst tiara that had once belonged to the Empress Eugénie.

But for all her splendor, Mrs. Astor is eclipsed tonight. It is upon the tall and smiling man at her side that all eyes instinctively fasten. His face has long been familiar to habitués of Europe's greatest opera houses: the wide forehead, the brilliant black eyes and heavy brows, the prominent nose, the full lower lip. Familiar, too, is the way that, in smiling, the right corner of his mouth draws up, creasing his cheek with deep lines of mirth and almost shutting his right eye . . . as if the warmth of his smile, so like the sunlight of his native land, causes him to squint even as it brightens everything it touches.

Mrs. Astor, standing with her hands clasped about his arm, flutters in the light of that smile like a netted moth; and if Alfieri seems amused that she forgets her imperial dignity in his presence, it is a kindly amusement—such lapses happen all the time and he is used to them by now: one German princess even forgot herself so far as to kneel to *him*.

"You are most kind to a stranger in a strange land," he says to those who crowd around him as the receiving line dissolves in the heat of the evening's excitement. "Thank you for inviting me." His voice is soft and very light, holding no hint of any hidden glory.

"The pleasure is New York's, we assure you, maestro," says one matron. "We only hope that you will enjoy your stay in our city, and come to think of it as home."

"Madame, if all of its people are like you, I cannot fail to do that."

It seems, in fact, that this night he cannot fail at anything. At the sight of him, New York goes slightly mad, its most exalted citizens jostling each other in their haste to be at his side, and he laughs as he shakes the hands of the gentlemen, and bends over the outstretched fingers of the ladies, and says charming and appropriate things to the glowing faces of both—such as how he remembers Mrs. Dobson from that reception in Rome two years ago, and hopes her daughter's wedding had come off as planned; and how, yes, he does recall Mr. Martindale from that small supper party after the performance of *Faust* last fall in Paris, and trusts that his gout is much improved; and no, he has never had the pleasure before, but surely Mrs. Pennington must be a cousin, and not a very distant one, of the delightful Comtesse de la Mercier-Trouville, for the resemblance is certainly remarkable . . .

And the city surrenders.

Thaddeus Chadwick watches it go down from a vantage point on the far side of the ballroom. Three broad, shallow steps lead up and into the conservatory, and he stands on the topmost of these and observes the debacle through gleaming spectacles, a small, mild, Buddha-like smile on his face. He is a portly man, all jowls and chins, with sausage fingers encased in tight white gloves, and an odd, bobbing quality to all of his movements, for his thin legs and small feet seem not to support him so much as to anchor him to the ground, much as a string holds a child's balloon.

". . . most *astonishingly* handsome," one substantial lady in blue silk and sapphires is saying as she passes by amid a knot of revelers, fresh from their introductions to the guest of honor. "And not vulgar in the *least*. I had expected him to be *quite* uncouth . . . and yet he seems a perfect gentleman, for all that he is *such* a notorious libertine . . ." And she gasps, turning bright pink at her own audacity.

Her companions laugh and murmur agreement, but a slender woman in dove-gray satin embroidered with pearls, replies: "Oh, no! My brother has written me from Florence. He says that the Alfieri family is most respectable. They can trace their line back to the fifteenth century, and are descended from the Medici."

"The Medici?" Chadwick says, lifting a glass of wine from the tray of a passing footman. "What of them, Mrs. Hadcock? If it is true—and I very much doubt that it is—they hardly seem to have done him much good. Your great Maestro Alfieri is no better than Little Tommy Tupper. He, too, sings for his supper."

It is the lady's husband who takes up the challenge. "Perhaps you would call it supper, Chadwick, but then, attorneys doubtless set far richer tables than do bankers, which—alas!—is what I am. I rather think of what Maestro Alfieri sings for as a twelve-course banquet. *With* an excellent vintage at every plate." Hadcock smiles faintly. "He earns twenty-five hundred dollars for each performance. A very rich supper," he says, and eyes widen as jaws go slack.

Chadwick clicks his tongue in disapproval. "Details of finance before the ladies, Hadcock? How shocking!"

"Only when the boodle's your own, old man," says another member of the little group, turning to Hadcock. "Is *that* his price? For each performance?"

"That, and twenty-five percent of the gross over five thousand . . . every time he steps onstage."

Another man does the calculations. "But that's upward of five thousand dollars a night! For twenty performances . . . that's one hundred thousand. You must be joking! Grau would never spend that kind of money . . . and even if he would, Morgan and the other shareholders would never stand for it!"

"He would and they have. In fact, Morgan and the others will hoist Grau on their shoulders. Grau knows what draws, and he's willing to spend in order to get. Alfieri will bring money into the house as it's never been brought before."

"Where did you hear all this?"

"Beeson told me over luncheon at the club. Grau called him in during the negotiations; they needed his expertise in foreign currencies and rates of exchange. Alfieri is no one's fool, by the way . . . he's being paid in pounds sterling and the money is going directly to his account in London."

"Beeson advised him, of course," someone else says.

"So *I* thought," says Hadcock. "But Beeson says not. He said it was one of Alfieri's own stipulations. He also said that he wished his own people had as much business sense."

"Quite a compliment, coming from Beeson," says still another. "But the man must get advice from someone. He's a singer, not a financier."

Hadcock shakes his head. "Perhaps he does. But it appears that he handles all his business affairs himself, and just today Beeson told me that in the week Alfieri's been here he's made inquiries about some very sound investments."

"Then perhaps he *is* descended from the Medici, after all," murmurs Mrs. Hadcock.

For these, at least, of Mrs. Astor's guests, it only remains to be seen if the tenor can make lame men walk and blind men see; there is plainly nothing else he cannot do.

Still talking amongst themselves about the prodigy they have just met, the little group moves on. Chadwick watches them go, slowly sipping his wine until, tiring of the noise and the heat, he retreats to the conservatory, to seat himself in the cool shadows and smoke a cigar amid the foliage. If he is surprised, halfway through his cigar, to have someone sit down quietly beside him, he gives no sign of it.

"Mr. Chadwick?"

"Yes?"

"Mr. Chadwick, I believe that you are the only man in New York tonight whom I have not yet had the pleasure of meeting. I am Mario Alfieri."

"I know who you are, signore, even though I did not join the lines of those waiting to shake your hand. I am not easy in crowds."

"On a warm night even I find them trying, Mr. Chadwick. There is no need to apologize."

"Apologize? I'm not apologizing, signore; merely explaining."

The tenor smiles in the darkness. "Then let *me* explain, as briefly as I can, why it is that I have sought you out. You are, in fact, the chief reason that I am here tonight, although I would hope that you would not say as much to Mrs. Astor. I understand from Mr. Upton that you were the late Mr. Slade's attorney."

"If this is business, Signor Alfieri, perhaps it will wait until tomorrow? You may not be particular about where you are when you break into song, but I make it a rule never to discuss business either after hours or away from my office." He stands and bows shortly. "Allow me to retire so as not to disturb you."

"I wish to buy Mr. Slade's house, Mr. Chadwick."

There is silence for several moments. "Did you say 'buy,' signore?"

"I did."

"Strange. I was not aware that the property is for sale."

"Nor am I. That, obviously, is why I am speaking with you now."

"But you are aware that the house is available for lease. Did Mr. Upton tell you why?"

"He told me that you are in no hurry to sell it, but wish the money for its upkeep to come from somewhere other than Mr. Slade's estate."

"Mr. Upton does not have a massive intellect, Signor Alfieri, but he shows houses very well, and his memory is excellent. What he told you is perfectly true. What, then, makes you think that we are prepared to sell the house, at this time—to you or any other speculator?"

"Because the sale of the house—for cash—which I am prepared to pay, Mr. Chadwick—would both relieve you of the burden of responsibility for it and enrich Mr. Slade's estate considerably. And surely a man as careful as yourself would welcome the opportunity to save time, as well as money."

"You are being presumptuous, signore, which is unbecoming to a so-called gentleman. And have you any idea of what the property would fetch if it were for sale?"

"I have a vague idea, Mr. Chadwick. I saw the house today. I have a few properties in Europe—a town house in London, an apartment in Paris, a country place outside of Florence. I would wish to buy Mr. Slade's house as it is, by the way. Completely intact," he says pleasantly. "Just as it was during Mr. Slade's lifetime."

"As an investment?"

"As a place to live. I will be here for more than a year."

"And what do you wish me to say to you, signore? Surely you do not expect me to quote you a price here and now?"

"Hardly that, Mr. Chadwick. I merely wish you to tell me if the house is for sale, and, if it is, whether or not you will see my attorney if I send him to you."

There is another pause in the darkness; then: "I will see your attorney, Signor Alfieri."

"Thank you. I am grateful to you."

"I have not said that the house is for sale, signore. Merely that I will see your attorney."

"But you have not said that it is *not* for sale, Mr. Chadwick, and I am an incurable optimist."

"Then I will take my leave now," Chadwick says, with another bow.

"Forgive me, Mr. Chadwick," Alfieri says as the attorney turns to go. "There is one more thing I must ask you."

"Yes? What is it?"

"I met Miss Adler today."

There is a brief silence. "That is not a question, signore."

"No, Mr. Chadwick, it is not."

"Would you care to tell me the circumstances of your meeting?"

"Gladly. Miss Adler was feeling better than usual this morning, or so she told me. She thought that a walk, to build up her strength, would do her good. You know, of course, that she will not go outside—not even into the garden—for fear that someone will see her unfortunate hair. She decided, instead, to walk in what she calls the 'shut-up' part of the house. I fear that she is not so well as she tries to be, Mr.

Chadwick. She became tired and could go no further, entered the music room and fell asleep. And that was where I found her."

"You would make an excellent trial witness, signore. You are succinct and very clear. Did you speak with Miss Adler?"

"We had tea, Mr. Chadwick, and spoke, yes."

"In her room?"

"In her sitting room."

"Of course. And just what is it you wish to ask me about Miss Adler?"

"Just this: I am prepared to make over one whole wing of the house for her exclusive use, and to provide her with a staff and a companion— a duenna, or chaperone, if you will—so that she need not leave the home she is accustomed to. She told me that you have made arrangements to have her moved elsewhere once she is strong enough to leave. She is frightened, Mr. Chadwick, and very much alone, and she does not wish to go. She is not of age, and you are her late guardian's attorney, and so I appeal to you. Will you permit me to do this?"

"Signor Alfieri, if your attorney comes to see me, and we find that the house is in fact for sale, and we discuss terms, and you are able, somehow, to meet those terms, and you buy the house, then you may do whatever it is you wish to do with it, including pulling it down around your ears. Miss Adler, however, is another matter entirely, which I have no intention of discussing with you, either now or in the future. I bid you good night, sir."

Alfieri listens to Chadwick's departing footsteps until they are lost against the distant sounds of a waltz coming from the ballroom beyond the conservatory. After several minutes, another figure disengages itself from the shadows and takes Chadwick's vacated seat.

"Forgive my intrusion, Mario, but when I saw him leave and you did not follow . . ." Alfieri does not answer, and the speaker says quietly: "Is it that bad?"

Alfieri shakes his head. "I fear that Mr. Chadwick and I will never be friends, Stafford. He is not an agreeable man and I—stupidly—let him provoke me." His tone is bitter. "You said your attorney was eloquent? He will have to be a perfect Cicero to win for me now."

"You tried your best, Mario."

"And failed."

"You don't know that."

"Oh, yes I do. He will not discuss the matter with me under any circumstances. That is what trying my best has led to—"

"Then let Buchan handle it. I have seen him win the most amazing battles. Leave it until tomorrow."

"—I could cut my tongue out!"

"Mario, Buchan knows him. Let him deal with it."

"He does not care that she is afraid. How could he not care? How could anyone be harsh with her? Such a small child, Stafford . . . such eyes. Did I tell you about her eyes?"

"All afternoon, Mario."

Alfieri turns to his friend, his smile returning. "You think I have gone mad."

"I think you have been struck by lightning, as they say in Italy. Are you in love with her?"

Alfieri's laugh is incredulous. "I? In love with a child? My God, Stafford, are there not women enough in the world? You think that now I must start with little girls?"

"She's not a child, Mario . . . I understand she's nearly twenty."

"An old lady, certainly! But only if one is your age, *ragazzo*." Alfieri shakes his head again. "Stafford, you know my family. My youngest sister—the baby, Fiorina—will be twenty on her next birthday. When she was born I was twenty, and already singing leading roles. How could Miss Adler be anything more than a child to me? And a little child, at that . . . when I first saw her I thought she was fourteen and no more."

"Then why this concern for her?"

Alfieri shrugs, his smile fading. "Can you see a child in pain, and not try to help it? Some can, maybe . . . Mr. Chadwick, perhaps. But I cannot. And then . . ." He stops, thinks, shakes his head again. "I tell you, Stafford, there is something about her. She is so like . . . and yet not . . ." He raises his hands, then lets them fall, helpless, to his sides.

"Let it go until tomorrow, Mario; wait and see what Buchan can accomplish. There is nothing more to be done, certainly not tonight.

Besides, all of New York must be wondering where Mrs. Astor's guest of honor has gone."

"You are right, my friend," the tenor says, as they make their way back to the ballroom. "At least I know that little Miss Adler is not in any distress now. Only musicians—and the very rich—turn night into day. At—what time is it?—two o'clock in the morning?—most of the world, and especially children, are in their beds and fast asleep." He lifts two glasses from the tray of a passing waiter and hands one to his friend. "To our success, Stafford, and her sweet dreams."

Rest of any kind, whether of mind or of body, has always eluded Clara. She cannot remember a time when sleep has come easily for her; perhaps it never has. Even in childhood, in the many beds and the many rooms of the many houses in which she had passed her years—more than a visitor, less than a guest—sleep had been a stranger. What wonder, then, that now, in her forfeited bed, in the room that is no longer hers, in the house she will soon leave forever, it should continue to pass her by.

She has left her childhood very far behind her; but she lies now, in her warm bed, as she did then, under the thin blankets and the mended sheets, in the hot rooms or the drafty ones; lies awake and staring at the chink in the curtain where morning glimmers like a star, listening to the birds wake and call—such a lonely sound—in the twilight world outside.

What was it he had said that morning? "You deserve a better life." She had thought so, once. "My dear child," he had said. "Have you no family to return to? No one at all?"

"No one."

"No parents? No brothers or sisters? No relations of any kind? All dead?"

"Yes," she had said. "All dead."

"Then where will you go? Has anyone told you?"

"No."

"How can you bear not to know?"

"They will tell me when it is time."

"Haven't you asked?"

"No. It doesn't matter."

"My dear, if that doesn't matter, then what does?"

"Nothing."

He had looked at her so pityingly. He had been so kind. He will take the house—he had told her so—and she will move on once more.

It occurs to her, now, lying in the gray light, that he must think her mind unsound; must believe her despair to be both symptom and proof of madness.

Not so. Her mind has already passed through that shadowy realm, like a soul sinking into hell, and fallen out the other side. To go mad again would mean an ascent, an upward journey; but she has tumbled out of madness onto a plain of such pitiless clarity, and there is no escape.

Madness would be a relief. Madness, at least, being shadowy, had offered her places where she could hide. But it has all come back to her now, one death resurrecting another, grief reviving grief . . . and here, in this boundless desolation, the vision stretches endlessly: the past remembered clearly, the present lived clearly, the future—oh, not the future of his tea leaves—seen clearly.

What she has done is always with her now, as is what is left to her; and the two are joined inextricably, the one engendering the other, and both are linked through what she is. It is like being the point where two lines cross; like peering through the wrong ends of telescopes into remote distances on both sides of her life at once; like looking forward and backward together.

There is no forgiveness in either direction. No pity. No hope.

She wipes her eyes. Waking to the sound of his voice, she had thought, at first, that she had died, and for the moment she had felt such joy, knowing that her misery was over at last. And then she had opened her eyes and seen him, and he was his voice made flesh, dark and beautiful, and she was glad she was not dead . . . forgetting, as she watched and listened, that alive or dead is the same to her now. If she were different, if she were not who she is . . .

Never mind. He had been kind. He had kissed her hand and read her tea leaves. How could he know that there was nothing to see in them because she had ceased to be long ago?

If she were different, if she were not who she is . . .

Alone in the dawn, Clara curls herself up, and cries.

Chapter Four

THE GRAY LIGHT WARMS and turns to gold, the creatures of the night melt away like dew, and the pace of the city quickens with the progress of the new day. Clara sleeps at last in her sun-warmed room and, mercifully, does not dream.

Thaddeus Chadwick, although he had bidden Mrs. Astor adieu only shortly before dawn, rises at his usual hour, which is eight o'clock. Chadwick needs little sleep—an advantage, perhaps the only one, of advancing years—but even in his youth sleep had been a luxury he could forgo at need. Far more important to him is the orderly management of time. If Mrs. Astor's life is measured in cotillions and balls and levées, Chadwick's is measured in hours and minutes and seconds, each day being so finely calibrated that one can be certain of exactly where he is at any given moment, just by looking at a clock.

Nine o'clock finds him at his breakfast in the morning room. His house is one of a graceful row of houses fronting the north side of Washington Square, its red brick faded by time to a rosy hue, and the morning room, at the back, looks out onto his small garden, where the lately radiant dogwood trees are now losing the last of their pink and white blossoms.

This is his favorite room of the house: a sunny chamber filled with shining, dark furniture lit by the gleam of brass, the table laid with a snowy cloth and fine china. It is a room with a clear conscience, a room

indicative of a healthy appetite and a good digestion, and it illustrates
the guiding principle that informs every aspect of Chadwick's existence:
serenity. As a bachelor, he can shape his life to suit his wishes, and he
does precisely that. No voice is ever raised in his presence; no untoward
emotions ruffle his days or intrude upon his nights. He floats through
life upon his small feet, his placid smile upon his lips, observing the
world benignly, and the occasional furor—such as the sudden death of
his friend Slade, or the equally sudden affliction of Slade's little ward—
falls into his life with no more effect than that of a pebble flung into a
glassy lake: the ripples soon die away, leaving the water as tranquil as
before.

Take, for instance, the unexpected approach of the tenor last night,
with his ridiculous offer to buy the Slade house. He—Chadwick—had
been irked at the time, it is true, but his annoyance was as much a
reaction to the high-handed manner of the man who made it as it was
to the proposition itself. Reflecting upon it quietly this morning, however, over his eggs and toast, it occurs to him that the Italian has done
him a very great favor. The sale will do more than merely fill the coffers
of the Slade estate to better than overflowing and relieve him of an
unnecessary burden (as Alfieri had so astutely pointed out, to give the
Italian devil his due); it will also provide him with the opportunity to
bring to fruition a plan—a most important plan—which has merely been
waiting for the right set of circumstances to occur before he could set
it in motion.

And this is the time. He has not grown rich in the service of others
by failing to know when the proverbial iron is hot enough to strike, and
the tenor's desire to own the Slade house has suddenly fired this particular metal to white heat. Chadwick is pleased, with himself as well
as with events. Alfieri's arrogance—and particularly his insolence in
requesting the girl—is something he can easily put by . . . for now. It
is important to maintain one's mental balance, however, for the mind
functions best when not clotted up with petty annoyances and ill humors;
and besides, as the Italians themselves say, revenge is a dish that is best
tasted cold.

But he is in no hurry. Nothing must disturb the routine—serenity, always serenity—and a glance at the clock tells him that he has the better part of an hour yet, before his scheduled arrival at his office. The documents needed to put his plan into effect are already prepared—they have been so for months—and are waiting to be filed with the courts; all that remains is for him to affix his signature.

With a small sigh of contentment, Chadwick folds back his newspaper, pours himself more coffee and, raising the cup to his lips, mentally salutes Alfieri. Because of the tenor, the greatest plum of his—or, indeed, anyone else's—life is almost within his grasp. And if it takes a little time for his fist to close about it . . . well, what of that? Lighting his first cigar of the morning, he gazes out into the flower-decked garden, a happy man with all the time in the world.

The clock moves on, and noon finds Alfieri en route to his appointment with the attorney who will do battle on his behalf for the house of the late Mr. Slade. The morning has not been easy for him; he has had the curious sensation, since waking from a fitful sleep—and a brief one, as he, too, had left Mrs. Astor at dawn—that every passing minute poses some increasing threat to the solitary child in the great, empty house, and he keeps a preoccupied silence during the ride downtown.

He is accompanied by his friend of the previous evening, Stafford Dyckman, who has known the tenor long enough to recognize when speech will be unwelcome; long enough, indeed, to be quite comfortable in the complete absence of any conversation. He sits wordlessly beside Alfieri as their carriage threads its way through the noontime crush of lower Broadway, intruding only occasionally upon his friend's thoughts to point out some feature of interest on the bustling New York pavements.

Their destination, the offices of Daniel Buchan, Esq., is very near Wall Street, and so close to the graveyard that surrounds Trinity Church that its second-floor windows look directly out onto the weathered, tilted stones of the green and quiet burial ground. Dyckman makes the introductions as the church's chimes ring out a quarter past noon.

"Your view is quite beautiful, Mr. Buchan," Alfieri says as he and the attorney shake hands, "but perhaps somewhat . . . suggestive for your clients?"

"Actually, Signor Alfieri, the view is for my improvement. I find it most helpful. On those occasions when I succeed for a client, this view helps me to maintain my sense of proportion. It serves the same function as the slave who would ride in the chariot with the hero during ancient Roman triumphs, whispering 'Remember, you are mortal.' " He is as dark as Alfieri, but small and balding, and his brown eyes are bright and very shrewd.

"On the other hand," he says, ushering his guests to their chairs, "on those occasions when I do happen to fail, I look out the window and take solace from the fact that, win or lose, we all come to the same end eventually."

"A comforting sentiment, to be sure," Alfieri says, smiling. "But as I am considering retaining your services, Mr. Buchan, I would be a great deal happier if you could assure me that the former occurs considerably more often than the latter."

"Often enough to pay the rent," the attorney replies with an answering smile. "Now, Mr. Dyckman has explained very briefly what it is that you wish to do, signore. Might I ask you to provide me with more detail?"

The matter is quickly explained.

"This is very intriguing. I know Mr. Chadwick well," Buchan says, leaning back with his elbows on the arms of his chair and his fingertips pressed together, forming a steeple. "He and I have been on opposing sides many times over the years, and I know that he is not an easy man to sway. And yet you say that he seemed open to consideration?"

"Of the purchase of the house, yes."

"But that is the important thing, surely?"

Alfieri shakes his head. "Important, yes. But not more important than the house's current occupant. I do not wish to disturb her, or be the cause of her displacement."

"And are you willing to make that a condition of the purchase?"

"Meaning do I wish you to tell Mr. Chadwick that if he insists upon moving the child I will retract my offer? If you feel that that will carry weight with him, by all means, Mr. Buchan, make that a condition."

"And if he still insists, Signor Alfieri? If he calls your bluff? Will you then withdraw your offer?"

"Yes, Mr. Buchan, I will."

"And yet you tell me that you want the house very much."

"Very much. But not enough to cause a little invalid to be made homeless."

Buchan sits up. "Signor Alfieri, there is one point upon which I must satisfy myself. I hope that you will not take offense if I touch upon a . . . well, a rather sensitive matter."

"I am here seeking your assistance, Mr. Buchan. Ask me whatever you wish."

"Thank you," the lawyer says. "But perhaps Mr. Dyckman wishes his luncheon? It is unfortunate that we have to meet at such an awkward hour, but I see no reason to deny him his sustenance, signore, even though you and I may be here for some time, yet."

Alfieri nods at the young man. "If Stafford wishes to leave, I certainly will not stop him. But I have nothing to hide from him, Mr. Buchan. We have known each other for years."

"As you wish, of course. I will be blunt, then. Before I agree to represent you, I must be confident of your intentions in this matter. You see"—he hesitates, choosing his words judiciously—"your reputation for more than merely singing has preceded you across the ocean. The rumors of your, let us say, 'expertise,' signore, with the ladies have been making the rounds of every gentlemen's club in this city for weeks."

Alfieri says evenly: "And you wish to know if they are true, Mr. Buchan?"

"I wish to know if they have any bearing on your desire to have the late Mr. Slade's ward remain in his house."

Dyckman, silent until now, turns red to his ears and opens his mouth to speak, but a swift gesture from Alfieri checks him.

"My tastes do not run to children, Mr. Buchan, if that is your concern."

"And Miss Adler is not a child, Signor Alfieri; she is a young woman, and therefore your tastes become very much my concern—especially as their catholicity has become a topic of general discussion." He stops, shaking his head. "I am truly sorry, signore," he continues more gently. "I do not enjoy treading on such delicate ground, nor do I wish to cause you undue embarrassment. But if I am to argue for Miss Adler to remain in your house, I must be absolutely certain that she will come to no harm."

"She will come to no harm. I promise you that." But Alfieri's own words remind him of the unease that has plagued him all morning. Disturbed, he says quietly: "You say she is not a child, Mr. Buchan. But I have seen her, and I have spoken with her, and I tell you that I have known real children half her age who were better able to care for themselves than she is."

"No doubt. But it is the duty of others to be responsible for her. That is frankly not your place."

"Is it not?"

"No." Buchan is firm. "Though you might wish to do it for the most unselfish of reasons, it could never appear other than highly improper. It is simply unacceptable, signore."

"So much for our Lord's teachings. Is it unacceptable to provide a haven for a bereaved child?"

"I repeat: she is not a child."

"For a bereaved young woman, then. I would allow her to stay safely beneath her own roof, in her own familiar surroundings, with her own things about her. And you tell me this is wrong?"

"No. I tell you it would *appear* wrong. Consider those rumors about you. She would be compromised forever in the eyes of the world."

"And what does it say for the world, Mr. Buchan, that it could read something indecent into the desire to do a kindness, or suspect the worst of a little invalid because she accepted it?"

Buchan says, almost sadly: "But that is the way of the world, signore. You know the world, perhaps better than most. Why do you deny what you know to be the truth?"

"Because"—Alfieri's words are sharp, his face dark—"because the way of the world is paved with hypocrisy, Mr. Buchan, which we both know; and I find no virtue in celebrating that fact."

Buchan leans toward him. "And do *you* speak of virtue, Signor Alfieri?"

Dyckman sucks in his breath. The tenor's eyes widen and he half rises from his chair—only to sink back, looking at the attorney with a frown and a small, puzzled smile.

"Do you know, Mr. Buchan," he says, after a pause, "I think you are trying to make me angry."

"Why would I want to do that, signore?"

"Perhaps to hear me admit, in an unguarded moment, that I am Don Juan and Lothario and Casanova rolled into one, and that I plan the imminent seduction of little Miss Adler. Well, I am sorry to disappoint you, Mr. Buchan; truly, I am. But she is so small, and so very much alone. Only a monster would take advantage of her; and I am many things, but I am not a monster. I do not prey on the defenseless." He spreads his hands helplessly. "I do not know what else I can say to convince you, and you must decide for yourself, of course. But if you could find it in your conscience to help her, I would be very grateful."

The two men regard each other in a silent appraisal that ends when Buchan's face relaxes. He extends his hand to the tenor.

"Signore, I will be pleased to speak to Mr. Chadwick on your behalf."

The relief is plain in Alfieri's face. "Thank you, Mr. Buchan, so very much. You cannot imagine how pleased I am."

"But you must not be too hopeful," the lawyer cautions. "You must realize that the odds are not with us."

"As I told Mr. Chadwick last night, I am an incurable optimist."

"Then let us hope that your optimism is justified."

"Amen to that." Alfieri rises and walks to the window, where he stands gazing out at the brown bulk of Trinity Church across the narrow street. "I should like, by the way, to speak briefly of those rumors you mentioned, if you would care to listen."

Buchan looks surprised. "There is no need for that now, surely? I brought them up only because—"

"I know why you brought them up. But I would rest easier in my mind if I thought that you understood. You see, Mr. Buchan, very simply put . . . women make themselves available to me. They do it in embarrassing numbers and with a regularity that astonishes even me. But do not be fooled, Mr. Buchan; I am not so irresistible as the numbers would seem to indicate, although I would not be honest if I said that I did not sometimes flatter myself on that score. Nevertheless, what most of the ladies are seeking is the carnal equivalent of an autograph; and while most delude themselves into believing that they are in love in order to justify what they do, their real desire is not for me—it is for the heady experience of being in the bed of someone world-famous."

He turns and faces the lawyer. "What is wrong, Mr. Buchan? You look uncomfortable. Are you having second thoughts about me? I have not yet mentioned the ladies who give themselves to me because they believe me to be Faust, or Hoffmann, or Lohengrin, or Otello. You think I should turn away all those eager ladies, and practice abstinence for the sake of their poor souls? But they do not care a whit for their souls, and I am no fool, to refuse a gift freely given. However, lest you think that I am utterly without self-control, I must point out that I do not accept the favors of every woman who makes her interest known: for one thing, there would not be enough time in this life; and for another, since I can pick and choose, I limit myself to those who are the most attractive."

"Are you certain you should be telling me this, signore?"

"You are my attorney now. My confidence is safe with you. And someone besides Stafford should know the truth. And, just perhaps, when you are next at your club you could put in a kind word for me, to counter all those rumors: poor Mario Alfieri—so many women, and not one of them but sees only her own reflection in his eyes."

"Forgive me, signore," Buchan says quietly. "But isn't that what each of us sees in another's eyes?"

Alfieri shakes his head, smiling. "We must speak of this further sometime, Mr. Buchan, at length, preferably over dinner. But now," he says, going to the attorney and holding out his hand, "I will leave you to your work. I am still unknown here, and free to walk about the streets like anyone else. I must take advantage of that happiness while I can."

"But the rest of our discussion?"

"All the rest I leave in your hands, Mr. Buchan. I trust you whole-heartedly. Stafford will stay and give you any further information you need. No, please do not get up, either of you. The day is lovely, and my time has so rarely been my own . . ."

The door closes behind him.

Chapter Five

A MOST UNUSUAL MAN, Stafford," the attorney says.

Dyckman looks at Buchan reproachfully, breaking his silence at last. "And also very discomposed, just now. He is not accustomed to having his motives questioned, Daniel. In Europe he is treated like royalty— no one would dare to throw his behavior in his face like that!"

"He took it well enough."

"As you said, he is a most unusual man. He is also a gentleman, in the old sense of the word. Was it necessary to bring up such matters?"

"Regrettably, yes. How else was I to get to know his nature on such short acquaintance?"

"You might have asked me."

"Stafford." Buchan looks at him mildly. "He is your friend. You are naturally biased in favor of the man, and while I trust your opinion, I needed to find out for myself what he is really like."

"And your little test did that for you?"

"Admirably so, yes.

Buchan leans back in his chair, settling himself comfortably. "Tell me how you came to meet him. I've never heard the story."

Dyckman relents finally, annoyance overwhelmed by memory. He is a pleasant-featured young man of twenty-eight, fair-haired, gray-eyed and tall, though not so tall as his friend Alfieri, and his smile now is tinged with embarrassment.

"It was during my first trip to Italy, just after college. Mario rescued me," he says, flushing slightly, "from a rather elderly—and extremely tipsy—lady of the evening."

To his credit, Buchan does not laugh. "Not an everyday predicament, to be sure. Would you care to share the full story with me?"

"On one condition, Daniel, and that is that you not tell my family. I've succeeded in keeping it from them all this time, and I have no intention of having them learn it now."

"As shameful as all that?"

"Don't be ridiculous. But Mother would be shocked beyond words, and even Father would find it less than amusing—the Dyckman name, you know. Truly a shame," he says, with a grin, "because it really was very funny . . . although I was the last one to think so, at the time.

"I had only been in Italy for about three weeks, you see—this was in Milan—and I had developed the habit of walking about late at night, in order to take in as much of the atmosphere of the city as I could. On this particular night, right behind La Scala, the opera house, someone hooked an arm through mine, and there I was, with this creature hanging on to me.

"I was pathetically green, remember, and knew no Italian. I tried my best to extend my regrets, and tell her that I wasn't interested, but she wasn't having any of it. Finally, in sheer desperation—well, I pushed her away. It was far from gallant of me, I admit, but I simply didn't know what else to do. At any rate, she stumbled, being none too steady on her feet. She didn't fall, and nothing but her pride was injured, you understand—but that was more than enough. She began to scream— gathered quite a crowd." Stafford laughs. "I had no idea of what she was saying, of course, and the people in the crowd were definitely less than helpful—some of them undoubtedly knew English, but didn't want to spoil the fun—and when the *guardia* came I had visions of spending the night in jail, and having to send to the American consulate in the morn- ing . . ."

His eyes narrow, smiling at the memory. "And then, suddenly, there was Mario. He had sung that night, and was just leaving the opera house, but he stopped to see what the commotion was about. I had no idea

who he was, of course, but the crowd certainly did—it parted like the
Red Sea to let him through, applauding madly all the while. He offered
to translate, listened first to the woman, then to me, and had the whole
thing sorted out in five minutes. It seems, by the way, that what my
lady was announcing to the assembled populace of Milan was that I had
enjoyed her services and then refused to pay.

"Mario paid her, of course, out of his own pocket . . . not to have
done so would have meant that he knew she was lying, and Mario would
never offend her that way." Stafford is thoughtful. "Just as an aside, do
you know what she did with the money? She kissed the bills, tucked
them inside her bodice, just above her heart, and said that she would
put them by her statue of the Blessed Virgin and never spend them
because they had been given to her by *il signore con la voce degli angeli,*
the man with the voice of the angels."

The young man shrugs and smiles. "Mario never told me that, by the
way. It was told to me later by someone else. All Mario said was that
I was a menace to his country, and then he invited me to join him and
a few friends for dinner the following evening. And that," he says, "is
the true story of how I met Mario Alfieri."

Buchan nods. "You are very fond of him."

"He is my dearest friend. He has been very good to me—and for no
other reason than pure kindness. But that is Mario's way."

"What are his people like?"

"Very much like him; very generous, very open. His family is large,
although not very, not by Italian standards. His mother died when he
was small, and had no other children, but his father remarried when
Mario was ten or so, and the present Signora Dottore Alfieri has more
than filled the breach. He has a host of half brothers and sisters—four
brothers, three sisters, to be exact—all very much younger than he,
and a perfect army of little nieces and nephews."

"Do you know them well?"

"I've met them all, at one time or another. I know some of them
better than others." Dyckman reddens slightly.

"Did you say, by the way, that he's never been married?"

"I never said anything about it, but yes, it's true. He's never been married. Most people, of course, think it's because he has no need to be . . . the plethora of ladies, you understand . . ."

The lawyer cocks his head and looks at Dyckman. "You don't believe that."

"No, I don't."

"Why not? Do you know the real reason?"

"I have my theory, which may or may not be correct. We've certainly never discussed the matter."

"And what is your theory?"

"Quite simply that he's never met any woman he's wanted to marry."

The lawyer lifts an incredulous eyebrow. "Among so many?"

Dyckman shrugs. "We each have our own criteria. You said yourself that he's an unusual man. Perhaps he's looking for something very rare."

"Which is what?"

Dyckman shrugs again. "Unless he finds it, we'll never know."

"Stafford," Buchan says, leaning across his desk, "I am not the enemy, and your friend is a famous—I will not say infamous—man. Anything more you can tell me about him may help me in my dealings with Mr. Chadwick."

"You still want to know about Mario's women."

"I want to know why a man extravagantly romantic enough to wish to buy a house for a young woman he never saw before yesterday should still be a bachelor. I simply refuse to believe that he could have escaped unscathed all these years. You say that you can tell me about him? All right, then"—he leans back in his chair—"tell me about him."

"Well, would it surprise you to learn that he's always had a penchant for the ladies? His stepmother . . ." Dyckman smiles at the memory. "His stepmother once told me that all her friends loved attending sewing circles and musicales and other such ladies' meetings at her house because Mario would go from chair to chair, kissing the hand of each guest and telling her how lovely she looked."

"Considering whom we're speaking of, is that so remarkable?"

"Daniel," Dyckman says. "He was twelve years old at the time."

The lawyer laughs and cocks his head. "So this is not something he's cultivated as he's grown older."

"Oh, no . . . it's bred in the bone. He told me once that since he was thirteen he's spent more time in the confessional, and on his knees, doing penance, than any three men he's known . . . and I think he was only half joking. Mario likes women a great deal."

"So do I, Stafford. But when I was thirteen I wanted nothing more than to go swimming with the boys in the summer, and watch the trains pulling into the station. That, I guess, is what makes the difference between Mario Alfieri and me."

"That," the young man grins, "and the fact that he can sing like a god."

"The clear implication being that I do not."

"I've heard that the minister asked if you would be kind enough to mouth the hymns," Dyckman answers, "because you were throwing the organist off-key. By the way," he says casually, "one of Mario's sisters did tell me that once, years and years ago, he did want to marry."

Buchan shifts in his chair. "Did he, indeed?"

"It was a very brief affair, very intense. Mario was wild about the girl. She was a year or two older than he . . . also a singer, apparently. She refused his offer of marriage . . . wanted her own career, and ran off with some German landgrave with a castle on the Rhine, several *schlager* scars, and a small private army, who promised to help her. Mario's family were pleased that she was gone: he was just becoming famous, singing all over Italy, and had refused several plum roles because he would not be separated from her. He went half mad when she left him, and tried to get her back, but the landgrave wouldn't let him near." Dyckman is smiling no longer. "He never saw her again."

"When was this?"

"About fifteen years ago. Fiorina—Mario's youngest sister—was only five when it happened, and remembers nothing of it herself . . . but it's still spoken of in the family from time to time."

"Fiorina told you this?"

"Yes. She's Mario's favorite." He stares down at his hands. "Mine too."

Buchan's lips twitch, but he chooses to ignore Stafford's confession. "And the woman he wished to marry?"

"Fared badly, or so the family heard, although they tried to keep it from Mario. The landgrave did nothing to forward her career, nor had he ever intended to . . . that had been a ruse to get her into his bed, nothing more. He tired of her after about a year and passed her on to the captain of his guard, who kept her for several more months." Dyckman lifts his shoulders. "After that she disappeared. I don't know if Mario ever learned what became of her, or if he would care any longer, if he did. It was all a very long time ago.

"Once she was gone he threw himself into his singing, sang everywhere in Italy—all over Tuscany and Umbria, in Parma, Venice, Modena, Turin, Naples, Genoa, Bologna, Rome . . . everywhere. Began to make a name for himself in other cities, too—London, Paris, St. Petersburg. And then he met Verdi.

"Back in the early sixties, when Mario was a child, his father had been at the center of the Risorgimento in Florence. Leading local and sometimes national figures would meet at his house . . . the writer Manzoni and Verdi among them. Mario auditioned at La Scala in eighteen eighty, for the role of Alfredo in *La Traviata*. Verdi was at that audition. He's a tough old bird, is Maestro Verdi, and he isn't easily impressed, but he asked to meet Mario afterward. When they were introduced, and he found out that Mario was the son of his old comrade . . . well, it would have made no difference if he hadn't had the voice, but between sounding like a god and being his father's son . . ."

Dyckman smiles. "And the rest, as they say, is history."

The chimes of Trinity Church ring out one o'clock, and Buchan rises from behind his desk. "Thank you," he says, clapping the young man on the shoulder. "But that is enough history for one day. Will you join me for lunch? There's a small restaurant nearby with an excellent cellar. I should like to hear what it's like to be an American expatriate living in Europe."

"Gladly. And I should like to know what you can tell me of Slade's ward," Dyckman says as he draws on his gloves. "Having been away for the past five years, I never even heard of her until yesterday. Who is she?"

"That, my dear young man, is a question to which many people would like the answer. I suspect, now that Henry Slade is dead, that only Thaddeus Chadwick really knows."

"Is he likely to tell?"

Buchan snorts. "Thaddeus Chadwick does not give things away. There is a pretty price tag attached to everything he touches, even knowledge. Signor Alfieri will have to pay handsomely for that house if he really wants it."

"He wants it, Daniel. I've never seen him like this before."

"It may prove too dear even for him."

Stafford shakes his head. "The price won't matter."

"Don't be naïve; price always matters, even if only as a point of pride. On the other hand, what a thing costs is not always measured in money."

"He will pay what he needs to buy the house."

"But not if Miss Adler is not there, or so he has said. Therefore, what price do you assign to her? What is she worth?"

"All I can tell you," Dyckman says as they make their way down the stairs, "is that for someone normally so reasonable, Mario becomes the most intractable human being once he has his heart set on something. *Nothing* sways him."

"Ah, Stafford; I fear he has met his match in Mr. Chadwick. Well, this should prove an interesting contest. My esteemed colleague has evidently made up his mind that Miss Adler is not to be an issue in the sale of the house, and Signor Alfieri has his heart set on having her under his roof. Which of them will prove stronger in the long run, I wonder?"

Dyckman laughs, as they reach the sidewalk. "And what, pray tell, happens to the young woman caught between them?"

"She is pulled to pieces, of course," Buchan replies, only half in jest, and taking Dyckman's elbow, steers him into the rushing Manhattan river called Broadway.

Chapter Six

Had he been asked where he intended to go upon leaving Buchan's office, Alfieri would have given no definite answer, but the vague response would not have been an evasion—nor would it have been a result of his discomfiture at Buchan's hands, for he is far less discomfited than Dyckman believes. It would simply have been a true reflection of his state of mind, which seesaws between a soaring elation at being so completely unrecognized in this city that he can melt, unnoticed, into the madness of a Wall Street lunch hour, and a gnawing apprehension concerning the welfare of the child—for so he still considers her, despite Buchan's denial—in the Slade house.

And yet the mere act of walking is the perfect answer to both moods, reinforcing his heady sense of liberty while diverting his mind. He begins, therefore, merely to walk, with no particular destination in mind; and because this simplest of all pleasures has been denied him for years, he studies everyone and everything in his impromptu journey— buildings, window displays, the dress, manners, speech, and gestures of his fellow pedestrians, the never-ending current of wagons, omnibuses, carts, and carriages jamming Broadway—with the greed of a starving man at a banquet and the smile of a discharged convict, causing more than one passing stranger to give him wide berth.

After a while, however, he settles upon a direction and bears northward at a leisurely pace, savoring his freedom, stopping here and there to enter a store and browse among the merchandise; even halting once on the crowded pavement to admire the sheer magnitude of the Post Office Building—a vast, layered wedding cake of a structure that dwarfs the simple, classical grace of City Hall immediately to its north—and to marvel at the swirling human stream, not the least specimen of which pays him any mind, unless it is to push impatiently past him as he slows the flow of traffic at this busiest of intersections.

His path up Broadway should lead him, eventually, right to the front door of the Fifth Avenue Hotel. It is a walk of slightly more than three miles, but he first takes a blissfully solitary midday meal in a dark little restaurant down a flight of steps, then simply loiters his way up the street. His frequent detours, his pauses, his brief excursions into this or that shop to inquire about some item in the window, or to make a small purchase to be sent on ahead—not out of any need, but solely for the pleasure of being at liberty to go into a shop like any other customer— take up the time, and it is nearly four o'clock when he reaches Union Square, where Broadway meets Fourteenth Street.

There, pleasantly tired, he seats himself on a bench and contemplates the final leg of his journey. In the last week, he has become sufficiently familiar with New York to be able to navigate its busiest streets more or less successfully. He knows, for instance, that to continue in a straight line up Broadway, which runs up the western side of Union Square, is to arrive at his hotel, now a mere nine blocks distant. But he also knows that to walk east, across the bottom of the square, and then one block further, is to come to Irving Place. And once on Irving Place, a left turn and six swift blocks will bring him to Gramercy Park.

Both wisdom and prudence dictate the former route and an uneventful arrival at his hotel. But his journey has left him quite drunk with forgotten spontaneity, and the amount of attention he has attracted on the street has almost convinced him that he has become invisible; and these facts, added to his still-lingering disquiet about the welfare of Miss Adler, and his sudden realization of her nearness, set up a siren song inside his head against which the sober claims of wisdom and prudence have small chance of being heard. Gramercy Park it is to be, if for no other reason than to put his concern to rest, once and for all, about his self-appointed protégée.

At least entering the Slade house poses no problem. The kindly disposed Mr. Upton, perhaps in gratitude for the sublime singing that he had been privileged to hear, had presented the front-door key to Alfieri when the two men parted yesterday; and whether the house agent's key had been the culprit then, or whether the lock had merely grown rusty from disuse, the front door gives no trouble today.

Upton has also left the generator in working fettle, and a simple push of a button is all that is needed to banish the darkness of the great hall. But Alfieri is reluctant to trouble that darkness now, overcome by the sense that such a disturbance in the house's hushed equilibrium—a rude thrusting of light into the echoing dusk—might break the enchantment and cause both the magical child and her chamber to shiver into nothingness before he can reach her. He steps into the hall, to be enveloped once more by its whispering welcome, and, leaving the twilight intact, climbs the stairs.

If some part of him had believed that he would find her in the music room again today—as if she were, in fact, a ghost, forever haunting that particular chamber—that part of him is disappointed, as is the part which looks for her in her own room. She is off again, on another wander, and the prospect of speedily locating someone so very small in a house of this size is not bright. But now that he has come this far, the thought of leaving without seeing her again is suddenly unbearable to him; and reasoning that it is still beyond her strength to reach, and return from, the ground floor, he begins his search on the floor immediately above.

His reasoning is sound. He finds her, after several tries, in a booklined study in the north wing, not far from the music room, seated by the window, gazing out at Gramercy Park. An open book lies forgotten on the table before her; and as the door swings open she turns her head, startled. At the sight of Alfieri her colorless face becomes even paler, and she rises to her feet, clutching the edge of the table.

Everything about her is as he remembers it, even her astonishing eyes with their burden of grief. They rest on his face now with something between shock and wonder, rendering him, once more, momentarily dumb.

"Forgive me," he says, slow to find words with the weight of her gaze upon him. "I have frightened you again. I seem forever destined to terrify you when we meet."

"You came back," is all she says.

"Did you think I wouldn't?"

"I didn't know. I thought—to see the house, maybe." And with the acknowledgment that she may not, indeed, be the object of his visit, a pink flush creeps up her face.

But Alfieri shakes his head, unable to take his eyes from her. "I have seen the house. *Piccina,* it is you that I needed to see again. I was afraid that—perhaps—I had frightened you, telling you that I would buy it."

"There's no one I would rather it belonged to."

"You are very kind. But if I have caused you any pain . . ."

"You mustn't think that."

"And yet—forgive me, again—but your eyes were not so swollen yesterday, I think. You have been crying."

"Ah, that," she says, looking away at last, her fingers fidgeting and twisting. "That's nothing. I slept badly last night. I often sleep badly."

He watches her hands tearing at themselves, wanting to take them in his own hands, to quiet them. "My dear," he says, "if I have been the cause of any discomfort, or troubled you in any way, I humbly beg your pardon. I would not hurt you for the world."

The pity in his eyes is almost more than she can bear.

"I'm so glad you came back," she whispers.

"I too. We had such a good talk yesterday."

"Oh, yes."

"And I am in no hurry today. Are you? Then, if you would—and if I am not imposing upon your hospitality—and if you do not think me so terribly ill-mannered for inviting myself—perhaps we might have another cup of tea together?"

Pausing for rest halfway up the stairs, leaning on his arm, she looks up at him, hesitantly.

"Will you forgive me for something too?" she says.

"Forgive you?" He smiles down into her face. "What could you possibly have done that would need my forgiveness?"

"I was very impolite yesterday."

"Impolite, my dear? In what way?"

"It was only after you left that I remembered . . . I never even asked what it is you do, and what has brought you to New York . . ."

He throws his head back in a shout of laughter, then raises her hand and kisses it . . . and still she is not afraid of him, for all his strangeness.

She is not naïve, and knows the reason for his return: his remorse at displacing her . . . and easing her loneliness may help to both soften the blow and relieve whatever compunction he feels for being the cause. But it does not matter why he is here; nothing matters, so long as she can watch him and listen to him—and, when he is not looking, hold the hand he had kissed against her mouth, or press it to her cheek.

If she is not changed from yesterday, neither is her room; it waits today just as it did then—as if time stands still here—and she pours out the tea and listens, her elbows on the table and her head resting on her hand. He speaks today of his country and his family, elaborating upon stories he only touched upon yesterday, taking inspiration from her bright, mobile face, for Clara says little but is an eloquent listener, and her expressions mirror his, nuance for nuance.

Both seem, in fact, to be listening as much with eyes as with ears. The face she watches is happy, wistful, darkly alive with the memories he tells, and she thinks that he must be lonelier than he knows, here in this strange land, and never takes her eyes from him until the tea is long gone and both suddenly realize that blue dusk has crept through the windows, and it is hard to see the other's face across the table.

He leans back in his chair, smiling at her in the gathering darkness. "I must seem," he says, "the most egotistical, self-indulgent man on earth. You should have stopped me long ago."

"I loved listening," she says. "You made them all come alive. I feel as if I know them now . . . especially Fiorina. I like her very much."

"The baby, yes. The two of you would get along well. She is only a little older than you."

Clara lifts her chin, her smile gone. "I am not a baby," she says, rising from her chair.

Alfieri rises with her, protesting: "Miss Adler, I meant no disparagement of your years . . ." But she does not answer. Instead she takes a box of matches from a side cupboard and goes from table to table in silence, lighting the numerous candles set about the room—ten, fifteen, twenty—until the pretty chamber glows and flickers like a magic cave.

Alfieri watches her move about. By the candlelight's soft sorcery he sees her for the first time as she should be: all traces of illness erased; and her body—as she bends to kindle a cluster of tiny flames, or stands on tiptoe to touch her lit taper to another on a high shelf—is not the body of a child.

"If you promise to forgive me," he says quietly, lost once more in some half-remembered enchantment, "I promise not to tease you again."

She does not answer at first, and he is wondering what to do to make amends when she says: "You spoke so much of your brothers and sisters." She does not look at him, all her attention centered on the candles. "You spoke of them, and their children, and your mother and father, but you never once mentioned your wife."

"Did I not?" He smiles at her, watching her light the last of the candles on the mantelpiece beneath her portrait. "That is because I have no wife to mention."

She says "Oh!" quite casually, crosses the room to place the matches back in their cupboard and turns toward him again, not quite looking at him.

"I must call Margaret," she says, "to clear away the tea things and lay the table for dinner. I usually dine alone, but if you would like to stay . . ."

He shakes his head and she falls back a step, as if struck, nodding quickly. Gathering her skirts about her, she moves toward the bell rope that hangs beside the mantelpiece, but he reaches it before her and takes her outstretched hand.

"I cannot stay," he says gently. "I promised to be somewhere else, never imagining . . ." Her head is down, her hand motionless in his. In the candlelight the curve of her cheek is achingly sweet. "I would stay if I could."

She raises her eyes to his. "Would you come again?"

"Whenever I can. As often as I can. Tomorrow."

"No." She looks away, distressed. "Not tomorrow. There will be someone else here tomorrow."

"Who?" he says abruptly, and the word is out before he realizes the arrogance of his question. Fool! What right has he to ask her whom she sees?

She does not seem to notice. "My guardian's lawyer."

"Mr. Chadwick?"

She raises her head again, wondering. "Do you know him?"

"Only by name," he lies. "As the seller of this house."

"Yes, of course," she says. "He comes for luncheon twice each week." Something in her voice makes him look at her more closely. "To see if I am mending."

"He is a friend?"

"Of my guardian. But he has been very good to me since my guardian's death," she replies. "He has paid for the doctors, so many doctors, and allowed me to stay here."

"Why would he not? This is your home."

"Not any more." Her voice is barely more than a whisper. "Not since my guardian died. Mr. Chadwick says that I'm here on the sufferance of the estate, and as executor he could put me out at any time, if he wished. But he lets me stay, though he needn't. Someone else, someone not as kind or as generous, would have sent me to a charity hospital. Or an asylum."

"Did he tell you all this?" Alfieri has gone very still. "Did he tell you this himself?"

"Everyone tells me. The doctors . . . even the servants. About how grateful I should be. And I am grateful."

He draws her over to the sofa, sits down beside her still holding her hand, wanting to quiet her fears, to tell her of his plans to divide up the house between them, but he says nothing. If Chadwick refuses, as he is likely to do . . . if the plans come to naught . . .

"Madonna," he says, "I will come back. The day after tomorrow, yes? And we will sit together, and have tea, and this time I will be quiet and listen while you tell me about yourself."

Even by candlelight he can see the uneasiness creep into her eyes. "I have nothing to tell," she says, and slips her hand from his. "Nothing. My family are all dead."

"So you told me yesterday. But what of you?"

"I have nothing to tell." The words flow from her like a litany, oft-repeated. "My family died when I was thirteen, I went to an orphanage, my guardian saw me there, he took me in." She makes a little gesture with her hands. "He took me in because he was kind and I had no one . . . he was my last hope. And now he is dead too. . . ."

"Piccola," he says, drawing her hands from her face, "there is nothing you need to say. We will sit quietly, you and I, and if we speak of anything at all it will be the weather, or the latest foolish fashions . . . have you seen the sleeves the ladies are wearing? They are called 'leg-of-mutton,' and indeed they look as if some poor sheep is missing an extremity . . ."

She laughs, wipes her eyes, folds her hands in her lap. Shamefaced, she says: "You are a guest. You don't want to hear my troubles . . . I am sorry I bothered you with them."

"There is no one whose troubles I would rather hear. I would help you with them if I could. Will you let me try?"

Her eyes lift to his—trusting, guileless—and his heart turns over. "You cannot help me," she says. "But I would be so happy if you came to see me again. I like you very much."

"The day after tomorrow. At three o'clock."

He takes a candle with him to light his way out, but stops at the door and turns back.

"And *madonna* . . . do not make plans for dinner with anyone else."

Chapter Seven

FOR THE PAST TWENTY YEARS, every Tuesday and Friday, Thaddeus Chadwick has taken his midday meal in the dining room of the house in Gramercy Park. It is his custom. Chadwick is a man of regular habits, and even though his erstwhile host is now no more, his custom it remains. Clearly, then, if an occurrence as momentous as the death of a beloved friend need cause no alteration in the established routine of a man of regular habits, it logically follows that mere illness, barring the threat of contagion, would certainly not be grounds for so much as a moment's deviation. And so, even during the blackest weeks of Clara's affliction, Chadwick had continued his punctual arrivals at half past eleven twice each week, whereupon he would confer with the doctor, gaze briefly at the patient, and then descend to the dining room, there to partake of a leisurely, and very full, luncheon.

And yet, for all his immutability, Chadwick has made one very recent modification. With Clara convalescent and able to take her meals at table once more, the attorney, unbidden, has changed the venue of his noon meals from the solitary splendor of the dining room to the more homely comforts of the girl's sitting room. Luncheon is now served, every Tuesday and Friday at precisely twelve noon, at the very same table where she had heard her future read in a cup of tea.

The question of whether Clara is pleased with this new arrangement has never been raised, as Chadwick had not found it necessary to consult with her before making it, doubtless assuming that since his meals would be more enjoyable if taken with her, it could only follow that hers would be more enjoyable if taken with him. Let it only be said, therefore, that she acquiesces in this as she does in all things.

Nevertheless, both as meals and as occasions for social intercourse, the success of these times together has, until today, been most emphatically one-sided: Clara eats almost nothing and generally says even less than she eats, leaving her companion to fill both himself and the silence. But today, with the remains of his usual hearty meal spread before him, Chadwick's conversation is full of Mrs. Astor's grand end-of-season gala, held the night before last. Chadwick's eye is good—none better at noticing things that others overlook—and his powers of description excellent; and although he has somehow neglected to mention the gala's raison d'être and the presence of its guest of honor, Clara listens raptly for once, seeing it all in her mind's eye.

"It must have been wonderful," she murmurs.

"Wonderful? My dear child! What jewels, what food, what music! Such a pity that you could not have been there to see for yourself. But then"—he reaches over and pats her hand, which she quietly withdraws into her lap—"you are not the giddy, thoughtless type of creature who delights in such frivolous pleasures. You are more sedate, more modestly womanly. Yours are the small joys of quiet evenings in your own cozy bower, with your books and your needlework, are they not? Why, I have always known you to be such a solemn little creature that I believe the very idea of frivolity bores you."

"No," she says dreamily. "Once, when I was very young, I watched two older cousins dress for a ball. It was so magical to me, like Cinderella come true, and I thought of the gown I would wear to a ball one day . . . and how I would waltz, and waltz, and waltz, until the sun came up . . ."

For all her illness and her shorn hair and her strange, solitary existence, for all that she belongs nowhere . . . she is still a young girl like any other; she had had dreams, once, of a gown like a froth of pearls and moonlight; had pictured herself, light as a bubble, the shining magnet of all eyes.

Chadwick watches her while she is far away, lost in the pretty dream. Not himself being prey to visions of pearls and moonlight, his passionless gaze misses no sign of her recent illness: the restless fingers folding and unfolding the napkin in her lap, the tiny, nervous twitch of a muscle at the corner of her eye . . . and yet her color is definitely better today, and she looks less drawn and exhausted. She starts suddenly, and flushes under his close gaze, catching herself.

"My dear, is something wrong?" he says, but it is another moment before she answers him.

"No . . . no, nothing," she replies in confusion, her head bowed, her hand at her throat. "I did not mean to startle you. I . . . I was only . . ."

"You were daydreaming. Was it a pleasant dream?"

"It was nothing. Only . . ." She colors again. "Nothing."

"As you wish, my dear. I hope my tales did not overexcite you. Rest is what you need, now, and quiet. Waltzing can be arranged when you are well, if that is what you wish."

But not in the arms that had held her in her dream just now. She can see him still, standing in the doorway with the candle lighting his face, but she is what she is, and he would run from her if he knew the truth . . .

"Come," Chadwick says jovially, "let us speak of something else. Let us speak of you." He drains his teacup and pushes it from him. "Well? And how have you passed your time since I saw you last?"

"Very quietly."

"Of course you have, my dear. As you always do, in fact."

"Yes." She avoids meeting his eyes.

"A life as constant as the North Star, as retired as a nun's. Never any change, never any new sights, never any company other than my own."

"No." The untouched food on her plate seems suddenly to take on new fascination for her, and she pushes at it with her fork.

"My poor child. How you must long, at times, for some company. The hours must pass slowly for you, with no diversions."

"Margaret keeps me company. And I have my needlework."

"But Margaret is only a maid, and she has her chores to do. And needlework engages the fingers, not the brain, leaving one a great deal of time to think."

He pauses.

"Tell me, my dear, do you still worry about your future? I have told you that you have nothing to fear. I will care for you, come what may."

Clara's fork clatters into her plate. "I am very grateful to you."

"I am certain of it. And yet I do not do this for the sake of your gratitude; I do it because to do anything less would be inconceivable. It is not merely a matter of Christian duty. You know, don't you, that in the years since my good friend Henry brought you here you have become . . . dear to me."

"Yes." The word is a whisper.

"And I had hoped that, over time, you might have been growing fond of me too."

"I am . . . fond of you."

"Are you, my dear? Thank you. You make me very happy by saying so. I think your dear guardian would be pleased as well. He was, after all, my closest friend. Nevertheless, I have noticed"—he is thoughtful—"that since his death you have ceased to address me as you used to. 'Uncle Chadwick,' you were wont to call me, once upon a time. 'Uncle Chadwick,' you would say, 'would you care for more tea?' Or 'Uncle Chadwick, won't you stay to dinner?' " He repeats the words—"Uncle Chadwick . . . Uncle Chadwick . . ."—drawing them out, admiring the sound of them. "I must confess that, as a man with no family ties, I had never been called 'uncle' by anyone until you began to do so. It was such a pretty habit, my dear; I quite enjoyed it. Why do you no longer call me that?"

When she makes no reply he probes further. "Have we become strangers to one another?"

"No. Not strangers." He can barely hear her.

"I am glad of that too, my dear. Please understand that I want neither your gratitude nor the approbation of the world for what I have done. Kindness, as we know, is its own reward, and I dislike even mentioning the matter. And what the consequences would have been—to you, child—had there been no one to step in and shoulder the burdens that my poor friend, your guardian, laid down when he died, leaving you— need I say it?—with nothing, I need not go into, for I know that you know them all too well. Just think, dear girl, of where you might be right now, had I not kept this roof to shelter you."

Clara bows her head. Months of constant reminders of what might have been have not accustomed her to her utter indebtedness to this man, or blunted the horror of what, without his continued goodwill, might yet still be.

The wretchedness that awaits her without his help almost stops her heart. She has no friends, she has no home, no income, no livelihood, no accomplishments. She owns nothing but the contents of her wardrobe, not even the furnishings of her two rooms. Work she would welcome, but to do what? She has neither skill nor strength enough to be a maid or a shop girl, nor sufficient education to be a governess. And who would hire her, after all, to care for their innocent children? As for references . . .

She stares blindly out the window. The streets are always there, waiting for her. She wipes her eyes with the heels of both hands, but the tears—always there, too, just behind her eyes—continue to well up steadily and quietly, dropping to land, like pearls, on the black lace of her bodice.

As before, Chadwick watches her, unmoved and unmoving.

"I am sorry to distress you, my dear," he says, "but although it is true that, as I said, I dislike mentioning the matter, it will perhaps be necessary to remind you, from time to time, of your position. I hope that I will not have to do it often; nothing would cause me greater pain."

Clara, unable to speak as yet, nods her head.

"What does that mean, my dear? Does that mean that we understand each other?"

"Yes."

"I cannot hear you, my dear."

"Yes. We understand each other."

"Say it again, please, so that I may be certain of what I think I heard."

"We understand each other."

"We understand each other . . . Uncle Chadwick," he says.

"We understand each other." She swallows her tears. "Uncle Chadwick."

"Good. Then tell me, dear child," he says, bringing his face close to hers, "just how long you intended to wait before telling me of your visitor of two days ago. Or were you never going to tell me at all?"

She shrinks back in her chair, the tears still spilling down her cheeks.

"I did not . . . I did not think . . . that it mattered."

"Did you not? Or did you merely think that I would never know? Oh, no, my dear," he says, "don't turn your head away. If that was your innocent thought, let me make one thing perfectly clear to you, so that we need have no misunderstandings, ever again. Everything about you matters to me. Everything you think, everything you do . . . everything that happens to you is of the utmost concern to me." He smiles. "Because I care for you."

He leans back expansively. "You are wondering just how I know, of course. I should let you believe that I can read your mind and hear your thoughts, that I am a magician—but you half believe that already. No, the explanation is much simpler than that: your visitor, himself, told me of his visit during the course of a delightful conversation we had the evening before last. You see, he was the guest of honor at Mrs. Astor's gala."

Clara stares at him, uncomprehending.

"What, my dear! Do you not even know the identity of the man you entertained so charmingly? He is only the finest singer in the world. But perhaps the two of you spent so much time speaking of your concerns about your future that he had no time to tell you of himself." He waves his hand. "Never mind. Whatever you discussed, you certainly impressed him most favorably."

And yesterday's visit? Does Chadwick know of that too? What if he does, and she remains silent? But what if he does *not,* and she confesses that her caller has been here, not once, but twice? Which will make him angrier? What should she say? Panicked, almost sick with fear, she stammers: "He . . . he stayed such a short while. We had tea. He asked me a little about myself—"

"And you wisely told him even less, I'm sure . . ."

"—and he told me a little of his family. That was all, truly! We never spoke of what he does." Not even last evening, when she had asked him. No doubt he had seen no point in telling her. How stupid he must think her, she realizes with sudden shame—how pitifully ignorant; no wonder he had laughed at the question—and even in the midst of her fear her tears well up again at the thought that she had repaid his many kindnesses with such offense.

"How very self-effacing of him," Chadwick says.

"But I should have known," she whispers, only partly to Chadwick. "I heard him singing."

"Did you indeed? Then you have been the recipient of a singular honor, my dear! How fortunate that Mrs. Astor was unaware of it. The good lady would doubtless have had a seizure had she known that some-one else had been the first to hear the great Alfieri sing in America, especially after trying so hard to cajole him into it at her party, and failing so abysmally. But getting back to your singer, did you know that he wishes to buy this house? Ah, so you did speak of something other than his family."

She wipes her eyes, her dread of imminent discovery beginning to ebb. "He likes this house."

"So it would appear," Chadwick says dryly. "It seems to contain every-thing he wants. Nevertheless, I wish that he had held his tongue. I had wanted the news I have for you to come as a surprise."

"News?" she whispers.

"About the impending change in your life."

She feels the trap closing around her, wants to run, to fly scream-ing into the street, away from what awaits her . . . and sits silent, in-stead, for there is nowhere to go, after all, and in any case it is no more than she deserves. Who will remember her when she is locked away? Oh, Mr. Alfieri . . . will he think of her sometime? She will never know . . . but at least he will be here when she is gone . . . he, and not some faceless stranger, treading the halls that were once her home. He had liked her a little, had made her smile, and his tales had opened a window for her onto another world, a world of happy people living happy lives. No matter that she will never be one of them . . . she aches with love for him, and always will.

"When does he want me to leave?"

"He? Want you to leave?" Chadwick corrects her. "Oh, no, my child, that is *my* decision. He wants you to stay! He feels that this house is large enough to accommodate you both. He even asked me if I would permit you to remain—with a female companion, of course, as a chaperone." He allows just enough time for disbelief, gratitude, and an almost pathetic joy to flicker across her face before saying, with a short laugh: "You don't believe that I would consider it for even one moment, do you?

"For one thing," he says, leaning back in his chair and folding his hands over his ample middle, as if discoursing upon a fine point of law, "the man has the manners of a peasant, and I would be remiss in my duty if I were to permit you to stay under the same roof with him. When I questioned him, civilly enough, as to whether he knew what this property was worth, he found it necessary to boast of his houses in London and Paris and Florence. He then had the effrontery to suggest that you should come with the house, as though you were some part of the furnishings. 'Just as it was during its owner's lifetime,' was the phrase he used, I believe."

"He seemed so very kind and polite," she whispers.

"You doubtless have charms that I lack, my dear. But you weren't there during my conversation with the man, were you? No, I fear that our sweet singer of songs has started off on the"—he smiles appreciatively at his bon mot—"wrong key, with me. For that reason alone I would not permit you to stay in this house with him, even if he hired fifty chaperones.

"And speaking of chaperones," he says, "I am reminded that he is as celebrated for his lechery as he is for his voice." His eyes gleam behind his spectacles. "Oh, my child, you cannot *begin* to imagine the stories I have heard of his women. Such things are not for your ears, of course, but surely you will agree that, in light of past events"—Chadwick smiles—"even with a chaperone it would be most unwise to put you in temptation's way."

He leans close, lowering his voice confidingly. "And yet even if those things were not of concern to me, I have still another reason for not letting you stay here. What reason? Why, my child, surely you've guessed? You must have realized that once you were well enough to leave this place your home would be with me? Signor Alfieri's desire for this house and my plans for you have coincided beautifully."

She is suffocating, dying. Swiftly, now, the walls are moving in— now a shutter slamming shut, now a door locking fast. She is going to be sick . . .

"I see that happiness has made you pale," he says to her white face. "And you should be happy. Who is more suitable to be your new guardian than your late guardian's dearest friend and counselor, after all? Who would know—who could know—better than I what he wanted for you? And I am certain the court will see it that way too, my dear. The petition to have you made my ward is already filed, and I expect a favorable decision within a fortnight. And while my house is not so grand as this, it is more than adequate for the two of us. There I will be able to watch over you, and see that you grow well again, and strong. You must believe me, dear child, when I say that your health is the most important thing in the world to me."

Rising to stand behind her chair, he lays his heavy hands on her shoulders, letting the thumb of one hand stroke her neck.

"You see now how much I care for you, don't you, my dear?" He bends low to murmur it, his breath against her cheek. "How happy we will be with a single roof to shelter us! Nearness fosters tenderness, you know. And you will call me 'Uncle' again, and someday, perhaps . . . well, we must wait and see what the future will bring."

She closes her eyes. "Please . . . please, Uncle Chadwick, I am so grateful . . . but, please . . . I would rather stay here."

"I am certain of it." His lips move against her ear; his hands tighten on her shoulders, holding her still. "And I don't care."

Letting his hands fall from her, he rings for a servant, then lights a cigar, idly following the blue smoke as it curls into the air.

"Clear the table, Margaret," he says when the maid appears. "I'll be leaving in a moment. And see that your uncle waits for me in the hall;

I need to speak with him and I don't intend to hunt him down all over the house, as I had to do last time. Should he not be there when I come down, he needn't stay on the premises after today."

The maid curtsies and vanishes to convey the message, and Chadwick turns back to Clara, sitting dumb and motionless.

"And now, child," he says, bending over her, "it is time for me to go. Your singer's attorney will be waiting in my office to discuss the purchase of this house. I would not wish to keep him waiting . . . not too long, at any rate. And as for your singer, I will ask his attorney to give him your farewell. I do not think you will be seeing him again."

Always he kisses her upon arriving and departing—it is his custom—and today is no different, except that here, too, there is a change of venue. Seizing her face between his hands, he kisses her mouth roughly, prolonging the pressure when she recoils and tries to pull away.

"Two weeks from today," he says, stroking her cheek, "you will come to live with me. Didn't I promise always to take care of you? You see how I have kept my word. Even now your room is being prepared . . . a pretty bower just for you, my child . . . and so very near to mine. What need have we for chaperones, you and I? It does my heart good, you know, to think how relieved you must be, now that you have nothing more to fear."

The maid, coming in with a tray a few minutes later to clear away the dishes, finds Clara curled in her window seat, sucking in great breaths of fresh air from the garden.

"It's his big cigars, miss," the maid volunteers as she scrapes and stacks the plates. "They do stink, don't they? The smoke stays in the curtains for days . . ." She looks up from her tray. "Why, Miss Clara, it must've took you awful bad—your eyes are watering dreadfully!"

Clara, her head against the window frame, sees no reason to contradict her.

Chapter Eight

THE NEWS OF CLARA ADLER'S imminent removal from Gramercy Park will cause hardly a ripple among those members of New York society who had followed the course of her illness with such devotion. For one thing, anyone capable of doing so has abandoned the city for summer quarters, leaving only a handful of the elect behind to marvel at the idea of Chadwick—who loathes domestic encumbrance in every form, and enjoys no one's company so much as his own—suddenly assuming familial responsibility in the form of a ward.

For another, the girl herself, since being reduced to the status of a penniless dependent, has ceased to be of any interest other than as a lingering oddity, and has come to be viewed in the same light as any other exotic creature housed by a wealthy owner to prove his eclecticism and the depth of his purse. One may expatiate upon a potential heiress at great length and in vast detail; one does not, however, spend any time at all discussing a pet monkey or a tame peacock unless the beast has done something untoward, such as savaging one of the servants; and unless Miss Adler turns upon Chadwick's household in a similar fashion (the chances of which seem relatively improbable), the public's fascination with her is not likely to be rekindled any time soon.

Outside of Clara herself, then, there are only three persons in the world to whom it matters that she is soon to disappear beneath Chadwick's roof: Daniel Buchan, who, despite his expectation of just such an outcome, finds Chadwick's intransigence galling in the extreme; Stafford Dyckman, who is concerned because Alfieri is, and also because his chivalrous young soul is roused at the rather romantic notion of a maiden in distress; and Mario Alfieri himself.

But the problem is more simple and direct for Alfieri than it is for either Buchan or Dyckman. Her loneliness calls to him, stirring something that has lain silent for years.

There had been a young woman, once, about Clara's age. How long ago? Before the world changed, before he had become "the nightingale." Her eyes had not been trusting—she had known too many beds before coming to his, and too much betrayal—but she had clung to him the same way, out of need, and he had loved her . . .

He is young no longer and the world has changed, and Clara is young enough be his child; he has met her only twice. But when she clings to his hands the old years are come again, and all the lost joy with them, and he is a better man, a gentler man . . . a kinder, more worthy man . . . and the thought of losing her is like Lazarus, dying a second time; he will not be raised from the dead again. God has given him his last chance.

The knowledge, therefore, that she will soon be beyond his reach—for there is not the faintest breath of hope that Chadwick will allow him to call upon her—has him staring into nothingness for most of the night after Buchan tells him the news, restlessly pacing from room to room, and rising early the next morning. Three o'clock is the appointed time for his return to Gramercy Park, and the hours between are all but unendurable.

The precious sophisticates of his world, the ones who know too much and care too little, how they would laugh at him! He has slept badly, and awakened in a jangle of raw nerves—he who can nightly face the close attention of a thousand pairs of eyes and ears with as little anxiety as another feels crossing the street—because of a young woman who does not know who he is, but says "I like you very much" with her heart in her eyes.

He fills the empty time by walking, even though the day is wet, first to St. Stephen's for Mass, then to Stafford Dyckman's club for an hour or two of absentminded conversation and a luncheon remarkable chiefly for the level of Alfieri's distraction. Shortly before three o'clock, he bids Dyckman an impatient farewell and walks through a misty spring rain to Gramercy Park.

She is in her own sitting room today, curled into a corner of the sofa. Of the improvement Chadwick had seen in her appearance yesterday, nothing at all remains. Her head comes up blindly at the sound of Alfieri's knock and the opening door, her eyes so swollen that he doubts she can see him at all, until she stretches out her hands to him. He is at her side in another moment, her cold fingers covered by his warm hands.

"Are you ill, little girl?" He says it into her hair because she has buried her face in his shoulder to hide her red and aching eyes.

"I thought you wouldn't come back."

"I promised you I would."

"He said I would never see you again." Her voice is muffled against him.

"Who told you this?"

"Mr. Chadwick."

"*Madonna,* it will take much more than Mr. Chadwick to keep me from you."

"He told me . . ."

"What did he tell you?" he says with great gentleness, and waits to hear what he already knows: that she is soon to be living in the lawyer's house.

"He told me who you are," she whispers.

A chasm opens up beneath Alfieri's feet. "Ah, did he?" he says, closing his eyes in sudden pain.

"I am sorry I didn't know. I am very stupid." Her voice trembles. "Don't be angry with me."

"*Bambina,* is that what you think? That I would be angry because you did not know who I am?"

"I meant no offense."

"And I took none. Is that why you cried, and made your lovely eyes all red?" He rests his lips against her hair, breathing in its fragrance.

"Listen, dear heart, I am not angry with you. I was happy that you did not know."

"Why?"

"The reason is not important now. Someday I will explain." He takes her by the shoulders and holds her away from him. "Did Mr. Chadwick tell you nothing else?"

She droops beneath his hands, and her bowed head touches his shoulder again. "I must go with him."

"*Cara,* tell me . . . do you want to?"

"No." Close as he is, he must strain to hear her. "He frightens me."

"*Grazie a Dio,*" he whispers. "That is all I needed to know."

"He told me what you tried to do," she says; "that you would let me stay here with you."

"Would you prefer that?"

"Oh, yes, I would like to stay." She raises her head and looks at him for the first time. "With you."

Red nose, swollen eyes: Alfieri thinks that he has never seen anyone so beautiful. "Then stay with me."

"He won't let me."

"He will have no choice. We will give him no choice."

"How?"

"By making certain he can never take you away from me."

"How?" she says again.

"By changing your name."

She stares at him.

"*Sì,* your name, Miss Adler. Oh, my dear," he laughs, seeing her bewilderment, "do you still not understand? I am asking you to marry me."

She has forgotten how to breathe, and her eyes brim with sudden tears. "You would do that for me?"

"No, *bambina*—for me."

"Why?"

"Don't you know, little girl?" He looks at her with a puzzled smile and touches her face. "I'm in love with you."

She smiles back tremulously, and shakes her head. "You don't know me. You don't know anything about me. I'm not clever, or talented, or wonderful." In her eyes is the deep sadness he had seen the day he found her, and a fear he does not understand. "I didn't even know who you are. I would disappoint you."

"I know what disappoints me. It is not you."

"How do you know? Why are you so certain? What if you're wrong?"

In answer he takes her face between his hands and kisses her, tasting her for the first time, and her mouth is young and sweet, and all the lost years have been found. When he lifts his head she lies against him, her heart beating wildly, fitting into the circle of his arms like a key in its lock: perfect, unfaultable, beyond all praise.

"Am I wrong?" he says.

She cannot think, she cannot reason, not here, pressed against him, warm and safe. Even before she had opened her eyes and seen him she had loved him, hearing his voice. What have right and wrong to do with it? What sane person would refuse such deliverance? Since yesterday she has been ill, sick in mind and body at the thought of what lies in store for her. This reprieve must have been sent for a reason, to give her another chance at life. She will tell him the truth, very soon, and he will not mind; he is in love with her. This is a miracle, a miracle . . . let me be worthy . . .

"I love you so much," she whispers, "so much, so much, so much . . . and I will try so hard to be a good wife, and to make you proud. Be patient with me, please. I will learn as fast as I can." She touches his mouth, still not quite certain that this miracle is real, that it has happened.

"Do you really love me?" she says.

THE RAIN FALLS in steady sheets, and the street lamps gleam twice over, their halos of light reflected off the wet and shimmering pavement. A small fire has been lit in Buchan's study to take the dampness from the air. The lawyer and his guest face each other from either side of the hearth. On a small table at Buchan's elbow are two glasses and a decanter of golden brandy that glows in the firelight like the longed-for sunlight of a happy future.

"My thanks, Mr. Buchan, for seeing me so quickly, and especially on a Saturday evening. I hope that your good wife will forgive me for taking you away from your dinner guests."

"Signore, you must know that the appearance of Mario Alfieri on our doorstep has raised Mrs. Buchan and me to new heights in the estimation of our guests. But besides that, did you really think we would turn you away? Especially when you come bearing the news that Miss Adler has agreed to become your wife?"

The lawyer nods thoughtfully, regarding his guest. "I am delighted for you, of course, signore, but I must also admit to you that I am amazed. Dumbfounded, in fact, would be a far more fitting word."

"Why?" Alfieri says. "Do you still doubt my intentions?"

"No, not your intentions. You have offered the young woman honorable marriage, and have informed your attorney of it. You would hardly have done either if your intentions were less than worthy."

"But still you do not approve." Alfieri's gaze is frank. "May I ask why?"

Buchan spreads his hands. "It is not a matter of either approval or disapproval. You are a grown man with much experience of women—"

"And Miss Adler is a very young woman. Is that what disturbs you?"

"Not precisely, signore. After all, we are not discussing the young lady's ruin and abandonment—"

"I have never been guilty of that, Mr. Buchan. With any woman."

"I never said you have. But now you wish to marry."

Alfieri says: "You make it sound as if I have taken leave of my senses. Well, in a way I have. I am in love, Mr. Buchan. Is that so difficult to believe of me?"

Buchan's voice softens. "No, of course not. But you have met the young lady a total of—what? Three times now? You have enjoyed each other's company for some eight hours. Is that sufficient to determine a lifetime's happiness together? I do not speak of her judgment—at nineteen, the capacity for judgment has not yet had time to develop. But what of yours, signore? Certainly you are old enough, and you appear to know what you are doing . . . but do you? Or could it be that, finding yourself in a new land holding no memories for you, with no affiliations . . . experiencing a freedom you have not known in many years . . . could it be that this has led you to see Miss Adler as a young damsel in distress?"

Alfieri smiles. "Whom only I can save? You think I have cast myself in the role of the knight from a far-off land, Mr. Buchan, who rides onto the scene to rescue the little princess from her tower and carry her away?"

"It is a flattering role, signore."

"Very true. But I am not delirious, or living in a fantasy, or spinning dreams, and this is neither an illusion, nor an infatuation. I have fallen in love. Why? Each man has his own reasons for loving whom he does, reasons that would make no sense to another. All you need to know, Mr. Buchan, is that I have asked Miss Adler to be my wife and she has agreed. I regret, of course, that it has all happened too quickly for your entire satisfaction, but I desperately need your help if I am to marry her . . . there is not much time!"

The lawyer smiles and holds his hands up in a gesture of surrender, reaches for the brandy on the table beside him and fills the two glasses. He hands one to Alfieri, then touches his own glass to the tenor's— "Mrs. Buchan and I wish you joy!"—and drinks.

Alfieri drinks too. "My thanks to you both. As to the necessity for speed," he says, "for that you must blame Mr. Chadwick. He has left me no time for a traditional courtship and engagement."

"You do know that you'll be making a bad enemy, don't you? He will not take kindly—a colossal understatement, I fear—to your stealing Miss Adler out from under his nose, just as he was about to carry her away."

"And should I be afraid, Mr. Buchan? Next year at this time I will be preparing to return to Europe. He can do nothing to me, so long as he cannot steal her back, or have her taken away from me . . . by having the marriage annulled, say, because she is underage, and did not receive his consent."

Buchan rises to refill Alfieri's glass. "I suppose there is no doubt of your intention to consummate the marriage rather quickly? Yes, well, once she is your wife, in fact as well as in law, no court would consider undoing it, regardless of the lack of Mr. Chadwick's consent. You have nothing to fear on that score. But let us discuss the question of the wedding itself," he says, returning to his seat and refilling his own glass. "Have you decided how it is to be done? Who, for instance, will perform the ceremony?" He hesitates, then says bluntly: "You are Roman Catholic, are you not?"

Alfieri laughs. "I am from Italy, Mr. Buchan, am I not? Italy is rich in many things, but not, I am afraid, in Lutherans and Baptists."

"But does it not pose a problem for you that Miss Adler is"—he hesitates again—"not Catholic?"

"Perhaps I am not so good a Catholic as you believe, Mr. Buchan. Miss Adler and I have discussed this matter—briefly, to be sure—and how we marry is of small importance to me. What is certain is that with less than two weeks remaining before I am to lose her to Mr. Chadwick, we must move quickly. There is no time for her to take instruction in my religion . . . even if she were so inclined, which I do not know."

"Then the ceremony will be a civil one?"

"If you will be so good as to provide us with a justice of the peace, or some other such dignitary."

Buchan cocks his head thoughtfully. "And will your church recognize a civil marriage to someone of another faith?"

"No, Mr. Buchan, it will not. In the eyes of my church I will not be married at all. But I am not so concerned with the eyes of my church as I am with the laws of your country. So long as she is married to me legally and Mr. Chadwick cannot take her from me, I am content." He smiles again. "And as for the state of my immortal soul . . . that is a matter for my confessor, not my lawyer. Do not let it disturb you."

Buchan says: "She means that much to you?"

"Yes," Alfieri answers. "That much."

Buchan leans over to stir the fire, blinking in the strong light. "Then it must be done quickly and it must be done in absolute secrecy." He looks up at Alfieri. "But discretion is vital, as I am sure you realize. What of Slade's servants? You will need their assistance, of course, but can they be trusted not to inform Mr. Chadwick of your plans?"

Alfieri says: "Oh, yes, I am sure of it. I spoke with them both, you see, before I came here this evening. Not surprisingly, I discovered that they are not especially devoted to Mr. Chadwick . . . something to do, I believe, with his pleasant manner when he addresses them. I assured them both that Miss Adler—Signora Alfieri that is to be—would be grateful for their services in her new home . . . she is very shy, and too many new faces around her would make her uneasy. In return, I have been given to understand that both the maid, who has already served as Miss Adler's ladies' maid in a small way, and the footman, will be perfectly content to follow their little mistress to her new home—and would sooner have their tongues cut out than give away her secret."

"But can you be certain?"

"They are faithful to their late master's memory, Mr. Buchan, and greatly attached to his ward. And with promised positions at half again their current wages waiting for them in my house, in addition to the opportunity to escape from Mr. Chadwick once and for all . . ." Alfieri smiles. "Oh, yes, I think we can trust them. And with the inclusion of Gennarino—my valet—such a staff should prove an excellent size for a newlywed household."

"Signore, you take my breath away. Are you always this meticulous and well-prepared?"

"Well, it does not pay to take chances, does it? Not with what really matters." He pauses, grows serious, and seems suddenly hesitant to speak. "That is why I would ask . . . although I know it is a great imposition . . . still, might I ask if you would undertake to help me in yet one more way?"

"Name it," the lawyer says.

"Actually, it would be for my young lady." The tenor picks his words with care. "She is all alone, Mr. Buchan. She has no friends or family to assist her through this time, no one to help her prepare. Most especially, she has no one to confide in . . . no *mamma* with whom she can share her hopes and fears, as brides must surely need to do . . . no one to tell her"—he gestures slightly—"what happens to a young wife on her wedding night." He pauses again. "I was wondering . . . and I know it is a great deal to ask . . . if your good wife would consent to be such a friend to her. When you introduced us just now, and I saw that Mrs. Buchan has such a sweet face, I knew that Clara would not be frightened of her, and I thought . . . perhaps . . . if it would not be too much . . ."

Buchan's voice is gentle. "Signore, consider it done. I would not normally speak for my wife in her absence, but I know that in this our opinions will agree. Frankly, she will be touched, as I am, that you thought well enough of us both to ask."

Alfieri leans back and smiles in pure relief. "Thank you, Mr. Buchan—and your wife too. There is such a great deal to do in so very little time, but with your help I know we will manage it."

"And after the wedding? You will want to go away, of course, on a honeymoon. Have you any idea where?"

"Here again I must rely on your kindness, Mr. Buchan. I have only been ten days in your city. I was thinking of somewhere quiet, in the countryside. Clara has been ill; she needs sunshine and fresh air, but it must not be too far away—the strain of a lengthy journey would be too much for her. Do you know of such a place?"

"I know of a place, signore, but it is very humble. Just a small farm, about two hours north of the city by train, outside a pretty little town called Hudson. The owner is a former client of mine: a widow with two daughters, who takes in guests to supplement her income. Mrs. Buchan and I have stayed there, and I can vouch for its excellence. The house is large—clean and very quiet—and the food is superb: Mrs. Noonan is a marvelous cook. Still, you may wish for something more imposing, such as a hotel . . . although many of them may already be filled for the summer . . ."

"No, no hotels. Above all I want my privacy, and a great deal of quiet for Clara. The place you speak of sounds ideal."

"Then I will make the arrangements. I know the family well; Mrs. Noonan and her daughters are very discreet. No one here will know where you have gone, and no one there will say who you are. But of what date are we speaking? For the wedding, I mean?"

"Wednesday, the sixth of June. Mr. Chadwick has told Clara that he will come for her on the eighth, and I want to be far away with her by then."

"Which gives us exactly"—Buchan does the mental calculation—"eleven days until your wedding." He melts abruptly into a broad, complicitous smile, shaking his head. "My God, who would have thought it? The notorious Mario Alfieri marrying Henry Slade's disinherited ward exactly a fortnight after their first meeting. You know, signore, that this will stand New York on its ear, don't you? And I cannot imagine what all of Europe will think when the news finally reaches them!" He laughs out loud. "I fear that many who go to the opera, come the fall, will be going to do more than just hear you sing. Everyone will want to see what Mario Alfieri looks like as a married man!"

"But it is his pretty young wife who is worth looking at, Mr. Buchan, not Mario Alfieri. Still, if it will make them happy, they are free to stare at me as much as they like . . . and I promise you, I will not allow Mr. Grau to raise the price of the tickets . . ."

Chapter Nine

Am I late?" Dyckman says, flushed with hurrying.

"No, sir." It is Peters who answers, the late Mr. Slade's footman. "The other gentlemen have just arrived." He takes the young man's hat and gloves. "Go right upstairs, sir; they are waiting for you. You do remember the way?"

Dyckman remembers the way. In the last ten days he has developed a nodding acquaintance with this great house; he has known it, however, only in its state of perpetual dusk, and is not prepared for the vast change which this morning has brought. His eyes widen with amazement as he crosses the entrance hall and mounts the stairs.

Light everywhere. Every curtain has been pulled back, every shade raised, every window flung wide, every door opened. From one side of the house to the other, from front to back and top to bottom, the gentle air of June wafts through the rooms, fluttering the pale muslin that still shrouds the furniture, and blowing away the darkness. What is left of it lingers in the high-ceilinged halls and on the alabaster staircase that runs up the center of the house, but it is a muted darkness now: a silvery, soft, underwater darkness that pools in corners and grows shallower until it disappears as it nears doors and windows open to the sun. Staring about him, Dyckman is reminded of a cathedral on Easter morning, and makes his way to the music room—stripped of its net and muslin shrouds, and restored now to its gleaming blue and gold glory—in a suddenly exalted mood.

Alfieri and Buchan are waiting for him with a third man, bespectacled and bearded; a man whom Dyckman does not know, and who is introduced to him as Mr. Wheeler. Alfieri is pale but very composed, and the hand that grips Dyckman's is both warm and steady.

"The train tickets?" he says.

"I have them here, Mario," the young man replies, patting his breast pocket.

"And the baggage?"

"Is at the station, waiting for you to arrive."

"Then there remains nothing to do." Alfieri rests his hands on his friend's shoulders. "Except to thank you."

Dyckman flushes. "There is nothing to thank me for. I have done very little. Besides," he smiles, "the thanks should be mine. I will be invited everywhere on the strength of this story, Mario; you know I will."

Alfieri laughs and bows to Dyckman with an elegant flourish. "Then may you have as much joy in telling it as I have in presenting it to you."

Buchan looks at his watch and nods to the tenor. "Ten o'clock, signore. We should start."

"Will you go upstairs, Stafford," Alfieri asks, "and tell the ladies that we are ready?"

When Dyckman returns, Alfieri has joined Messrs. Buchan and Wheeler by the mantelpiece. Wheeler stands behind a small table upon which are a book and two small glasses, one containing wine, the other empty.

Dyckman nods. "They're coming."

Buchan presses the tenor's hand and walks to the door to wait.

Three servants—the two belonging to this house and Alfieri's own valet—slip quietly into the room and stand a little distance away. The room falls silent, and in the stillness the rustling of skirts is heard in the passage. A fair-haired woman of middle age appears in the doorway; leaning on her arm is a very small, very young woman—hardly more than a girl—in a dove-gray gown. The young woman's hair is covered by a soft lace veil that falls to her shoulders, and she carries a nosegay of three white roses.

Relinquishing the arm of the older woman, and never raising her eyes from the floor, the young woman takes the arm Buchan offers to her. He walks her slowly toward the little group formed by Alfieri, Dyckman, and Wheeler, but before they have covered half the distance, Alfieri comes forward and holds out his hand to her; and she looks up, for the first time, to see him smile.

At the sight of her face, an old verse of Spanish poetry, learned for practical reasons in the days of his own wooing, and for decades unre- membered, springs unbidden into Buchan's mind: "So pale she is with love, my sweet child, I think that never will the rose return to her cheek . . ." As Buchan falls back, the tenor folds the young woman's arm under his own, and together they walk to where Dyckman and Wheeler wait.

Wheeler clasps his hands and looks at each of them; then clears his throat lightly, and says: "Dearly beloved, we are gathered together in the sight of this assembly . . ."

The wine is shared, the lovely words spoken. Alfieri's voice is low and clear in the responses, Clara's very faint. Buchan gives the bride away; no one steps forward to declare any impediment, or to state why this man and this woman should not be joined together. Dyckman pro- duces the ring, which he hands to the justice, who hands it to Alfieri, who slips it onto Clara's finger . . .

And it is done. So quickly that it seems a dream, Mario Alfieri and Clara Adler are pronounced man and wife.

The justice reminds the groom needlessly: "You may kiss the bride."

"No," Alfieri says, "not yet." And before the perplexed eyes of the as- sembly he takes the empty glass from the table where it has stood during the ceremony, unused and unnoticed, wraps it in his handkerchief, places it on the floor, and brings his foot down hard upon it, smashing it to bits. Dyckman and the justice merely stare at each other, dumb, as do the ser- vants and even Mr. and Mrs. Buchan—for the fair-haired woman is none other than the attorney's wife—and each may be forgiven for thinking, understandably, in the face of such bizarre behavior, that perhaps the sudden strain of long-deferred matrimony has proved too much for the tenor.

But the little bride watches with enormous eyes and her hands pressed to her mouth, looking as if she will faint, and when Alfieri has crushed the glass beneath his foot she rises on tiptoe to fling her arms about his neck. And now, it seems, there is no more reason to wait: cupping her face between his hands, Alfieri takes heed at last of the justice's reminder and kisses his wife, so long and so deeply that the assembled guests use the time to slip silently away.

A FTER THAT KISS it is all a blur for Clara: the wedding breakfast, which she gets through somehow, managing to speak normally, and taste what is placed before her, and raise her glass to her lips, all as if she were really there when she is not; the toasts to the happy couple, which she hears as strings of words that she forgets before they have been completely uttered; even the last, poignant farewell to the dear, familiar rooms, which she utters silently as, numbed and unresisting, she allows herself to be changed into traveling clothes for the wedding trip which will be the beginning—and the end—of her marriage.

He has broken the glass. When he had asked her, so tenderly, if she minded being married outside her faith, she had confided—with no thought that he would ever take her words to heart—that she would miss only that ancient custom, because it had always seemed to her to seal the wedding vows before God and to mark the actual instant of marriage . . . and, therefore, if it was not done, no real marriage had taken place.

And he has done it; he has broken the glass for her sake: not merely to humor her foolishness, in his infinite kindness, but to assure her, as no words ever could, that they are truly married, before God. And his reward for such kindness? Very soon, now, he will know what she is . . . and what she is not . . . and how much pain she might have spared him, if she had only been decent, and brave.

And she had wanted to be; she had meant to be, truly. The mad rapture of the day he proposed had lessened, day by day, and fear had grown in its place . . . because when she was not in his lap with her head on his shoulder, when he was not kissing her—then she could think again, clearly, and understand that she owed him the truth. And each day she had meant to tell him . . . except that she could not, because she knew what the truth would do. Just one more day, she had begged herself each day; just one more. And now it is too late, and the thought of his hurt leaves her numb with grief . . . but her remorse will do neither of them any good. He will leave her, once he knows, sickened both by her and her silence—and in two short weeks he has become her light and her air and the blood in her veins—and she will die when he goes away.

And that is only fair. That is right, that is good; that is just as it should be. That will finish what had started so long ago, when a part of her died in the tiny room above the carriage barn while the sun crawled across the cracked plaster wall . . .

The floor creaks behind her and she raises her face from her hands.

"Little love," Alfieri says, slipping his arms around her and pressing a kiss on the top of her head, "our guests are all gone and it is time we were gone too. Have you said your farewells to this house?"

"Yes, Mario."

"I wish that I could have saved it for you, *sposa,* but I had to choose between you and the house . . . and I had to have you. And in any case, you could not have stayed. One way or the other, it seems, your fate was to leave this place." He strokes her hair. "Are you glad to be leaving with me?"

"Yes, Mario."

He knows her well in two weeks. Seating himself on the sofa, he turns her around and pulls her to him, smiling and frowning. "What is it, dear heart? What's wrong?"

"Nothing."

"Something, I think. Won't you tell me?"

Coward from the start; coward still. She has not lived these two weeks in silence, only to tell him now and see the loathing in his eyes. She will be his wife first, for just one day. "Nothing. Only nerves."

"Truly? There is nothing else?"

Paler than ever, she says: "What else could there be?"

He shrugs and busies himself straightening the brooch at her throat. "I do not know. I thought—perhaps—you might be frightened because everything has changed so quickly . . ."

She stares at him.

"Are you frightened, little girl?"

"Yes," she whispers. "Are you?"

"I?" He raises her chin. "Terrified. I have never been anyone's husband before."

Her laugh is like a sob. "Mario, listen . . ." But he puts his finger to her lips.

"Dear heart, this is so new for both of us. I must unlearn forty years of bad habits in order to be fit for my new wife, and you must learn that, in all things, I am for you. We must learn to be patient with each other, yes? Both the learning and the unlearning will take time." He kisses her forehead. "And now the carriage is here to take us to the station. You would not wish to miss the train?"

Rising, he takes an envelope from his pocket and places it on the mantelpiece, leaning it upright against the wall beneath her portrait.

"What is that?"

"Nothing. A letter."

"To whom?"

"To Mr. Chadwick. I think it only right that he learn from me what has happened to you."

"You're leaving it there for him?"

"For when he comes to collect you on Friday . . . and finds you gone."

"What does it say?"

"I thanked him—very graciously, I think—for making it impossible for me not to marry you. It is a scrupulously polite letter; I only hope that he takes it in the spirit in which it is intended."

Taking her hand, Alfieri leads her out of the room, shutting the door behind them for the last time, and down the stairs to the entrance hall.

She falters only once. To step over the threshold into the outside world from which she has hidden for so long—to calmly walk to her

own extinction—is suddenly beyond her strength, and she draws back before the noise, the light and heat, of the open front door. As Alfieri, a step
ahead and already outside, turns back to her with his hand outstretched,
Clara seems to waver and vanish into the shadows before his eyes.

"Love," he says, "don't slip away. You have come so far."

She stands just inside the doorway, a small ghost in gray half-
mourning, staring out at the light with longing eyes.

"*Sposa*, this is not your home any more. Come with me." His voice
is very low. "The glass is broken. It can never be mended again."

"I know." The glass is broken. Her home is with him until he no
longer wants her, but still she cannot take the last step, and looks at
him helplessly.

"Come with me, *madonna*," he says again. "Shouldn't we begin our
blessedness on such a beautiful day?"

Clara takes the hand he holds out to her, and steps into the sunlight.

Chapter Ten

THE HUGE CLOCK SITS on the mantelpiece of Mrs. Noonan's parlor, each sweep of its pendulum ending in the sharp, metallic snick of blade meeting bone. The room is otherwise silent, the close country stillness broken only by the occasional sound of a page being turned, the creak of a chair, or the faint clink of ice settling in a glass . . . and always, always the clock, endlessly butchering time.

Clara looks down at her hands. Each wears a ring, now, a gift from her husband: the right hand bears her engagement ring, a ruby flanked by two pearls in an intricate setting; the left, a wide, gold wedding band of carved leaves and flowers. She twists them around and around, first one, then the other, the feel of the hard metal the only real thing about this nightmarish, endless day.

They had arrived at Westerly, as Mrs. Noonan's farm is called, at three in the afternoon, and the good lady had herself shown them up to what is to be their home for the next two months: a high-ceilinged, spacious apartment at the head of the stairs, consisting of bedroom, sitting room, and bath, with wide windows overlooking the view which gives the farm its name—west to the wide river and then across to the shaggy blue crests of the Catskill Mountains flowing, wave on wave, into the distance. Mario had been delighted. There had been just enough time to unpack—Mrs. Noonan's elder daughter, Ruth, had performed that function for Clara—and to bathe and change from their dusty trav-

eling clothes into fresh garments, before they had been invited downstairs for a special, five-o'clock supper in recognition of the fact that
newly arrived travelers are generally parched and hungry. The Noonans,
it seems, keep country hours: dinner at Westerly is served at midday,
and supper, ordinarily, at seven.

No servants accompany them on this trip: Gennarino has stayed behind in New York to settle their belongings into the house on Madison
Avenue that Mario has taken—through the kind auspices of Mr. Upton,
the house agent—for their eventual return to the city, and the other
two servants have been given time off before commencing their new
duties. Mario will look after himself for the eight weeks of their stay,
and Clara's needs will be attended to, as in the unpacking, by one or
the other of Mrs. Noonan's daughters.

There are two of them, Ruth and Rebecca, both older than Clara.
Ruth, who appears to be about twenty-three or -four, is dark. Rebecca's
coloring is closer to Clara's, but her hair is a lighter red and it gleams
in the sun; she may be two years younger than her sister. Both of them
are everything that Clara is not: tall, handsome girls with thick plaits of
hair that fall below their waists, and the healthy, red-cheeked, slightly
windblown look that comes of farm living. Clara had disliked them both
on sight.

She in fact dislikes everything about this place, even their rooms,
which are too bare for comfort: there are no rugs on the wide-planked
floors, no pictures on the plain, whitewashed walls. She had murmured
this last complaint to Mario, who had laughed and said that no one
needed pictures with such a view beyond the windows . . . like Tuscany,
he said, but bigger and more wild; but Clara had barely noticed the
scenery. Her eyes had been drawn back, again and again, to the high,
old-fashioned bed that dwarfs the broad bedroom, its vast white iron
bulk canopied and draped with sheer netting like bridal veils.

Supper had been another trial. Mrs. Noonan is the cook at Westerly.
She is a thin, slightly stooped, hard-bodied woman with large hands who
has won local fame, and numerous blue ribbons at county fairs, for her
skill in the kitchen; but despite Mario's praise of the food Clara had
merely pushed at it with her fork—she does not even know what had

been placed before her—listening with barely half an ear to the lively conversation at the table between Mario and the sisters, which she remembers not at all.

And after supper they had retired here, to the parlor, where Mrs. Noonan and her daughters sew quietly and Mario reads, glancing up at her occasionally with a small, encouraging smile and a look of concern. Clara's head has begun to throb, but now and then she glances idly at the Noonan girls' handiwork, and forgets her aching head long enough to feel a faint urge to go upstairs and bring down her own embroidery, to let them see what *she* can do. But her workbasket is not in the sitting room; to fetch it means opening the door to where the great bed stands like an altar in the center of the room—and so, her temples throbbing, she twists the rings on her fingers and watches the hands on the mantel clock move relentlessly and with agonizing slowness, the passing minutes never seeming to pass at all as each tick of the clock shears off another second from the time she has left.

But at half past six, with the sun still well above the mountains, Mario lays his book aside, citing the fatigue of their long day and, courteously bidding Mrs. Noonan and her daughters good night, asks her if she is ready to retire. Face scarlet, heart hammering, Clara looks from one to the other, unable to believe how calm everyone is, how civil and polite, pretending not to know what they are going upstairs to do; and when her husband holds the door open for her, she rises from her chair and walks to him with leaden feet, her palms clammy against her sides, her eyes fastened to the floor, mumbling an unintelligible good-bye to the three women who calmly observe her departure as if nothing very special is in store for her—as if every night they watch someone stumble to her death.

The stairs loom before her and she climbs them slowly, her heavy feet dragging her down, the panic rising higher within her at each step until they reach the landing. Her husband shepherds her gently into their room and closes the door; the latch clicks behind her like the bolt of a trap springing shut, and she is a prisoner in this wide, sunlit chamber, staring at her deathbed—high and white and piled with pillows—with the eyes of a terrified child.

While she stands nailed to the bare, wooden floor, Alfieri moves easily about the room, humming a snatch of melody under his breath, pulling off his coat, his tie and collar, rolling back his sleeves, unlacing his boots and placing them neatly beneath the wardrobe, all as serenely as if he has forgotten she is there.

He has not forgotten. When he turns to her at last, it is to take her hand and draw her gently to a nearby chair. He sits on the edge, places her before him like a schoolgirl, holding her between his knees, and begins to kiss her softly, his lips brushing over her eyes, her ears, against her neck . . .

The layers of her clothing are no protection at all; he reaches behind her, his musician's fingers deftly undoing the tiny buttons of her dress until it slips, rustling, to the floor, and the rest of her garments— petticoats, stockings, corset—fall away slowly, like so many petals beneath his kind, remorseless hands. She makes no protest, only stands there with her eyes tightly shut until nothing at all remains but her little chemise.

His hands stop and Clara opens her eyes to see him staring at the outlines of her body, clearly visible beneath the thin fabric. He raises his dark eyes to her face.

"*Amorosa,*" he says, and his voice is not quite steady, "do you know what happens between a man and a woman?"

"Yes," she whispers. "I know." This fear has a taste; it fills her mouth and swells into her throat, choking her. "Mario"—her voice breaks— "couldn't we wait until tomorrow? Just one more day . . ."

"Why, my darling? Are you so very frightened?"

She moves her lips but no sound comes out, and the tears begin to slip down her cheeks.

"Little girl," he says, clasping her around the waist and drawing her close, "do you love me?"

"Oh, so much." She hides her face against his neck.

"Do you think that I would hurt you?"

"No, Mario . . ."

"Then why, *bambina?*" Alfieri strokes her hair. "I will love you so gently."

"Please, please . . ." Her body trembles with grief. "Tomorrow, Mario . . . we can do it tomorrow. Let me be with you one more day, just one more day . . ." Small fingers clutch handfuls of his shirt.

Gathering her up, he carries her to the great bed and lays her down gently upon it. She looks up at him through her tears, stark terror in her eyes.

Alfieri shakes his head sadly. "No, love, I will not force you. When you are ready, *piccina,* and not before." Lying on the bed with her, he holds her tightly, brushing his fingers along her face. "We have had a long day, my darling, and in my happiness I had forgotten that you are still a little girl. Rest now, *amore. Dormi, mia stanca diletta,* sleep . . ."

Warm against him, she listens to the soft sound of his words, very near sleep already, worn out by the feverish excitement of her wedding day, by the journey, by her terror and his kindness and this sudden, miraculous reprieve. It had been impossible, of course, from the very beginning; she is not a happy-ending kind of person; nothing she has dreamed of has ever come true. But it had been so pretty, for a little while, to dream of being his wife. And when he has gone away, and the streets have claimed her, she will still have this to remember.

"Sleep," he says, laying his hand across her eyes . . . and she sleeps.

It is the sun that wakes her, sinking behind the mountains, its dying rays warm on her face, and her eyes open onto a room glowing red-amber, like a heart of fire. She lies still, enchanted by the radiance. Mario is enchanted by it too; he stands leaning against the open window nearest the bed, staring into the sunset, his black eyes half-closed against its splendor; and at the sight of him Clara forgets the light, and watches him, instead.

She recalls, suddenly, the faces of Mrs. Noonan's daughters as they watched him across the dinner table; and after dinner, in the parlor, how their eyes had lingered on him. She remembers how they had caught his eye at every opportunity; how they had laughed and smiled, so eager to please, so agreeable, playing with their long braids, smoothing their skirts, for all the world like moths around a flame, her own presence utterly irrelevant. He had seemed not to notice at all, but it had been a revelation to her, which only her panic had blotted out, and she remembers it now. She has never seen him before in the presence of other women: why has it never occurred to her that they would find him as wondrous as she does?

Her brief sleep has left her very calm; and the tightness in her throat, the ache as she looks at him, is stronger now than her fear. Oh, God, to lie in his arms, just once. And once she does, and he discovers what she is—what does it matter whether he leaves her today or tomorrow? What good is it to put off the inevitable? Nothing will change. How much better to meet the end bravely . . .

She moves slightly and he slowly turns his head. In the ruddy light his face is smooth and expressionless, his half-closed eyes cold, and for one moment she shrinks back from this stranger—and then he smiles and moves toward her, Mario once more.

He sits down beside her on the bed, smoothing her tangled curls, and she looks up at him, finding it hard to breathe, the ache almost unbearable.

"Now," she says.

He knows at once what she means. "Are you sure, *madonna*? There is no need to hurry. We have all the time in the world."

"Now," she says again, before she can lose her courage, but she shuts her eyes against the sight of him bending over her, and he laughs at her terror.

"Lord," he murmurs, his mouth on hers, "let now thy servant depart in peace . . ."

He is gentle, as gentle as he had promised, but there is no going back from this and no stopping, even if she wanted to; and she twists beneath him soundlessly until she is climbing the air to meet his hands and his mouth, until her bones melt and her silent shivering becomes something else entirely. She speaks just once, saying, in a voice that is not her own: "Mario . . . please . . . I want to tell you . . ." But she has waited too long, for he is past hearing, and in another moment she has forgotten what she meant to say.

He takes her slowly, whispering to her, kissing her hair, her eyes, her mouth, her throat, her breasts . . . until she cries out at last, straining upward, frantic hands clenching the iron bars of the bed. Head thrown back, body arched, small fingers gripping the coverlet, Clara's only sound is the breath sobbing in her throat; and Alfieri is too drowned in her warmth, and the sweetness of her moving beneath him, to notice how easily he enters her. In the last moment before oblivion, her eyes open wide—pleading—and then close again as she shudders, turning her face into the pillow to silence her final cry.

Chapter Eleven

An evening breeze has sprung up, fluttering the curtains, and an amber glow still lights the clouds above the distant mountains. Alfieri watches it fade to deep crimson and purple, and the sky shade from pale blue to apple-green to the deepest azure, with one clear, winking star in its depths.

His young wife lies sleeping at his side, her breathing light and even. He is, in his way, a student of sleep—too many have shared his bed for others' sleep to be a mystery to him—and enough of a connoisseur to have noticed that, with age, sleep changes. Children, for instance—and here he thinks of his brothers and sisters in their infancy, and their babes in turn—sleep intensely, bringing the same energy to their repose as to all else they do. Their eyes tightly shut, as if in concentration, children work at their sleep; not for them the easy slumber of old age, the effortless slide from waking to dreams to waking again, as if one were merely an extension of the other, and both merely a preparation for the endless night to come.

Clara still sleeps like a child, in an awkward splay of arms and legs, a slight furrow between her brows. He has covered her against the night breeze, but the light blanket cannot conceal how very young—how completely defenseless—she is. She lies with her back toward him, half on her side, and as he traces the line of her bare shoulder with his fingers she murmurs something unintelligible, sighs, and turns away; and without warning his eyes fill with tears.

He is not the first . . . not the first . . .

He cannot bear to finish the thought, but even incomplete it is true; and it is not the absence of blood on the sheets that has betrayed her—he has played at these games too long not to know the fallibility of that test. It is, for want of a better phrase, her lack of ignorance that has given her away. Not that she knows a great deal. Wiping his eyes, he almost laughs at the terrible irony: had he been less experienced, he might never have noticed; and she—poor little girl—had she been more experienced, she would have feigned innocence.

And yet what a fitting punishment he has been dealt, after all; what perfect—what sublime—retribution for the many men who wear horns courtesy of Mario Alfieri. Only a stupid man would fail to see the justice in it; only a graceless one would rail at the pain. God knows that he has given hardly a thought to the anguish of the men he has cuckolded.

But this, at least, is in his favor: all of his victims have been willing ones—seasoned women, who have known other beds—and none has suffered more at his hands than a few sweet moments of regret when the affair ended. Why, then, has Clara been made to suffer so much more than they? Oh, my Father, he thinks: she is so very small; to make her the instrument of my correction, was it necessary to hurt her so badly?

He had believed her terror to be no more than an innocent young bride's fear of the unknown. But if she is no stranger to the act of love—and she is not—then it must have been the knowledge of what was to come, and not the ignorance of it, that had so terrified her. And fear of that magnitude could only be caused by . . . what?

The western sky holds only the faintest light now, and in the almost total darkness Alfieri's mind conjures up cruel pictures that make him twist and sweat. He presses his hands to his eyes, as if he can gouge out the visions, but they do not yield, either to his fingers or to the commands of his brain, and he starts up, shaking, groping for the matches on his bedside table. To lie in the darkness, haunted by the image of her trapped beneath another man's body, will surely drive him mad . . .

The match rasps loudly in the silence; the flame flares up, the candlewick catches and gleams steadily, a small, clear beacon of sanity in the peaceful room. Clara still sleeps, curled on her side, and he watches the gentle rise and fall of her breathing.

He has never known before what it is to be utterly helpless, but he knows it now. When he carried her to the bed, could she have denied herself to him if he had chosen not to wait? They both know the answer, but her knowledge has come from brutal experience: the terror in her eyes was testament to that; and he can no more prevent what has already happened than she could prevent it when it was happening. And so they are equals, finally, he and his little wife: he is as helpless as she.

She stirs next to him. Reaching over, he readjusts the coverlet, which has slipped from her, but the breeze is stronger now, and carries with it the smell of rain. A low peal of thunder rolls in the distance, and Alfieri rises mechanically to close the windows, taking the candle, which he sets down on a small table before a narrow pier glass between two of the casements. The blackness outside is complete, broken only by an occasional flare of lightning on the horizon to the south, and one tiny point of light across the river that flickers, vanishes and reappears as invisible trees toss in the rising wind.

With the windows shut, Alfieri can see more behind him, reflected in the panes, than he can outside. The candle burns clearly, its brightness magnified by the pier glass, casting a ring of pale golden light that encompasses the bed, and he gazes at the reversed room mirrored softly against the night; at his new wife, curled small, a pillow clutched in her arms. He had wanted to show her that there was nothing to fear, to watch her joy as he taught her about pleasure . . .

Her eyes are open, watching him.

In the brief time since they met, he has discovered that she possesses none of the little feminine wiles that other women employ as a matter of course to emphasize their femininity—the coy glances, the artless laughter, the ineffectual, fluttering hands. She is so free of artifice, indeed, that he wonders, sometimes, if she has spent all her young life in the kind of solitude in which he found her, with invisible hands to attend her and no one to emulate. Now, for instance, any other woman would drop her eyes, would pretend to be asleep, or to have awakened at just this moment. But Clara's eyes remain fixed on him as he approaches her, searching his face with a desperate intensity as he kneels beside her and touches her cheek.

Dear heart, he thinks; you know that I know, don't you? That was your fear all along—not that I would hurt you, but that I would blame you, both for what you could not prevent and for keeping silent about it. You believed that I would never want you once I knew; and believing that, *innocenza,* how could you not be terrified, knowing all the while that I would discover it for myself . . . as I have done. And now that I know, my darling, and you know that I do—do you still believe that I could stop wanting you?

But all he says is: "*Sposa,* did I wake you?"

She moves her head slightly, no, but does not speak; one escaping sound would be the crack in the fortress wall of her rigidity, and all her grief would come spilling out . . .

I am so sorry, she wants to say; but I was lonely, and so afraid. And I loved you. There is no other excuse.

But she will not be the first to speak. She is waiting for his anger, waiting for him to demand an explanation for her shame; he must say something. Yet what words can he possibly use? Listen, my dear, it does not matter? But it does matter: to her, because she believes herself worthless; to him, because he loves her. How could it not matter? It is with her always, this cross she cannot set down.

Listen, my dear, he thinks; in your own eyes you have been shamed already, and to force you to admit it would only shame you more . . . and if I bring it to the light—if I speak of it, no matter how gently— my words will drive it between us at the very beginning of our life together, and its shadow will fall across all the happiness that should lie before us. *Cara,* if I could take the burden from you and carry it myself, I would do it—do you know how gladly? But it is your secret, dearest, and you must deal with it in your own time and in your own way, for

I cannot help you, except to be here for you always. Until the day you speak of it, I will say nothing. When you are ready, *piccina,* and not before.

Gusts of rain spatter against the windows, thunder rolls across the mountains; the old room sighs and creaks in the dark night-wind. There are just two of them in a pale circle of light, and beyond that there is nothing. Still touching her face, running his thumb across the curve of her lips, he bends very low, until his head touches hers, shutting out everything but the sound of his words.

"I've waited for you so long, little girl—tell me again that you love me."

For a moment she is as still as if she has not heard; then she turns her face up to him, lips parted in wonder, the first hint of hope widening her eyes, and he pulls her into his arms, pillow and all . . .

She is not so afraid, this time; not so afraid, at least, that she does not watch him through lowered lids, only closing them when his eyes lift to her face; but she is silent once more, her lips pressed implacably together as his skin glides over hers, and his soft words go unanswered except for the ceaseless whisper of flesh slipping against the sheets, and the quickening creak of the ancient bed springs.

Afterward she sleeps profoundly, her head resting in the hollow of his shoulder, her legs still tangled with his, while Alfieri listens to the rain hissing against the glass, his cheek against her hair.

Chapter Twelve

IT IS NOON ON FRIDAY, the eighth of June, and the rose-brick house on Washington Square is at peace once more. It has suffered, in the last fortnight, beneath the trampling feet of what have seemed, at times, to be whole armies of strangers, as painters and paperhangers, plasterers, upholsterers, and drapers strode through the servants' entrance in ceaseless, steady lines, bearing the implements of their respective trades. Those acquainted with this particular house, and with its master, would surely marvel at its being thus disturbed and wonder at the cause, for change is as antithetical to a placid existence as night is to day, and no alteration has been permitted within these walls for years. But it is early June, and New York is empty of everyone but those chained to it by necessity, by poverty, or by having nowhere else to go; and there is no one left behind to care.

Such massive disinterest suits Thaddeus Chadwick to a nicety. Some of the alterations he has made to his house would, perhaps, raise eyebrows, were there any about to raise. He has chosen, for instance, to vacate his own quiet, spacious bedroom and sitting room at the rear of the house, and to move to new, smaller quarters facing onto Washington Square; and the austere rooms he left behind have undergone a metamorphosis of paint and paper, and emerged gorgeous, like a butterfly from a dull cocoon.

Flowers now adorn the formerly sober walls, and lace curtains veil the windows. Against one wall, where his writing desk used to stand, a pretty new table twinkles in the light, skirted in tiers of silk and covered with those silver-stoppered crystal bottles so dear to the hearts of young ladies; and in place of his sedate, mahogany bedstead there stands a wonder of carved rosewood hung with pale blue satin, a bed out of a fairy tale. Everything within these two rooms, in fact, has been purchased and installed with only one object in mind: to appease and comfort its awaited occupant.

Other things as well have been purchased and installed, but they are outside the rooms, and provide comfort of another kind to the house's owner. The new iron bars that have been welded across the windows, for instance, and the new locks for the doors, which can only be turned from the outside, are details which simple prudence dictates. The future resident of these rooms, having proved unstable in the past, is not to be trusted now; and it is only sensible to take precautions against her demonstrated tendency to madness.

And as if to make his point, during the past two weeks the girl has been more silent than ever, hardly ever meeting his gaze, and his keen eye has detected a heightened fear in her nervous starts and stammers, and a morbid excitement as she watched her things being made ready for the journey to her new home. That she will relapse into hysteria under the strain of adjusting to her new surroundings is all but inevitable, and he has already had his own staff advise the servants in the neighboring houses that strange sounds issuing from the barred windows are to be ignored.

In fact he has left nothing to chance, even to the extent of overseeing the whole vast and complex process of packing her belongings. In less than a fortnight, with the assistance of hired laundresses and seamstresses, every article of clothing she possesses has been inspected, mended, washed, ironed, folded, and packed away in deep trunks, ready to be conveyed to Washington Square. His most recent—and penultimate—visit to Gramercy Park, on Tuesday last, had seen her trunks and boxes piled man-high in her sitting room, waiting for the carters to come and take them away, which they are to do later today.

Chadwick sighs and leans back against the cushions of the carriage, his gloved fingers tightening, easing, then tightening again around his walking stick as he recalls the past two weeks. Another ten minutes will bring him, punctual as always, to the Slade house for the last time, to collect the girl and carry her away with him. No, he has left nothing to chance, and nothing—and no one—has been forgotten.

Certainly not the tenor, Priapus *redux*, whose happy interest in Clara has made today possible. It was amazing how quickly the man's desire for the house had disappeared, once he learned that the girl would not be in it. Chadwick, who has heard that the Italian has already leased some paltry town house or other on Madison Avenue, thinks approvingly of the hot place in hell reserved for hypocrites, and smiles.

Having spoked the tenor's wheels, Chadwick could almost feel sorry for him, were it not for the fact that he loathes him so thoroughly. Of course, there had never been any real contest. He—Chadwick—had been perfecting his own fine Italian hand when Alfieri was still in his cradle. Considering what he has done to get to this point, no one—and surely not an arrogant debauchee—will be permitted to stand in his way. Today is the culmination of years of slow, careful work, requiring the utmost delicacy and finesse.

Anyone, for instance, who believed it an easy task to get Henry Slade to extend himself, at the possible risk of his reputation, knew nothing of the man. That great philanthropist, as he liked to think of himself, would have been perfectly content to let the girl remain forever with her mother's people—a miserable little gypsy, shunted about, sometimes as often as once a month, from one grudging relation to the next. It had been a clear stroke of genius on his—Chadwick's—part to arrange for her to be boarded with Fauvell and his wife. Only by putting her in Fauvell's way and letting nature take its course could he be certain of being able to convince Henry to take her in.

And it had worked, exactly as he had foreseen. Is he not about to gather up the fruit of his labors?

The carriage jingles to a stop before the Slade house as the bells of St. Paul's ring out the noon hour. Chadwick has dressed with particular care today, in honor of this special occasion, and he steps onto the pavement carrying his gold-knobbed walking stick as if it were the emblem of some weighty office, his boots, buttons, and eyeglasses gleaming in the sun. Looking neither to the right nor the left, he mounts the two low steps to the somber front door, fits his key into the lock, and passes into the cavernous darkness.

He climbs the two flights of stairs without difficulty, whistling a merry tune beneath his breath, knowing his way so well that, even sightless, he never stumbles; raps at Clara's sitting room door impatiently with the head of his stick, and without troubling to wait for an answer, pushes it open and walks in—

To emptiness.

Stripped, silent and dim, it is a room like all the others now: sunk in the same vast slumber, its blinds drawn behind its thin lace curtains, its windows shut fast. Chadwick stares about him, gaping, a man who has stepped off a precipice into empty space. Nothing remains but bare furniture and the pictures on the walls. Even the piled trunks have vanished. He walks to where he last saw them standing, solid and very real, and moves his hands about disbelievingly in the air, as though expecting to feel them there.

Stumbling to the bedroom door, he flings it open without bothering to knock, knowing, even as he does so, that he will find the same emptiness; that she is gone . . . fled . . . vanished along with her things . . . that in the very act of clutching his prize, his hand has closed upon thin air. He stands between the two rooms, breathing heavily; and his eyes, glazed with shock and confusion, flicker incredulously, back and forth, until they come to rest on the girl's portrait, above the sitting room mantelpiece.

Something is resting against the wall beneath it—a white square— and Chadwick walks toward it. It is an envelope with his name upon it, written in a large, fluid hand that he does not know. He reaches for it, suddenly afraid, breaks the seal with trembling fingers, opens the single, folded sheet of paper, and reads.

He is less than two lines into the closely written page when he begins to scream.

. . .

IT IS SIX O'CLOCK in the evening on Friday, the eighth of June. The dull brick house at Gramercy Park is at peace once more. There had been sounds earlier: unsettling sounds, shrill and jagged in the darkness, like tremors in the dead air, but they have long since ceased, and the whispering silence has come flowing back. It is not disturbed as the front door opens once again, for the man who steps quickly inside is more circumspect than the previous visitor, and moves across the entrance hall like a shade among the shadows.

He is of medium height, and wiry, and in the brief flash of the sun by the open door his hair shone iron-gray. Pausing briefly in the twilight to remove his boots, he continues silently upon stockinged feet and mounts the stairs, treading warily, certain that the old man has already come and gone, but wishing no surprises.

He is here to be certain that nothing has been overlooked. He should have been here yesterday afternoon, with a safe distance of twenty-four hours between himself and Chadwick, but a burst pipe in the kitchen of the new house had disordered his plans—and so he is here now, for the sake of the small signora who has come so suddenly into Maestro Alfieri's life. It will be a brief visit—a quick inspection of wardrobes and bureau drawers, a final glance around bedroom and bath—and he will be on his way, out of this echoing marble vault and back into the sunlight.

After the maestro and his bride had left for their wedding trip, he and the two other servants had gone about, floor by floor and room by room, shutting windows, drawing blinds, and closing curtains, returning the house to its state of everlasting night. Now, reaching the third-floor landing, he turns in the direction of the room of Miss Adler that was, ready to keep count of each door as he passes it by tapping it with his hand, lest he become disoriented and lose his way in the blackness. But there is light—daylight—ahead of him, streaming into the corridor just where her doorway should be; and, very much on his guard, he tiptoes to the open door and peers inside.

Five minutes later an ashen-faced Gennarino is in a carriage on his way downtown, urging the driver in Italian-laced English to go faster, faster . . .

Chapter Thirteen

THE DAY HAD BEGUN foggy, the sun a silver disk behind low, pearl clouds. "It will burn off," Mrs. Noonan had said, looking at the sky from under her hand. "It will be a fine day. Will you come to Mass with us, signore?" Alfieri had said simply: "Thank you, no. Clara and I were not married in the Church," and she had replied, with no hint of censure, "then it will be a fine day to spend in the meadow." And she had been right.

They were in the meadow by noon, the red-checked cloth spread for their picnic in the shade of an old, twisted oak at the edge of the woods, listening to the sound of church bells, very faint and far away, ringing their Sunday praise. Alfieri smiles. The afternoon is hot, the still air loud with the shrill of insects in the tall grass. If he cannot go to church again there are worse places to be than here, in a field of flowers beneath a blue sky with his wife resting beside him, her small face tilted up to the sun.

He had been right to bring her here. The quiet, the sunshine and fresh air, are already working their healing magic. Her appetite is returning: she had done her part in emptying the hamper of food that Mrs. Noonan had prepared for them this morning, and the hired man who had carried it over the fields with much huffing and blowing will find it no great burden, now, to carry back to the house. And as for sleep, her rest would be unbroken if only he would not wake and reach for her so often in the night . . .

Alfieri leans back against the tree and closes his eyes, drawing Clara to him, and she sighs and settles against his side, clasping his hand in both of hers, twining her fingers with his.

"I wish we could stay here forever," she says. "Just like this."

"Here?" he says gravely. "Just like this? We can try, love, but in a few days you will begin to wish I had my bath . . ." When she giggles he kisses her head and holds her close. "My darling little girl, four days ago you were unhappy because there are no pictures on the walls of our room."

"I know," she murmurs. "But that was before . . ."

He tilts her chin up, looks down at her. Her face is serene and foolishly soft, and he brushes the damp curls back from her forehead, marveling that four short days could have wrought such change—there are faint roses in her cheeks, now, and a powdering of freckles has blown, almost magically, across her nose. But more important than what has appeared is what has vanished: the stiffness from her young body, the terrible fear from the eyes that smile up at him. Dear heart, he thinks, smiling back at her; when did it happen? You have set down your burden, at last.

"What are you thinking?" she says.

"That it is nearly time to go back."

"No, Mario," she pleads, "not yet. It's early still."

He shakes his head, smiling. "Remember our visitors? Mr. Buchan's telegram said that he and Mrs. Buchan would be here in time for supper. If we are to be ready when they arrive, we should start back fairly soon."

She wrinkles her nose at this reminder, and he says, surprised: "Why, my dear? Don't you like the Buchans?"

"Of course I like them," she says. "They have been so good to us. But we haven't been away long enough to want visitors."

"They will only be staying the one night. Mr. Buchan's telegram said that he needs to speak with me urgently about some matter . . . and you would not be so unkind, *madonna,* and have him come so far, only to turn around again and go straight back? And Mrs. Buchan, who is so fond of you?"

"No, of course not." Her sigh, this time, is one of genuine regret. "We can come back here another day, can't we?"

"Any day you like."

"For another picnic?"

Alfieri strokes her hair. "I think," he says, "that we should save our picnics for Sundays."

THE SUN is slanting steeply from the west when their guests arrive. Alfieri greets them at the bottom of the walk, helping Mrs. Buchan down from the open carriage before grasping Daniel Buchan's outstretched hand.

"You got my telegram," says the attorney.

"Yesterday," Alfieri says. "I am glad to see you again."

"You are a gallant liar, but I rather think not," Buchan says dryly, as they turn up the path to the house. "Not so soon, at any rate. I would not be glad, either, if someone intruded on my honeymoon. Please forgive us, and believe me, *signore,* when I say that if I did not need to speak with you, we would not be here now."

Mrs. Buchan simply says: "Tell us . . . how is your wife?"

"Well, I think. But you must judge for yourself," Alfieri says as Clara appears on the front porch.

"But, my dear!" Mrs. Buchan says, reaching for the young wife's hands, "how fine you look!" Her eyes grow wide as she draws Clara out into the sunlight where she can be seen more clearly, holding her at arm's length and looking her up and down. The girl wears a gown of soft blue, with a dark blue ribbon in her short, shining hair, and Mrs. Buchan touches the ribbon, and then Clara's face, with gentle fingers.

"How fine you look!" she says again.

"Then you see the same improvement I do," Alfieri says, never taking his eyes from his wife. "Thank you, I was hoping that it was not merely wishful thinking on my part."

"No, indeed."

"No, indeed," agrees Mr. Buchan, remembering the pale little bride of less than a week ago.

"*Cara,*" Alfieri says, "will you show Mrs. Buchan up to her room? I am sure that she would like to rest after her long journey. And Mr. Buchan and I will step into the parlor for a few minutes, to discuss this urgent matter that has brought them here."

Freed from scrutiny, Clara escapes into the front hall with a grateful look at her husband, followed by Mrs. Buchan, and Alfieri and the attorney make their way to the parlor.

"In honor of your visit," the tenor says to Buchan, "Mrs. Noonan is preparing what, for her, is a late supper, so we should have time to complete our business—whatever that is—before sitting down to eat."

"I look forward to it," Buchan says, looking around the comfortable room with a sigh of pleasure as he settles into a chair. "If Mrs. Noonan would only listen to reason, I could provide her with an excellent position as cook in the house of a deserving attorney and his wife. But, strange as it seems, she refuses to leave this place and move back to the city . . ."

He studies Alfieri closely as the tenor hands him a glass of brandy. "You will not be offended, I know," he says, "if I mention that you look the way a new husband should: happy, preoccupied, and more than a little fatigued."

Alfieri laughs and seats himself nearby. "The fatigue is the result of the long walks we take to build up Clara's strength. That is what accounts for the new color in her cheeks. But I am so much older than she, you see, that the same exercise tires me out."

Buchan laughs too. "You are a gallant liar, signore, as I said, and a plausible one. But remember: I have been a newlywed too. However, if that is the story you wish to tell people, so be it." He raises his glass in a salute, takes a long swallow of brandy, then sets his glass down, his smile fading.

"All right, to business. I wish to get this over with, so that we may enjoy the rest of the evening. But let me begin by saying that I am glad you are safely away from the city, and will be, for a lengthy period of time. There has been an ugly incident."

Alfieri says quietly: "It is Mr. Chadwick, isn't it? I knew it when I got your telegram. Is Gennarino well? And the others?"

"Everyone is fine."

"Then . . . ?"

"Two days ago I received an unscheduled visitor in my office. Yes, you are right, it was Mr. Chadwick. He had just come from the Slade house, where he had discovered Miss Adler's flight . . . and your letter." Buchan leans forward. "Oh, signore, signore," he says, shaking his head. "That was a mistake!"

"Eloping with my wife?" Alfieri says lightly, but Buchan is not amused.

"Why did you not tell me of the letter before you left it?" the attorney says. "That was never a part of our discussions. We had agreed that you would allow *me* to tell Mr. Chadwick."

"I was never happy with that arrangement, Mr. Buchan, and you know it. The matter was between Mr. Chadwick and myself."

"And so you left him a letter to let him know what you had done."

"I preferred it to stealing away with my wife as if we had done something shameful by marrying, yes."

"Did you, signore? You preferred personally rubbing his face in the fact of your victory over him, at the very instant he found your wife gone? And you thought that wise?"

"I thought it civil."

"You thought it civil," Buchan repeats impatiently. "I could tell you what he thought it, but I do not wish to foul the air in this room. I tell you, signore; this man will make a dangerous enemy. You still smile? You think I exaggerate? Chadwick is not a man who accepts defeat well, signore. In fact, he is not a man who accepts defeat at all."

Alfieri still looks amused. "Very well, Mr. Buchan, I am sorry. That is what you want me to say, isn't it? Yes, I am sorry, very sorry that I left the letter for him—"

"That is just what I am afraid of, signore . . . that you will be sorry."

"—but I find it incredible that you have traveled all the way up here just to reprove me because, in freeing my wife from a man who terrifies her, I have ruffled Mr. Chadwick's feathers. Frankly, Mr. Buchan, I do not care if he is furious. What can he do to me? Take me to court, perhaps? For what? I owe no money, I have broken no laws. I have fallen in love and I have married, which, the last time I looked, was not a crime, not even in America, not even in New York. And at the risk of sounding self-important, I can truthfully say that I am here at the invitation of many highly placed people—people whom I am sure even Mr. Chadwick would not wish to antagonize. And in a year's time I will return to Europe with my wife. So how can he harm me?"

Buchan stares at him. "Don't you know?" he says quietly. "Can't you guess? You, who are so clear-sighted, so well prepared? You astonish me, signore. To harm a man, you strike him where he is most vulnerable. What is the most precious thing in the world to you?"

Alfieri's smile fades as the lawyer's meaning sinks in. "But that is not possible," he whispers. "You told me he could not take her back. You told me . . . you *promised* me, Mr. Buchan . . . that he could not take her from me!" There is real fear in the tenor's face. "Are you telling me now that you were wrong? You said that once she was my wife, no court in your country would undo our marriage . . ."

"And I say it still."

Alfieri's face is white with anger. "Then you frighten me for nothing! Why, Mr. Buchan? For what reason?"

Buchan says: "Listen to me, signore. When Chadwick came to see me he could hardly be called rational at all. Certainly he was not rational when he made threats against you before witnesses. Yes, threats." He shakes his head. "It was not a pleasant interview. He continued to rant until I warned him that I would have him bodily removed. He left then, under his own power, but not before promising, quite clearly, to destroy you . . . and your wife with you."

"How?" Alfieri demands.

The lawyer looks at him narrowly. "I said he was irrational, signore, not stupid. Chadwick would never disclose his plans, unless it was to intentionally mislead. I came here merely to warn you about what he said . . . and to tell you what your manservant, Gennarino, came to tell me later that same day. He went first to my office, but I had already left, so he called upon me at my house. He wished to alert me, you see—and have me alert you—about what he had seen."

Alfieri stares at him. "Seen where?"

"At the Slade house. Your man had gone back to Gramercy Park in the late afternoon, when he was certain that Mr. Chadwick would be long gone, to make one last search for anything belonging to your wife that might have been left behind."

"Why Friday?" Alfieri says sharply. "We had agreed that he would go on Thursday, to lessen the chance of discovery."

" 'The best laid plans of mice and men,' signore. A pipe burst in the kitchen of your new house, and took the entire day to repair. Your man did not know the plumbers, of course, and would not leave them alone in the house with all your belongings."

Alfieri nods. "Go on."

"Your man went back, therefore, on Friday. Be glad that that pipe broke, signore, and that it took all day to repair. He said that when he entered Miss Adler's rooms he found them quite"—he hesitates, trying to remember the exact words—"quite torn apart . . . as if a madman had been at them. The furniture was overturned and smashed, pictures and mirrors shattered, curtains ripped from the windows . . ."

Buchan pauses, marshaling all his powers of description. "And on the wall, over the mantel, the portrait of Miss Adler was—quite literally—battered to bits. What was left of the canvas was hanging in shreds from the frame, which was itself in splinters. In fact, whoever destroyed the portrait had swung at it with such fury that the wall around it was deeply gouged. The marble of the mantelpiece was cracked as well, and large pieces broken from it. Marble is, of course, relatively soft. But the walls of that house are solid plaster, signore. They do not dent easily. On the floor nearby lay one of the fire tongs, horribly bent and twisted—clearly the weapon that had inflicted the damage."

He muses silently upon the assault. "I am, of course, only repeating what your man told me. But I must tell you, signore, that he was shaken by what he had seen. He said that it looked as if the portrait had been beaten to death . . ."

Both men are silent now, envisioning the destruction. "I have no doubt as to who wielded the weapon," Buchan says at last. "And neither do you, I am sure. And I confess that I am worried."

Alfieri shakes his head. "But it is not possible," he says. "Even if Mr. Chadwick is beside himself over Clara's loss . . . surely . . . surely he would not put himself in jeopardy by trying to harm her?"

"Have you been listening to me, signore? Mr. Chadwick is far from stupid, and he values his own life as much, if not more, than the next man, but he wants revenge. Nevertheless, despite the smashing of the room, despite what he said in my office, I do not believe that he will attempt to harm either of you physically. That is not his way. He will be more circumspect, more subtle."

"And do what, Mr. Buchan?"

"If I knew, signore, I would not be here now, disturbing you on your honeymoon. I can only tell you that I expect some form of retaliation, and that that expectation is based in large measure upon what was told to me by your valet. Still, you know your man far better than I do. Is he the type to give way to lurid fancies?"

"Gennarino?" Alfieri smiles faintly. "Gennarino has been with me for fifteen years. He has no nerves in his body. He is as sound as they come."

"Yes, that is what I had assumed. And that is why I am worried. Because when he told me what he had seen, signore, he was frightened. And when a man like that is frightened, then there is something to be frightened about."

In the stillness the men can hear the murmur of women's voices through the open windows, and Clara's sudden, bright laughter.

"Signore," Buchan says quietly, "I have never asked you before—I have not needed to, of course; but tell me now, if you will—how much do you know of your wife's history before she arrived at Slade's house?"

Alfieri's face betrays nothing at all. "Little," he says. "Very little. We have been together such a short time. Why do you ask?"

"I would like to look into it, if I may. I will only undertake such a thing with your permission, of course . . . but such knowledge may prove helpful to us."

"How so, Mr. Buchan?"

The attorney is thoughtful. "There are many ways of doing harm, signore."

Chapter Fourteen

THERE IS NO RELIEF from this heat. Shade might help, but there is no shade here, only flat, bare fields under a white July sun that hammers the land and everything that crawls upon it; and the thick air, when it does stir, serves merely to draw attention to the moisture that plasters the shirt to one's back and drips into one's eyes. Beneath the cart's wheels and the slow, shuffling hooves of the horse, the baked dirt road sifts up a fine brown dust that clings to glistening faces and damp hands, and seeps into the folds of wilted clothing. Gradually, around a bend in the road, a house shimmers into being through the haze, immaterial one moment, substantial the next, growing ever larger and clearer as the open cart draws near.

The house must once have been imposing, with its high, peaked roof and long windows, but the years have not been kind. Although the ragged hedges are clipped just enough to show that some vestige of self-respect—however haphazard—remains to those within, the front steps sag, and crickets shrill in the waist-high weeds where flower beds used to be; and the paint, once white, but now stained with weather and time, flakes in scabby patches from the walls. Seen from the road, the general decay combines with the impenetrable mat of ivy engulfing the pillars and porch roof to give the house the look of a worn and blowzy woman with her hair in her eyes.

To the left of the missing gate, the name "Fauvell" is just legible on the mailbox.

Plodding ever more slowly, the tired horse comes at last to a complete halt and stands, head down, before the path to the house, as if exhaustion has finally triumphed over both good sense and the will of its driver. But that sweating man, no less exhausted than his horse, wrestles a large valise down from the cart and carries it up the walk with some difficulty, the smooth leather slipping twice from his wet palms and tumbling noisily to the ground before he succeeds in setting it down on the porch.

The cart's single passenger is benignly tolerant of the driver's clumsiness, if the slight smile he wears is any indication. Certainly he remains seated, his small eyes behind his spectacles vastly busy with the house itself; as unperturbed, by either the heat or the struggles of driver and box, as any stone in the road. It is not until his valise has come to rest on the porch, with the spent driver panting beside it, leaning over with his hands on his knees, that the passenger finally rouses himself and steps down from the cart.

"My good man," he says amiably, still smiling as he mounts the sagging stairs with the help of his gold-headed stick, stepping adroitly around places where the wood is too rotten to support his ample weight. "I must thank you. I had begun to think that my case would remain pristine forever, but you have provided just the amount of injury that it needed to appear properly broken in. My compliments upon your achievement."

The driver mops his glistening face with his sleeve and shuffles uneasily, muttering apologies, but his passenger is a man of exquisite reasonableness, and waves the words away with an airy gesture.

"No, no. Accidents will happen. However, in light of the damage inflicted, it is, of course, out of the question that I should pay for your services." He smiles again, the soul of magnanimity. "But I would not have you think that I bear you any ill will because of so small a mishap. I will allow you, therefore, to call for me here tomorrow, and drive me back to the station. Be here at precisely a quarter of nine in the morning. I would not wish to miss my train . . . and you would not wish me to miss it either, I assure you."

A dismissive flick of the white-gloved hand, and the driver finds himself hurrying back down the steps to his cart, grateful for escaping with only the loss of his fee. The door of the house opens as he drives off, and a consumptive-looking maid peers out.

"Is it Mr. Chadwick?" she inquires, and the still-smiling man turns in response to his name and, doffing his hat, enters.

The heat is here before him, despite closed windows and drawn blinds, having found its way in without invitation, and the stifling, stagnant air has a faintly unpleasant, musty smell. Chadwick's heels ring against the uncovered wooden floors as the maid leads him up the stairs and along several narrow, bare corridors, past dim, empty rooms stripped to the walls, and brings him at last, by a sudden turn, to yet another chamber . . .

It is a room so laden with carpets, rugs, cushions, swags, pillows, tassels, drapes, throws, runners, shawls, and curtains that it is impossible for the eye to discern any right angles in it whatsoever, or even to determine where the windows might be. Myriad whatnots, cabinets, chests, tables, cases, and stands rise like islands in the sea of fabric; and upon every horizontal surface are objects assembled from every nook and cranny that the wide world holds: marble busts, flower domes, urns, carved wooden ornaments, mirrors, figurines, peacock feathers, paperweights, seashells, daggers, decorative plates, clocks, glass miniatures, inlaid boxes, painted masks, wax fruit, picture frames, oriental fans, vases—as if the house had been lifted by a giant, turned on its side, and shaken vigorously, emptying the contents of every other room into this one, vast jumble.

"It is Mr. Chadwick." The maid, not venturing within, possibly for fear of being lost in the utter profusion of *things,* makes the announcement at the doorway of this incomprehensible agglomeration and then departs, leaving Chadwick—whose eyes cannot distinguish any figure amid the clutter—gazing in and waiting for an answering voice.

It comes from somewhere toward the center, and is accompanied by movement, as a rounded shape emerges from one of the chairs and rises to its feet. "Ah, Mr. Chadwick," the shape says, and holds out its hand, "it has been a long time, has it not?"

Picking his way carefully through the chaos, Chadwick reaches for the outstretched hand and bends over it. "Miss Pratt," he replies, "it has been long indeed."

Miss Pratt is very pink-and-white, with yellow hair, eyes which, even in the half-light, are a bright china blue, a small, upturned nose, and a rosebud mouth; but the pretty face rests atop a corpulence which defies tight-lacing—that which her corsets attempt to compress in the middle is simply forced out at either end—and even her perfectly manicured hands, with their oval pink nails, are dimpled and fat. As with many fleshy people, her age is difficult to guess, and a stranger's eye would put her somewhere between twenty and thirty-five. Chadwick, who is not a stranger, knows her to be twenty-four.

Gesturing to a nearby divan, which is almost buried under its numerous pillows, Miss Pratt sinks once more into the depths of her own chair, gracefully arranging her skirts about her, and waits for Chadwick to speak.

He studies her for several moments. "I do believe that the years stand still for you, Miss Pratt. I can say in all honesty that you have changed not at all." The sound of his voice, soaked up by the encompassing curtains, drapes, and cushions, is curiously flat in the dead air.

The young woman gazes at him, wide-eyed. "You flatter me, of course. It must be—why how long has it been, Mr. Chadwick? I believe it must be fully five years. We last met—"

"At the funeral of your dear mother, yes. I regret that business has kept me so constantly occupied these past years that I have not been able to call sooner. I have, of course, striven to write, but even my letters have been less frequent than I have wished."

"They have been welcome, nevertheless. Were it not for your letters, I would have wondered, many times, if my maid and I were not the last people on earth." She sighs and settles herself a little deeper in her chair, her gaze wandering around her. "The world has pushed us away, Mr. Chadwick. Even my neighbors will have nothing to do with us . . . not that the feeling is not mutual, you understand . . . and all because of the way my stepfather and my brother died. Dying violently would seem to be something shameful, not something for which to be pitied.

No, the world did not want Mama and me; and I have returned the compliment. Little by little I have retreated further and further from it. I scarcely ever leave this room, now."

Chadwick's gaze follows hers. "Is that why you have gathered all your stepfather's things about you?"

"His treasures, yes. All the things he collected in his travels when he was a young man—before he took up teaching, before he married Mama and settled down with us here. It is a vast collection, as you can see, and I have devoted myself to labeling each item, and recording the information about it in a great book, so that future generations may come to revere this man whom his contemporaries so callously threw away."

Chadwick nods. "A noble sentiment, to be sure, joined to a noble task. Your devotion should be offered as a model for sons and daughters everywhere, Miss Pratt—and all the more so because Dr. Fauvell was not your natural father."

"And what natural father ever loved his daughter more than he loved me, Mr. Chadwick, I ask you that?"

The lawyer is left to ponder this question in solitude, for Miss Pratt is required, by the delicate state of her health—her size makes the heat difficult to bear—to rest during the most oppressive part of the day; and after a light lunch eaten off trays set down amid Dr. Fauvell's trove, she retires to her bedroom, a small room leading off the treasure chamber, to nap until the comparative cool of late afternoon.

But Chadwick, having unpacked his valise in the room assigned to him—a stale-smelling and none too clean apartment on the upper floor, which Miss Pratt has kindly thought to render habitable by provisioning it with what she designates "the cream" of her stepfather's collection—takes advantage of his hostess's absence by walking around her property and inspecting the damage that time, and the elements, have wrought upon it.

He remembers it in a more prosperous time, shortly after Fauvell had taken up residence here, eager to restore the house, the small crop of outbuildings, and the surrounding few acres with the monies he had received from the school as an inducement to leave quietly. Chadwick had represented the school in those negotiations and, despite Miss Pratt's exalted opinion of her stepfather, knew just how damning was the case against the man. Still, say what you like of his morals, Fauvell's nerves had been of steel: had he not been bought off, he would have fought the allegations through the courts, insisting that his accusers face him openly. It had been a brazen gambit, but a spectacularly successful one, for the value of his destruction had to be weighed against the children's certain shame . . . and what parent would blast a daughter's chance for honorable marriage later in life with an admission of involvement in such sordidness—especially at so tender an age—if another solution could be found?

Chadwick shrugs inwardly and continues his trudge up the overgrown path to the outbuildings. Fauvell had gambled and won. He had resigned from the school with his dignity, and his reputation, intact, and retired here to embark upon a new life as a landed gentleman of leisure, living off his wife's estate from her first husband. There was no reason, therefore, for anyone to be alarmed (nor was there anyone who cared enough to be), when he—Chadwick—had arranged for the Adler girl to be sent here for her further education. Frankly, it had been an excellent arrangement from every angle . . . except, if one thought it mattered, from the child's point of view.

Certainly the timing could not have been more impeccable. Henry Slade had already agreed to remove her from her mother's family, where she was so clearly miserable, and send her somewhere—at the family's expense—for her schooling; and the family had been so impatient to be rid of her that they were willing to pay any price to see her gone. But the choice of *where* she went was left entirely in Chadwick's hands . . . with the result that Clara had come here, the sole student in a school of one, situated miles across bare, board-flat southern New Jersey fields from the nearest neighbor, with only Lucy and her mother, a bitter invalid, for her female companions, and Edward Fauvell for her teacher.

Chadwick's neat boots crunch on the gravel. The abandoned outbuildings form a loose semicircle up ahead—summer kitchen, icehouse, toolshed, stable, carriage barn—of rotting beams and rusting hinges, broken glass, weed-choked doorways and crumbling walls, and he steps over piles of debris at the entrance to the last building on the right.

A wooden wheel lies broken and half-buried in the dust, weeds sprouting up between the spokes, all that remains of the carriages that once stood here in the cool darkness. Chadwick walks through the barn, his feet kicking up great puffs of dust with every step, listening to the tiny explosions and startled scurryings around him of the small animals who now make this their home. An open flight of stairs at the back leads up to the apartment under the eaves where a coachman once made his home.

Chadwick mounts the stairs, pushes back the door, and steps into a large, empty room. The afternoon heat, directly beneath the tin roof, is ferocious. In the far corner to his right, where the roof slants down to meet the floor, another wooden door stands ajar, opening onto another, much smaller room: a simple square box of a room with bare walls, bare floors, bare ceiling.

A room with no place to hide.

The ceiling is lower here, hardly high enough for a grown man to stand, and with the sun caught full in its two square windows of wavery glass, the tiny chamber is little better than a furnace. But the dirty walls are flecked with a thousand drops of color, glowing like jewels across the rough, pocked plaster, and Chadwick, unmindful of the heat, ducks his head and enters. His footsteps shake the plank floor, and a dozen bright crystals, suspended from a length of string drawn across the dirty windows—a child's forgotten toys—wink and bob in the light, splintering the sun into tiny rainbows that dance and tremble around him. A horsefly buzzes angrily against the panes.

He notices the stains at once: a deep brown, almost black discoloration, soaked into the wood, that slants across the floorboards and pools behind the door; an abrupt, rust-colored splatter across the opposite wall that someone had tried—vainly—to sponge away. They seem to fascinate him. He stares at the mark on the floor, runs his bare hand across the smeared wall. Hair comes away on his fingers.

This is it, then. This is where it happened. He breathes the suffocating air in deeply, wondering what it must have smelled like on that other July afternoon, six years ago. It had been just as hot.

He ducks through the door once more, and out into the larger room, absently wiping his hands with his handkerchief . . . then stops, remembering what he had almost forgotten, and returns to the little room and its window. Seizing one of the dangling crystals, he pulls at the string that holds it. For a moment the thousand drops of color dance madly across the walls; then the old thread snaps, scattering prisms across the floor like bits of ice, and the rainbows vanish.

Pleased, Chadwick pockets the crystal in his hand and abandons the little room to the angry fly, still banging against the window. Only a rusty stain remains to lend color to the blank plaster walls.

You have been most kind," he says to Miss Pratt as they conclude their dinner. "You have not asked me why a man who has not seen you for five years, and who has written to you only sporadically during that time, should suddenly write and request a meeting." He dabs delicately at his lips with his napkin.

"I have complete faith in you, Mr. Chadwick. I knew that you would not leave me in the dark for long." She smiles as she pours out the coffee and hands the attorney his cup.

They sit at a small, round table in the midst of the treasure room's disorder, their two places carved out of the surrounding jumble. Miss Pratt folds her plump hands on the table before her, and gazes at the attorney with rapt attention, her eyes wide and guileless.

"Then, not to prolong the suspense," says Chadwick, "I have news of Clara Adler that I must share with you."

The pink face turns crimson, the blue eyes seem to start from Miss Pratt's head. She takes several deep breaths, as if breathing itself has suddenly grown difficult for her.

"You must forgive my agitation," she says, with a little shaky laugh, her hand at her throat. "You, of all men, can appreciate how hard it is for me to hear that name spoken in this house."

"To be sure," says Chadwick. "But what I have to say about her will seem even harder to you . . . and yet you, of all people, have a right to be told." As she stares at him, slack-jawed, he leans forward.

"She has done well for herself, you see. She has grown, and prospered . . . and was recently married."

"*Married?*" The word is a stifled shriek. "She is married?" The rosebud mouth turns hard and thin, and the several chins tremble.

Chadwick nods sympathetically. "I knew that you would wish to know. And it was not something I felt I could tell you in a letter."

Miss Pratt nods, pressing her napkin to her brow, composing herself with a visible effort. "Who?" she says, after a while. "Who would have the little bitch?" She takes a deep breath and straightens in her chair, recovering her poise. "And yet, after all, what is it to me? No one would want her except someone as foul and twisted as she is herself."

"So one would like to think," Chadwick says quietly. "But we both know how unfair life can be, don't we? No, my dear Miss Pratt, I am afraid . . . I wish that I could spare you . . ." He breaks off and begins again. "It is my misfortune to have to be the one to tell you—she has married a man whom many would consider to be the prize of the century."

The blue eyes bulge. "Tell me!" she demands. "*Who* is her husband? *What* is he?"

"A man whom the world calls great," Chadwick replies. He smiles sourly. "A very eminent man—gifted, handsome, and rich."

Each word seems a blunt stake driven through Miss Pratt's heart. "And he chose *her*? How is it possible? No one ever wanted her, not even her own people. Papa only took her in out of pity . . . you know that, don't you? Out of pity! And she repaid him, didn't she? She repaid all of us! Papa was in his prime when he died; Thomas, my brother, not even twenty-one! And when they both were gone, how could my poor mother, sick as she was, be expected to live? No, Mr. Chadwick, my mother was murdered as well . . . just as surely as if she, too, had been shot!" She has had ample time to dwell on this topic, and she warms to it quickly, her voice growing high and shrill.

"And what of me? What of *me*? I rot here, alone . . . no mother, no father, no brother . . . all alone, because of that bastard, with nothing left to me but these . . ."—she gestures furiously around her—"these *things* you see . . . and you tell me that she has found happiness as the wife of a great man?"

"But my dear Miss Pratt," Chadwick says, "after all . . . what can we do about it?"

She does not hear him. "She can't have told him!" she says wildly, beating the table with her fists. "She must be keeping it from him!" Miss Pratt's cheeks are streaked with tears, and her blue eyes swim. "Oh, the poor man . . . the poor man. It isn't fair! Someone should tell him, someone should let him know the kind of poisonous, wicked piece of *filth* he has taken for a wife . . ."

"Ah, yes," Chadwick says. "Someone should."

"Then why don't you?" she cries. "You know what she is!"

The lawyer protests swiftly. "I, tell him? *I?* I know the man, in a small way, of course, but who am I, after all? A stranger, nothing more. There is no reason for me to—"

He stops, chagrined, at the sound of his own words. "You shame me, Miss Pratt. Yes, you do. You, with your noble nature and delicacy of judgment, have instantly perceived what I, with all my legal experience, have been too blind to recognize. I have been looking at the matter in terms of law, but you see it, rightly, in terms of justice. And you *are* right . . . the poor man needs to be told. He *deserves* to be told." Still, he shakes his head, dejected. "And yet, why should he believe me? What do I know, myself, of his wife's corruption?" His eyes narrow and he leans forward again, struck by a new thought.

"But what if he were told by someone who had truly suffered at her hands? Think of that, my dear! Just *think* how much more weight such a revelation would carry!" He waits, watching her, his head to one side, and when she remains silent he sighs, lost in thought. "But who would do it? Her family would not, I know—no, they will not even acknowledge her existence. Who, then? If I could find someone with courage enough to come forward and expose her, I might be willing . . . in the interest of justice . . . and because I owe the man for something he once did for me . . . yes, I would be willing to arrange an introduction to him."

He sips at his coffee, watching the drowned blue eyes envision the scene. It does not take long.

"I will do it, Mr. Chadwick."

"Ah, Miss Pratt, if I thought that you were really sincere . . ."

"I consider it my duty."

Chadwick sets down his cup. "It will not bring back the dead."

"No. But it will go far toward balancing the score."

He bows his head in agreement. He knows much about balancing scores. "It means leaving your home, and putting yourself through the trouble and discomfort of a journey to New York."

"Is that where they are?"

"It is where they will be."

"Then that is where I must go. I would willingly go to places much worse for such a pleasure as this will be." She wipes her eyes with her napkin. "How soon can we do it?"

"Not for a while." He smiles at her impatience. "They are not in the city now."

"Are you certain they will be there?"

"I am certain. The husband has commitments to keep."

"Good." She leans back, smiling tremulously, and widens her eyes. "I have not been to New York since my school days, you know. Just thinking of seeing it again makes me feel quite giddy . . . but then, a holiday *anywhere* away from Rosebank would do me a world of good, I'm sure."

"I have no doubt of it. And there is always so much in any great city to keep a woman of taste and culture—such as you are, my dear— thoroughly entertained. It will be my personal pleasure to be your escort in New York City during your stay, to introduce you to the best people, and take you to the very finest places." He smiles suddenly.

"Tell me, Miss Pratt . . . do you like the opera?"

Chapter Fifteen

B y l a t e J u n e they have established a kind of routine, although it can be broken or changed at a whim—his or hers. Mario, very self-disciplined in all matters pertaining to his art, does not believe much in rules for others, but insists, for himself, that he vocalize every day for at least an hour. The time of day is not important, other than it be well past noon—Mario is not at his best in the morning, and despite the fact that they have quickly fallen into step with the Noonan household— going to bed an hour or so after sundown, and waking with the dawn— Mario's voice is still a creature of the night, and refuses to ring free before one in the afternoon.

But this is well for the rest of the household because the best time for him to practice is in the early evening, while the sun is still up but the day has begun to cool; and every evening, once supper is over and the dishes cleared away, Mrs. Noonan and her daughters and Clara arrange themselves on the wicker chairs and settees on the porch with their needlework, and listen to Mario singing in the parlor.

All the windows are open, of course—the parlor is large and airy, the heavy drapes taken down for the summer, the carpets replaced with cool rush matting—and the old piano, although only an upright and none too fine an instrument, seems to understand that something special is happening to it when Mario begins to play: its ordinary, tinkly sound changes, somehow, grows deeper and sweeter with his hands on the keys. Clara knows, in her mind, that it is because he is such a superb pianist, but also believes, in her heart, that Mario's hands can make anything sing; a month after their wedding, Clara knows all about Mario's hands . . .

But it is of his music that we are speaking. With Mrs. Noonan and the others seated on the porch, Mario vocalizes, beginning with scales. For anyone but a musician, it is impossible to lend interest to the practice of scales. Do, re, mi, fa, sol, la, ti, do . . . do, ti, la, sol, fa, mi, re, do . . . re, mi, fa, sol, la, ti, do, re . . . re, do, ti, la, sol, fa, mi, re . . . Then there are chromatics, then arpeggios, then thirds, then octaves, until the minutes crawl and the listener wants to scream. But not when Mario sings them. The sweetness of his voice brings tears to Mrs. Noonan's eyes, the power of it makes the Noonan girls slightly faint. And then the scales are done, and he begins to sing, really sing— arias, hymns, lullabies, melodies from his native land, even the parlor songs that Mrs. Noonan adores, such as "Love's Old Sweet Song" and "After the Ball," which become positively exotic, their lyrics flavored with his strong Italian accent . . .

It is usually right after the scales that the farmhands appear. They come quietly, moving around from the back of the house, gathering silently, wiping their hands on their handkerchiefs and mopping their red faces. Some of them squat on the grass of the wide lawn, or under the elm that grows by the long drive; some, more respectful, stand and listen, their tribute not to the ladies on the porch but to the voice that pours out to them from the windows.

Mrs. Noonan never hurries them off, or shoos them away. There is no need. Once Mario has done, once the last, lovely note has faded away, they rouse themselves, nod, replace their hats and shuffle off to their nightly rest, and a few moments later Mario himself comes to join the ladies on the porch and take the evening air.

There is never any acclamation from the gathered listeners. Early on in the Alfieris' stay, Rebecca had burst into fervent applause after an achingly beautiful rendition of "Jeannie With the Light Brown Hair," and that evening Mario had shortened his practice by a good quarter of an hour, for which Rebecca's disturbance was blamed. Neither she nor anyone else has made the same mistake since. It is as if a pretense is needed—he pretending not to be overheard, they pretending not to listen—but it works, and that is all that matters.

Other than that there is no formal routine for the Alfieris at Westerly. They are not pampered, but neither are they expected to share in the farm's work: as paying guests they are, for the most part, benignly ignored, except during meals and the cherished nightly concert; but they fall, fairly soon after their arrival, into a pattern of their own within the larger context of the farm's activities. They wake, as does the rest of the household, with the sun, are bathed, dressed, and down to breakfast by seven. They help themselves from the sideboard in the dining room . . . no one has the time to wait table in the morning, when there are the pigs to be fed, the eggs to be collected, the cows to be milked, and the house to be cleaned from top to bottom. After the first week, Clara takes to helping collect the eggs, although the hens frighten her in the beginning, pecking at her hands as she reaches beneath them, and the smell of the coop makes her wrinkle her nose in disgust. But the pigs are something else again: too large and bristly to be approached with comfort; and she cannot be induced—no, not for anything—to milk the cows. Their large, liquid eyes are gentle, but their hind legs can administer a killing kick, and Clara greatly admires the way that Ruth and Rebecca lean their heads into the great flanks as they milk surely and steadily, their capable hands moving rhythmically as they talk and laugh, the warm white milk foaming into the pails.

Most often, unless Mario plans to drive the pony cart into Hudson—he grows hungry, sometimes, for sidewalks and shops and cobbled streets—Clara spends the morning in the kitchen with Mrs. Noonan, watching her cook and bake, helping her prepare the midday dinner, learning from her. Mrs. Noonan's own daughters already know much of what their mother has to teach—experience will do the rest for them—but Clara is utterly untutored in the ways of the kitchen, and wants desperately to learn. Two months is not much time in which to absorb what Mrs. Noonan has to impart, but it is a beginning; and Clara is an attentive, eager student, grateful to her teacher, humble in her recognition of her own abject ignorance.

Someone with less understanding—or more means—than Mrs. Noonan might wonder why she bothers: Clara, after all, has married a man of remarkable wealth, and will always have sufficient cooks and servants to need never lift a finger in her own house. But Mrs. Noonan is old-fashioned: she understands well Clara's desire to make a true home for herself and her husband, and her motherly heart goes out to the motherless girl who has had no one to show her the way. She herself is a patient teacher, and loves what she teaches, so that it is a joy to her to answer questions; and Clara asks a great many of them, some of them so foolish that she blushes as she stammers out the words. But Mrs. Noonan never laughs, or finds a question too foolish to answer— and Clara has Mario buy her a little copybook on one of their trips into town, and takes careful notes, and watches, and tastes . . . and learns.

And every skinned knuckle, every parboiled finger and sliced palm held out for her husband's rueful inspection, brings a kiss on the wounded spot and another on her mouth, making the pain well worth having. Mario's pleasure in her progress is profound: this she is doing for him. He regards her efforts with pride, and when her first perfect loaf of bread is brought to him, still warm from the oven, baked from scratch and presented to him with shining eyes, he slices and eats it with deep delight, declaring it the best he has ever tasted because it was made by *i dolci mani della mia carissima sposa* . . . even Mario's spoken words sound like music.

In the matter of needlework, however, Clara cedes pride of place to no one. Her small hands are nimbler with the needle than the Noonan girls' larger, rough ones; her stitches are tiny and uniformly perfect, her embroidered designs intricate and lovely. In the hot, still evenings, when the mosquitoes have driven them indoors, they retreat to the parlor, and Clara works at her embroidery while Mario pre- tends to read . . . but more often than not he watches her, seated with Ruth and Rebecca at the small table in the center of the room, her head with its queer, short curls bent beneath the light of the oil lamp, and his eyes go from one to the other of them and back again. The three young women make a pretty *tableau*—Mrs. Noonan's daugh- ters are well aware of the impression they make—but his wife far outshines them . . . softer, prettier, sweeter. Clara can feel his gaze, but whenever she lifts her head Mario is deep in his book, not looking at her at all, and it becomes a game to her, to see if she can catch him looking . . . but she never can.

But when her attention returns to her work he lifts his gaze again, taking in the prospect of all three young women, two of them with the frank admiration one bestows on any object of beauty, admiring it for the pleasure it brings simply to see it. But he gazes at the third—his wife—with his heart in his eyes: a look of tenderness, and of longing, and of miraculous surprise . . . as if his joy in her is still so new that he has not fully grasped it yet, and so unlooked for that its existence leaves him shaken.

Mrs. Noonan understands, as the younger women cannot, how difficult it must be for him, poor, happy man that he is, to be so very drunk with his own wife; and Alfieri, if he knew her sentiments, would agree. Certainly he is in what he frankly describes to himself—in those rare, lucid moments when his years and his natural intelligence reassert themselves—as a pitiful state. Common sense, dignity, any wisdom he may have acquired . . . it has all vanished. He is a boy again, right down to the sweaty palms, the dry mouth, the racing pulse. And like a boy, given half a chance he would talk about Clara to Mrs. Noonan, to her daughters, to anyone who would stop and listen . . . except that he retains just enough of his faculties to recall that there is nothing so boring in this life as a lover reciting the perfections of his beloved, and just enough mastery to hold himself in check.

It is his twenty years on the stage, learning how to keep himself outwardly under control, that saves him now, and for that knowledge and ability he is profoundly, and humbly, grateful. What is as droll, after all—what could be as droll—as a worldly-wise, middle-aged gentleman with a vast experience of women being reduced to a schoolboy stammer by his own nineteen-year-old wife? The answer, of course, is "nothing" . . . which accounts for the plenitude of Italian opera farces about imbecilic older men who take pretty young brides.

Yes, he is ridiculous, and he knows it. But then, what man could have been with Clara day and night for the last month, as he has been,

and retained his good sense? What man could have watched her changing, almost by the hour, from a sickly, fearful child into a rosy young
woman with smiling eyes and an upturned, eager mouth, and held on
to his reason? She is so softly round, now, that it is difficult to keep his
hands from her, even when there are others present—when he is alone
with her he does not even try—and what man could be her accomplice
in the little game she has invented, all on her own, and not be very
nearly mad?

Two or three days a week, on any afternoon at all—he never knows
which it will be, or why—after their midday dinner, with her morning's
lessons with Mrs. Noonan behind her and the table cleared of dishes,
she will stifle a yawn, murmuring that she really must not be quite well
yet, to feel so tired, so early in the day. And then, begging her pardon
of Mrs. Noonan with as chaste a face as he has ever seen, and never
once looking at him, she will vanish up the stairs to their bedroom.

The first time she did it he had followed her swiftly, frightened,
cursing himself for allowing her to do too much. He has learned to wait,
now, muttering his concern for her health before taking the stairs two
at a time. He deceives no one, of course—Mrs. Noonan and her daughters look the other way, smiling, and say they hope he finds Clara feeling
better—but he cares nothing for what they think because on the other
side of the door will be Clara's clothing, strewn in a path from the door
to the bed, and then Clara herself, waiting for him behind the bed's
gauzy curtains like some pasha's houri, wearing nothing at all but the
rings he has given her, holding out her arms . . .

He tries, afterward, as she lies drowsy against his heart, to recall the
faces and bodies of other women who have shared his bed . . . and
cannot. The way she has of lifting her eyes to his while she kneels before
him, her mouth and hands busy with their indescribable work, has
witched his mind clean of everyone else. The way she moves in the
darkness, crouched on him in love, her silhouette rising and falling above
him, black against the pale netting that walls them in—silent until she
throws her head back, crying out his name—has stolen all his memories.

But when did she learn such things? And who had taught her? He
knows that his own sins will not be easily forgiven, and that the slow,

knotting agony of jealousy that twists his heart when he thinks of her swaying in the darkness above someone else, and the triple torture—of believing that she had been forced . . . and fearing that she had not . . . and never knowing the truth because he has vowed never to speak of it until she speaks first—are part of his punishment still.

He knows, too, that he did not find her by chance—he has known since his earliest days that nothing ever happens to him by chance, that he has been touched by God, although for what reason it has not been given to him to know, no more than any man ever knows why he has been singled out for special curse or blessing.

He has come to believe, in the last month, that Clara is his penance: both his punishment, and his reward for bearing its pain in silent submission. The image that comes to him, of the pain, is from a story his mother had read to him as a child, long years ago: of a nightingale who pierces his heart on a thorn for love of a rose, pressing it ever deeper into his heart . . . and Clara is his thorn, and Clara is his rose.

And when she looks into his face, flushed and sleepy with lovemaking, and murmurs: "Oh, how I love you!" and there is no one else but him in her eyes, he thinks he will die of happiness. He had said that to her once, foolishly—just once—and she had turned white, silly little girl, and her eyes had filled with tears. "Please," she had begged, "please, now that I have you, don't leave me!" . . . and he had spent the next hour swearing to her that he would never leave her, showing her how he *could* never leave her . . .

Completely forgetting, wrapped in her fragrance, that in the tale of the rose and the nightingale, the nightingale dies of a bleeding heart.

BOOK II

Clara

Chapter Sixteen

THE TRAIN SPEEDS south with a rush and a clatter, holding to the river, its whistle trailing through the summer morning like a comet's tail. It rides light on its rails, barely burdened by the weight of passengers, for it is early August, and few go willingly to the city: it will be weeks, yet, before the thick swelter of summer gives way to the dry, baking heat that signals the approach of autumn.

The dearth of riders—there are hardly more than a dozen in each car—is surely the reason that the couple who board at the town of Hudson attract such attention. After all, who would care about—or even notice—an additional two passengers (with or without a basket of kittens, such as these have brought with them) on a crowded train? And yet there is no doubt that they are a singular pair: the man tall and powerfully built, in a white suit of perfect cut, the face beneath his wide-brimmed hat as dark as any Gypsy's; the woman very young and very small, her dress a soft blue, the unfashionably short cut of her dark hair only partially concealed by her bonnet.

There is a story here, that much is plain; something more interesting than the usual fare, something that causes fellow passengers to lift their heads and steal furtive peeks above the edges of books and around open newspapers, wondering . . .

The tall man, for instance, may or may not be an exile from the Argentine, very possibly a millionaire; certainly he is foreign—those sitting nearest him can clearly detect an accent when he addresses the young woman—and carries himself with an air. The young woman may or may not be his daughter; the care with which he settles her into her seat by the window, the smile in his eyes as they light on her, the way he leans toward her when she speaks: all could be equally the expressions of a husband, a father, or a lover. The kittens, at least—there are two of them in the covered basket—are merely kittens, although the young woman fusses over them as they roll and tumble over each other as if they are rare and precious things; and the man watches, not them, but her face as she watches them, and laughs with her laughter.

The curious, kindly onlookers laugh, too, at the sight and sound of her merriment; and as kindly laughter has the quality of making friends of strangers, as well as making time brief, the dozen passengers are soon sharing the contents of a deep hamper that has come aboard with the singular couple and their kittens, and the tall man—who, all are agreed, is the Argentine's loss and America's gain—pours out the wine with a liberal hand until it is but a memory, and wishes them *"buona fortuna"* in the authentic, Spanish way; and a dozen strangers part as friends when—two hours later and much too soon—they arrive in New York, not one of them knowing, as each goes his separate way, that he has broken bread with the great Italian tenor Mario Alfieri, and his young wife . . . but all of them a great deal happier for having done it.

Gennarino is at the station to meet the maestro and his bride, and collect their baggage; quiet and watchful as always, he has not altered in their absence. Neither has Stafford Dyckman, newly returned from his father's summer cottage in Newport for the express purpose of handing Signora Alfieri down from the train and presenting her with a huge bouquet of yellow roses. New York itself is the same as when they left, only much hotter, when Alfieri—who is bearded, now, and burnt brown from two months of going about hatless and in his shirtsleeves beneath the summer sun—steps from the train.

Stafford's gaze, as he grips his friend's hand and clasps his shoulder in welcome, lifts to a young woman who appears, smiling a little uncertainly, on the train's steps just behind the tenor—and for a moment he is confused, thinking that Mario, having left with one woman, has returned with another; and then he catches his breath and merely stands there, staring, while Alfieri bursts out laughing at his expression. Turning, he lifts the pretty stranger down from the train, his hands around her waist, and sets her gently on the ground.

"She has changed, Stafford, has she not?"

The loving pride in Alfieri's voice registers in Dyckman's mind, to be recalled and pondered later, but now he can only gape. "Changed" is not a word that does justice to the transformation that his eyes behold. The gaunt and wasted child has been replaced, that is all; and in her stead is an enchanting young woman with a dusting of freckles across her nose. She is not beautiful, nor will she ever be: her features—always with the exception of her eyes—are too ordinary for real beauty; but she is pretty enough, and Dyckman stares at her, and stammers.

Alfieri leans toward him. "The flowers," he murmurs into the young man's ear, and Dyckman flushes and proffers the bouquet to Clara, who accepts it with a smile.

The carriage which brought the young man to the station has waited, at his request, to make the return trip downtown; and as they clatter down Madison Avenue, Dyckman, feeling that it would be less than delicate to inquire too deeply into what has clearly been a most successful honeymoon, chooses rather to entertain the newlyweds with anecdotes of Newport society during his stay there.

But Clara's is not the only transformation. It does not take Dyckman long to discover that his friend, too, has greatly altered: where before Alfieri would have listened keenly and laughed, he now merely listens dutifully and smiles, his eyes rarely leaving his young wife, who is leaning forward in her seat, watching the familiar streets pass by with a half-smile of recognition, as if she has never quite seen them before.

Who should know better than Dyckman that Alfieri is now a married man? He had, after all, been present at the occasion that made the two, one. But so many women have passed through the tenor's life that, despite the wedding—despite the ring, and the vows, and the strange, broken glass—it has never really occurred to Dyckman, until this moment, that this one would be different; would be something more than the others had been. He falls silent at last and watches the newlyweds with a dawning sense of loss, suddenly aware that Mario's attention has shifted forever.

This feeling does not abate as they approach their destination. Standing out clearly among the row of nearly identical brownstones, most of them closed and shuttered, Alfieri's house is conspicuous for its look of lively habitation: for the dark green awnings that shade the windows, and the garlands of fresh flowers that curve up the stone balusters to the open front door, to welcome the couple home.

The interior, too, has been decorated for the signore and signora, with colored paper streamers dangling from every chandelier, and vases of roses in every room. Maid and footman, their faces familiar from the Slade house, stand smiling in the foyer as Alfieri lifts his bride across the threshold with no more effort than if she were a china doll; and Dyckman, lagging behind to pay the driver, is forgotten in the general excitement as the tenor shows his wife around her new home.

Feeling more than a little sorry for himself, and also disloyal to Alfieri for begrudging his happiness, Dyckman wanders into the darkened drawing room, unsure of his welcome. All these sensations—self-pity, disloyalty, uncertainty—have been hitherto unknown to him; none is conducive to sobriety; and as the drawing room is cool, and the day hot, he pours himself a whiskey at the sideboard and settles into a deep chair to probe his hurts. He is well into his third glass when the soft rustle of skirts makes him lift his head.

"Mrs. Alfieri," he says, rising unsteadily to his feet, but Clara takes the chair near him and looks up into his face. He seats himself again, wondering, somewhat foggily, what she wants with him.

"I should like you to call me Clara," she says, "if you wouldn't mind. Whenever someone calls me 'Mrs. Alfieri,' I turn around to see who's behind me. It sounds so important . . . not like me at all."

It is the first time he has ever been alone with her, only the second or third time he has ever heard her speak.

"Thank you," he says stiffly. "But won't Mario mind?"

"I don't think so," she says. "You have been his friend for so long, and he is so kind. Besides, it's my name."

"Clara, then," he says, still unsure of her purpose. "You've come looking for Mario, I suppose. I haven't seen him since we arrived."

"Oh, no. Mario is upstairs, going through some letters from Italy that Gennarino put aside for him. While he was busy I thought I would come down and talk to you. I was hoping you hadn't gone."

"Why?"

"Ah," she says. "You are angry with me. I felt it, in the carriage."

"Angry? What nonsense!" he says, loathing himself for being ill-mannered, and resenting her for making him so. "Why should I be?"

"Because you think that Mario won't want your company any more, now that he has a wife."

Whatever answer he expected, it was not this one. Dyckman stares at her, appalled by her frankness. Decently bred people clothe their meaning in layers of indirection, as a cushion against the sometimes sharp edge of truth.

"And now I've shocked you," she says. "But I could see how you felt." She looks down, playing with her wedding ring, turning it round and round on her finger. "My being here won't make a bit of difference. You know Mario so much better than I, and for so much longer. Do you really think he could be so unkind to a friend?"

Suddenly ashamed of his doubts, Dyckman murmurs: "No, of course not." But she has not finished.

"I really came to ask you . . ." She stops, draws herself up and starts again. "I came to ask if we might not be friends too. *He* would be happier for it, and I . . ."—she makes a small gesture, an eloquent movement of hands and head—"I would be so glad. Even if you don't like me, we have Mario in common, now; and I love him so much. Shouldn't that make us friends?"

Against indirection he might have prevailed; but what defense can there be against such simplicity? Leaning over, he takes the hand that still twists her wedding ring.

"I am Stafford to my friends," he says, "if you do not think Mario will mind."

"I don't think so," she says. She is so very pretty when she smiles.

. . .

Dinner that same evening is a festive affair, although somewhat unconventional. The happy couple are fêted in their own home by Mr. and Mrs. Buchan and a much blither Stafford Dyckman, who calls his hostess "Clara" with a look of pride that seems to defy anyone—even Alfieri—to challenge his right to do so; and the new bride, Mrs. Noonan's teachings still fresh in her mind, oversees her table with almost perfect poise . . . although the intervals between the courses are lengthened—much to her husband's amusement and the detriment of some of the dishes—by her need to absent herself for quick trips to the upstairs spare bedroom, where her kittens have been installed, to relieve her anxiety over their well-being.

The cook, new to the establishment, and hired in anticipation of the Alfieris' return by Mrs. Buchan and Gennarino working in concert, must wonder what sort of topsy-turvy household she has joined, for at one point the table is abandoned by *all* the diners in response to a crisis in the "nursery"—an emergency which has the guests crowding around and calling out helpful suggestions as a laughing Alfieri, standing on a chair, gingerly plucks a tiny, clamorous and very adhesive cat down from the top of the draperies and restores it to the arms of its frantic young mistress.

Order restored, and the kittens packed off to the servants' hall where Margaret, the maid, can oversee their safety, the party troop back downstairs in high spirits to resume their interrupted dinner. Mrs. Buchan watches Alfieri privately wrap his handkerchief around his hand as they go, to bind up the bloody scratches received in the fray. She murmurs: "You indulge her shamelessly, signore." And the tenor merely smiles and replies: "You have discovered my secret vice, madame. Don't take it from me . . . it's the only one I have left, now."

The remainder of dinner is a triumph, with a penitent Clara on her very best behavior; and when she lays down her napkin at last and rises from her chair to signal the end of the meal—flushing slightly at the newness of the sensation as all the gentlemen rise to their feet—not even the severest social critic could pick holes in her deportment.

The gentlemen remain in the dining room for their port and cigars,

and she and Mrs. Buchan retire to the drawing room, where, in a bow
to the summer heat, the windows have been opened wide and the curtains tied back to let in the evening breeze. No more than a dozen
candles flicker in the spacious room, leaving the corners in darkness,
the walls softened by shadows, and Alice Buchan sinks back into the
sofa, slipping off her shoes with a sigh of pleasure and smiling at the
blessed reprieve from formality that the absence of men brings.

"Do you know," she says, fanning herself languidly, while Clara stands
before a window, eyes shut and arms open to welcome the cool night air,
"when I was young I thought that women had gotten the poorest end of the
bargain socially. Oh, yes, I was very put out at having been born female. I
envied the fact that the men stayed behind after dinner, to smoke and talk
of whatever grave, momentous things men talk of when women aren't
there. But I've learned, over the years, that all we really miss is spending
more time on those hard chairs, arguing about foolishness while breathing
in air like the inside of a chimney. No, not over there," she says as
Clara turns from the window, laughing. "Come sit by me." She pats the
seat next to her. "I want to have a good look at you."

Clara sits, obediently, and Alice sets to studying the blooming young
wife, so different in every way from the frail bride of two months ago.
The small face glows and there is no hint of shadows beneath the lovely
eyes, but what impresses Alice the most is the fact that Clara does not
try to turn away or hide from her gaze. Her face stays raised for the
inspection, and her eyes meet Alice's resolutely, guileless and clear; and
the room is not so dim that Alice cannot instantly see the reason for
the wondrous change.

"He has made you very happy," she says, and Clara's only response
is a sudden, joyous laugh, like a ripple of water. She tries to speak but
her voice fails, and she slips from the sofa to kneel at Alice's feet and
hide her burning face in Alice's lap.

The older woman strokes her hair, running her fingers through dark
curls grown long enough, now, to make a halo of shining ringlets about
Clara's head.

"I told Daniel that his fears were foolish. He thought that the great
difference . . . well, never mind. You have begun well, my dear, and,

God willing, you and your husband will go on, from happiness to happiness, for many years to come. And now will you pour the coffee?" Alice bends over the head still resting in her lap. "You are mistress here, and it is your place to pour."

Clara lifts her head, her face still scarlet, brushes the happy tears hastily from her eyes, rises and seats herself at the table. Her "lessons" at Westerly had included the serving of coffee and tea to guests, and she works now with quiet deliberation, sitting very erect, so as to look properly dignified and formal, striving to do everything as she had been taught. Holding a cup and saucer in one hand, she lifts the coffeepot in the other and pours slowly, a tiny frown of concentration on her face.

"Milk?" she says. "Do you think I will ever learn to entertain? Correctly, I mean. And what will I do if Mario wants to bring important people to dine before I'm ready? Sugar? One or two?" Setting down the coffeepot without a drop spilled, she heaves an almost inaudible sigh of relief and hands the cup to Alice.

"It will all come with time and experience," Mrs. Buchan says. "You have done extremely well tonight, particularly as this was your first dinner party."

"Except for the kittens," Clara says, the color rising in her face again.

"Now, you mustn't fret," Alice says. "Little disturbances happen in the best-regulated households." She sips her coffee. "Besides, no one minded. Certainly not your husband."

"Well, no," Clara says, "but then he does spoil me shamelessly," and she laughs again, another, longer ripple of laughter, at the sudden blush that now spreads across Mrs. Buchan's face.

Clara reaches across the table for her hand. "Forgive me," she says. "I heard what you said to him, and I don't mind. You were right, of course, and, oh, I do so *love* it when he spoils me! But Mario is a great and famous man, with important friends, and I must learn to be elegant and to know everything about being a great man's wife. That's why I tried to learn as much as I could while we were away . . ."

Mrs. Buchan listens, nodding her approval, both of the desire to learn that had prompted the studies with Mrs. Noonan, and of how much had been learned in eight short weeks.

"I only wish that I had had time for more," Clara says.

"But you *do* have time," Alice protests, "a great *deal* of time! My dear, I am no Mrs. Noonan, with blue ribbons for my great deeds in the kitchen and a farm to run besides, but I have managed a city household well enough for twenty years, and there are things that I can teach you too.

"You and Signor Alfieri leave for Philadelphia in three days, do you not? And you return at the end of October? Well, then, I will be your Mrs. Noonan in the city, if you'd like. When you return to New York we can begin regular lessons, and by next summer, when you and your husband sail for Europe, you will be able to hold your head up among any collection of wives on the Continent."

She puts down her cup. "And in the meantime, until we can begin your studies, my advice to you is simply to continue doing whatever it is that causes your husband to look at you in that way." She tilts her head, observing Clara with a smile. "You may be less than proficient at housekeeping, my dear, but no amount of housekeeping has ever brought that sort of smile to a man's face. I wonder if you shouldn't be giving *me* lessons . . ."

Could he hear it now, the sound of Clara's laughter would doubtless bring just that sort of smile to Alfieri's face. But he is immured, instead, in the dining room with Messrs. Buchan and Dyckman; and despite the admirable port and excellent cigars, and the presence of good friends, he is restless. He is not used to having Clara out of his sight for many minutes at a time, and he finds himself irritable without her, and craving her presence as an opium addict craves his pipe. The spirited comparison of political corruption in New York and Milan in which Buchan and Dyckman are engaged is simply insufficient recompense for the loss of his wife's nearness.

Tapping his fingers on his knee, he waits for a lull in the conversation. "Shall we join the ladies, gentlemen?" he says, rising from his chair.

Stafford looks up, takes his cue from Alfieri and also rises to his feet. Only Buchan remains seated. He, too, looks up at the tenor.

"If you please, signore." He turns from Alfieri to Dyckman, smiling. "You will not mind entertaining the ladies alone for a few minutes, will you, Stafford? There is something of a business nature that I must discuss briefly with our host."

Surprised, Alfieri resumes his seat, curious at the way Buchan refuses to say any more until the door is shut fast behind the young man.

"You are being very mysterious, Mr. Buchan. God knows what Stafford will think, and what he will tell our wives."

"Stafford's flights of fancy do not worry me, signore. But I have not seen you since that day at Westerly, two months ago . . . and as you are leaving the city again in a few days, and may not have time to meet with me again, I wanted to let you know what my investigations have— and have not—brought to light thus far."

"Investigations?" The tenor's eyebrows lift. "What investigations are those, Mr. Buchan?"

"Into your wife's history, signore, which, if you recall, I requested your permission to undertake."

"Ah, yes; my wife's history." Alfieri's smile is bland. "Frankly, I had forgotten that I gave you such permission, Mr. Buchan; perhaps it is time, now, to rescind it."

Buchan is very quiet. "You do not wish to know what I have learned?"

"Two months have passed with no sign of this dreaded retaliation from Mr. Chadwick. Let us say that I do not think you need to pursue your investigations any further. I do not think that we have anything more to fear from him."

"Don't you, signore? Well, doubtless, you know best. Certainly, if you tell me to stop, I will do so. But before you make a final decision, I would be grateful if you would allow me to tell you what I have learned thus far. It would be a pity, don't you think, to let so much good, hard work go to waste?"

Alfieri glances at the clock on the mantelpiece. "Very well," he says, "we have a few minutes. Please begin."

"Thank you, signore. Please understand, by the way, that as far as any danger from Mr. Chadwick is concerned, I never said it would be immediate. The purpose of my research into your wife's history was to be the discovery of anything that he might ultimately use to injure the two of you, either now or in the future. I have found nothing of that nature; nevertheless, I think you will find what I have to say interesting."

He smooths his hand across the tablecloth. "When we spoke at Westerly, signore, you very graciously told me that you had learned from your wife that she was born in New Jersey, on October the fourteenth, eighteen seventy-four. She had not said where in New Jersey, and you, not wishing to alarm her, did not wish to ask. Armed with just that information, therefore, and thinking it best to begin at the beginning, I had the birth registers for the years eighteen seventy-two through eighteen seventy-six examined in every county in New Jersey—I added two years on either side of the year you told me, to allow for possible errors."

He leans back in his chair and looks at the tenor. "*Three* Clara Adlers were born during those years, signore. The first Clara Adler was born in Cape May on the seventeenth of June, eighteen seventy-three. Her father was—and still is—minister of the Lutheran church there. The girl was married a year ago, and recently became the proud mother of twin boys. Her married name is Hoffmeier.

"The second Clara Adler was born to an Episcopal family in Little Ferry on January the twenty-third, eighteen seventy-five. She died on the ninth of July, eighteen seventy-six, of scarlet fever. The local doctor—retired, now—remembered her well. Losing the little ones was always hardest for him. He even told me where she was buried. I went to the grave." He shakes his head at the memory. "The family still leave flowers there.

"The third and last Clara Adler is the child of German immigrants who arrived in this country just days before her birth on the fourth of November, eighteen seventy-five. She was, tragically, born simple, probably as a result of an accident her mother suffered on board the ship from Hamburg. She still lives with her parents in Camden, and her mind will never be more than five years old."

Alfieri is very still. "The English of which is what, Mr. Buchan?"

"I think the meaning is very clear. Either Mrs. Alfieri was born somewhere other than where she told you, or she was born with a different name." His eyes never leave Alfieri's face. "But as of right now, signore, as far as I have been able to determine after two months of searching . . . your wife does not exist."

Chapter Seventeen

Alfieri's voice is low. "Be very careful, Mr. Buchan."

"I have been careful, signore—so careful that I could not possibly have made an error. These records have been checked and checked again."

"And my wife is therefore a liar . . . that is what you are saying."

"No, signore, you mistake me. That your wife is sincere and has told you what she believes to be the truth I have not the slightest doubt. But clearly there is some inconsistency here; and since I do not believe that, once grown to womanhood, an intelligent child would forget either her name or where she was told she was born, I have no choice but to believe that she has been intentionally misinformed about either one or the other . . . perhaps both."

"Why should anyone wish to misinform her about her name or her birthplace?"

"That would depend upon who she is, would it not?"

The chair creaks as Buchan leans forward. "Let me mention some random thoughts that have been going around my brain lately, signore, and that all seem to converge at the same point. Perhaps you will think me foolish, or even mad; perhaps not. You must judge for yourself."

A moth flutters its wings against the glass of a lampshade; Buchan watches it absently, then begins: "As I am certain you know, signore, your wife's late guardian died of heart failure. But were you aware that

Henry Slade did not have a weak heart? On the contrary: his own doctor thought him likely to live another twenty years. Not a definitive point, as outwardly healthy people die of heart failure every day, but an interesting one nevertheless.

"Perhaps you have also heard that he was one of the cleverest and most careful businessmen in New York, a man who had, for years, turned a profit on everything he touched. That is all true. And yet, when this clever and supremely careful man suddenly dies, it is discovered that he has made no provision for the young woman he took in four years earlier, and of whom, by all accounts, he was absurdly fond. Don't you find that strange? I do. His very real affection for your wife, by the way, was confirmed to me earlier this evening, in a conversation I had with your maid and footman."

Alfieri's expression is guarded. "A miscalculation, nothing more. As you said, Mr. Buchan, he thought he would live for another twenty years, and did not bother with a will."

"You are forty years old, signore, not sixty-six, and I would lay odds that you, too, believe you will live long. But you established a trust shortly before your marriage—I know, I drew it up for you—in order to provide for your wife, of whom you are absurdly fond, in case the worst happens. And, if you will forgive me, signore, you are very wealthy indeed, but Henry Slade was rich . . . rich to the tune of thirty millions. He had not gotten that way by making miscalculations.

"Besides," Buchan smiles, "you have forgotten: he *had* a will—one that had been drawn up twenty years earlier, before he bought the house at Gramercy Park, before your wife was even born. It was that will that was probated. So why, signore, would he draw up a will in his younger days when he had no legatees but his estate and various charities, and yet not change it once he had taken in a child whom he grew to love?"

"Why, indeed?" Alfieri says impatiently. "And what has any of this to do with Clara's identity being kept from her when she was a child?"

"I do not know, signore, but I can guess. Isn't it becoming plain to you too? I cannot be certain, however, until I have worked backward along the thread that connects her to Slade. But always we are led, again and again, to the question that all New York has been asking for five years now: who is the young woman known as Clara Adler, and why did Slade take her in?"

"She is my wife, Mr. Buchan; that is who she is." Alfieri rises to his feet. "That is her identity, and the rest of the question will have to remain unanswered, for I want your investigation to stop, now. As to why Mr. Slade took her in, whatever his reason, his soul has my eternal thanks; but I am equally grateful that he left her penniless, because, had she inherited his fortune, I never would have found her. And now I think we should join Stafford and the ladies in the drawing room—our absence must appear unconscionably rude."

His hand is on the door when Buchan's voice stops him.

"And are you so sure, signore, that she did not inherit his fortune?"

The tenor turns back swiftly. "Are you quite well, Mr. Buchan? The will made no mention of her—"

"The will, the will!" Buchan brings his hand down on the table with such force that the glasses ring. "That will was twenty years old, man! Don't you see? Can't I make you understand? It's not possible that Henry Slade would have died without a more recent will, it would have gone against every fiber in the man's body! And who would have drawn up that new will, who would have known the disposition of every last nickel? Who, besides you, signore, wanted your wife very badly?"

Alfieri is suddenly pale. "Go on, Mr. Buchan," he says. "You begin to make perfect sense to me. She was to be taken to live with him . . ."

"Yes," Buchan says quietly. "You understand me now. I think he would have forced her to marry him, once she was locked safely away in his house. And I doubt that it would have taken long—after all, what choice would she have had? As she told you, she had nowhere else to go, no one else to go to, and he would be hectoring her day and night. If she refused, he could threaten to turn her out with nothing once she reached her majority. He might even—forgive me, signore—but he might even have forced himself on her, if she proved particularly obstinate, then persuaded her that refusal to make their intimacy legal was pointless, and would only lead to disgrace, especially if she bore a child . . . whose paternity, if she still refused, would be charged to a servant, or one of the local tradesmen . . ."

Buchan shifts in his chair. "But it matters not how he accomplished it: the wedding would have been soon, followed by a few months of conjugal bliss for the happy couple, and then—oh, wonderful! A new will, miraculously found, and young Mrs. Thaddeus Chadwick in sudden possession of thirty million dollars and a mansion on Gramercy Park!"

He is quiet, watching the moth batter itself against the glass shade. "Frail Mrs. Chadwick, I should say. If it makes you feel any better, signore, I do not think he would have mistreated her, once they were married. It would have been in his interest to keep her well . . . for a little while, at least. Still, everyone knows how ill she was after Slade's death; no one would have wondered if, in spite of the tender care Chadwick lavished on her, she slipped quietly away in her sleep after a year or two . . .

"This is, of course, all only conjecture," he says to Alfieri's bowed head. "You understand that, don't you, signore? I have no proof whatsoever . . . only a shattered portrait in a shattered room, and a raving man's promise to see you destroyed."

"And Slade?" Alfieri replies dully. "His death?"

"I have known such handy coincidences to occur naturally, but they are rare. I rather think that Chadwick helped him into the next world, but the only way to find that out would be to have Slade's body exhumed for autopsy, and I have not the slightest shred of evidence to offer as my rationale for such a request. So all of this remains merely my theory."

"But surely," Alfieri says, "surely he would have been caught in his own lies? Surely when the new will was brought to light, someone would have asked him why he had substituted the old will for it?"

Buchan shrugs. "The new one could not be found when Slade died."

"But that is absurd! Would he not have a copy? A document as important as that would have to have been copied, perhaps many times."

"The copy was lost, or destroyed. In fact, my memory tells me that there was a fire in Chadwick's office a few months before Slade's death . . . small, and easily extinguished, but causing fairly extensive damage. Chadwick would have pointed to that, no doubt. He had meant to make a new copy of the will, of course, but had waited, thinking that he had all the time in the world. Then Slade died before that could be accomplished, and the original could not be found." Buchan shrugs again. "Is it a weak story? Certainly. But men have taken far greater risks for far smaller prizes.

"Then, too," he says, "Chadwick's silence on the subject of the new will would add more weight, not less, to his story. If *I* had been so lax as to lose the only copy of a crucial document, signore, the original of which could not then be found, do you think I would wish to tell anyone about it, and advertise my carelessness? I cannot think of a better way to lose clients. And besides, who had suffered from the substitution? Only an insignificant child, an unimportant little Jewess with no known family, no connections of any consequence, and a dead guardian.

"And, finally, we must not lose sight of the fact that Miss Adler would have inherited after all . . . even though she would have been Mrs. Chadwick by that time. Could anyone say, then, that she had truly been cheated of her inheritance?"

Alfieri straightens up slowly. "What you are saying, then, is that Mr. Chadwick's design was nearly foolproof. And yet he has failed, has he not? For all his well-laid plans, he is left with nothing—God will pardon me, I know, if I rejoice in his loss—and I have Clara, and she is safe."

"Safe?" the lawyer says gently. "You must pardon *me,* signore, but I cannot agree with you. You and your wife have deprived Thaddeus Chadwick of thirty million dollars. If, in fact, he did murder his dearest friend for that sum, what do you think he would stop at in your case?"

Alfieri shakes his head. "Gennarino—"

"Is your bodyguard," Buchan says. "Yes, I know. He told me so on the day he came to my office, the day Chadwick found your wife gone. But as I have said before, I do not expect Chadwick to use violence against you, despite his outburst that day. That was his fury speaking, and it was over quickly. No, he will never do anything that could possibly be traced back to him, especially since he was heard to threaten you and Mrs. Alfieri. He will be more subtle, signore. More ingenious."

Alfieri looks away. "Continue your investigation," he says quietly. "I hope to God you find nothing."

"I would prefer it, signore, if there were nothing to find."

Rising from his chair, the lawyer leans over the lamp. He cups his hands and gently scoops up the moth which still beats its wings against the shade, walks to the open window and releases it into the night, looking after it until its flutter is lost in the blackness. He remains by the window, looking out at the backs of the nearby houses, most of them dark and empty, across the rustling garden space between.

With his back to Alfieri, he says: "When we last spoke, signore, you said that you knew nothing of your wife's earlier life because you had been acquainted such a short time. Two months have gone by. Have you learned anything that can help me?"

"No, Mr. Buchan, I have not."

"Even knowing how important it is? Even if it will safeguard you both? You still know nothing?"

"I cannot help you."

"Signore . . ."

"I cannot help you; I would, if I could . . ." He stops and Buchan turns to look at him. The two men face each other down the length of the table. "What I know . . . let us say by accident, Mr. Buchan . . . is another's secret, and not mine to tell."

"Not even if it will protect her?"

"I do not know how your knowing would do that. But no, not even then. I will protect her all I can; Gennarino will do the rest. It is a matter of honor."

"Yours or hers?" the lawyer says shortly.

"Both of ours." Alfieri plays idly with an empty wineglass. "Do not think that I am not grateful for what you are trying to do. But you must find what you can on your own, Mr. Buchan; and if you find it, you will understand my silence."

Neither man stirs. Then Alfieri says: "Tell me, Mr. Buchan . . . who do you think my wife is, really?"

Buchan smiles. "I think she is a gentleman's wife, signore."

The gentleman turns away. "Thank you," he says quietly, and leads the way into the drawing room where Clara, very proper, is waiting to serve them their coffee.

Chapter Eighteen

THE CITY IS MOTIONLESS. It lies panting and prostrate in the August sun like some dusty, treeless hamlet on the prairie, broiling in a pitiless white glare, the only sound on its deserted pavements the high, electric whine of the cicadas, rising and falling like current in the wires that tie street to street. On this stifling day, Trinity Churchyard is no more still than the sidewalk beyond its railing, and far more populous than Broadway; and the men toiling stoically in the surrounding offices loosen ties and sodden collars, and mop their streaming faces, looking dully up at ceiling fans which seem powerless to move the leaden air, fanning themselves with whatever papers may be to hand and dreaming of September's salvation.

Such heat makes men irritable. Buchan, listening to the faint, slow scratching of his two clerks' pens in the sweltering silence, finds himself staring out the open window at the churchyard, and twisting over and over in his mind the seemingly insoluble problem of finding the identity of someone who does not exist. As I was going up the stair, he thinks, I met a child who wasn't there . . .

Irked at the way his thoughts are drifting, he shakes his head, sending drops of moisture spattering onto the freshly copied paper before him, blotting the page with circles of running ink, and he sweeps his arm across the desktop in a sudden spasm of annoyance, sending books, pens, papers flying to the floor, then sits glaring at the mess, wiping his face with his pocket handkerchief.

The door from his inner office to the outer one, where his clerks sit, is open to permit the free flow of any air that might stir—a painfully comical illustration of the adage that hope springs eternal in the human breast—and the crash of books in the silence is enough to pique the curiosity of one clerk, who appears in the doorway, wordlessly surveying both his employer and the havoc at his feet.

"Yes, Lennox? Is there something I can do for you?"

The clerk clears his throat, but before he can answer there is the sound of the outer office door opening and shutting, and a quiet voice asking the other clerk for an audience with Mr. Buchan.

"Who shall I say is asking for him, please?"

"My name is Peters."

"Have you an appointment, Mr. Peters?"

"Why, no." The voice is hesitant. "If you could just tell him that I'm here. I work for Maestro Alfieri, you see."

Buchan skirts the papers on the floor and steps into the outer office. "Peters," he says, extending his hand, "what brings you onto the streets on such a day? It's no cooler indoors, God knows, but out there the sun is enough to fry a man's brains. There's no trouble at your master's house?"

"Oh, no, sir." The footman, clutching his hat in his hand, finally relinquishes it to one of the clerks in some confusion, being unaccustomed to this reversal of roles. His somewhat sparse dark hair is plastered to his head, his normally ruddy face deep red, now, and covered with perspiration. "The master and mistress left for Philadelphia this morning."

"Indeed," Buchan says, guiding the man to a chair in his office as the clerks swiftly and silently gather together the spilled books and papers and vanish into the outer room, pulling the door shut behind them. "Did Margaret and Gennarino go too?"

"Yes, sir." The footman blots his brow with his sleeve. "But Cook and the kittens are staying with me."

The lawyer nods and smiles faintly. "So you remain behind in the city," he says, reaching for a pitcher on his desk and pouring part of its contents into a glass, the sides of which turn instantly opaque with condensation. He hands the man the iced water. "I cannot help but think," he says, watching as the footman gratefully takes several huge swallows, "that you and the kittens have the better part of the bargain. If New York is this bad, Philadelphia must be even worse, being farther south."

Peters smiles for the first time, sighing with relief, and carefully wipes the moisture, first from his upper lip, then his brow. "I can't say that I mind staying behind, sir. The house is cool enough, especially down in the servants' hall, and there's little enough to do with everyone away."

"Well, then," Buchan says, seating himself and folding his hands in front of him, "tell me what has brought you out of a cool house into this inferno."

"Yes, sir." The footman clears his throat. "Actually, sir, it's my niece. Well, you know, I think, that Margaret is my niece—Margaret that's now Mrs. Alfieri's maid, sir—she's my sister's girl, and it was I that got her her first position with Mr. Slade, God rest his soul." Buchan nods politely at this bit of information, and the servant, encouraged, continues.

"She thought she should tell you herself, sir, but first she worried that she might be thought disloyal—as if either of us would do or say anything to hurt Mrs. Alfieri—or the master, either, for that matter, as generous a gentleman as God ever made, for all that he's Eye-talian— and then there was no time, what with readying Mrs. Alfieri for her trip. And so she asked if I would tell you for her, and I said I would, as soon as they had all gone . . ."

Buchan merely waits for the man to take a breath and another swallow of water.

"Thank you, sir, for your patience. The point is that—without listening on purpose, you understand, sir—Margaret overheard you, the other night, speaking to Maestro Alfieri. She truly couldn't help herself: she was in the master and mistress's room, turning down their bed for the night, and it's at the back of the house, right above the dining room.

Well, she heard your voice out the window, sir, asking the master if he knows anything about Mrs. Alfieri's past, and that it could protect her if he did."

Buchan's eyes are suddenly bright. "Yes? And?"

"Well, Margaret helped care for Miss Clara—Mrs. Alfieri, now—all through her illness this past winter and spring. Margaret's good with the sick, you see, being quiet and gentle-fingered, and she stood watch in Miss Clara's room all through the worst part, when we thought the child—Miss Clara, sir, meaning no disrespect—would surely die." The footman clears his throat again. "Margaret never left her side for days, sir, and even slept there, in a chair, for Miss Clara was delirious, and raved out of her head . . ."

He shakes his own head. "The child said things in her illness, sir, sometimes talking, sometimes pleading with people . . . and Margaret thought that you might wish to know, sir, of the names that Miss Clara repeated over and over."

"Christian names or family names?"

"Both, sir, although Margaret can't always be sure which went with which: sometimes Miss Clara would say names together, sometimes separate."

"Did Margaret tell you the names?"

"She did better than that, sir. She wrote them down." He hands Buchan a folded sheet of paper, very wilted, from his breast pocket. "She can't be sure that they're all spelled right—but she told them to me and we tried to spell 'em as they sounded, if you follow me, sir."

Buchan eagerly unfolds the paper and stares down at a vertical list of some fifteen lines printed in a large, childish hand. "Are they in any particular order?"

"The ones Miss Clara said most often are the ones Margaret remembered best, and put down first. She says if she thinks on it, more will probably come to her."

"I doubt if that will be necessary. The ones mentioned most frequently will probably prove to be the most important." Folding the sheet again, Buchan slides it into a desk drawer. "Will you be writing to your niece? When you do, thank her for me. Tell her that she has done Signor and

Signora Alfieri a real service. But remind her, too, that she is not to tell anyone about giving me this information. This is our secret; it stays among the three of us."

"Yes, sir." The footman looks dubious. "Not even Signor Gennarino? He is most devoted to the master, sir, and because the master is so wild about her, to the little mistress as well. He would be greatly put out if he thought we were dealing behind his back . . . and I should not like to have him for my enemy."

"Not even Gennarino. I will inform Signor Alfieri myself when I am ready; you will not suffer for this. Believe me when I tell you that you and your niece have done right."

"Thank you, Mr. Buchan." The footman drains his glass and starts to rise to his feet, but the lawyer waves him back into his chair and smiles companionably.

"You know, Peters," he says, "you and Margaret are in a most enviable position. Everyone has wondered about Mrs. Alfieri, but there is precious little that anyone really knows about her." Buchan refills Peters's glass as he speaks, this time pouring in a generous amount of whiskey, as well—he holds the bottle up for the footman's approval—from a collection of bottles in a cabinet nearby. "You, on the other hand, have been in the same house with her since her arrival here. Tell me"—he hands the footman his glass—"what was she like when she first came to Gramercy Park?"

Peters waits, drink in hand, while the lawyer mixes a similar libation for himself. "Like?" he says. "Like nothing I had ever seen, sir. I know children, in a small way—my sister had eleven of 'em, of which Margaret is the youngest—and a sadder child than Miss Clara was then, I don't think is possible. You saw for yourself what she was like on her wedding day. Well, she was far worse when she first arrived . . . a white, pinched, sick little thing, skinny and so scared . . . too scared even to raise her eyes from the floor."

Buchan lifts his glass to his visitor and leans back again, nodding for him to continue. The footman takes a generous swallow of whiskey, as if reviving his memories.

"The first year she barely spoke to anyone except Mr. Slade, and even him rarely, and almost never came out of her room. We all pitied her, sir; the whole servants' hall. It was impossible not to. Cook would make her special little treats, to try and get her to eat, and the maids handiest with their needles would turn out dainty little things for her—handkerchiefs and pincushions and suchlike. And we cheered her on, Mr. Buchan, year by year, as she grew braver and stronger.

"She turned out a sweet child, with a smile and a greeting for every one of us whenever she spied us, whether scullery maid or butler. All the kindnesses that were showered on her she returned tenfold. She remembered birthdays with little trinkets bought with her own pocket money, and she became friendly like with some of the younger girls, never forgetting the difference in their stations.

"And many belowstairs would go to her when problems arose between us—bad blood and ill feelings—for no one could smooth things out faster than Miss Clara, and see that all were neighborly again. Ah, she would sit there in this great chair, listening to both sides and dispensing justice like a little Solomon, but with a smile. She had a way of listening, so that you knew you were being heard, and a way of explaining one side to the other, so that everyone could see the other's point. A fairer-minded little creature you could not imagine, as though she knew herself what it was like to be unjustly treated. Well, there was twelve of us belowstairs, so Lord knows we kept her busy enough with all our squabbles and spats . . ." He stops then, and his grin fades.

"And then the master died, and his will was read, and all the gains Miss Clara had made . . . gone, sir"—he snaps his fingers—"just like that."

Buchan nods. "Because she got nothing," he says. "Doubtless she had come to think of herself as quite the little heiress, in the month between, and was already making plans to spend her fortune. A horrible shock, of course, but that's what comes of counting one's chickens—"

"Ah, no, sir! No!" The footman's hand jerks with the force of his vehemence, slopping the whiskey from his glass. "Them that wasn't there shouldn't be passing judgment on them that was! I was there, I saw how his passing went to her heart! It *wasn't* losing the money that made her sick, for I don't think she would know what to do with it if it were dumped in her lap in hundred-dollar bills . . . she never pined after jewelry or Paris gowns like other young ladies do, she never asked him for anything . . ."

He sits back abruptly, mortified at his outburst. "I . . . I do beg your pardon, sir," he stammers, pulling out his handkerchief and mopping up the spilled whiskey from the desk. "I meant no disrespect, truly I didn't. It was just . . . well, hearing you say what you did—and I know that many others have said it—about her being disappointed over the fortune. But it wasn't his fortune that she wanted, sir. She was so worried, you see . . . so deathly afraid of having to go and live with strangers. She told Margaret—after Mr. Slade's death, but before the will was read—that he had promised her that she would be taken care of, in case he died, and that she would always have a home of her own, and not be at the mercy of strangers. And then the will was read, and there was nothing for her, sir—nothing." He shakes his head sadly. "Nothing at all."

He drinks his whiskey absently, wipes his mouth with the back of his hand. "Poor little girl, her worst fear come to pass . . . and then, on top of it, the thought that Mr. Slade had never really cared for her, after all—and truly, that was the way it must have seemed to her, sir, for it looked so even to us, who knew better. And she couldn't bear it, she went to pieces. I was one of the ones helped carry her to her room that day. It was like the four years had never been. Worse, even, for there were such unnatural things in her head after she was struck down . . . ugly, ugly things. Margaret said often that Miss Clara's ravings gave her nightmares of her own."

"Why?" Buchan says quietly. "What did Miss Clara say?"

"Nothing that made any sense at all, that was the worst part. She would babble about horrors—about flies, and men with no heads, and blood everywhere. Fever dreams, of course, but how a little girl could ever know to dream of such things was beyond all of us."

"Fever dreams, as you say." The lawyer's face is sympathetic. "She must have been the topic of much talk in the servants' hall over the years. Did no one, in all that time, ever discover what had happened to her before she came to you, or who her people were?"

"No, sir. We only knew that her father was a businessman, and acquainted with Mr. Slade."

"But why was she there at all? Truthfully, Peters, I've never understood it. Mrs. Buchan and I have not been blessed with children, but it's long been my belief that doting fathers—and especially wealthy ones—do not surrender their young daughters to strangers, even strangers as kind as Mr. Slade. Did anyone ever speculate as to how she had come to be with him?"

Peters laughs shortly. "Did anyone ever not speculate? The talk, of an evening, was often about that, of course. But that's all it was, sir. Just talk."

"Of what sort?"

"Oh, some thought that her father had lost everything in a business venture and killed himself, which would account for the state she was in when she came to us. Others thought that he was perhaps recently widowed, and had married again, and that the new wife—young, maybe, and pretty—couldn't abide the child of the old one, and insisted he get rid of her."

Buchan leans back, stretching his legs out in front of him. "And what about you, Peters? To which school of thought did you subscribe?"

"I put my money on the first, sir. It made more sense, in light of what she was like."

"Very wise," the lawyer says, nodding thoughtfully. "But, of course, both of those theories only serve to explain why she was no longer in her own home. They don't explain Mr. Slade's reasons for taking her in. To be honest," he says, "had I been in the servants' hall with you during those discussions, I might have made a suggestion of my own. I might have suggested"—he smiles and shrugs—"that she was Mr. Slade's own child."

His words catch Peters with a mouthful of whiskey and water, which the footman just manages to swallow. "Mr. Slade's own . . . ?" he says, shouting with laughter. "Forgive me, sir, but it's plain that you didn't know him. I don't believe that there was *ever* a gentleman so indifferent to the ladies as Mr. Slade was!"

"Always?"

"Pardon me, sir?"

"Was he always so . . . indifferent?"

"So far as I know, sir. He never married, of course, and certainly there was no woman in his life during the whole seventeen years I was with him. He lived for his work and his charities. Taking Miss Clara in was just like something he would do—he was very big on educating the heathen in foreign lands, and such, and making the Lord's word known—and Miss Clara not being a Christian, it was like he was practicing what he preached, only nearer to home."

Buchan nods. "And did Miss Adler receive instruction in any branch of the Christian faith during her time in Gramercy Park?"

"Not to my knowledge, no, sir. But then, she was in no condition to do much of anything when she first came to us, and later on it didn't seem to matter. Perhaps Mr. Slade hoped that, just by living with Christians, Miss Clara would learn by example. And he must have known what he was about—don't you think, sir?—for it seems to have done the trick. She stayed behind when the master went to church on Sundays, it's true, but I've never known her to do anything very different from what other people do, or say any strange mumbo-jumbo, or turn up her nose at a nice bit of pork."

Buchan smiles. "So Mr. Slade had no interest in women and he supported Christian philanthropies. But what sort of man was he, Peters? Vain? Proud? Affectionate? How would you describe his character?"

The footman takes another deep pull at his glass, his eyes pensive. "He was most particular about his good name, sir. And he could be a bit cold, at first, and standoffish, so that some who didn't know him might think him unfeeling. But once he knew you, once you fit into the household, and were *his* . . . why, there was no kinder master."

"And he was fond of the girl, you said."

"Of Miss Clara? Oh, he set great store by her. That's why we were all so shocked, sir, when his will never even said her name. He liked to have her by him. Evening was their special time. She would read to him for hours, or else he would work in his study and she would sit with him, stitching away at her embroidery, both of them together and not saying a word, but just fond of each other's company, if you know what I mean. Not that he made a show of it, you understand, for the master was always very quiet in his ways."

Feeling the whiskey at last, the footman shakes his head. "No, sir, Mr. Slade was always very correct, sir; very reserved, very proper." He smiles brightly. "Not at all like the present master," he says, then adds hastily: "Oh, not that Maestro Alfieri is *un*proper, sir! Please don't misunderstand me; he's a true gentleman. But it's something to see—don't you think, sir?—watching him with the little miss. It's like he's drunk with her; quite drunk indeed. Why, you've seen the way he pets her, like she's one of her own kittens, and never takes his eyes from her. Quite, *quite* drunk with her, he is"—he nods emphatically at each iteration of the word "drunk"—"but then, of course, he's her lawful husband, not her guardian. And she? Ah, sir, it's enough to make a man repent of being a bachelor, just to see her face when she looks at him— for a devilish handsome man he is, too, though he is a foreigner, and"— he lowers his voice confidingly—"old enough to be her father—"

"Yes," Buchan smiles, interrupting his visitor's disquisition. "Well, newlyweds will be newlyweds. A toast to them, Peters," he says, raising his glass. "Long life and much joy to them."

The footman raises his glass in his turn. "Amen is what I say to that, sir. Happiness, health, and the fullness of years!" He drains his glass again. "It's true that Maestro Alfieri talks funny," he says, as he gets to his feet, "but whatever he says is music to that little girl's ears, as anyone can see. And I'm that glad to see her happy at last."

And with that he is gone, first thanking his host with great politeness before reclaiming his hat from the clerk, then trudging unsteadily up Broadway with his head down, his shoulders sagging beneath the sun's assault.

Buchan takes the list of names from the drawer and stares at it, drumming his fingers impatiently on his desk. They mean nothing to him. He calls: "Lennox!" and the clerk appears at his door.

"You're still working on that Howe brief? That can wait. Put it aside," Buchan says, handing over the sheet of paper, "and begin on this."

The clerk stares down at the list. "What shall I do with it, sir?"

"Find out who and where those people are, if you can. They are, or were, all known to our young lady who does not exist. Try ward lists, census reports, tax rolls, anything. Yes, it's a needle in a haystack, I know, but there's nothing for it. Oh, and look in New York first, Lennox. I won't have you combing every county in New Jersey again, just to wind up with a fistful of smoke, like the last time."

Mumbling "Yes, sir," the clerk turns away, still reading the list. Buchan picks up a thick file from a stack at his elbow, but allows it to rest unopened on his knee. As before, he finds his attention wandering. Peters's description of a child too frightened to raise her eyes from the floor has made a deep impression on him. My dear, my dear, he thinks—what was it that terrified you so?

"Mr. Buchan? Would you look at this, sir?"

The clerk stands in the doorway, a piece of yellowed newsprint in his hand. At Buchan's nod he comes forward and lays it, along with Peters's list, on the lawyer's desk. Buchan gazes down at it, then says, impatiently: "Lennox, is this something from your 'mayhem' file?"

"Yes, sir."

"Lennox, we have had this discussion before. The fascination you have with tales of violence and mutilation is lost on me. Think, man!" he says sharply. "On a day when the heat can drive a man to kill, is it wise to show me an article on murder? Why aren't you looking into those names, as I asked you?"

"But I am looking into them." The clerk, with a faint smile, points to the first name on the handwritten list. "See this, sir?" He moves his finger to the piece of newsprint, culled from one of the city's more lurid tabloids. "Now look at this."

Buchan's gaze moves from one to the other, then lifts to his clerk's face.

"Yes, sir. The spelling is different—'F-a-w-v-e-l' on the list, 'F-a-u-v-e-l-l' in the newspaper—but it sounds as if it could be the same, doesn't it?"

The lawyer nods slowly. "So it does, by God." He stares at his clerk again. "Enlighten me, Lennox. How did you happen to remember this name, to make the connection?"

"Why, it's a most unusual name, sir, as you must admit. And this is one of my favorite cases, in that it's never really been solved—not properly, at any rate. You might as well ask me how I could remember the name Lizzie Borden. Lizzie Borden, sir? The double murder in Massachusetts, two years ago? The lady was tried for killing her father and stepmother with an ax. Oh, no, sir, she was acquitted. At any rate, I didn't have to remember Fauvell's name, you see, for it's not one I've ever forgotten, and when I saw it, even spelled wrong . . ."

Seeing Buchan's growing interest, he says: "It's a simple enough story, sir: a young man named Thomas Pratt followed his stepfather, Edward Fauvell, into a deserted barn one afternoon, blew the man's head off with one barrel of a double-barreled shotgun, then turned the second barrel on himself. It seems, on its face, to have been just an ordinary murder and suicide . . . except that there was apparently no motive at all. Certainly no motive ever came to light. Nor were there were any witnesses, sir: the farm was very isolated; and the boy left no note behind to explain why he had done what he had done. The whole thing appeared to be an act of quite pointless violence.

"What makes it even more interesting, sir? The boy had just graduated from Princeton, with honors, and was preparing to enter the ministry. Neither his mother nor his sister was able to provide any explanation for the tragedy: Thomas Pratt had never been a wild boy, or done any violence before. The local constabulary, in consultation with the local doctor, who was also the coroner, could only assume that he had gone suddenly mad. Death by reason of insanity, they said, and closed the case, declining to pursue the investigation further."

"Over the protests of the mother and sister, no doubt?"

"Wrong, sir. Still more interesting. Mother and sister made no effort to press the case, or push it higher. They simply let it . . . die."

Buchan grunts, his absent gaze fixed on the gravestones in the churchyard. "But how does our young client fit into this story? Tell me that, Lennox. Explain to me where the connection lies. By what magic could Clara Adler, ostensibly the child of a wealthy Jew businessman, get to know a farmer on a very isolated farm—a farmer with a fledgling minister for a stepson, no less—well enough to call his name over and over in her delirium?"

He consults the paper. "This happened six years ago, in July of eighty-eight. When farmer Fauvell died, she would have been not quite fourteen. We don't even know where she was, then: she didn't arrive at Slade's house until more than a year later."

The clerk's voice deepens with satisfaction. "But I've not told you the most interesting part, sir. I don't know how Miss Adler might have known him, or when, or even where . . . but farmer Fauvell wasn't a farmer, originally. He only moved to the farm five years before his death. Prior to that he was headmaster of a rather exclusive girl's academy, right here in the city."

The lawyer stares at his clerk, then reads the article through closely.

"Fauvell died six years ago," he murmurs, when he is done, "and had been away from the city for five years before that. Eleven years ago Clara Adler was only eight years old—and it pains me to say that she could not have been a pupil at his academy." He taps the paper. "Look for yourself, Lennox. The school was Episcopal. How many schools do you know of named St. Justin Martyr that admit children of the Hebrew faith?"

The shrill of the cicadas is deafeningly loud in the silence. "I owe you an apology, Lennox, for being short-tempered and hasty. You are quite right: there are some very singular features about this story. I want you to find out all you can about this man Fauvell . . . who he was, where he was from, what his professional credentials were—and above all, why he left the school. Headmasters don't normally metamorphose into farmers, like caterpillars into butterflies.

"As for me," Buchan says, "all this talk of farms has given me an urge to see green grass again, and pigs and chickens and cows. I was already thinking that Mrs. Buchan and I could use a few days in the country to escape this heat, but now I'm certain of it.

"Please get me information on trains to"—he consults the article—"Rosebank . . . why, it's in New Jersey." He smiles up at his clerk. "And while we're there, perhaps Mrs. Buchan and I will look around and see if anyone by the name of—what was the stepson's name? Pratt?—still lives there. It occurs to me that I knew a young man in my college days named Pratt, who was, perhaps, this young man's relation. Surely no one could blame me for trying to look up the family of an old and dear friend . . . ?"

Chapter Nineteen

THE CROWD WAITING at the station is over five hundred strong, despite the August heat.

They have been gathering since morning—the cognoscenti, the admirers, the merely curious—and nothing could be more natural, for one of the constants in the life of any star is that he will draw crowds the way sugar draws ants. The earliest arrivals have claimed the choicest locations, those best situated for watching the welcoming ceremony; the later arrivals have arranged themselves along the edges of the red carpet upon which he will walk; the tardy and the hopelessly delayed are even now—with the train pulling into the station—pouring themselves into the spaces remaining, clambering onto baggage carts, perching on ledges, and climbing up pillars, so that someone looking down from the roof of the vast station would see a sight like bees swarming over a honeycomb.

Into the equally vast noise of crowd and train, of hissing and shouting and cheering, the waiting orchestra hurls its welcome—Wagner's "Entrance of the Meistersingers"—in a kind of frenzied pantomime of music-making, bow arms sawing the air, trumpeters' faces purple, all dripping with the effort of making themselves heard above the massed voices, the chuffing and clanging of the locomotive . . . and Mario Alfieri arrives triumphant in Philadelphia to a sound like the sea in a high gale.

Hungry for a first glimpse of the great tenor, the throng surges toward the still-moving train, heedless of their own safety, a human wave sweeping toward him, their upturned faces peering into all the cars, mouths gaping, fingers pointing, searching for the one in which he rides, and the first well-wishers to find it begin to hammer on the windows with their hands. The windows have been shut, for safety's sake, and it is hot inside; the car vibrates with the howl of the crowd and the pounding of fists.

Clara stares out at the bedlam beyond the glass, her eyes wide, a fine line of moisture beading her upper lip—fully aware, for the very first time, of what it means to be Mario Alfieri, and of what it therefore means to be Mario Alfieri's wife. Never once raising his own eyes to the clamor outside, the tenor draws her away from the window, acting quite as if no one is there at all. "Hush, dear heart, they will not hurt you. They mean no harm."

She nods, but her lips are stiff, and her voice faint. "Is it always like this?"

He strokes her face, not telling her that this is a small crowd as crowds go; that usually it is much worse. "Not always," he says quietly, "but often enough."

Gennarino stands nearby, silent, a calm eye in the hurricane, and Alfieri turns to him—"You know what you are to do?"—then, at the valet's nod, turns back to Clara.

"When I leave the car, my darling, you will remain here with Margaret. Gennarino will stay with you. When the crowd has thinned, which should not be long, he will take you both to the hotel."

"No, Mario."

"Clara . . ."

"*No!*" Her chin sets stubbornly.

"Clara, my sweet child, you have told me that you fear crowds, that they make you ill. To come with me means walking through the midst of that . . ."—he gestures to the raucous mass of bodies beyond the window—"then sitting on a stage before everyone in this heat while the mayor and others make tedious speeches. Why would you want to do that?"

"Because I'm your wife."

"And will be for many years to come, please God. There will be other days and other speeches. Go to the hotel, *cara,* for my sake. It will be cooler there. Bathe, change, rest. I will be with you again in time for dinner, I promise. The country has done you so much good, and you are so much improved, but too much excitement in this heat . . ."

She draws herself up to her full height—a sight that never fails to make him smile to himself, but still he listens gravely, holding her hands in his. "So long as you're with me I won't be afraid. I can sit on a stage just as easily as I can sit anywhere else."

"But why, *madonna?* We have been through all this. You do not need to prove to me how brave you are. There will be time enough for you to face these things when you have grown more accustomed to them. For better or worse, love, so long as the voice stays, there will be crowds."

"Then if I must begin sometime, why not now?"

"The heat, if nothing else. *I* must think of your health, if you will not."

She stares at him, mutinous. She will walk alone into the middle of the mob, if need be, to prove to him that he has not made a mistake in choosing her, that she is worthy of his name and his faith in her, that he need never be sorry for giving her both because she would rather die than disgrace him . . . and then her expression changes, and she looks away.

"Mario, are you ashamed of me? You can tell me. I know I'm not very impressive, not at all what people would expect your wife to be, and that was all right in the country, but we're not in the country anymore. Maybe when my hair is grown . . . maybe next time . . ."

He stops her mouth with his hand.

"Am I ashamed of you? Of you, my happiness? Don't you know that everyone who sees you envies me? Come with me, then, *cara.*"

Gennarino is the first to descend from the train, planting himself to the left of the steps, his light eyes flicking across the myriad faces of the crowd. Alfieri descends next, to a great roar of welcome. He bows his thanks—once, twice, three times—then turns, reaching for Clara, who, flinching as the wall of sound strikes her, has moved haltingly out onto the steps behind him. He lifts her down gently, and an excited whisper—"Pretty . . . very pretty . . . who is she?"—sighs across the station like a wind. Margaret descends last, taking up a position directly behind her mistress, and the four of them wait as a sizable deputation of dignitaries—the mayor and the city council, accompanied by the general manager of the Grand Opera House and its entire board of directors—approaches along the red-carpeted path, kept clear by threescore stalwart policemen.

Mario frames the introductions to cover her shyness, saying simply, "And this is my wife, gentlemen," with his arm around Clara's waist—if there is any surprise that the notorious Alfieri has descended upon them with a bride, it does not show—and she is spared the ordeal of saying anything at all by the noise, which makes conversation virtually impossible, and by the mayor's desire to move them back along the red carpet to the station's cavernous main waiting area, where Alfieri is to be officially welcomed to the city.

For Clara, who cannot see over the heads of the crowd, the carpet is a narrow ribbon of safety, a path between two high walls of swaying, cheering, goggling humanity. The mayor leads the way, puffed with importance, and she and Mario follow directly after, his arm still about her, her hand in his. With Gennarino immediately to her left, Margaret behind her, and all the many councilors and board members bringing up the rear, she has a sudden vision, as they walk, of Moses leading the Hebrew children across the bed of the parted Red Sea, the solid waters rearing up on either side, wanting only a slight distraction of the Lord's attention to come smashing down again, sweeping them all away—and even as panic sucks the air from her body she stifles a sudden urge to laugh, for the Moses leading them is a small, plump man with a tall top hat, a little, waxed moustache, and a gold chain stretched tightly across his middle, and she pictures a long, patriarchal beard on his double chin and a great, rough staff in his fat, manicured hand . . .

And then the waters spread themselves and fall away, and they are at a clear, open space, looking up at a high wooden platform draped with bunting, and Gennarino and Margaret stay below while she and Mario mount the dozen steps that lead to it, as if climbing to their execution. There is a moment's confusion while an extra chair is brought—she was not expected, after all—and they wait, so close to the edge that one enterprising spectator, lifted up by his laughing neighbors, tugs at the hem of her gown so that she gasps and stumbles in the circle of Mario's arm, nearly pitching into the crowd, and then the chair is in place next to the flag-draped podium, and she is seated, staring out over the ebb and flow of a sea of hats, a sea of faces bobbing like whitecaps in a stiff breeze, an ocean of eyes fixed on her and on the man who sits so calmly beside her, holding her hand in both of his.

There is another, smaller platform a short distance away against the station wall, but a wooden scaffolding surrounds it on three sides, and a white curtain, suspended from the scaffolding, obscures whatever rests upon it. One man, trying to peek beneath the curtain's edge, is shooed away with a cautionary word by one of the dozen policemen who ring the platform. Clara tries to imagine what might be behind the curtain, but cannot, and soon turns her attention to the various speakers who rise to the podium, one after the other, addressing the now-quiet multitude, speaking of Philadelphia's pride, her devotion to Culture, her rightful place among the world's great cities . . . but the day is stifling and the sound of the crowd beneath the soaring station roof is a vague, murmuring sigh, like a seashell held against the ear, and after a while she finds herself growing sleepy.

This is not so very bad, she thinks; what was I afraid of? The past is past and I am Mario's wife. I need never be afraid again . . .

A loud burst of applause draws her attention briefly. The mayor has commenced his speech. ". . . a tremendous honor," he is saying, in round, rolling cadences, "marking not only his debut performance on our continent but the American premiere of a magnificent new work"— he consults his notes—"*Manon Lescaut,* by the brilliant young composer"—another consultation—"Gia-*co*-mo Puccini!" and she sees Mario wince as the mayor's tongue wraps awkwardly around the strange name. She smiles at him from the corner of her eye and he squeezes her hand, but now the mayor is saying ". . . proud recipient of yet another honor, for the maestro has come to us straight from his honeymoon, bringing his lovely bride to our city . . ." and she feels the scarlet flooding her cheeks as the applause rolls around them; but the faces around her are friendly enough and the moment soon over, and the mayor moves on, recalling Philadelphia's history from the days of William Penn, and her long dedication to the Arts, and Clara's mind wanders again.

Her eyes grow heavy in the heat; the speaker's voice and the vague, murmuring sigh of the multitude merge, and behind them both, very gradually, she hears a new sound, deeper, a low, humming sound in the distance. She shifts uneasily. She has heard that sound before, but where? An endless, swelling drone, louder now. A multitude, yes, an infinite assembly; but not of people. Flies. The buzzing of flies. Great flies, black ones, and small, shiny green ones, so many. Why had she never known there were so many flies in the world? Clouds of flies, settling on the still forms on the floor, blanketing them, and on the darkening red pools that dry inward from the edge, covered now, bristling with great black flies, and small, shiny green ones, more and more, the wall opposite furred with flies, arranged in a great, erratic starburst, a moving, droning black splatter on the white wall. Where do they come from? The window is closed, despite the heat, the prisms hanging motionless on their string—Papa had wanted no noise they made to betray them—so where are they from? So hot. So hard to breathe with the air thick with flies, and the sweet, sickening smell, and the buzzing loud in her ears, and louder . . .

She opens her eyes with a sudden jerk. Mario is staring down at her, a little thin line of worry between his brows. He holds her right hand in his; his left arm is about her shoulders. She must have slumped in her chair. She straightens up and tries to smile, but her heart is hammering almost audibly in her throat, dampness trickles unpleasantly down the back of her neck, and she knows from his expression that she must look white and ill. She begins to say something, but they are both caught up in a sudden burst of excitement, a shout of approval from the crowd as the mayor extends his arm and the white curtain falls away from the scaffolding around the other platform.

The cloth has been hiding the pièce de résistance of the welcoming program, a *tableau vivant* of the nine Muses, designed specifically to honor the newly arrived Lord of Song. It is a striking picture, composed of a graceful grouping of nine extremely pretty young women, their unbound hair streaming about their arms and shoulders, wreaths of flowers on their brows, their arms full of blossoms meant for strewing in the conquering hero's path, each clad in a gauzy white wrapper of a brevity which would have been scandalous had the costumes not been certified as being historically accurate.

Each of these young ladies is the maiden daughter of a prominent Philadelphia family; each has volunteered—freely, thinking only of the honor of her city—for this solemn ceremonial duty. Each has sacrificed her modesty on the altar of welcome for this great occasion, and agreed to appear before the public in a state of *déshabille* which would normally be unthinkable outside of the boudoir, in order to inject an aesthetic note into the momentous instant of Alfieri's reception. And so, each blushing Muse, feeling the gaze of her city upon her, bravely keeps her sacrificial pose—squaring her lovely shoulders and raising her chin, biting her lips to redden them, tossing back her hair to display to best advantage the authenticity of her costume—although the injunction to gaze skyward, as if contemplating the glories of Art and Science, is utterly forgotten as nine pairs of eyes fasten on the tenor, each pair of eyes bright with the hope of catching his.

Clara rises to her feet, her face burning now, and Mario rises with her. How brazen they are! How shameless, to allow men to stare at their bodies, their loosened hair, their legs, bare almost to the knee. The crowd is cheering, some of the men waving their hats excitedly at the cluster of graceful girls. Mario is still holding her hand, still has his arm about her, but she looks up at his face and he is looking at them, and smiling. "Oh, my child," she hears Chadwick telling her, "you cannot *begin* to imagine the stories I have heard of his women . . ." and she looks away from him and down into the crowd, almost weeping, then stops, sucking in her breath.

Every face but one is turned toward the *tableau vivant*. Only one, in all the many hundreds, looks the other way, is raised to her alone. It is almost directly below her: a fat face; a smooth, pink and white, many-chinned face with a smiling rosebud mouth, framed by yellow curls, with china-blue eyes that stare up at her and never waver; a face from long ago, from the past that cannot ever come again; a face that peers at her between their shoulders, watching as they try to wave the flies away—they barely move now, too bloated to fly—watching as they wrap her in something and carry her from the reeking, buzzing room, watching as the murmuring crowd stares at her legs, at her hair, at her face, pointing, whispering, nudging each other, smiling . . .

Mario says something sharply, but the buzzing is deafening now and she cannot hear him, and it is hot, so hot and still, so hard to breathe, the air so full of great black flies . . .

Chapter Twenty

IT WAS THE HEAT, the doctor said; the heat and nothing more. Mario had laughed, later, when he could laugh again—his face, when she opened her eyes, had been sick with fear—and said that her fainting at that precise moment had shown a genius for timing that Duse might envy . . . but he blames himself. If he had remained firm with her, and followed his original plan to send her to the hotel, she would not have fainted from the heat. She has not told him that if she had listened, and gone, she would not have seen what she had seen, would not have remembered what she had almost forgotten. She has not told him about the face, or the flies, or Chadwick's words, haunting her. She has not told him that she is afraid.

The honeymoon is over. Mario is absent during the day, busy with his rehearsals, and she has been confined to bed: three days, the doctor had said, of rest and quiet; seven days, Mario has said; one full week of absolute inactivity and calm—only rest, he tells her, only rest, only rest. He will not make the same mistake again; this time no amount of pleading on her part will sway him. She is permitted no books, no needlework, absolutely nothing which might tire eyes and hands and brain, and Margaret has been charged with ensuring that nothing reaches her which might interfere with her repose. For four days now she has lain alone in this great, hushed room, where the ceiling fan and drawn shades drop the mercury fifteen degrees below the temperature on the pavement, in this vast island of a bed, with its ornate, carved headboard soaring ten feet against the silk-covered wall, listening to the muted voices of the people who come and go beyond the heavy bedroom door.

Gennarino is kept fully occupied by them: well-wishers, opera-lovers, sycophants, would-be hangers-on; all utter strangers who come to the hotel suite bringing flowers, asking after her, paying their respects to Maestro Alfieri's ailing young wife. No one is admitted—Mario has left instructions about that that Gennarino would ignore to his peril—but Clara hears them in the outer room. Lying in the dark with nothing else to do, she strains to follow their murmured words before Gennarino thanks them on Mario's behalf and shuts the door firmly upon them; and then Margaret, careful not to trouble her, tiptoes in with the flowers—the vases crowd the windowsills, the mantel, and all three dressers—and withdraws again as silently as she had come. The cool air of the bedroom is heavy with the scent of massed flowers, like a room where someone lies dead, or dying, and there is nothing to do but listen for the next knock at the door, to strain to hear the muffled voices; nothing else to occupy her mind, nothing to drive the fear away.

Only rest, he says, only rest, only rest . . . dear God, if she only could! But her mind will not let her, will not be still; and when she closes her eyes, willing herself to sleep—desperate for sleep—then the memories come back, round and round, of the half-naked Muses, and Mario, smiling at them, and Chadwick's voice in her ears . . . and then the bloated pink face is staring up at her again, smiling from the crowd with a look of such steadfast hatred . . . and in the cool and quiet room, fragrant with flowers, with no one to chase the sight away, she remembers what she is.

But had the face been real? Or had it been only a mirage and no more, an invention of her fancy, brought on by the heat, like the flies, like the still forms on the floor? Lucy Pratt has a place in such visions, after all; she had been there, fat and panting, screaming as she ran— Clara had heard, and Papa, too, but by then it had been too late, the feet already thudding up the stairs, and there was no more time and nowhere to go . . .

Clara wipes her eyes. It—the mirage—had appeared close to where

Margaret and Gennarino had been standing. Had they seen it? Had anyone seen it? She knows, by now, that Gennarino's eyes miss nothing.
Dare she ask? And what would she say? Did you see a woman near you
in the crush? A very pink woman, enormously fat, with yellow hair? I
knew her, once.

And her stepfather.

She turns feverishly, the sheets hot, tangling around her. Only rest,
Mario says, only rest . . . but *why* is he so insistent that she rest? Why
has he not touched her in four days, not made love to her since the
tableau, since he had seen the half-clad Muses at the station, and smiled
at them? She can still see their rounded breasts and flowing hair, their
parted lips, their naked arms full of flowers, and Mario's eyes . . . he
had bit his lip as his eyes traveled over them, to keep himself from
laughing. They had been pretty, so pretty, and none of them had fainted
and ruined the ceremony in his honor, disgracing herself—disgracing
him—before the whole city; and she cannot believe that any of them is
shut away now in the dark. No, they are all free to come and go, all
nine of them; free to step lightly into their carriages and call on whom
they please. Why else does he not want her? Why else, when he lay
down beside her last night and she slipped her arms around his neck,
pressing herself against him, begging for him—why else had he gently
pulled himself free and pushed her away, kissing her on the forehead
and whispering: "Only rest, *bambina,* only rest . . ."?

Her skin is hot in the cool room, her head throbbing. The bedclothes
smell of him and she buries her face in his pillow, twisting, seeing him
smile again . . . "my dear, his women," Chadwick's voice says . . . and
Lucy's face stares up from the crowd, mocking, hating, and Clara
writhes in the sheets, frantic, desperate for a way to stop the endless
thoughts that circle round, and round, and round . . .

Mind racing, one arm flung across her face, she lies against the pillows, unable to still her thoughts, unable to run from herself, remembering, the images flickering faster until they blur and mingle, Mario
and Lucy, Lucy and Chadwick, Chadwick and the nine Muses, and her
body is so heavy, the room so still, the distant street noises unusually

clear, comforting in their ordinariness. Little by little the sounds fade away. And now there is a light behind her closed lids, and someone moving against the light, someone who bends over her and says tenderly: "How is my darling today?" and she does not have the heart to tell him the truth, but reaches for his hand and clasps it to her.

She feels him gather her in his arms—he is younger than she remembered, alive, smiling and happy, his hair silver in the light. "Papa?" she whispers, her eyes filling with sudden tears. "Papa? It's been so long; I'm sorry you died," and a great agony rises inside her . . . Lucy is screaming down in the yard, and the footsteps pounding up the stairs make the rainbows tremble on the walls, and soon the door will burst open and there will be no time to say good-bye, only for him to push her away, and then the clap of thunder . . .

"Don't let me go," she begs, "not this time," and opens her eyes to see him better, to find that it is not Papa, after all, who cradles her, looking down at her with the little thin line of worry between his brows, stroking her hair; and she clings to him bewildered, the dream still so real that the dust and plaster of the carriage barn seem to burn through the silk walls around her.

"Dear heart, hush, it's nothing but a dream," he says. "Hush, my darling, it's gone now, I promise, it was only a dream."

She buries her face in his shoulder, crushing herself against him, feeling his arms tighten about her. "Tell me what it was," he says. "*Cara*, tell me, and it will not come back again, not ever." He smells like the sheets around her, warm; he smells of soap and a faint memory of cologne and his own, clean scent, and she presses her mouth against his coat to stop herself from sobbing, the dream still so strong that she cannot speak . . . but even when she can, she will not tell him. He has forgiven too much already, and there are things that cannot be forgiven in this world, and too many pretty women waiting.

"Tell me," he urges again, and she begs: "Mario, let me get up, let me get dressed. Please, please don't make me stay here anymore . . . let me go with you to rehearsals. Please, Mario, don't make me stay here. I need to be with you, Mario, please . . ."

"No. You need to rest, my darling. If I needed anything to prove that to me, this has. You are tired, you need rest, and I will not be talked out of it this time."

"But I don't rest, Mario, I don't, I can't."

"Why? Tell me why! *Anima mia,* how can I help you if you won't tell me?"

And except for him there is no help for her in the world, and suddenly she cannot live with the fear any longer, the fear that will go on forever if she does not find out the truth, and she whispers, with her forehead against his shoulder: "I'm afraid, Mario. I saw someone, and I'm afraid . . . I'm afraid."

"Saw someone, dearest? In your dream just now?"

"No, not in my dream. Before. In the crowd, Mario. At the station."

"At the station?" He looks down at her, incredulous, almost laughing in his disbelief. "At the train station? Four days ago? You saw someone who frightened you four days ago, and you have said nothing all this time? But why, *cara?* Well, then I must hear it . . . yes, all of it," and she tells him, haltingly, of the terrible mirage, forgetting to mention, in her terror, that the face has a name, and that she knows it well.

He listens soberly—"She looked how, my dear? A fat woman? With blue eyes?"—prying it from her, bit by bit, a man used to dealing with frightened children, and when she is done she lies empty, waiting for his words.

"Little love," he says, nodding, his fingers touching her cheek, "you are right. There was such a woman. I know who you must have seen, for I saw her, too . . . everyone saw her. No, no, hush, *cara!* . . . no, don't tremble so, she is no one for you to fear! She and her husband came here that same evening, to ask after you while you slept."

Her lips form the silent words. "Her husband?"

He smiles then. "Her husband, the mayor, my darling . . . yes, dear heart, the little mayor has a great, big wife. To see the two of them together is like looking at a tugboat with an ocean liner. How old is she? It is impolite to ask, but I should say fifty, at least, and hoping to be thirty years less. A cheek that color was never painted by Nature, and that yellow hair is surely from a bottle. Poor creature . . . how hard she tries to be young, and how sadly she fails."

Clara only stares at him. "Promise me?" she whispers. "No one else, Mario? There was no one else?" And he kisses her forehead and smooths her hair back from her face.

"Poor little girl," he says, shaking his head. "Frightened of a foolish old woman and suffering all alone. No one can harm you, love. I will not let anyone harm you, not ever, you know that. It was the heat, my darling, just as the doctor said; the heat and nothing more."

Weak with relief, she floats between exhaustion and the sweet joy of escape, lost somewhere between laughter and tears. A mirage, it had all been a mirage, not Lucy at all—a play of light, the mayor's wife, the heat, and her own feverish brain, already full of the memory of flies, all combining to trick her eyes—not Lucy at all, but an old lady, bleached and rouged, and the heat, and the deadly monotony of lying in a darkened room with nothing to do but think, and remember, in a bed smelling of Mario . . .

But now he presses her back against the pillows, and his smile is gone. "I am disappointed in you, *piccina,* you know that, don't you? Four days of such unnecessary fear, and for what? For a stout old lady who never wished you a moment's harm. You must promise me that you will never torment yourself in that way again."

"You think I am silly," she says.

"I think . . . ? I think Mrs. Buchan is right. I think I spoil you shame-lessly." He shakes his head again, slowly, to emphasize his words. "I do not want such a thing to happen again, do you understand me?"

She lowers her eyes. "Yes, Mario."

"When will you learn that I am here for you? That I am not an enemy, to hide things from? Have you learned your lesson? Will you tell me the next time something frightens you?"

"Yes, Mario."

"*Bene.* That is all I ask. And now you must rest," he says, and starts to rise from the bed, but Clara clings to his arm, drawing him back down.

"There is more," she says, looking up at him from under her lashes.

"More?" He sits back down. "Something else has frightened you? All right, tell me."

She tells him, keeping her face averted. "All those young women on that platform . . . I saw how they looked at you, and how you looked at them. You smiled at them."

He smiles again at the memory. "Did I, little girl?"

"You know you did," she says. "I saw you."

"And that bothers you? That I smiled at nine foolish young ladies standing on a stage in their underclothes? *Sei tu una moglie gelosa, piccina?* Are you a jealous wife?"

"No . . . I don't know . . . maybe they come to the opera house to watch you rehearse," she says, her words coming very fast, "and to speak to you, and to flirt . . . there were so many of them, Mario, and they were all so pretty, and I have to lie here . . ."

He has the kindness not to laugh. "Yes, I see. And you think I have been making love to all those pretty young ladies while you have been lying here. Very well, which version would you care to hear? The one where they called upon me at the opera house en masse, to invite me to join them in a group assignation? Or the one where each came to me separately, begging to be ravished behind the scenery?"

"Don't make fun of me." Her voice trembles. "They were pretty, and you smiled at them, and maybe . . . because last night, when I tried . . ." Still unable to look him in the face she raises her hand to his cheek, and he covers it with his own hand and presses his lips into her palm. "Last night, when I tried"—she can barely say the words—"you didn't want me."

He is smiling no longer. "You think that, little girl?"

"You pushed me away."

"Did you hear the doctor say that you must rest? That you were to do nothing? That there was to be no exertion of any kind?"

"That's not exertion," she says, and turns scarlet, her eyes filling with tears at his sudden burst of laughter. "No, don't laugh at me! He meant things outside of bed—"

"Ah, so you asked him about that, did you?"

"—and he said three days, only three. It was you who said one week!"

"Now," he says, "now I understand completely. Because I want you to rest, because I want you well, you add two and two in that lunatic little mind"—he taps her forehead—"and decide that I have taken nine lovers, yes?"

He takes her face between his hands. "Listen to me, my sweet little fool. No, *cara,* listen! In three weeks' time I must sing in a strange house, with a conductor, singers, chorus, and musicians I have never met before, in a brand-new opera of which not one of them has seen or heard a performance, never mind performing it themselves. Already they have been rehearsing for two weeks, and I should have been here with them. *Sì,* mid-July I was supposed to be here, but instead I was with you, in the country. I kept you there as long as I could . . . for your health, yes, but just as much because being there with you was more happiness than I have ever known . . . and now you accuse me of taking up with nine absurd women when the real truth is that, because of my selfishness, there is now much work to be done, and very little time in which to do it!

"Do you hear me, *cara*? How do you think an opera comes to be? Magic? It is my work, it is what I do. There has been no one at the rehearsals except those who belong there. There have been no visitors, no Muses, no pretty girls wishing to flirt . . ."

He looks down at her as he scolds her: at her lashes wet with tears, at her trembling mouth. She is impossibly young, impossibly small in the huge, rumpled bed, all wrapped in a cocoon of gauzy white night-gown and twisted sheets.

"Clara?" he says, his voice suddenly hoarse. "Have you heard me at all? Do you know what torture it has been to lie beside you all night long, night after night, and not touch you, knowing that all I had to do was reach out my hand to be in paradise? There is no one else, *madonna,* I swear it—before God, I swear it—and if a hundred pretty Muses called on me it would make no difference. That other life is over, *finito per sempre.* No young ladies any more. No old ladies, no middle-aged ladies, no one else at all, of any age, or size, or shape. Only my wife . . . are you listening to me, Clara? . . . only my ridiculous, impossible, adorable . . ." He kisses her nose, her forehead, her eyes, her mouth with each word. "Only my love, my darling . . ."

"Promise me," she says once more, whispering, "promise me." And he answers, still kissing her: *"Dio m'assisti, ma mi fai impazzire, piccola mia, e t'amo, t'amo tanto . . ."*

She understands imperfectly, but well enough; understands his hands and his mouth and the look in his eyes, if not his words. "It's all right," she says, beneath his caresses, "I can rest now, Mario . . . I couldn't before because I was afraid, but now I can . . . now that you're with me . . ."

But he has already pulled the last bit of sheet away, and his fingers have finished with the little pearl buttons of her nightgown. He parts the fabric, kisses her breasts, covers them with his hands.

"Little love," he says, "now that I'm with you . . . what makes you think you can rest?"

Buchan climbs down from the hired buggy, dusting the dirt from his clothes. His wife remains seated, staring with dismay at the shabby house, the overgrown yard, the ivy massing over the front porch, the filthy, crusted windows, all closed and shuttered on the inside.

"Daniel, are you certain this is the right place? It looks abandoned."

He points to the empty mailbox, its door hanging down in the sunlight like a parched tongue, the faint name "Fauvell" still visible on its side. "The hotel manager swears that someone still lives here. I am only sorry that I dragged you down here with me, my dear. My intentions were good, but Rosebank does not seem to be the garden spot that I had anticipated. Certainly it is a queer place for the headmaster of a fashionable school to choose for his retirement. Let me see if either Mrs. or Miss Pratt is at home."

He climbs the rotting stairs, picking his way cautiously around loose or missing boards, and knocks at the door. He waits for a long time, his eyes traveling narrowly over the peeling clapboards and cracked panes, looking with some apprehension at a huge wasps' nest growing from an angle of the porch roof like a large, buzzing fungus. Thinking he hears a faint sound within, he knocks again, louder, calling: "Is anyone at home?"

The door opens with a noise like a cemetery gate, parting only a few inches. A small, sallow girl in a limp maid's cap and dirty apron peers out at him dully, evidently disturbed from her sleep, and says nothing.

Buchan removes his hat. "Is this the Pratt residence?"

The girl shifts, thinking. "Yah."

"Might I speak with Mrs. Pratt?"

More thought. "Nah. Mrs. Pratt's been dead five years."

The door starts to close and Buchan stops it with his foot. "What of Miss Pratt? Is she at home?"

The maid's eyes go vacant for a moment, narrowing with the effort of recall. "Nah," she says finally, and begins to close the door again.

Exasperated, Buchan pushes the door with his hand, opening it again, widely enough so that he can glimpse the bare walls and floors behind her, stretching into the darkness. "Is she expected back today?"

"Nah."

"Well, when *will* she return?"

"Dunno," the maid says, swinging the door shut again with more strength than Buchan would have credited. "She left three days ago, on a visit. Went to Philadelphia to see someone she used to know . . ."

Chapter Twenty-one

THEY SIT AT THE TABLE, a perfectly respectable couple—uncle and niece, perhaps, or grandfather and granddaughter—taking their respectable tea: he an elderly man, all jowls and chins, with a bland smile and gold-rimmed glasses, she a fat young woman, inordinately pink, with an upturned nose. Her eyes of china-blue wander happily among the pots of palms that give the vast room the air of an indoor garden, then up the soaring marble pillars to the gallery, from which a string quartet is showering Strauss waltzes down upon the heads of a largely oblivious public, and lastly to the waiters who move between the tables bearing tiered serving trays laden with dainty cakes and sandwiches of almost transparent thinness. She sighs contentedly, a pilgrim who has found the end of her search, and the elderly man breaks his silence.

"You enjoyed your tea, then."

"Yes, thank you . . . it was lovely. I had forgotten that such places exist. These past four days have meant more to me than I can say—meant so much, in fact, that I do not even mind having to return this afternoon." She flutters her eyes. "I feel like the character in *A Tale of Two Cities*—'recalled to life!' " she says dramatically, her hand on her breast.

Chadwick says dryly: "I would not personally equate your experience with eighteen years' confinement in the Bastille."

"Then you must never have lived in Rosebank," Miss Pratt replies. "I assure you, it is *quite* like being walled up alive." She sighs, folds her napkin daintily and places it beside her empty cup. "I am so grateful for your suggestion that I come to Philadelphia for a few days."

"Regrettably, we must leave for the station soon if you are not to miss your train," Chadwick says, pulling out his watch, then snapping it shut. "But in light of your enjoyment of these more, shall we say, stimulating surroundings, let me leave you with a thought that has been much on my mind recently. I am convinced, Miss Pratt, that you should move away from Rosebank. There is no reason, any longer, for you to stay shut away there, mourning your family. They are gone, and you are alive. You are still at a tender age, and have much to offer the world. Think not only of what you are missing," he says, gesturing around him, "but what you are denying to others by remaining—as *you* say—buried in such a place as Rosebank."

"How kind you are." Miss Pratt gazes gratefully at him. "But there is the work of labeling my stepfather's collection."

"And are you a nun?" Chadwick says. "Have you taken holy vows to remain in your cloister and devote your life to your stepfather's memory, caring for his relics? No, Miss Pratt, such a fate would be unnatural, to say the least. You are a young and vivacious woman! Your stepfather, devoted man that he was, would not have wanted you to wall yourself up alive in his memory. Did he not send you to France for your education, to make you a woman of the world, as he was a man of the world . . . cultured, well traveled, refined? And would you thwart his ambitions for you? Let his intentions die with him?"

She murmurs: "There is much in what you say . . ." and fidgets with the hem of her napkin.

"I am pleased that you can recognize that. Certainly, I would not be saying it if I did not believe it to be the absolute truth for you. You know that I am not in the habit of advising my clients wrongly."

"Oh," she says, looking away. "Your clients . . ."

"Or my friends," he adds, and nods as she blushes.

"I had hoped," she says, "that I might call you my friend. I have no others, you know. I am so different from the other ladies of Rosebank, having been educated in New York, and abroad"—Chadwick nods again, understandingly—"and all my schoolmates from St. Justin's were left behind when Papa retired. I am utterly on my own, now . . . and friend-less."

He reaches across the table and covers her hand with his. She does not pull away. "Not friendless, my dear. Not while I am alive. But what good is a friend," he says, sensibly, "when you are so far away? Letters, even if a friend had the time to write, are no substitute for talk, or a chance to take in a concert or attend a play with a kindred spirit. In any case, my practice keeps me so busy that letter writing, as you know, is well nigh impossible for me. And as for visits, to travel to Rosebank on any but the most sporadic basis . . ." He lifts his thick hands at the sheer absurdity of the idea.

"But the collection," she says, clearly torn between past and future. "What would happen to it? And then there are the financial considerations . . . Papa's annuity ended with his death, of course, and I must stretch out the last of his savings as long as I can, in order to have something to live on."

"Have you never considered selling your property?" Chadwick says, clicking his fingers at a passing waiter and motioning for the bill. "Yes, that's right, sell it. Sell it all—house, grounds, land. You certainly will not need it if you move to Philadelphia . . . or New York. I will venture a guess, and say that the entire property should bring enough to set you up for life—not lavishly, of course, but comfortably—wherever you choose."

He waits as she thinks over this novel idea. "And—forgive me, my dear Miss Pratt, for what I am about to say—but . . . have you ever given a thought," he says, lowering his voice and leaning toward her as the waiter lays the bill at his elbow, "to selling the collection?"

Her eyes fly open in horror. "Oh, Mr. Chadwick, I could never . . . how could you even suggest! All the things Papa loved so! Oh, I couldn't *begin* . . . !"

Heads turn in their direction and Chadwick raises his hands in a calming gesture.

"It was merely a suggestion, my dear, there is no need for you to become upset. No one will force you to part with a single feather, if you do not wish to let it go. I only mentioned it because it struck me, when I visited you last month, that there are some very good pieces lying about your treasure room—pieces that would fetch handsome prices from collectors who know their worth. Some might even find their way into museums. Think how proud you would be—how proud your dear stepfather would be!—to walk into a room at the Museum of Art on Fifth Avenue, step up to a fine glass case, and see within it a familiar treasure . . . and next to it a card, stating that it is from the collection of Edward Otis Fauvell, donated by his own, dear child . . . and know that the world has recognized, finally, what a man of culture—of fine aesthetic sensibility—he truly was."

Her eyes look into the distance and he sits back, smiling mildly. "*That* is what I call a fitting tribute to a great man, my dear. Not that your idea of keeping it all together does not have merit. But can it compare with knowing that connoisseurs the world over would be daily saluting his memory and paying homage to his exquisite taste? Think, my dear: would Edward Fauvell wish his treasures to remain in Rosebank—unseen? gathering dust in a farmhouse?—or would he prefer to have them displayed in elegant surroundings, where people of delicacy and superior judgment can thrill to their beauty, and have the opportunity to appreciate those things he loved so much?"

Her eyes are bright. "Put that way," she murmurs breathlessly, "of course there is no question . . ." She stops. "But how? Dear Mr. Chadwick, I know no one who might be interested, no one expert enough to put a value on the things . . ."

"Why, my dear young lady," Chadwick says gently, reaching into his pocket, extracting some coins, counting them and dropping them upon the table, "whatever are friends for? I would be delighted to be of assistance in this matter. I am privileged to know, both in my professional capacity, and—if I may be permitted the sin of pride in a small way—socially, some of New York's most respected authorities in the matter of *objets d'art*. If you will allow me, I will be the happy conduit between you and them. I will also help you, should you decide to pursue the other matter we discussed—as a friend, you understand—to negotiate the sale of your house and land."

"How good you are to me!" she says. "How can I ever thank you?"

"Dear girl," he protests, going around the table and pulling out her chair for her, "do not thank me . . . nothing has been accomplished as yet. Return to Rosebank, and in three weeks' time I will come to you there. Yes, I know we are supposed to meet here again, for the opera's opening, but if I come to you a day early we can begin to choose pieces for transport to New York, discuss bringing in an agent to view your property, and then travel on together . . . a prospect which, I must confess, I find most gratifying!"

Strangers nod to the pleasant-looking couple as they make their way past the tables, and Chadwick returns their salutes, touching his walking stick to his hat. "You can have no idea how delightful it is," he says, as they stroll through the hotel's lobby and out onto the pavement, "for me to have an opportunity to mix business with pleasure in this way."

Once settled into a cab, Miss Pratt clasps her hands together over the handle of her parasol and sighs: "This is the perfect end of a perfect holiday."

"Yes, it has been enjoyable," Chadwick agrees, watching the parade of traffic as they move through the busy streets. "And certainly it started well enough. I do not think I would be exaggerating if I said that the unexpected sight of you at the station made a *great* impression upon the young lady who was, after all, the original reason for this excursion of ours. It was all—and more—than we could have hoped for."

A dreamy look comes over Miss Pratt's face at this reminder. "It did my heart good," she says, "to know that she remembered me so well— and I look forward even more, now, to the day when I tell her husband what she is. Now that I've seen him, I can rehearse it all the better in my mind." Her smile is blissful. "I would be happy to do it when we return, in three weeks."

Chadwick clucks his tongue gently. "Miss Pratt, you disappoint me. You must remember," he says, "that we do not do this to be vindictive. It falls to us to inform her husband of her character, yes; but we do it to rescue him from her lies and to wake him from his pretty delusion, not because we wish to gloat. We are not vengeful people, you and I! It is probable, by the way, that, having seen you, she is suffering even now, anticipating what you intend to do, waiting for your knock at the door. And we would not wish to be too hasty. No, I rather think that instead of telling her husband in three weeks' time, you should send her a small wedding gift." He nods. "In fact, I have already selected a gift especially for you to give her . . . I assure you it will move her deeply."

Miss Pratt's voice rises shrilly. "*A gift?* Are you quite mad? I would sooner die!"

Chadwick gazes at her furious face until she drops her eyes. "Do you trust me, Miss Pratt?"

"You know I do," she says desperately. "I must! No one else is on my side."

"I am glad of it. Trust is the single most important quality that can exist, both between a lawyer and his client, and between friends. Without trust nothing good can be accomplished. You will therefore obey me in this, and do as I instruct."

She endures the little homily in sullen silence. "And what is the gift I will send her? May I be permitted to know?"

"All in good time. You must learn, dear girl, that I am to be deferred to in all matters of judgment. I will tell you everything you need to know—and even many things that you do not—but only when I am ready. Of course," he says, shrugging, "if you think you can carry this off successfully by yourself, and interest buyers in your stepfather's collection, and arrange for the sale of your property . . ."

Miss Pratt leans back against the cushions. "Forgive me," she says. "You know best, of course. You are my legal advisor, after all."

"And your friend, dear child," he adds, waggling his thick finger at her. "Do not forget that. Your very *good* friend." As the cab makes its way through the traffic, his hand covers hers, lying on the leather seat. She gazes out the window, biting back a smile, and does not pull her hand away.

Chapter Twenty-two

THE GRAY-HAIRED MAN puts down the letter. He is a thin, clean-shaven man with papery skin, sharp lines and angles to his face, and the pale blue eyes that go with such features. He removes his gold-rimmed glasses carefully, unhooking them from behind his ears, and polishes them with his handkerchief.

"Bill Sheridan asks me to answer your questions," he says, tapping the letter with the earpiece of his glasses, "although since, you've already spoken to the sheriff I don't see what use the doctor can be to you.

"Still," he says, "still, Bill's asking cuts a lot of ice with me. I have a lot of time for Bill Sheridan—he's one of the finest men I've had the pleasure to know—for all that he's spent his whole life as sheriff here." He cocks his head and addresses Buchan. "Not much of a way to waste a life, is it?"

The lawyer waits as the old man fumbles his glasses back into place, his eyes taking in the room. Like everything else in Rosebank, the doctor's office has a curiously halted, defeated air, as if time has somehow gotten the better of it, and run off to brighter, more exciting places, leaving only memory behind. This is possibly more understandable in the doctor's case than elsewhere, for he is retired now—out to pasture, as he has already told Buchan—and the office is rarely used.

"Just the odd patient, every now and then," he says to Buchan across the corner of the old rolltop desk, "the occasional boil needing to be lanced, or a cut that one of the farmhands has let get septic. Maybe a sore throat in the winter. Nothing big." He smiles tiredly. "The town is emptying out. More and more of the young folks head for the cities— New York or Philly—and the old folks die, as old folks will . . . so there's not much to do any more. There's a bright, young doctor in the next town to take care of the big cases. I'm just here for the stubborn old rubes like myself, who insist on staying on.

"No choice, really," he says, meaning staying on. "Can't abide cities myself—never could, not even when I was young. Noisy, smelly things, cities, with too much going on all the time. They don't leave a person time to think, much less live. And all that excitement isn't good for the health—ruins the digestion. Causes palpitations."

Buchan smiles. "Dr. Ogilvie, whole years go by when I couldn't agree with you more. But Mr. Sheridan says you can tell me about the occurrence six years ago."

The doctor snorts. "Occurrence? You mean the killings, over at the Pratt place. Always call a spade a spade."

"Killings." Buchan allows himself to be corrected. "But why the Pratt place? The mailbox says Fauvell. Didn't he own it?"

"No, he married it." The doctor's eyes are bright behind his glasses. "It was Pratt's place for years before the widow Pratt married Fauvell. Pratt's daughter, Lucy, went to school up in New York—some snooty place, Saint Something-or-other, I forget just what. Mrs. Pratt always had grand ideas—she never could believe she had gotten herself hitched to a hick farmer and stranded down here in the sticks . . . even though the town was bigger then, had more life to it."

"When was that?"

"When they got married? Oh, thirty years ago. Right after the war. Rosebank was still pretty busy then. All the young men back from the fighting—those of them who came back in more or less one piece, that is—were looking to pick up where they had left off. But the place had already changed, in five years. The country had changed. That was when people started to leave." He pauses. "What were we talking about?"

"Mrs. Pratt sending her children away to school . . ."

"That's right. She couldn't leave them here; had to send them off to

the city, to get them itching for the kind of life she could never have."
He shrugs glumly, then smiles and shakes his head. "Some favor she did
them, don't you think?"

"But just sending her children away to school—what harm could there
be in that?"

"Oh, it wasn't where she sent them. It was what came of it." He
shrugs again and seems to change the topic. "You've been to the Pratt
place? Pretty horrible, isn't it? You should have seen it twenty years
ago—lace curtains at all the windows, fancy carpets, chandeliers full of
crystal dangles . . . Nothing too good for Annabelle Pratt. Flower beds
out front, and lining all the walks, like she was in Versailles, for Christ's
sake."

"What happened?" says Buchan, truly interested now.

"What happened? What happened was that Curtis Pratt got himself
kicked in the head by one of his own horses." The doctor shakes his
own head. "That was in eighty. My wife died that same year. We had
a bout of influenza down here—carried off a lot of people." He shakes
his head again. "Anyway, Curtis lasted for more than a year—eating,
breathing, sleeping, and with no more mind in him than that stove," he
says, nodding toward a black iron hulk at the side of the room.

"Unfortunately," he says, allowing himself an almost invisible smile,
"Annabelle Pratt was like that without benefit of horse—a sillier woman
God never made. May He rest her soul," he adds, in an afterthought.

"Curtis, now, he was a good, straight man, honest and plain, with
no varnish. What you saw, with Curtis, was what you got. His wife,
though, was a romantic fool, and an hysteric. She took to her bed, when
he died—from grief, she made it plain, although she had paid precious
little attention to him before the horse kicked his head in. Too busy
finding ways to spend his money."

He sighs. "Maybe I do her an injustice. Maybe she came to realize,
during the year she watched him lying there, like a great big vegetable,
just what a good, straight man he was."

Buchan listens, fascinated, not daring to breathe for fear of breaking
the flow of thought.

"At any rate," the doctor says, "she disappeared into her room after that—the children were youngsters, still—Thomas was fourteen, I believe, and Lucy not yet twelve—and sent them off to school, the better to wallow in her widowhood. Of course, she couldn't send them to just *any* school. Being Annabelle Pratt, she had to send them to New York."

The doctor sighs again, and stretches, then gets to his feet. "Can I get you something?" he says hospitably to Buchan, realizing that he has been talking for a long while and that his own throat is rather dry. "Whiskey or gin?"

"Whiskey," Buchan says, "thank you," and waits impatiently for the doctor to seat himself again and continue.

Settling down with his glass in his hand, Dr. Ogilvie says: "I guess Bill Sheridan told you something about the Pratt children, so I needn't elaborate. Thomas got the idea, somewhere along the line, that he had a calling to the ministry, although there had been no ministers in the Pratt family ever, so far as anyone knew. Annabelle was Episcopalian— of course, being Annabelle—but the boy was different. No High Church frills for him, he was Presbyterian, like his daddy, and a bright enough boy in his way too. Did well in school. Always had a bit of an hysterical streak in him, though, like his mother. Looked like her too—slim and fair, blue eyes, not too tall. Never thought, though, that he'd be the one to go funny. Lucy, now . . ."

Ogilvie's eyes grow speculative. "I don't know about Lucy. She has her father's build, of course—Curtis Pratt was a large man, built like one of his own plow horses—and that can't be easy for a girl. She got her mother's coloring. Spent two years abroad, came back the summer of the killings. Went to school in France, I believe it was. Can you imagine a girl from Rosebank, New Jersey, going to France for her education, Mr. Buchan? At any rate, she was at what I believe is called a 'finishing school.' " He takes a mouthful of gin. "She came back finished, all right," he says flatly. "Have you seen her? No? Well, probably just as well. Not what I would call appetizing—but that's just my taste, don't mind me. Some men might find her appealing."

He shifts in his seat. "That snooty school I told you about, in New York? That's where she met Fauvell. He was the headmaster there."

Buchan waits, but the doctor's flow of words appears to have stopped, and he sits staring with narrowed eyes, seeing something in his memory.

"Dr. Ogilvie?"

The man stirs and looks up. "Sorry," he says. "Woolgathering. It happens when you get older—you find that so little of what goes on around you is as interesting as the things you remember. Where was I? Oh, yes, Lucy Pratt and Edward Fauvell." He purses his lips. "Fauvell came here with her over one Christmas vacation. The girl had evidently developed a great infatuation for the man, and had written all kinds of wonderful things to her mother about this paragon in academic robes—and Mrs. Pratt, ever the climber, invited him down for the holidays. Invited his wife, too, and was pleased as punch, I'll be bound, when she was told that the good headmaster was a bachelor. It must have been difficult for Lucy when she returned to school after the holidays, seeing as how the headmaster was now affianced to her mother."

His smile is bitter. "Say what you will about schoolgirl infatuations, they can be painful, and I can't think of many things nastier than having your knight in armor stolen away by your own mother, can you? That was probably one reason . . ." His voice trails off.

"What year was this?" Buchan says.

Ogilvie rubs his thin cheek. "Curtis Pratt died in the summer of eighty-one . . . that would have been Christmas of eighty-two."

"Were people surprised?"

"Surprised, Mr. Buchan? Annabelle Pratt was giving Queen Victoria a run for her money as the professional widow of the age, and suddenly she was engaged to be married to a man she had known for a fortnight. I'd say people were surprised. They were less surprised, though, after they'd gotten a look at the man."

"Handsome?" Buchan says.

"More than handsome—striking. Silver hair and blue eyes, fifty years old, but looking at least ten years younger. A good smile, a strong handshake, a winning way with children. You could understand how thirteen-year-old Lucy could worship the man, and how her mother could have succumbed so quickly. Only the boy seemed immune, but that was understandable—he'd always been closer to his father than his mother, and here she was, the grieving wife, throwing off her weeds with a suddenness which must have seemed like a slap at his father's memory, at the very least."

Buchan stares at him for several moments. "Dr. Ogilvie," he says quietly, "how do you know all these things? Meaning no disrespect, sir, but do you listen at windows, or press your ears to walls? These are things that people don't tell other people, except in the confessional, or on their deathbeds . . . and Thomas Pratt didn't have a deathbed, not in the usual sense."

The doctor smiles. "Ever lived in a small town, Mr. Buchan? I mean a *small* town. At its height, right before the war, Rosebank had nine hundred inhabitants. By eighty-two, the population had dwindled to about five hundred fifty. By eighty-eight, the year of the killings, it was down to four hundred fifty. Now? Now it's—maybe—three hundred seventy-five, although I haven't checked with the mortician or the post-mistress today to see who's died or moved away since yesterday. There's almost nothing that the living don't know about their neighbors . . . and as doctor, I know more than most."

Buchan shakes his head. "I'd either go mad or kill myself."

"Many do both, Mr. Buchan. Of course, they do it in cities too, but there are too many of them to notice, there. Here, now, when a Thomas Pratt unloads one barrel of a shotgun into his stepfather and turns the other on himself, it makes a vast impression."

The lawyer leans forward. "Do you know what happened?"

"Did Bill Sheridan say I know?"

"He said that you were the only one who does."

Ogilvie shrugs and smiles. "He's a good friend, but he's a liar, of course. He knows just as well as I do—he was there with me when we went into the carriage barn. He just doesn't like to talk about it, so he saddles me with it every time." He shrugs again and leans back in his chair.

"If you'll let me ramble on a bit, Mr. Buchan, I'll get to what you want to know, I promise. It's just that I've got to reach it in my own way—work up to it slowly, if you will. Humor an old man, Mr. Buchan, won't you?"

Buchan sits back too, trying to still his urge to grab the old man by the shoulders and shake the story from him.

"Fauvell and Annabelle Pratt were married just after Easter of eighty-three, up in New York, at the school. She made a very pretty bride, and Lucy was maid of honor. Thomas refused to take any part in the ceremony, although he did attend. The happy couple went to Niagara Falls for their honeymoon. It was when they got back that the trouble started at Fauvell's school. You know about that, of course."

Buchan nods. "Mr. Sheridan . . ."

Ogilvie nods back. "Fauvell was an intelligent man, Mr. Buchan. He had timed his marriage perfectly. What could his accusers say, when he produced his pretty new wife, whose own daughter was a pupil at her husband's academy, and then threatened to fight the charges through the courts?" Ogilvie smiles, shaking his head. "You've got to admire a man with guts like that. Anyway, the charges were hushed up, no legal action was ever taken, and Fauvell resigned—with a sizable settlement—to go and live with his new family on his wife's property and become a gentleman farmer."

He sighs and rises to his feet, grimacing and rubbing at an arthritic knee, then flexes the leg slowly. "Forgive me," he says. "I've got to walk around, every now and then, or I stiffen up. It's a thing you never think about, when you're young. Come walk with me, Mr. Buchan. We'll sit in the garden for a while. Bring your glass."

He hands Buchan the bottle of whiskey, picks up his own glass and the gin, and heads for the back hallway and the door to the garden. A few lawn chairs and a table are gathered beneath a huge elm, whose rustling shade is welcome after the close, faded air of the office.

"This is better anyway, isn't it?" Ogilvie says, acknowledging the expression of relief on Buchan's face as the lawyer sinks into his chair and stretches out his legs. "It's also better for the last part of the story. I always find it difficult to tell that part surrounded by four walls—it gets kind of—" He breaks off abruptly.

"Anyway, Fauvell and Annabelle stayed in New York while all the commotion was going on . . . they arrived here, with Lucy, in the late fall of eighty-three, and things seemed fine, for a while. Fauvell turned out to be a likable man—I enjoyed his company, myself . . . he was well read and well spoken. He had a good, hearty laugh, too, and liked a good joke. Christmastimes he would do readings in the town hall— Dickens, mainly—and at other times of the year he would lecture on all different kinds of things . . . it seems he had been everywhere and done everything. The men liked him, the women—well, what can I say?—they thought he was a wonder."

There is real regret in the doctor's eyes. "Fauvell brought a whiff of the outside world to this place, you see . . . just enough to add some spice, you understand, not enough to change the flavor altogether—and we couldn't believe our good fortune that little Rosebank had acquired such a prize.

"Everyone was happy—except for Annabelle, who should have been the happiest of all. By the spring of eighty-four she was looking ill . . . drawn and thinner, as if something were eating away at her from the inside. I couldn't find anything wrong with her, she was just . . . suffering, but wouldn't tell me why. Lucy, on the other hand, was almost bursting out of her skin with health, plump but not fat, not yet, and she seemed to have recovered completely from the shock of her mother's engagement and marriage to her idol. Tommy was away at school, still—it was thought better that he be at home as little as possible, an arrangement that all sides agreed to.

"That same fall, Annabelle took to her bed again, and never left it. In one year she had gone from a pretty, smiling woman to a pinched, silent, red-eyed invalid who lay most of the day with her face to the wall, and who pounded on the floor with a stick she kept by her bed if she needed anything."

"What was it?" Buchan asks quietly.

"Don't you know yet, Mr. Buchan? I'm sure I didn't, not then. Fauvell was genuinely concerned about his wife—he would carry her trays to her himself, and watch while she ate, would brush her hair and read to her by the hour. Little Lucy seemed oblivious to her mother's illness—hardly ever went into her room, spent the days outdoors, a rosy, healthy child—but what fourteen-year-old wants to be shut up with an invalid, even if the invalid is her own mother? Sickrooms are boring for

children, and frightening. Thomas would come home holidays and summers, and grew closer to his mother, as if he and his sister were changing
places. Now he was the one who became her companion and confidant.
And that was the way things stayed, pretty much, for the next two
years: Fauvell solicitous of his sick wife, Lucy turning into a young
woman . . . she was beginning to grow fat, by this time, and looking
less happy than she had before; Thomas getting the calling and deciding
to enter the ministry; the farm and the house, which no one had
touched, really, since Curtis Pratt died, falling apart a little more each
season."

Ogilvie falls silent, woolgathering once more. Buchan listens to the
thousand noises that make up a sleepy country stillness—the high, lulling
drone of the insects, the soothing hush of bending grasses and leaves
stirring in the hot breeze—lost in his own thoughts. Ogilvie's voice
seems to come from far away.

"And then the little girl came."

Buchan's head jerks up. "What little girl?" he says, a sudden knot
growing in his belly.

"Child named Clara," the doctor says, almost dreamily. "Small
thing, pretty. Enormous eyes and a smile—when she smiled, which
was rare—like a morning sky." He sighs and rubs his knee. "Unfortunate history. Mother no better than she should be, to use the polite
English way of saying it, father unknown. Mother left the child with
her family—well-off immigrants, if I remember rightly, German Jews—
and headed out for greener fields, presumably where her past
wouldn't catch up with her.

"The little girl was a scandal for the family, of course. Ever known
any Germans, Mr. Buchan, of the better class? I knew some in the
army—they make Baptists look like loose livers . . . rigid, correct,
highly proper people, for whom respectability is God. I have no reason
to suppose that German Jews would be any different from their Christian
neighbors, in that sense, although I guess I could be wrong. In any case,
the child had been passed around from relation to relation like a sack
of trash—as if being a bastard were somehow contagious, and all her

good, respectable kinfolk would be contaminated by having her around too long.

"How they heard about Fauvell, or got the idea that he might take her in as a private pupil, I don't know; Bill Sheridan was never able to find out. But it seems that it was decided to send her away to school somewhere, as a way of getting rid of her while seeing to her education, and someone had the bright thought that boarding her at the house of a retired headmaster of a girls' school would be just the ticket. I don't know if they knew about the whispers surrounding Fauvell—as I said, the thing had been pretty much hushed up—and maybe, even if they had known, they wouldn't have cared. What I do know is that she arrived here in the summer of eighty-six."

"Eighty-six," Buchan whispers. "She would have been . . ."

"She was eleven, I believe, but she looked eight. I met her one day when I was paying a medical call on Annabelle. She stepped out of the shadows on the upper landing—a little thing with big eyes, dressed in some cousin's hand-me-down that was miles too big for her, so that it nearly touched the floor—and I nearly dropped my bag, she startled me so."

"How long was she there?" Buchan says.

"How long?" Ogilvie smiles, but the smile never reaches his eyes. "Long enough. Lucy hated her—she would, of course—but it made no difference because Lucy was packed off to her finishing school that fall— at the suggestion of her stepfather, I should mention, although France was her mother's idea . . . bedridden, but still a climber. Lucy was sixteen, by then, and growing very large. Thomas was indifferent to the little girl, at least the first summer, and then he went back to his school. Annabelle disliked the child on sight—part of the boarding arrangements were that Clara was supposed to keep the sick woman company during the day, reading to her, fetching her things, but Annabelle couldn't abide the look of the child—the ugly brown mouse, she called her—and refused to have her in her room."

Buchan stares at the doctor. "And Fauvell?"

"Fauvell? Fauvell adored her, as he adored all little girls. No, I do him an injustice. I believe she was special to him. I surely hope she was. She was why he died."

The lawyer feels the beads of moisture forming on his forehead. Pulling out his handkerchief, he blots them away, then wipes his hands, which have also grown damp.

"Dr. Ogilvie, you have no idea how grateful I am for all this history. But please, now—for the love of God—tell me what happened in the carriage barn."

Chapter Twenty-three

THE DOCTOR GAZES at Buchan mildly. "It occurs to me, Mr. Buchan, that you're showing an awful lot of concern for people you've never met. How is that, sir?" He cocks his head, noting the strained expression on Buchan's face, then waves away his own question. "Never mind," he says. "I'll finish my story, and then you can tell me why a big-city stranger is so interested in two men he never knew that he traveled down to nowhere in the middle of an August heat wave to hear how they died." He takes another swallow of gin, settles into his chair and continues.

"Both Lucy and Tommy returned home for good in the summer of eighty-eight, Lucy in June, Tommy a month later. Lucy stayed at the farm after she got back, never came to town. Nobody minded much; we just figured she had gotten too Frenchified to bother with plain folks. But Tommy came into town early the morning after his return, to take care of some business. Went to the bank, went to the store, ran a couple of errands . . . met some people who congratulated him on his graduation—that's a big thing, you know, in a little farm town where most don't learn to do much more than read a newspaper and sign their names."

The doctor picks his words with care and watches his listener's face to gauge their effect. "And while Tommy was in town, Mr. Buchan, Fauvell took the little girl to the carriage barn. There's a room upstairs there, under the roof, not much bigger than a closet. I don't know what it was used for originally, but at the time I'm speaking of there was an old straw mattress on the floor. That's where they would go when Fauvell wanted to have her."

He pours more gin into his glass. "A man only needs to make one mistake, if it's bad enough, and Fauvell's was. He forgot to remember the old saying, see, the one about a woman spurned. Thomas came back from town early, while Fauvell and the girl were still in the barn—and Lucy was waiting to tell him. She'd been nursing her pain, saving it up for when Tommy came home. He was to be her champion, and fight for her. She still loved Fauvell, you see. She told Tommy everything— about her mother, about herself, about the little girl. I don't know what she thought he would do about it—I don't even know if she knew what she wanted him *to* do—scare Fauvell, maybe, or force him to send the child away. Anything but what he did.

"But put yourself in Thomas's head, Mr. Buchan, after she told him. He was utterly ignorant of the situation, of course—he'd been away from home for seven years, except for holidays and summers, and Lucy and her mother had hugged their shame close. Try to imagine Thomas's state of mind when Lucy told him that she had become Fauvell's lover at the age of twelve, that Fauvell had only married their mother as camouflage, to fool the worried, frightened parents at his school, then had chucked her, once he was safe, and gone back to Lucy. And now poor, ruined Lucy had been chucked too. She had grown up, and grown fat, and Fauvell didn't want her any more—it wasn't women that he wanted—and he had taken up with the child who had been sent to them for her education, was with her right now, and if Tommy hurried he could catch them . . ."

The doctor sighs and rubs his knee, speaking absently, as if the memories are speaking for him. "Poor, innocent Thomas—it was a lot for him to hear at one go. Lucy had told her story too well, of course. Thomas grabbed a shotgun and ran for the barn. Lucy ran after him, but she couldn't keep up. She was still on the path when she heard the explosion."

Ogilvie shuts his eyes and falls silent, staring into his memory, and

Buchan waits. "When she reached the room, Thomas was just standing there, staring, still holding the gun. Fauvell was dead, of course. Lucy screamed, seeing his body . . . or what was left of it . . . and Tommy seemed to wake suddenly. She said that he walked over to where Fauvell's body lay, looked down at it, and said, 'God forgive us both.' That was the kind of boy he was, Mr. Buchan. He would have asked God's forgiveness, even knowing that neither of them was likely to get it. And then he put the gun under his chin and pulled the second trigger."

The doctor raises his eyes to Buchan. "That was what you wanted to know, wasn't it, Mr. Buchan? You wanted to know what happened. Now you know."

Buchan says: "Dr. Ogilvie . . ." But the doctor holds up his hand.

"Not yet, Mr. Buchan. It's almost over. Let me finish. Lucy went for help. She had to go to the next farm over to get someone to send for me and Bill Sheridan, and instead of hitching up the buggy, she just started to walk—said later that she didn't know why, she must not have been thinking straight. It's five miles from the Pratt place to the Mulverhills, Mr. Buchan, and Lucy is built for comfort, not for speed. Fauvell and Tommy died at around eleven o'clock in the morning. Lucy didn't get to the Mulverhills until two, and Bill and I were out to the Pratt place by around four."

He downs another mouthful of gin, looking suddenly haggard. "Were you in the war, Mr. Buchan? No? No need to apologize . . . you were probably still in school. I was a field surgeon, attached to the Second Corps. The Second was at Gettysburg . . . also Spottsylvania, and Chancellorsville, and the Antietam, to name a couple of other minor engagements . . . and I frankly got so used to blood and the stench of corpses rotting in the sun that after a while I didn't see or even smell them any more. But that room . . ." He blinks. "It was a sunny July day, sunny and hot, with the kind of heat that makes you fear God, and the bodies had been five hours in a south-facing room that was hardly bigger than the mattress on the floor, directly under a tin roof with the sun pouring through a closed window. You could smell them downstairs in the yard—smell them and hear the flies. Bill and I tied handkerchiefs over our noses and mouths and went in . . .

"It was hard to see what we were looking at. The flies were so thick that the walls and floor seemed to be moving—the bodies too—and we had trouble shooing them away. Fauvell's body was naked, under the flies. Tommy had shot him at close range—no more than six feet away—with a twelve-gauge, and the blast had caught him at the top of his chest. There was nothing left above the sternum. Tommy's head . . ." Ogilvie's breathing is loud in the silence.

"And then we saw the third body—except that she wasn't dead . . . not yet, not quite. Lucy had bolted the door shut when she left for the Mulverhills' farm—she said later that she couldn't remember, that she must have bolted it in her panic without realizing what she was doing, but I don't know, Mr. Buchan, I don't know. She never told us that there was someone else in the room with the dead men, someone alive; she just let us take our own, sweet time getting there—she forgot, she said, to tell us about Clara, and that little girl had been roasting slowly, locked in that furnace with the bodies and the flies, for five hours.

"To this day I don't know which was worse: finding them dead that way or finding her alive and realizing that she and Fauvell . . ." He runs his hands through his thin hair. "Like him, she was . . . her clothes were over in a corner of the room, with his. I covered her with my coat, and carried her outside."

He blinks again, suddenly much older than he had been a few minutes before. "She was in shock, and almost dead from the heat, but the blasts hadn't touched her. I didn't take her to Tommy's house—didn't think it would be right, in the circumstances—I brought her back here to look after her. Bill went back to the house with Lucy, to break the news to Annabelle, who was frantic. Fauvell wouldn't keep any servants on the place—said he couldn't afford them, that all his money had gone to Lucy's fancy French school, although it was suddenly clear why he hadn't wanted anyone around—and Annabelle had been alone in the house all day, banging on the floor with her stick and calling for her son and her daughter and her husband, only there was no answer. She knew something was wrong, but didn't know what—an accident, maybe. She never did recover from the shock. She died about a year later, in her sleep."

Ogilvie rises stiffly to his feet, flexing his arthritic knee. "That's about all there is, Mr. Buchan. Bill got the whole story from Lucy and Annabelle over the next few days. We decided, between us, to leave everything out of the official report that concerned Fauvell's reason for being in the barn that morning—everything, in fact, about the girl, and Fauvell's inclinations—and to say that there had been no special motive, just bad blood between him and Tommy. And Annabelle—poor, grieving Annabelle—agreed with us. It was the first sensible thing I'd ever known her to do. But it was over, now, you see—Fauvell was gone, and Thomas, and it wouldn't bring back the dead to let such a story get out, just shame the living."

He upends the last of his gin into his mouth. "The little girl stayed with me for a few days, then Bill's wife took her in—she had raised six of her own, and could look after her better than I could, and anyway it wasn't medicine the child needed. I was worried about her mind. The sound of a door slamming two houses away would start her screaming, and she cried a great deal. She had to be reminded to eat—she'd sit at the table and just stare, with the food right in front of her. Sometimes, even with the food in her mouth, she'd forget to chew and swallow. She stared a lot.

"Bill got the address of her family from among Fauvell's papers and wrote to them about her. He told them the truth; he couldn't lie about a thing like that. They wrote back, a month or so later, saying that they couldn't possibly take her back—there were other children, innocent children, to consider—and that their lawyer would be in touch with Bill, to arrange for her to be taken off his hands and sent somewhere. Isn't that a pip, Mr. Buchan? Makes you wonder, sometimes, about what God intended when He made people. The lawyer came about a week after that—I didn't see the man—and took her away with him. He told Bill that she was going to a home for wayward girls, but wouldn't tell him where. I never saw her again.

"Wayward girls," he says again, his voice cracking. "I never met a less wayward girl in my life. I've had children, Mr. Buchan, two sons; they're grown now, and have kids of their own. What happened to her wasn't her fault, no more than being a bastard was her fault. What does a child know? If her folks had kept her at home and cherished her a little . . . but they sent her away to live with strangers, then called her wayward when someone finally wanted her. She wasn't wayward, Mr. Buchan, just sad, and that lonely that I guess it didn't matter why Fauvell wanted her, or for what. He was a charmer, and then Tommy pulled the trigger. You can't blame a child for something like that."

He checks his flow of words, biting his lip. "Anyway, she left, and I don't know where she went, or what happened to her. Maybe she's in an asylum somewhere, maybe she's on the streets. Maybe she's dead.

"Never mind." He falls silent at last, staring out beyond his garden.

Buchan lifts his head. He is numb and shaken, as close to tears as he has ever been. "Dr. Ogilvie," he says. "I'm so sorry."

Ogilvie walks around the table and rests his hand gently on Buchan's shoulder. "I'm sorry too." He pats Buchan comfortingly. "Which one of them did you know, Mr. Buchan? Fauvell? Tommy? Well, hell, why else would you care?"

The lawyer stares up at him. "Neither, Dr. Ogilvie. I know the little girl."

The old man's eyes widen behind his glasses and grow suddenly wet. His lip trembles. "You don't say," he says, as he removes his glasses with shaking hands and wipes his eyes. "You don't say."

It is dark when Buchan returns to the hotel, walking wearily down the nearly deserted main street, his heavy steps kicking up little puffs of dust from the old wooden planks of the walk. The desk clerk nods to him as he enters, and watches him, as he slowly climbs the stairs, with the passive, slightly sullen curiosity that strangers always elicit in small towns, then turns back to his ledgers.

Closing the door of their tiny suite behind him, Buchan slumps down onto the ancient horsehair sofa and leans forward, his face in his hands. The door to the bedroom is open, and although he cannot see her he can hear his wife moving about, opening and closing drawers, packing their belongings for their trip back to New York, but he does not call to her, to let her know that he has returned; he merely sits, letting the sadness wash over him. He has never been so tired in his life.

"Daniel, my dear?" his wife says, appearing in the doorway, then crosses to him, seeing his despair. Kneeling at his side, she touches his cheek and is rewarded by the lifting of his head, and then with a sudden movement he seizes her and holds her close. They have been married for more than twenty years—happy, contented years, for the most part—and in the way of good marriages they have grown together, like two arms joined by a single body: but they have never been a demonstrative couple, and it is rare for him to clutch her to him with such passion.

When he finally straightens up, holding her by her shoulders, she gazes into his face.

"You know, don't you?" she says. "Something about Clara. And it is very bad."

"It is very bad," he says, tiredly.

"Can you tell me?" She grips his hands. "I have never pried into your business matters, Daniel, you know that, never asked you about your clients or cases, and Signor Alfieri is your client, I know . . . but he and Clara have become more that that to us . . . to me . . ." She stops. "You have had your practice and I have been busy with my ladies' groups and church committees . . ." She rises to her feet and turns away. "Our lives have been full, and I have never really minded that there were no children . . . but . . ." She stops again. "If we had had a daughter . . ."

Buchan says quietly: "You are very fond of her, I know. But I cannot tell you, my dear. It is not my story to tell. It is hers, and it is not a story that I think she wants many people to know. I doubt that she has even told her husband, although I believe that he must have discovered some part of it. And how can I tell you what she has not told him?"

Mrs. Buchan nods in reluctant agreement, still with her back to him. "What will you do, now that you know?"

"Tell Alfieri. He needs to know."

She turns swiftly. "You have just said that it is her story. If she does not wish him to know, what right have you to tell him?"

"I have a duty to protect my client."

She is indignant. "From Clara?"

"No, my dear." Buchan rises to his feet. "From Thaddeus Chadwick. If I am right—and I am almost certain that I am—then Chadwick already knows what I have just learned. And I believe that he will use that knowledge to hurt them." He sighs and runs his hands through his thinning hair, in an echo of Ogilvie's earlier gesture. "I must tell Signor Alfieri what I have learned so that he will be prepared when Mr. Chadwick makes Clara's . . . misfortune . . . public . . . as he will."

"But why?" Mrs. Buchan says. "Why should he wish to harm her? She has done nothing to him."

"She disordered his plans, Alice. She inconvenienced him—badly, I'm afraid—by marrying someone else. And Thaddeus Chadwick is not a forgiving man."

His wife stares at him. "Are you saying that he wanted to marry her? But he's an old man, Daniel, and she's hardly more than a child!" And Buchan looks away.

"Such things have been known to happen," he says.

Mrs. Buchan stands silent, clasping and unclasping her hands. "This— this thing," she says, after a while, "this . . . misfortune that Clara suffered—what will happen if it is made public?"

"I suspect that Chadwick will wait until shortly before opening night to tell what he knows—and once it is common knowledge, I doubt that Alfieri will be able to face an audience again."

His wife turns pale. "What if they leave New York? If they just go away?"

"It will make no difference. It will be there before them, wherever they go, like a bad smell. And even if he divorces her—"

"Oh, Daniel, no!"

"Even if he divorces her," Buchan continues, ignoring her cry, "Alfieri will never live it down. How could he? His own notoriety almost eclipses his fame as a singer. Many will say that he deserved it, that it's a judgment upon him. People will laugh. 'Mario Alfieri,' they will say, 'he married the girl who . . .' "

He breaks off suddenly, aware that his wife is staring at him with her eyes filled with tears. "Hush, my dear, hush," he says contritely, taking her in his arms. "Forgive me for upsetting you. We will try to convince Mr. Chadwick to keep quiet. No doubt I am overly concerned. You know what a worrier I am. I should not have told you any of this . . . hush, Alice, it will be all right . . ."

But after she has dried her eyes and returned to the bedroom to finish packing, Buchan stands despondent in the little parlor. Less than a week ago they had welcomed Alfieri and his bride back to the city from their honeymoon, and the joyous flush on the young wife's face, the pride in her husband's eyes, lie on his soul like lead.

I must tell him, Buchan thinks, for he must hear it from me first, and not as some gossip in the street. But dear Lord, how do I do it? And how do I live with myself, once I have?

He sinks down into a chair, praying mutely—and then he sighs, and begins to put together the words that will shatter two lives.

Chapter Twenty-four

ALTHOUGH OFFICIALLY CLOSED to the public, the dress rehearsal of *Manon Lescaut,* on August the twenty-seventh, had, in fact, been attended by a small number of influential citizens known both for their capacious pockets and their abiding willingness to reach deep inside them for the greater good of Art; and their reports of the new opera—that it is a work of the most gorgeous melodies and the most desperate passions—augur the most unqualified success for the premiere itself.

Which means that tonight, the twenty-ninth of August, at eight o'clock, the curtain will rise on what, for Philadelphia, will surely be the crowning musical and artistic event of the decade, if not the century. All across the city, those fortunate enough to be attending make their eager preparations, while those who are not urge their luckier friends to remember every detail, and the entire populace seems to fizz like bubbles in fine champagne.

Oh, the bustle and scurry! Sounds of bathwater running, bells ringing, silks rustling, feet flying; the fragrances of flowers and soap and perfume mingling with the steamy smell of flounces being smoothed to perfection beneath flatirons, and the burnt smell of hair papers crackling around curling tongs; the flash and twinkle of precious stones on regal bosoms and white-gloved hands, the shimmer of gold and pearls in elegant ears . . .

Gleaming carriages and their no less gleaming horses stand ready, by

a thousand front doors, to whisk le beau monde through a purple summer dusk to the opera house, where black-cloaked ushers stand solemnly
at attention, and gilded doors swing wide to reveal two thousand red
plush seats in a gold and crimson wonderland ablaze with a million lights.

The preferred pastime of those already seated, as the glittering tide
rolls in, is to watch the new arrivals: searching especially, through
raised glasses, among the first tier of boxes that rings the auditorium,
the destination of those who glitter most gloriously of all. One box in
particular holds their attention, empty until moments before curtain
time . . . and then there is a general stirring and a low, rippling murmur as heads turn and glasses lift to watch its occupants' arrival.

The gentleman is young, tall and fair; but it is the very young woman
with him who draws their stares, and she shrinks from their upturned
faces as she steps into the box, then turns and smiles gratefully at the
young man as he guides her to a seat, partially screened by a velvet
drape, that offers her some protection from the peering eyes. Her gown
is like a froth of pearls and moonlight, gleaming white; her dark hair is
pinned back and covered by a delicate fall of lace held in place by a
coronet of white silk roses; and around her throat and falling to the
swell of her smooth, young breasts is a gossamer web of gems, a rare
and wonderful necklace of antique pearls and diamonds that winks and
glimmers in the lamplight, its delicate pattern repeated in the matching
jewels that twinkle in her ears.

The stares and whispers seem likely never to end, even when the
conductor mounts the podium to a burst of applause; but the pair have
timed their arrival well, and in another minute they are swept from
every mind as the houselights dim and the curtain parts to the lilting
rush of Puccini's music, on the busy village square of eighteenth-century
Amiens . . .

The dark young man who appears a few moments later is far too
engrossed in the book he is reading to concern himself with the group
of young men and girls laughing and flirting in the twilight. They stroll
the square before the inn—students, peasant youths and maidens—and
chaff him pleasantly as he continues to ignore them. He is a handsome
young scholar, tall and well made, soberly dressed, his curling black

hair pulled into a neat club at the back of his neck, and he pays the others no mind until the leader of the students gently mocks his preoccupation.

"You don't answer?" his friend asks. "Why not? Are you pining away with love for some unattainable lady?"

The young man raises his head at last. "Love?" he laughs, closing his book. "Love? With that tragedy—or, rather, comedy—I have no acquaintance!" And a sigh escapes from two thousand throats like a breeze on the summer air . . .

Alfieri has sung his first words in America. The audience, leaning forward in their seats since the tenor's entrance, collectively willing him to sing, now fall back into the music bubbling over and around them, only to rise again and again, drawn irresistibly upward—Orpheuscharmed—by the sound of that one, matchless voice.

And when the houselights rise at last upon the first interval, heads swivel to the opera box of the young woman in white, curious to read in her face her impression of the wild applause, the full-throated cheering, that greets her husband as he returns for his single, modest bow . . .

Except that she is no longer there. She and her escort have cheated the curious of their voyeurs' pleasure by slipping out during the last third of the act, once Alfieri's character had fled the stage. The box is deserted. Disappointed at being denied their glimpse of her, but exhilarated by the opera itself, the glittering crowd streams back up the aisles to refresh themselves with champagne and conversation. Upon the couple seated directly above the empty box—a stout, pleasant, elderly gentleman in spectacles, and an even stouter, pink-faced young woman dressed in blue with an aigrette of ostrich feathers in her yellow hair—not a single glance is wasted; but then, why should it be? Except for the accident of vertical proximity, what have these two to do with Alfieri's shining young bride, that anyone should look at them?

In the huge foyer, beneath the golden lamps, on the grand staircase and on all the marble landings, there is talk and laughter. ". . . pity Alfieri's wife doesn't sing, what a Manon *she* would make! . . . love at first sight, they say; eloped with her two weeks after they met . . . she's a *Jew,* I hear, and penniless besides . . . *handsome* man, and *such* a voice!

One might actually begin to understand why some women . . . must be a love match; he certainly didn't marry her for her money or social standing . . . just a child, really, can't be much more than a school-girl . . . whom he *hasn't* bedded? Why yes, but they're either too young, too old, or he hasn't met them yet . . . please him? Well, I should think so! Have you seen her necklace? My dear, definitely *not* a prize for best penmanship! . . . be fascinating to see them together after the opera, at the ball . . . yes, at the ball . . . afterward, at the ball . . ."

Even now the vast rotunda of City Hall is being transformed into a garden, a festival hall, a palace; for this night's exertions have only just begun, and the mayor and the city's leading citizens have arranged for a modest supper and dancing for five hundred, in Alfieri's honor. And Clara Adler Alfieri—the favored one, the fortunate, the blissful bride of the man no woman could capture—will waltz the sun up in her husband's arms.

How can they know that she is as unnerved, tonight, as she is ecstatic? The eyes of so many are on her; she feels them seeking her out even when the lights are down and the curtain up: the men staring openly, appraisingly, searching her up and down to discover what it is she pos-sesses that a thousand other women had lacked; the women gazing side-long, curious and envious; some merely wistful, others arrogant and bitter, each one absolute in the conviction of her own superiority. "Why you?" all their eyes say. "Why you?" And Clara might feel better if she could answer the question, but she cannot because he has never told her and she has never thought to ask.

The women are another thing, like the crowds themselves, to which she will have to become accustomed; for as Mario has said, so long as the voice lasts there will be crowds; and—and this she has learned for herself, not needing Mario to tell her—so long as there is Mario there will be women wishing themselves in her place, staring at her, willing her to imagine what they have imagined themselves doing with her husband, utterly assured, knowing beyond all doubt that they are in-comparably better suited, and infinitely more worthy, to be the great Alfieri's wife . . .

But tonight she must not let them bother her. Tonight she must simply nod and smile and sip champagne, and comport herself like a queen, and make Mario proud. Until the final curtain, Stafford Dyckman, who has not missed an opening night of Mario's in seven years, is her escort. He has come down from Saratoga for this gala occasion, and it is his pleasure to ferry her obligingly from the opera box to Mario's dressing room and back during the intervals, fetch champagne for her, tell her tales of her husband's other great stage triumphs, expound upon the finer points of opera, of which she still knows pathetically little, and be an altogether agreeable companion until he restores her once more to Mario's care.

It is Stafford who leans over, as the strings sigh the ending of the lovely intermezzo that precedes act three, and whispers the secret of her gift in her ear.

"Did he tell you, by the way, why he chose those jewels for you? I was with him when he picked them out. He said that he wanted you to look as if you had been dipped in diamonds."

But she has no time to answer. Act three is the tenor's act. The parting curtain reveals the Le Havre docks, and the dark student pacing distractedly beneath a looming prison with one barred window set high in the wall. Clara knits her fingers together as if in prayer, watches and listens with her knuckles white. The stage is his, belongs to him, and every soul in the darkened house, including hers, moves with him, breathes when he breathes . . . except that for Clara the sights and sounds are different, filtered through days and nights of sharing his life, his thoughts, his bed. He is passionate and anguished and note-perfect, but still he is Mario, *suo* Mario, her Mario . . . the Mario who never shuts his dresser drawers, who always wears something red for luck, who peels his breakfast orange with a knife in one continuous, winding strip and sprinkles his melon with salt, and each of whose gestures is as familiar to her now as morning coffee.

And yet there is another Mario on the stage, a stranger: not just the young French lover, but another Mario still . . . a Mario who belongs, not to her, but to a hydra-headed beast that fills the opera house, devouring him and drinking in his voice with its thousands of eyes and ears. She does not know this Mario: he inhabits a different plane, glorious, one that common mortals cannot reach, as far above her as heaven.

She cannot find her balance tonight. She, too, is more than one being: her own self, but also some new and astounding creature, a happy, envied, impossibly blessed creature, dipped in diamonds, unrecognizable to anyone, including herself, who knew her before. The urge is almost irrepressible to constantly turn and look behind her, to try and discover who this person is that people address when they speak to her, for surely it is not she. And if it is not she who wears her skin and looks out from her eyes, then where has she gone . . . and who is this someone that she is impersonating?

The double metamorphosis, hers and Mario's, is unnerving: neither of them is who she knows them to be; there is no firm center to this alien world. There are some moments when she finds herself unable to breathe, gripping the velvet arms of her chair and afraid to look down at herself, certain that she is naked, and her guilt plain. But she must not—she will not—let her terror emerge to spoil the evening. Tonight is Mario's triumph, and she must keep reminding herself that she is his wife, clad like the fairy-tale princess of her childhood dream, in a gown of pearls and moonlight . . .

Never mind! Nothing matters but the stage! Watch him! Watch them watch him! He is weeping on his knees, begging the ship's captain not to separate him from his Manon—see him? He weeps, the tears real on his face, offering his life, offering his blood to go with his Manon, and they all weep with him, all of them, every single one . . . leaning forward in their seats, hands at their throats, at their mouths, watching the ecstasy on his face as the captain relents, as the rapturous music suddenly soars, sweeping the two lovers up and onto the ship, wrapped in each other's arms, bound for the New World. Oh, Mario! Listen to them cheer, hear them scream for him! Tonight there is only *his* triumph, here on this giddy height where nothing is as it seems, and the certainty is that she is safe in his arms, now and forever beyond the reach of harm . . .

The gleaming throng, wildly elated, keeps its eyes on Mrs. Alfieri's empty place—she is gone again, before he takes his bow, but the third interval seems barely begun before she is back again, for the start of act four—and, conscious of being present on a night of nights, at a place where history is being made, the swarm settles down, in happy expectancy, for the final act. But this is opera, after all, where, like life, happy endings are rare . . . and the audience sits silent as the doomed and wretched lovers stumble across the barren land to the close of their tragedy, until the young student—in rags, now, and exhausted—lies down beside his love, holding her dead body in his arms, and *Manon Lescaut* sighs to its mournful, bitter end.

Many in the audience are weeping openly as the last, heartbreaking chord dies away, and the curtains slowly fall. There is a hushed sigh, for a moment, while eyes are wiped and breath is gathered—and then the opera house seems to heave into the air on one titanic burst of sound, the audience roaring to its feet, shouting, cheering, whistling, stamping until the walls and the floor, and even the distant roof, vibrate with the din. *Bravo,* Puccini, successor to Verdi! How beautiful! How wonderful! How heartbreaking! And, oh, God! Oh, God . . . Alfieri!

The singers appear, one by one, to receive their share of the acclaim. Manon, miraculously resurrected, makes her curtsies, holds her hands to her heart, blows kisses to the frenzied crowds, accepts her bouquets and vanishes. By rights she should be the last; hers should be the place of honor. But this night is different, and she has yielded her place, having no real choice in the matter.

And then the curtain moves and Alfieri steps out onto the stage. There is a second's silence, a momentary filling of lungs—and a second roar erupts from two thousand throats: a vast, frightening sound, like the bellow of some huge, primeval beast. He stands before it all alone, Saint George in rags, looking drawn and exhausted, almost stunned, like the grieving lover still, bowing tentatively, his eyes half shut against the houselights' glare as flowers rain down from the boxes on either side of the stage, and soar upward from the orchestra to land at his feet.

"*Orfeo!*" someone screams at the back of the house. "*Maestro Orfeo!*" And he looks toward the voice, smiling at last, and raises his hand, and others take up the cry. Only once do his eyes light on the box where his young wife stands, her face incandescent; and he smiles a different smile and touches his fingers to his lips, an almost incidental gesture, but the wild crowd sees it—it misses nothing in its adoration—and goes even wilder . . .

Neither Stafford nor Clara hears the knocking at the door of the box. How long the usher may have been there they have no idea, for the deafening roar of the audience drowns out everything else, but he suddenly appears, touches Clara on the arm, hands her a small, wrapped package, bows and leaves. She looks at Stafford, who shrugs his ignorance but smiles and gestures to the stage, as if to say "Another gift? Well, why not . . . ?" then discreetly turns his attention back to his friend and continues his own applause, allowing Clara her privacy as she opens the little parcel.

Flustered, she breaks the seal of the plain brown paper and uncovers a flat black velvet box, rectangular in shape, of the kind that jewelers use. She raises the cover; from the corner of his eye, Dyckman sees something glitter.

Perhaps she gasps, but no sound is audible in that uproar. There is no other warning. She does not crumple as she faints, but falls all of a piece, like a statue; and as she falls the little jeweler's box falls, too, to lie unnoticed beneath her chair, to be forgotten in the commotion as Dyckman bolts into the corridor, shouting desperately for a doctor, clutching at the bewildered ushers while the cheering still goes on . . .

He is an old hand, the house doctor; a solid, experienced, capable man with a passion for opera and a venomous hatred of tight-lacing— a practice he believes responsible for almost the entire panoply of feminine ills, from migraine to monthly indisposition; and he administers the *sal volatile* with confidence, fully expecting that this is merely another case—there is at least one at each performance—of an overexcited female who cannot draw sufficient breath. But when her eyes finally open, this young woman clutches his hand, dazed, and does not seem to know where she is, or even who she is, or to hear any questions put to her. Kneeling beside her, he chafes her wrists and gives her a sip of brandy from the small flask he carries for just such emergencies; but still she is confused, and her eyes wander.

Alfieri has left the stage, the lights are fully up, and even as the opera house empties, the opera box and the corridor beyond are filling up with strangers come to murmur, and stare, and share in the excitement as the word goes round that Alfieri's wife has been stricken; and the doctor orders them back in a rage, directing the ushers to clear them out while Dyckman kneels at her other side, almost in tears, fanning her with a program and whispering "Deliver us from evil, deliver us from evil . . ." over and over in his panic.

Someone—perhaps a good Samaritan, but more likely someone eager to be the first with bad news—has rushed backstage to tell Alfieri . . . and now the pandemonium in the corridor outside the box is magnified to near riot as he appears, still in his ragged costume and ashen under his makeup, pushing his way through crowds of people who cling to him as he goes, slowing him, bawling their names in his ear, trying to introduce children and wives, to congratulate him upon his performance, to shake his hand, to make small talk about anything at all. He will remember this, in time to come, as a nightmare come true: the hideous, universal dream of trying to run and being unable, of plodding through air that slows and drags, thick as treacle. Three ushers rush to his assistance and thrust the clawing, shouting well-wishers back from him, clearing a path through the madness to the opera-box door.

Dyckman looks up as Alfieri enters. His friend gives him one look only—of gratitude, shock, and utter fear—as he drops to his knees beside his wife; and the young man slips out into the chaos of the corridor, still perilously close to tears, wild with the desire to do *something* for Mario, to make amends for the fact that he has, somehow, not been sufficiently heedful of the treasure that Mario had placed in his care.

It is not until later—in the unimaginable silence that falls once Alfieri has carried his wife back to their hotel, and the crowds, with nothing more to stir their frenzy, have all drained away—that Dyckman remembers the jeweler's box and its glittering contents, and thinks to look for them. The opera house is eerily still now, peopled only by Dyckman himself and by the gray, stooped men and women who appear—like mice, from holes—to clear away the debris each night, once the theater is empty; and he takes the stairs two at a time, maddened by the thought that the cleaners might already have done their work, that he might be too late.

He is not. He finds the little box quickly enough. But it is empty, and he spends the next quarter of an hour on his hands and knees, searching for what it had contained. All that he finds, however, rolled beneath a chair, is a solitary crystal—a slim, transparent prism that might have hung from a lamp or a chandelier—which he tosses aside as a worthless bit of trash. He stalks from the opera house as the lights are going out, furious at the baseness of whoever had pocketed Clara's gift while she lay helpless, sick at the thought of having failed Mario twice, the soft summer breeze drying the tears that, finally, are spilling down his face.

It is well past midnight as Dyckman stumbles back to his hotel. In City Hall the dancers glide and whirl, but the ball will go on without him, just as it will without its guest of honor and his wife. There will be no dancing for them; no waltzing till dawn for Clara, in her gown of pearls and moonlight. Her husband has brought her home; has undressed her and put her to bed, letting no one else, not even her quietly weeping maid, come near; has written out his apologies to the mayor and the other guests and sent them on, in his and Clara's place; and now he sits by her side, stunned, the evening's triumph crumbled to nothingness around him.

He watches her for a long time as she sleeps, grateful to the doctor for the injection that had at last closed her eyes, thinking that nothing could be more dreadful than that vacant, wandering stare, not even her death—and then he crosses himself, terrified, denying that he had ever thought it, his mind flailing about for something to cling to, and, too exhausted to pray, he merely thinks: please, God; please, God; please, God . . . until that, too is impossible, and he is too exhausted even to think any longer; and then he turns down the single, dim lamp and, still in his clothes, lies down beside her; and he, too, sleeps.

He opens his eyes in the very early dawn, wakened by her movement. The curtains, hurriedly drawn last night, lift and stir gently in the early morning breeze. She is sitting upright in the bed, silhouetted against the silver-blue light, staring out at the first thin strands of pink that are beginning to streak the sky.

"*Cara,*" he says, and she holds her hand out to him without turning her head, groping for him until he catches her fingers in his own.

"I always watched the sunrise." Her voice is thin, a little ghost of a voice, perfect for the dawn. "I could never sleep, so I watched the sun come up every morning, no matter where I was. So many places. So many years. Listen." She lifts her head slightly. "Do you hear the birds?"

He raises himself on his elbow, still holding her hand. "Little love, you frightened me so last night."

"How beautiful they are . . . the birds and their morning songs. So sweet. I'd almost forgotten how sweet."

"Last night, my darling. What happened last night that made you so ill? Do you know? Can you remember?"

She turns her head slowly. In the half-light, to his tired imagination, her face is the face he had first seen in Gramercy Park . . . bruised, lost, haunted.

"But I stopped listening," she says. "You were there beside me, every morning, when I opened my eyes. I didn't need them any more."

"And I am here this morning too, *piccola*. Where else would I be but with you, my heart?"

"So many places," she says. "So many years. And I was tired, Papa, I wanted to rest . . ."

He eases her back against the pillows. "Hush, my dear," he says, "my dearest dear. No more talking. Close your eyes."

He lies down next to her again, laying his head beside hers on the pillow, drawing her against him, holding her close. She is weeping almost soundlessly, and he tightens his arms about her. Slowly, the first rays of sun pierce the curtains, painting a patch of wall molten gold.

Father, he thinks, don't take her from me. Always I believed that to be alone for all my life was the price I had to pay for Your many blessings. And then one day, long after I had given up hope, I walked into an empty house and found my happiness waiting for me. O my God, I am heartily sorry for having offended Thee . . . for my sins You sent her to me injured, and I have welcomed the pain, knowing the reason, and that You are merciful and just in all things. But if my punishment must be greater still, God, let it be some other way, not through her. Take back all the rest that You have given me; take everything else I have . . . only let her stay with me. O my God, I am heartily sorry for having offended Thee . . .

Outside, in the sunlight, the birds are making a tremendous noise.

Chapter Twenty-five

THE ANGELS, PRESUMABLY, do not tire of heaven. Mankind, however, being mortally flawed, quickly wearies of perfection, which is doubtless why God invented the seasons. For New York's patricians—who know themselves to be created only a little lower than the angels—even summer, that earthly mirror of Paradise, begins to pall before many weeks have passed; and such is their suffering, through the languorous, golden days, that by late August the more seriously bored are already shaking the rude dust from their dainty feet, and rushing back to the city pavements.

Others, however—Mrs. Astor among them—choose to remain behind in their summer cottages, using the last of their leisure to rest in anticipation of the autumn's grand exertions, secure in the knowledge that nothing of any consequence will occur in their absence because nothing of any consequence can . . . except that this summer something has occurred, something in which neither Mrs. Astor nor New York has played any part at all—and from city to country and back again, the news from Philadelphia moves with the speed of a thunderclap.

Word of the clandestine—and truly staggering—marriage of Mario Alfieri, infamous bachelor, to the penniless, friendless, and insignificant little nullity who had been Henry Slade's ward, had struck like a burst of heat lightning—quick to flare, slow to die away—in early August. Even now, in early October, its glare still lingers on the horizon.

Compounding the shock of the marriage itself, however, is the fact that the liaison had been two months old before the world—meaning, specifically, New York—had heard of it. And New York, having extended its hand to Alfieri—having wooed him, won him, and accorded him pride of place in its esteem—has developed what it considers proprietary rights to anything having to do with him . . . and that such a momentous event as his wedding should have been undertaken utterly without its knowledge, much less without its consent, has been adjudged rude, inconsiderate, and most definitely thankless.

Further magnifying New York's sense of injury is the fact that Philadelphia, and not its far more deserving self, had been the city granted the honor of having the first look at the newlyweds. Leaving New York's claim upon Alfieri aside altogether, there is always the matter of the bride. Is she not, after all, one of New York's own, through the agency of her late guardian? Well, then, even though New York's gentry would be the last to acknowledge her if they passed her on the street, certainly the ability to be the first to cut her should have been theirs by right. Add to this the twin facts of Philadelphia being the first city to hear the great tenor sing—this, in particular, is the thorn in Mrs. Astor's substantial side—and especially in a new and wildly praised opera, and one can gain some understanding of the grievance under which New York is laboring.

But the ultimate outrage, the most galling thing of all, is to have missed the final, incomparable excitement. It has been said that easily half of Philadelphia was on hand to see the gray-faced Alfieri carry his young wife from the opera house. For sheer, unalloyed sensation, the events in Philadelphia will never be surpassed; and New York, which—if there were any justice in the world at all—should have watched them played out before its own eager eyes, has had to obtain its information secondhand, smarting beneath the obvious and wholeheartedly smug pleasure that Philadelphia is taking in its achievement.

There is only one possible form of retribution. New York must have an opera season the like of which has not been seen before in any American city, commencing with an opening night of consummate magnificence. This should not be difficult to achieve: if Philadelphia's premiere of *Manon Lescaut,* by a new and relatively unknown composer, had been a victory, then New York's opening-night presentation of the great Verdi's masterwork, *Otello,* with Alfieri in the title role, should be a triumph of positively herculean proportions, and place New York firmly back in its rightful position of supremacy.

For if any role can be said to be Alfieri's, and Alfieri's alone, it is Otello. Verdi himself had reached out his revered hand and chosen the tenor to breathe life into this child of his old age; and Alfieri had done just that, singing the Moor at the opera's world premiere in Milan eight years ago, in a performance so terrifying, so heartrending—so superb— that it will be the performance by which all Otellos are measured for decades to come. It is a role, as its composer well appreciated, for which Alfieri could not be more supremely suited, for his dark and powerful voice is perfectly matched by his looks and size, and his dramatic skills are the equal of any thespian's on the stage today.

There is a story told that he had been so icily brutal at the climax of one particular performance, and murdered his Desdemona so horribly convincingly, that numerous ladies had fainted in their seats, and the soprano's husband, watching from the wings, had had to be bodily restrained by two stagehands to prevent him from shrieking and rushing onstage to rescue his wife. Whether this story is apocryphal or not is beside the point. The fact is that seeing and hearing Alfieri in the role of Otello is the event of a lifetime—and New York, for all of its displeasure at the singer's cavalier treatment of it, is not about to let that displeasure stand in the way of an experience of such transcendence.

Stafford Dyckman, of course, comes in for his share of blame. Alfieri's closest friend he may be, but he is also a scion of one of New York's oldest families, and it is clear where his loyalties should lie. His words to Alfieri, on the day of the tenor's wedding, about being invited everywhere on the strength of his role as best man, have proven prophetic, although far from the manner in which he had anticipated. That he is in demand as never before is only too true . . . but even as every host and hostess and all his fellow guests interrogate him, posing endless questions about the groom, the bride, the wedding itself, there is an air of disapproval in their manner; as if, while thankful that he can answer them, they nevertheless think less of him because of it. The fact that he also happened to be with the young Mrs. Alfieri when she was struck down on opening night in Philadelphia merely adds to the sense of his betrayal—although it makes him even more desirable as a dinner guest.

But the superfluity of invitations soon becomes a burden, even to the ever gregarious Dyckman: he is forced into untold repetitions of the events of the infamous evening, at which his tireless audiences probe and pluck, turning them inside out, groping among the facts like pagan diviners peering at chicken entrails for answers to the mystery of what had caused Clara Adler—which they willfully persist in calling her, despite her marriage—to collapse on the proudest night of her life.

The especial point of interest is the mysterious, empty jewelry box. Hypotheses about the author of the inexplicable gift run the gamut from practical jokers to murderous former lovers, with the vast weight of opinion favoring the latter, it being the most agreeably lurid, and Dyckman's earnest portrayals of the new Mrs. Alfieri as a shy and utterly charming young lady make little headway among an audience determined to search out just what sensational attraction she holds for the notorious philanderer who had married her. After a fortnight of well-bred smirks and insinuations, Dyckman grows so tired of preaching his disregarded truth to willfully deaf ears that he begins to refuse, very politely, when asked to tell his tale yet again. People being what they are, of course, this unwillingness to aid them in resolving the enigma—and in confirming what they wish to hear—is taken not as a gentlemanly desire for fairness, but merely as a further example of his defection from the ranks of those to whom he had once belonged.

No matter. He is still useful. He serves as an admirable foil for Thaddeus Chadwick.

Since the revelation of Alfieri's marriage, Chadwick, too, has been invited everywhere. The acid tongue for which he is famous had, in the past, made many a distinguished hostess hesitate before penning his name onto her guest list. But considering that he knows the Adler girl well, having been her guardian's intimate friend, New York's foremost matrons have concluded that his acerbity, after all, has a tonic effect, and is therefore a great aid to the digestion; with the result that he and

Dyckman have met often this September, and nodded to each other very much less than cordially, across numerous dinner tables.

Not that Chadwick's behavior is discourteous. Those who had anticipated that blood would flow have thus far been sadly disappointed. The razor tongue is less sharp than it used to be, and less ready to flay. Astonishingly, for one who knew of it so soon after the fact, Chadwick, like Dyckman, had kept silent about the elopement until it had become public knowledge. Even more amazing, he, like Dyckman, is unwilling to discuss the matter in the kind of loving detail that his fellow guests would wish to hear; and he is truly wonderful in his forbearance when speaking of the Adler girl, whom he has neither seen nor heard from since her flight from Gramercy Park.

His characteristic acrimony, in fact, seems to be reserved solely for her husband: it is only when Alfieri becomes the topic that the old Chadwick appears in all his corrosive glory. Chadwick has heard, of course, along with the rest of the world, about Clara's fainting spell at the train station in Philadelphia, and has wondered just what her husband could have been thinking of, to subject a young woman of delicate health and fragile mind to such an ordeal: set up on display in the suffocating heat, to be stared at by a thousand leering strangers as if she were a common strumpet, for sale to the highest bidder?

Chadwick has likewise heard—as who has not?—of Clara's far more serious collapse on the night of her husband's debut, and cannot help but have very serious doubts about Alfieri's conduct toward his bride. One can only imagine what he must demand of her—and here Chadwick's eyebrows wordlessly insinuate debaucheries beyond description— to leave her so weak and ill. And the result of the tenor's appetites? A young wife who, more than a month after the night in question, sits staring into nothingness, and trembles violently at the sound of a knock at the door, if Chadwick's informants—whose reports he has no reason to doubt—are to be believed.

There is little that Dyckman can say to counter these imputations. His own visits to Philadelphia to inquire after Clara's health have found her much as Chadwick describes her. They have also found Mario half-crazed with anxiety, and nearly sick with exhaustion from watching over her every moment he is not at the opera house; but Dyckman balks at offering up his friend's anguish for dinner-table conversation. Making it even more difficult for him to reply is the invariable presence at Chadwick's side of a young relation, orphaned and of rather distant connection: a young blond woman of agreeable features, china-blue eyes, and enormous circumference, who has come up from the country to live with her "uncle" Chadwick and be introduced to society.

At twenty-four, Lucinda Pratt is past the age where she can "come out" formally, but she is nevertheless welcomed into the homes of her "uncle's" acquaintances. Her years at an exclusive finishing school on the Continent have given her the manners, speech, and perfect French diction of a cultured lady; and while there is unquestionably too much of her to suit the average gentleman's taste, there is certain to be some New York bachelor or widower for whom an abundance of Lucinda—fair, amiable, and possessed of a significant fortune in the form of property and movables—will not be a deterrent. And if there are some of Chadwick's acquaintance who gaze at her and recall a flaxen-haired pupil, named plain Lucy Pratt, who was playmate to their own daughters at a once-troubled girls' school named St. Justin Martyr, they evidently prefer to keep such memories to themselves.

Clearly, she dotes upon her "uncle" Chadwick, and, just as clearly, he returns the compliment; and they are a comfortable-looking couple as they sit companionably side by side after dinner, enjoying their coffee, Chadwick slipping his barbed comments neatly between the ribs of the absent Alfieri, Lucinda listening intently, her admiration evident in her shining eyes and demure smile.

When they leave, equally companionably—Dyckman will have departed considerably earlier, able to ingest only so much venom in one evening, however well disguised—their destination will be Washington Square; and there, on the landing of Chadwick's handsome, well-ordered house, Lucinda will bid her "uncle" a fond good-night and retire to the rooms he has had prepared especially for her arrival: lovely, dainty, feminine rooms facing back over the garden, with flowered walls and lace curtains at the windows, a dressing table skirted in silk, twinkling with crystal and silver, and a delicate rosewood bed, carved like a blossom and hung with pale blue satin . . . a fairy's bed, or a princess's.

The iron bars across the windows, which might well disturb the dreams of a less blameless occupant, do not dismay Lucinda; they have been installed for her benefit, to keep both her maidenly virtue and her belongings inviolable from any danger without; and the lock at the door, which can be thrown only from the hall side, is there to ensure her safety as well, making it impossible for her to bolt herself in . . . a prudent precaution as, with the windows barred, the door is her only means of escape in case of fire. Besides, a lock on the inside would be purposeless; her "uncle" has overlooked nothing in his desire to secure her comfort and well-being, and it would be an ungrateful "niece," indeed, who would wish to bolt the door against such a generous giver.

The fact that he has never yet availed himself of the opportunity her unlocked door presents simply means that, being the gentleman that he is, he would never take advantage of a defenseless young lady living beneath his roof—it is inconceivable to Lucy that any man would not desire her—but he is courtesy itself, and he is on her side in the battle for decency. And that, of course, is why she is here . . . that, and her need to see justice triumph at last.

Because the mouse, the ugly brown mouse who had murdered her family and destroyed her life, has been caught at last. Once in the past Lucinda had trapped her and left her to die; but being hard to kill, like all vermin, the mouse had escaped, and disappeared. For six years she has cheated the hangman.

There is more. For the last five years, while Lucinda has been buried alive, all her perfections hidden from the world in the rotting backwater that is Rosebank, the mouse has wallowed in luxury, the pet whore of a New York millionaire. Uncle Chadwick has told her the truth, finally; told her—hesitatingly, unwillingly—of the wicked deception into which he had been forced, and the sham by which his client, Henry Slade, had gulled all the world into believing Clara Adler to be his ward, when all the time she was not only his mistress but his reward for anyone who furthered his financial success, a night's prize for every businessman who met his terms.

Well, Lucinda has found her at last; and having found her, will never—*can* never—lose her again, for the mouse has proven to be stupid, as well as ugly: she has married the one man in all the world whose whereabouts will always be known. The long-delayed sentence is even now being carried out, and there will be no quick drop or sharp blade, not after all this time. It will be a long dying.

As for her husband, Lucinda has seen him on only two occasions: once at the station, on the day of his arrival in Philadelphia; and again, four weeks later, on opening night. On the second occasion she had been a part of the crowd that had closed about him as he struggled to reach the opera box where the mouse lay, stunned, already beginning to die. He had made not a sound, never answering the people who clung to him and shouted into his face, saving his strength for the battle through their ranks, and Lucinda had lunged forward as he fought past the grabbing hands around him. She had caught at the shirt of his ragged costume, ripping it more, and as he tore himself free he had turned to face his tormentor, looking at her without seeing her.

His face was cold, even in the midst of that madness, cold and furious; but he sweated, and his eyes were black with fear. She had clutched at his shirt—his skin was hot beneath her fingers—and then he was gone, swallowed up in the surging mass of bodies around him. Lucinda has thought of that moment often: of his coldness, and his fear, and the heat of his body against her hand.

Uncle Chadwick had asked her, afterward, what she thought of him. "There is violence in him," she had said at last. "He is capable of killing." Chadwick had smiled. "We will see about that," he said.

What she has neglected to tell him is that, since that strangely intimate moment, she has felt an unaccountable bond between herself and Alfieri. What will the tenor's expression be, she wonders, when she finally tells him of his wife's sins? Will there be the same icy fury she had seen that night? Or will he burn like the sun, in an all-consuming rage? She does not know, and the uncertainty fascinates her. Of one thing, however, she is certain: he will not be indifferent. He will see her when she stands before him on that day.

And the outcome? The tales she has heard of him onstage fire her fancy. She sees him in her mind's eye as he has been described to her, killing his Desdemona with glacial, relentless savagery; and she sighs with pleasure, envisioning his hands curving around the little mouse's throat, or raised like a hammer to strike . . .

Lucinda will be there for him, of course, to bear witness to his provocation, to take the stand in his defense, enumerating the sins that had driven him to murder; and his gratitude will be profound.

In the meantime, there is Uncle Chadwick to keep her entertained. It is diverting to sit with him, night after night, amid the cream of society, and listen to him berate Alfieri for being heedless of his wife— Alfieri, who had sweated with fear—when all the while it is Lucinda who waits, like a great, silent cat, for the mouse to creep within reach.

"Of course," Uncle Chadwick had said mildly, not so very long ago, "we cannot be certain that she will not tell him herself. And if she does, what happens then to your lovely revenge?"

They were seated in the darkened drawing room of his house, just re-turned from yet another dinner. Neither of them was sleepy, or in the least mood to retire. The cool night was full of moving shadows and the rustle of leaves tossing in the autumn wind, and they sat and watched the lights of Washington Square flickering through the tall windows.

Lucinda had smiled into the darkness. "She won't tell him. You know that as well as I. Would you have come to me in the first place, to initiate our little plan, if you thought she would tell him herself?"

Chadwick said dryly: "I am not infallible, my dear. But tell me why you are so certain. Surely she must see that her only hope is to tell him before you do?"

"Perhaps. But she will not. She is too frightened of what he will do." Lucinda had hugged herself in the darkness. "Can you imagine her fear, Uncle? I think of it often; I try to imagine what it must be like. When she saw me at the train station she knew she was destroyed. But it was when she opened the box and saw the prism—oh, Uncle, you clever, clever man! How can I ever thank you enough for that gift?—it was then that she knew the end was near, that it was only a matter of time before I made her husband a gift of what I know. And every morning since that night she has wakened knowing that this day could be the one. The hours crawl by, and every knock at the door might be the end, but the end never comes. And each day that it does not happen is not a relief, not a reprieve, but only the end of one more day, and the promise of yet another tomorrow when it may, at last, happen . . ."

Chadwick had lit a cigar, a ruby ember in the darkened room; his face glowed as he drew upon it, and the pungent smoke made swirling patterns through the flickering shadows.

"You have a talent for hating, my dear. A genius, even. Whom will you hate when she is gone, I wonder?"

"No one," she replied, smiling at his jest. "There will be no need."

She could almost hear the sound of his eyebrows arching in the darkness. "Oh, my dear. People who do things well tend to do them often. Haven't you noticed? You have lived such a long time hating her. She has given your life meaning, and purpose . . . far more than cataloguing your stepfather's trinkets has ever done. You will miss your little mouse, I think, when she is no more."

For a long moment Lucinda had paused, openmouthed . . . uncertain . . . and then the humor of his words had struck, and she had melted into laughter which had grown even louder when she heard his own laughter answering hers from the shadows. They had gone upstairs shortly afterward, companionable as always, and as they parted on the landing, she wished him good night with a special warmth, grateful for the excellence of a joke that could end her day so happily.

She had drifted to sleep, that tranquil night, with a sense of particular contentment; and if she dreamed any dreams they were evidently not worth remembering.

Chapter Twenty-six

THE DAY IS BRIGHT but chilly for early October, and the fire in the drawing room grate is welcome. Two months have passed since Buchan last sat here, and much has changed, although not the pleasant room itself. It is the room's occupants who have altered, neither for the better.

The slanting sun of late afternoon, reflected from the windows of the houses across the wide avenue, combines with the low flames of the fire to produce a mellow, golden light of the kind beloved of women of a certain age, for it glides sweetly over the evidence of years that time etches in mortal faces. And yet, even the kindliest light could not hide the exhaustion in Alfieri's face, or the deep furrows now permanently engraved between his brows, or fail to pick out the silver in the once absolute blackness of his hair. In the two months since Buchan has seen him, he appears to have aged ten years.

But the lawyer, too, looks careworn, as he would be the first to admit; weighed down by something. He listens silently as Alfieri, staring into the flames, speaks in a voice of dull despair. He has been speaking for a long time.

". . . the doctors, of course, can find nothing. Well, that merely proves what good doctors they are, does it not? They can find nothing because there is nothing to find."

He laughs suddenly, a low, dispirited sound. "Although, to be fair, one medical gentleman did think he had identified the cause of the problem. He drew my attention to how very small my wife is, and how terribly young. He declared—with the utmost tact and delicacy—that he believed Clara's trouble to be one common to newly married young ladies, a condition he referred to as 'conjugal disharmony between husband and wife.' He went on to assure me, quite earnestly, that many young brides find their husbands' grosser needs to be repellent in the extreme, and the act of satisfying those needs almost always physically painful, so that having to perform frequently their 'compulsory spousal duties'—his words, Mr. Buchan, not mine—becomes an unbearable burden. This would be particularly so in the case of a large and vigorous man, like myself, with a small and very young wife, like Clara."

The tenor's smile is bitter. "Lest you think the good doctor unreasonable, by the way, he did allow that children—for those who might want them—can be gotten only in the old-fashioned way, regrettable as that way may be. Should fathering children be my intention, then I should confine my demands for Clara's 'compulsory spousal duties' to that time of month when they are most likely to produce the desired results." His voice, taut with temper, begins to rise, his words to come faster.

"As for the balance of the month, the doctor submitted to me that if I would only find a regular outlet for my more 'urgent needs' among the lower types of women—women for whom 'the act' is no more disgusting than it is to dogs or sheep—I would find my wife greatly improved in a very short space of time.

"I thanked the doctor for his opinion, of course, but informed him that in my vast experience of women there have been astonishingly few for whom 'the act' was physically repellent. The doctor was dubious, of course, but how could he doubt the word of such an expert?" Alfieri's fists are clenched on the arms of his chair; the words spill from him. "I also informed him that I have no intention whatsoever of moderating my attentions to my wife, and that he could set his mind entirely at ease about my—yes—very frequent demands for her 'compulsory spousal duties,' because no such 'conjugal disharmony' exists between us."

The tenor's voice is ragged with anger. "The gentleman bowed, therefore, to my clearly superior knowledge, pocketed his handsome fee, and left me, as all the others have done, not one shred nearer to knowing what is wrong with her, or how to make her well!"

As he utters the last word he slams both fists down onto the arms of his chair and heaves himself to his feet, then paces up and down the length of the room, slowing only gradually, stopping at last before one of the tall windows overlooking Madison Avenue, where he stands pressing his fingers against his eyes. After a long silence he turns back to his guest.

"Will you forgive me?" he says, and his voice is quiet again. "That was inexcusable, and I beg your pardon for it. I am not usually so crude. But I am so tired, Mr. Buchan, and there is nothing I can do for her, except watch her fade before my eyes. There is nothing *to* do, you see, because there is nothing to find, or so all the doctors tell me.

"Do you understand? There is nothing in the least wrong with her . . . except that she seems to be dying, and no one can tell me why. And I can do nothing for her, Mr. Buchan, nothing at all . . . except to be with her as much as possible. And in a few days rehearsals begin, and then I cannot do even that."

Buchan nods in commiseration and makes no reply. After a few moments he says: "How was the journey from Philadelphia?"

"Uneventful, thank God. We took a late train. I did not notify the hotel of our departure until we were ready to set out for the station." Alfieri smiles the faintest of smiles. " 'Like thieves in the night' is, I believe, an eminently suitable description of our leave-taking. But I wanted no send-off, no ceremony, no crowds. Especially no crowds."

Buchan nods again—"And how is she today?"—and the smile is gone again.

"The way she is every day: weaker than yesterday, not so weak as she will be tomorrow. Frightened and sick, like the child I first found in the music room. You remember what she was like, don't you? You saw her the day of our wedding. And yet this is worse. She eats nothing—she can keep nothing down—and she sleeps even less than she eats. And on those rare occasions when she does fall asleep, too exhausted to keep her eyes open any longer, then her nightmares wake us both. And always she seems to be listening, straining to hear, keeping a kind of mad vigil, as if any moment she expects someone or something to hammer at the door. It does no good to tell her that she is safe, that the doors are bolted and the windows locked, that Gennarino will allow no one inside, that nothing can reach her, or harm her. The sound of a delivery at the tradesman's entrance . . ." He spreads his hands eloquently, then drops them.

"And she will not say what happened on opening night," Buchan says, "or what was in the mysterious package that she received?"

"She insists that it was empty, that it must have been a practical joke."

"You do not believe her."

"No, I do not believe her!" Alfieri begins to pace once more, unable to keep still. "What is there about an empty box to cause a young woman to faint? But I do believe Stafford . . . and Stafford swears that he saw something glitter as she raised the lid. Besides, I have only to look at the change in her since that night to know that she is lying to me."

"And when you point these things out to her, signore? What does she say?"

"She asks why she should be faulted for Stafford's failing eyesight, and insists again that the box was empty."

"Have you tried reasoning with her?"

"I have tried everything, Mr. Buchan. I have tried reasoning, coaxing, begging, even anger." He stops pacing and turns away. "Oh, yes," he says, with his back to Buchan, "even that."

"And?"

Alfieri presses his fingers to his eyes once more, as if to shut out the memory. "And she cried, Mr. Buchan. But she would not change her story."

There is no answer to this. Alfieri returns to his chair, drops wearily into it, closes his eyes. The silence stretches out, broken only by the hiss and crackle of the flames in the grate, the occasional creak of footsteps overhead, and, once, the barking of a dog in the street outside.

"Have you spoken to Stafford recently, signore?" Buchan says into the stillness. "No? Then probably you have not heard that Thaddeus Chadwick has taken a young woman into his house."

Alfieri barely lifts his head: Chadwick's desires, so long as Clara is not their object, are of less than no concern to him.

"Has he, indeed?" he murmurs. "No, I had not heard . . ." He shrugs. "Someone to help him over his disappointment, no doubt. Well, men will be men, Mr. Buchan. I only wonder whether his friends will receive her."

"No, the woman is not his mistress, signore, at least so far as anyone knows, although one can never be entirely certain of what goes on behind someone else's closed door. What their relation is is anyone's guess. She is, however, being introduced as family, a distant cousin . . . but that she is no kin of his is the one thing of which I am certain. Her name is Lucinda Pratt." Buchan cocks his head. "The name means nothing to you?"

"Nothing at all. Should it?"

"Mrs. Alfieri has never mentioned it to you?"

"Clara?" This time the tenor does lift his head. "Does Clara know this woman?"

"Better than anyone alive, I should say."

Alfieri hesitates, then shakes his head. "I have never heard the name."

"Well, but your wife is, as you have said before, reticent about her early years. Lucinda Pratt, however—she was just Lucy when your wife knew her—will probably prove less reticent, signore, less reluctant to speak than your wife. In fact, I believe that is why she is here . . . either to make public what she knows, or to assist Mr. Chadwick in that task."

Alfieri stares at Buchan, suddenly wary. "What she knows?"

"About a very great tragedy in which your wife was involved, signore. Years ago, when she was still a child." Buchan meets the tenor's eyes. "Few people know of her role in it. Lucy Pratt is one. Thaddeus Chadwick is another. There are a doctor and a sheriff in a little town in New Jersey who know it too. And I. And that, I think, is all . . . for the moment. But if I am not mistaken—and Miss Pratt's presence in Chadwick's house tells me that I am not—many more people will know of it soon.

"I only learned of it two months ago. I would have told you then, signore . . . I had planned, in fact, to call upon you in Philadelphia . . . but then I heard that Mrs. Alfieri had fallen ill upon your arrival, and I thought it better not to disturb you. It seems, now, that that was a mistake. Now there is no more time left. I believe that Chadwick or Lucy—or both of them—sent your wife something at the opera house, something to let her know that her past would soon be known, to you and to others.

"But I do not think that her present suffering, however great, is Mr. Chadwick's final goal. I believe that he wishes to make your wife's role in this tragedy known to the world. That will be his revenge upon you. And I am afraid that if you do not hear it from me now, signore, you will hear it from others, very soon . . . and I would spare you that pain."

After a long pause, and in a low voice, Alfieri says: "Tell me what it is that I must know, Mr. Buchan."

He listens, motionless, to the lawyer's tale of his visit to Rosebank, trying not to hear, the words spilling over him like water. Gradually some of them sink into his mind.

". . . Edward Fauvell . . . unfortunate inclinations . . . very young pupils . . . none over the age of fourteen . . ."

Alfieri's palms are suddenly damp. He rubs them against the arms of his chair, blinking rapidly into the fire.

". . . generous stipend . . . allowed to resign quietly . . . retired to Rosebank with his wife and his stepdaughter, young Lucy—whom he had seduced long before he ever met her mother . . ."

There is a fine sheen of sweat on Alfieri's face. He is listening, now; listening closely, against his will. "It was some three years later," Buchan says, "that your wife's family decided to send her away for her schooling."

Alfieri presses his head back into his chair and shuts his eyes, sickness rising in his throat. He knows what is coming now, and can do nothing to stop it; Buchan's voice seems to come from a great distance away.

"She stayed with Fauvell for two years . . . from the time she was eleven to the time she was thirteen . . ."

Images of his wedding night crowd Alfieri's mind: Clara curled small, her silence, her eyes as she watched him, waiting for his anger. He sits with his head turned away from Buchan, so still that he might be asleep, except for the convulsive working of his throat, and the tears running down his face.

Buchan keeps his own face to the dying flames. "I am almost done, signore. In the summer of eighty-eight Fauvell was murdered, killed by a blast from one barrel of a shotgun, after which his murderer—his young stepson—turned the other barrel on himself. The murder took place in an old, abandoned carriage barn on the property." He forces the words out, telling the last of it in an unsteady voice. "Your wife was there, signore, when it happened. She and Fauvell were . . . together . . . when the young man burst in on them . . ."

The fire is only embers now, the sun nearly gone; the silent room is lost in gray shadows. Buchan gets to his feet slowly, staggering a bit, like an old man.

"I will leave you for a while, if I may," he says into the darkness, expecting no answer, receiving none. "With your permission, signore, I will go upstairs and see the ladies. My wife must be wondering why I have not yet been to pay my respects to Mrs. Alfieri . . ."

He closes the door behind him. Peters is in the hall just outside, preparing to enter to draw the curtains and light the lamps. Buchan stops him with a hand on his arm.

"Don't go in," he says. "Wait until he rings." And whatever the footman sees in the lawyer's face, he merely bows silently and walks away.

With the lamps lit, the little sitting room is a pretty picture of domestic peace: warm and bright, with drawn curtains shutting out the night beyond. From the soft rugs on the floor to the scattered books and the tea things upon the table, it is almost identical to the room Clara had left behind in Gramercy Park. Alfieri, striving to make her feel at home in this strange, new place, has had her old, familiar surroundings copied as closely as possible.

The door opens quietly. Buchan, not wishing to disturb those within, does not enter but stands still and listens. The murmuring voice he hears is familiar to him, loved and very welcome: Alice, reading aloud.

" ' . . . and thus the Treasure Valley became a garden again, and the inheritance, which had been lost by cruelty, was regained by love. And Gluck went, and dwelt in the valley, and the poor were never driven from his door . . .' "

Buchan watches her as she reads, her bent head golden in the lamplight. A little way away, Clara is curled into a chair in the half-dark, just beyond the lamp's reach, although whether awake or sleep, Buchan is unable to say. His eyes travel from the bright head in the light to the dark one in the shadows and back again.

What would he do if someone came to him, one day, and told him that the wife he loved was not what he had always thought her to be; was not merely his wife, but a sword suspended above his head by the slenderest of threads, a peril to his livelihood, his reputation, his honor; the potential, and wholly inadvertent, undoing of everything that he had worked a lifetime to build?

The story ends. Alice closes the book, looks up at him standing by the door, and does not need to ask if he has told Alfieri what he has never yet told her. She lays the book down and looks towards Clara. "She's asleep," she says. "Don't wake her, Daniel."

No, he would not wake her for the world. Let her sleep on, unaware of what he has done, of what duty has led him to do. Alice draws him to a dim, far corner of the room where they sit side by side in silence, waiting, although neither of them is certain of what it is they wait for.

"Read again," Buchan says to her after several minutes, after the stillness has begun to press in on him. "You read so beautifully, your voice is so lovely. And I'm in need of a story now, Alice . . . something pretty, with a happy ending."

Alice retrieves her book, lights the lamp, turns the pages. " 'Once upon a time,' " she begins, " 'so long ago that I have quite forgotten the date, there lived a king and queen who had no children . . .' "

Buchan listens, but not to the words. The sound of his wife's voice, rising and falling with the story, flowing in a smooth, clear stream in the lamplit room, is like balm to his sore heart, like music. He finds himself staring, his eyes half-closed, at the shapes of shade cast against the walls and ceiling; finds himself sinking deeper into the cushions, so still, so languid, that even when the door opens and Alice looks up and shuts the book abruptly, he turns slowly, and looks at Alfieri with great composure.

The tenor bends over Clara's chair. She does not stir, even with his hand resting on her hair, and her breathing is deep and even. Alice watches his hands—beautiful hands, strong and square, with long, blunt fingers—curve to smooth his wife's sleeping head, to touch her cheek.

"She has not slept like this in so long." He raises his head; his eyes are wet. "Thank you," he says to Mrs. Buchan. "I owe you more than I can say."

"Not I," the woman says gently. "You have brought her home, signore. All the stories in the world would not have lulled her to sleep if she were not finally safe at home."

Alfieri's hand caresses Clara's hair. "But I am a nomad, madame, and a citizen of all the world. And yet, wherever we are, I will keep her safe. That I promised; that I still promise." Bending, he murmurs something to Clara as she sleeps, something that sounds like "It can never be mended, the glass I broke . . ." but Mrs. Buchan cannot be sure.

He straightens up, wiping his eyes with the back of his hand. "Mr. Buchan, that matter we lately were discussing . . . there remains much to finish, all of it vital to making certain that my wife is indeed safe. Will you join me again in the drawing room? Mrs. Buchan will, I know, forgive us for abandoning her once more in such a good cause."

"I would forgive you both for a great deal more than that," Mrs. Buchan says, smiling, "in such a good cause."

Alfieri would be surprised, therefore, to see her burst into tears once the door has closed behind them. He would be deeply moved, as well, to learn the reason, but he will never know it, nor of her struggle to silence her sobs, or the fervent, silent prayer of thanks that ends her long weeks of fear: "He will not leave her; he will not leave her . . ."

It is Clara, instead, wakened at last by the sound of her tears, who stares at her white-faced, with terrified eyes, rising from her chair. "What's wrong? Why are you crying? Oh, Alice, my God . . . oh, my God . . ."

Alice starts up; the book tumbles from her lap. "Nothing is wrong, dearest, nothing at all." She hurries to Clara's side, still dabbing her eyes with her handkerchief, and kneels beside Clara's chair. "There's nothing to fear, I promise you."

She takes the frightened girl's hands in hers. "I did not mean to wake you, sweet. I have only been reading one of Mr. Wilde's stories while you slept." Easing Clara back into her chair, she smiles and touches her face where Mario had touched it only a few moments before. "Mr. Wilde's stories are so beautiful, and they always make me cry. Shall I read one to you? But you mustn't mind if I sob at the end . . ."

Plucking a blanket from a nearby cushion, she wraps it around her small charge's shoulders. Clara's hands are icy, and Alice covers her well, tucking her into the warm folds of wool, placing a pillow behind her head. Then she returns to her own chair to pick up the hastily dropped book. She arranges herself beneath the lamplight, looks up and smiles again. Clara's face is lost once more in the shadows.

"Do you know this one? Surely you do. Listen . . . 'High above the city, on a tall column, stood the statue of the Happy Prince . . .' "

Chapter Twenty-seven

THE LAMPS HAVE BEEN LIT, the curtains drawn. Alfieri listens silently, his face expressionless. It seems to him that he has never done anything but listen to Buchan's voice.

". . . Her mother was not married," Buchan is saying. "She ran away for good when Clara was three. I have met the family, signore, and I cannot blame her for leaving, even knowing as I do what happened to her child. I believe she would have taken Clara if she could have, and I do not believe that she would have gone if she thought Clara would suffer by staying behind . . . but that may be only my wishful thinking. Her family have no good words for her, certainly. All that I know of her, of course, I learned from them, and they are not any kinder to her memory than they were to her, twenty years ago.

Buchan shifts in his chair. The story falls from him easily now—now that the worst has been said—and he tells it evenly, with no hesitations.

"From the day her lover abandoned her, forcing her to return to them, until the day she ran away, the family kept her confined to the house, not wishing any of the neighbors to see her condition, or know of her shame. When she first returned home and it somehow became known that she was back, some of her young lady friends came to call upon her. They were told that she was permitted no visitors, and turned away. Even after her baby was born—there was neither doctor nor midwife in attendance, and the birth was never registered—she and the infant were not allowed outside: not even to walk in the garden, or sit on the back porch after dark on hot summer nights.

"On those pitifully rare occasions when there were guests to dinner, or a visitor for someone else, she was locked in her room with her child, and instructed to silence it quickly if it should happen to cry. Writing letters was forbidden to her, too, and any that she happened to receive were opened, read, and burned before she could see them. She was twenty when she gave birth, signore; only twenty-three when she ran away. She was still young and very lovely, and the knowledge that her life was over must have driven her mad. She had been buried alive; the future held only endless decades of imprisonment and abuse. Can you blame her for running away?

"She escaped, finally, by throwing some clothes into a carpetbag and climbing from a window during a rainstorm. Her flight was only discovered because Clara, frightened perhaps by the thunder, began to cry—and after two hours, when she did not stop, someone went upstairs to find out why her mother did not quiet her.

"Once she was gone they either discarded or destroyed everything that had belonged to her—gave every scrap of clothes she left behind to the ragman, burned every document, letter or photograph, rid themselves of anything they could that she had owned or even touched. In other words, they expunged her thoroughly from the family's memory."

He shakes his head. "Except for the one thing that they could not expunge, even though officially it did not exist: the little living reminder of her shame."

Buchan rises from his chair and walks aimlessly about the room, Alfieri's eyes following him.

"I was able to find the family through the sheriff in Rosebank—he had found a piece of paper with the name and address among Fauvell's things, and had kept it, I don't know why. I wrote to them to arrange a meeting." His lips curve slightly. "They were exceedingly disinclined to grant me an interview until I mentioned that I knew what had happened at Rosebank, and the nature of Clara's involvement, and that I would be willing not to spread the story among their neighbors if they would speak to me.

"I met with them, finally, about three weeks ago. They told me a great deal after all, and the rest I have been able to piece together. I will tell it all to you now, both what I know to be fact and what I believe to be true. You be the judge, signore, of whether it sounds plausible.

"I would imagine, by the way, that Mrs. Alfieri looks today much as her mother did when she first met her lover . . . certainly Ida Adler was about the same age that your wife is now. And her lover, like you, signore, was a man in his forties . . . exceedingly wealthy, a great bene-factor of many good causes, including the arts. They met at a musical soirée in New York, at which the young lady sang. She had hopes, you see, of becoming an opera singer—rather an irony, don't you think?

"Her family were vehemently opposed to her doing anything of the sort, of course: they believed that only harlots went on the stage, and predicted that singing would be her ruin . . . in which they were un-fortunately correct. Instead, they would have had her marry the son of a friend who had expressed interest in her, and who owned a prosperous business. But she had achieved some modest success despite their dis-approval, and was desperate to find a patron who would agree to finance her musical studies before she was forced by her family to marry the man they had chosen for her, and to abandon her dreams forever.

"During an intermission in the soirée, after hearing her sing, the wealthy man introduced himself and offered, then and there, to pay for the rest of her training, and to present her to his friends in the opera world . . . and the girl, overwhelmed, no doubt, by the advantages he could obtain for her, and by his very evident admiration, slipped away with him sometime during the evening. No one saw them leave."

Buchan stops his wandering, sinks down upon a sofa. "She did not return to her home that night; instead, a messenger appeared the next day. He carried a letter from her, saying that she was well, and very happy, and that her musical studies were to commence immediately, but that she could not tell them the name of her new benefactor because, although she had assured him that they would never press him for money, he had a rich man's fear of relations with outstretched hands.

"After that, of course, she was dead to them. There was just one family member—a spinster cousin with a foolish, romantic nature, despised by the rest of her relatives—with whom Ida kept up a correspondence of sorts, and I was able to read those letters. They spoke of singing lessons, and splendid gifts of clothes and jewelry, and the kindness of her lover, and were full of happiness and the certainty of a bright career." Buchan tilts his head quizzically. "Was the man's offer sincere then, signore, or merely a way to seduce an innocent young girl? I don't know. Perhaps if she had not gotten so quickly with child . . . but in that case, of course, we would not be having this conversation now." He shrugs the conundrum away.

"In any event, both her happiness and her career were very brief, no more than a few months. She was soon in the family way, and her benefactor promptly ended their acquaintance. He was scrupulous about his good name, you see, and would not risk soiling it. Keeping a charming young mistress and grooming her for the opera stage was one thing; fathering a bastard by a Jew tradesman's daughter was entirely another. Marriage to such a girl was, of course, utterly unthinkable.

"Consequently, he did what he had to do . . . and what, by his lights, must have seemed most generous: he cut all ties to her and refused to see her ever again . . . but, through the mediation of a discreet third party, he arranged for her to be sent back to her family with a large gift of money and his promise of continued financial support for her and the child. Did he know that he was consigning her to hell by sending her back to them? Perhaps not. But he would have done it, regardless."

Buchan rises again and walks to the window, draws back a curtain and gazes into the October darkness.

"To her family, of course," he says, watching the lights of the carriages passing by, "there was, and is, no difference between a kept woman and the lowest dockside whore—and I have no doubt that they would have seen her on the streets before taking her back, except that the lover paid them so handsomely. But there was no amount of money that could compensate them for their disgrace—or for the bastard she bore. And there was absolutely nothing they could do, you see, no action they could take against the seducer . . . because Ida had promised, in exchange for lifetime support for her child, never to disclose her lover's name. And she never did. The family still do not know who he was."

Alfieri speaks at last. "Where did she go? Where is she now?"

Buchan lets the curtain fall back into place and turns to the tenor. "No one knows, signore. Nor do they care, so long as she does not come back."

"And the lover? Do you know?"

"The lover went on to lead an eminently respectable and prosperous life. He never married, not having, apparently, a taste for matrimony; and he had, so far as anyone knows, no other mistresses after Ida, and no other children."

Buchan pauses. "Do you know, perhaps the saddest irony of this wretched little tale is that, had the fact of their respective stations in life not created an insurmountable barrier, Ida's lover and Ida's family might have pleased each other very much. There was the same passion for unimpeachable rectitude on both sides. But the barrier *was* there, and in the normal course of events Ida and her lover would never have met. In this case, however, the normal course of events was contravened by fate: the simple accident of two people attending the same musical soirée."

Alfieri's voice is ragged. "And what of a child sent to a seducer's bed, Mr. Buchan? Was that, too, just a simple accident? Could such an obscenity be just a simple accident? Because if it could, then God's pity is a lie . . ."

"Do not blame God, signore." Buchan's dark face looks wolfish in the lamplight. "Surely you remember your Scripture? 'For it must needs be that offenses come; but woe to that man by whom the offense cometh.' It is man who makes the obscenities, signore . . . not God."

He crosses the room, drops back into his seat. "You never asked the identity of the discreet third party, did you, signore? The liaison between the lover and Ida's family? The family never learned the lover's identity, but they became quite familiar with the go-between, and they told me his name . . . reluctantly, of course, but they had no choice. It was he whom they called upon some eight years ago, when they finally grew tired of having a bastard underfoot. It was he who told them of the place where she could be sent for her education, never mentioning the schoolmaster's little weakness, although he knew it well; it was he who advised them on making the arrangements. And the happy outcome? She never came back to trouble them again, for she proved that she was indeed her mother's daughter—and at a much, much younger age—and there could be no place for her with them."

Buchan leans forward, laying a confiding hand on Alfieri's arm. "And he planned it all, signore, knowing exactly what would happen . . . intending for it to happen. As lawyer to many wealthy and important people, he had represented the interests of Fauvell's school during the talks that resulted in Fauvell's resignation. And he knew Clara's father too . . . well enough to know that when the family refused to have her back, the father's own guilty conscience—made even more guilty by the lawyer's constant harping upon the father's paternal duty—would be great enough to induce the man to take her in. And once he took her in, signore? If the father grew to love his child, his *only* child— which pity, and proximity, and the child's own sweet nature might be counted upon to accomplish—might he not leave her his fortune? And once the will was finalized . . ."

Alfieri's eyes are full of tears. "Slade was her father," he says.

"Yes, signore." Buchan's hand still rests on the tenor's arm, and his voice is gentle. "And the man who gave her to Fauvell was Thaddeus Chadwick."

Chapter Twenty-eight

He knows first that he is cold, nothing more; opens his eyes in the darkness, uncertain. He blinks, raises his head; his neck is stiff from leaning awkwardly against his shoulder, and his eyes ache. The tall clock in the entrance hall finishes striking; the mantel clock above his head takes up the theme, hammers out four sweet notes, is echoed faintly by four more chimes from the dining room. He pulls himself upright in his chair, leans forward, peers into the grate. The ashes are dead and cold. Slowly he straightens up, runs his hands across his face, looks wearily around him.

The street lamps throw faint bars of watery light across the ceiling. Rising slowly to his feet, Alfieri stumbles to the long windows—hours before, suffocating in his anguish, he had flung the curtains wide—and stares out into the empty, early-morning avenue at the dead leaves and the dust, the tumbling bits of paper that rattle down the gutter in the gusting wind.

"It will be a rumor, signore." He can hear Buchan still in the silence, a gentle Jeremiah, quietly prophesying ruin. "An ugly, anonymous rumor, attributable to no one. Certainly he will not want his name linked with it in any way, nor the name of the young woman living in his house. Some surely will remember that Lucy Pratt was Fauvell's stepdaughter, and that surely will provoke questions—in light of Fauvell's fondness for little girls—that I am confident Mr. Chadwick would much rather not have to answer. No, he will wish to keep her name far removed from any association with the rumor and its origins. As for the timing, I suspect that it will begin to be circulated a few days before opening night, and that by opening night there will be no one in New York who has not heard it . . . except, possibly, your wife.”

Alfieri had nodded slowly, not needing Buchan to tell him how the tale of Clara’s wretchedness would be clutched, devoured, and vomited back whole, passing from mouth to mouth, made immeasurably more satisfying by the fact that she is his wife. She would be fascinating to the world for that reason alone; but the full story of her two years with Fauvell, and especially of his death and her part in it, would make her notorious in her own right; and the fascination with her shame would be magnified a millionfold by his own past: Mario Alfieri, with an unclean wife, repaid in kind at last.

“Can he be stopped?” he had said to Buchan, knowing the answer before he even asked the question.

“How?” Buchan had answered. “How does one ask a man not to do what he will deny ever even thinking of? After all, we do not know for certain that he will do this . . . we never will be certain until the rumor has begun . . . and by then, of course, it will be too late. But even if I went to him and he admitted his intent, what would there be to stop him from carrying it out?”

“Money?” Alfieri had said. “I do not have thirty millions, but I can give him a good amount. I can have my bank transfer the funds from London . . . and then there are the houses to sell, if he would only wait. The house in London alone . . .”

“This is not blackmail, signore,” Buchan had said. “He does not want your money, or your houses. He wants you destroyed, you and your wife together. And what is there to stop him, in any case, from taking your money and, after you have impoverished yourself, spreading the rumor anyway?”

Alfieri had nodded. “Yes, you are right, of course. Still . . . will you call on him for me, Mr. Buchan? Sound him out, as delicately as you can? I will give him everything I have . . . except my wife. It will kill her, you know . . . having this thing known. She has never even told me . . . but you know that too, of course . . . and I have never asked. I swore on our wedding night never to speak of it until she spoke first. She was so frightened, you see, Mr. Buchan. And I would not shame her."

"I will see him for you," Buchan said gently. "But if I am unsuccessful?"

"I will leave New York at once and return with her to Europe. How could I stay here, and subject her to such agony? I will say that her health is growing worse, that she needs a warm climate for the winter. God knows that is the truth."

"The season is planned around you, signore. Regardless of the reason, if you break your contract only six weeks from opening night, Maurice Grau and the Metropolitan Opera will sue you for everything you possess."

"I want my wife alive and well, Mr. Buchan. If I can secure her life and her health by running away tomorrow, I will do it, even if it means losing everything else." He smiles faintly. "What difference does it make, after all, if it goes to Mr. Chadwick or to the Metropolitan Opera, once it is gone? I will take Clara to my family in Florence. They will welcome us even if I am poor, and even if we are disgraced. And perhaps the story will not follow us there."

"You know better, signore. A story like this will follow you wherever you go, even to Florence."

"Then perhaps the noise of it there will be less loud."

But he knows better than that too. He stands now, staring out onto the windy street, looking at the end of his career.

Through the blackness in his mind there is a faint sound, a scrabbling at the drawing-room door that a mouse might make . . . someone trying the handle. He raises his head, scraping his sleeve across his streaming eyes. *"Chi è là?"* he says hoarsely. "Who is it? Who is there?"

No one answers. The rattling continues, soft and insistent, like small fingers at the door. *"Cara?"* he whispers. *"Cara, sei tu?"* And runs across the room, turns the lock with shaking hands, flings the door wide . . .

Only blackness in the hall, made deeper by the paler sky glimmering through the fanlight above the front door; by the feeble lamp, set like a grave candle in the niche at the turn of the stairs. She had come to the door around midnight, pleading to be let in, and he had sent her away without opening the door . . . sent her to bed without him for the first time in their marriage, wanting loneliness in his agony; and she had gone. A sudden terror comes over him now, and he takes the stairs two at a time, needing to see her again, needing to know that she is safe where she belongs, in his bed.

The westering moon, low over the rooftops, slants coldly through the windows. No nightmares disturb the stillness. Clara sleeps the sleep of exhaustion, her face in shadow, one arm curled around her head, the other flung wide, palm up, across his pillow, a sodden handkerchief still crumpled in her hand. Alfieri stands by the bed for a long while, watching the covers rise and fall with her breathing, until he is calm once more, and then he seats himself on the bed beside her, bends and kisses her. She stirs, sighs.

"Mario?" Her voice is hoarse with sleep.

"Sì . . ."

"Did I dream? Did I wake you again?"

"No, amore."

Still more than half-asleep, she lifts her hand to his face. She is so tired, and he . . . he is so pale in the moonlight, his eyes invisible, black hollows beneath his brow . . . so filled with sadness. And now a line of silver slips down his cheek to meet her fingers, and she touches it, and stops, and her eyes open, clear. Once more she touches his cheek, awake now, feeling his grief wet beneath her fingers.

She does not have to ask why, or what it means; she knows that he knows, though not how he has come to know it. Sometime tonight he has learned the truth. For the last thirty-six days, since she had received Lucy's message, she has waited for this moment; has spent lifetimes picturing it in her mind, preparing herself, trying out the million different ways in which she might find out that he knows.

But she has never imagined this: never the deep night, with the moon hanging beyond the window like a silver lamp, and not a word said.

I'm the same, Mario, she wants to say. I'm the same as I was before you knew. Nothing has changed, there's no difference in me. I'm the same. You loved me before you knew. Why should knowing matter?

Why should anything change, just because you know? Whatever you saw in me the day you found me . . . it's still the same, it's all still there, only then you didn't know and now you do, and what difference does it make when I'm just the same, just the same . . .

"Do you remember?" she says, holding her voice together, feeling it unraveling. "Do you remember the summer, and the peaches we bought at the side of the road?"

His eyes never leave her. "Tell me about Rosebank, Clara."

"They were warm from lying in the sun," she says, "and the juice ran down our hands when we ate them, and when you kissed me you tasted of peaches. That was my favorite day, Mario. That was the best day."

He whispers, "Oh, my wife," and shuts his eyes in pain, and she sits up, frantic, reaching for his hand, holding it to her cheek, kissing his fingers.

"But I never meant to hurt you," she says, "never, never, never! If you knew how much I loved you, from the very beginning, from the moment I woke and saw you . . . before, even, just listening to your voice, before I opened my eyes. And I wanted you to like me a little . . . that was why I lied to you. Do you remember? The very first day, when you asked me about my family, and I said that I had none, that they were all dead? That was a lie, Mario . . . I was the dead one. My life was done, but how could I tell you that? You would never come back again, and I loved you already, and I was so lonely . . . so lonely. So I told you a lie, and you came back, and I was glad I had lied . . . I would do it again. But I never meant to hurt you.

"And then—oh, God!—you asked me to marry you, and that was a miracle, a chance to escape, to live again. And the wedding drew closer, and I knew I had to tell you because I couldn't hide it, not once we were married . . . I had to tell you before you found out for yourself, I *wanted* to . . . only I couldn't, because you would leave me, and I wanted more time with you, another day, just one more . . . and then there were no more days. So I waited, on our wedding night . . . I waited for you to ask me . . . and you didn't. You never said a word. And that was when I knew that it was *all* a miracle, all of it . . . truly a miracle, and that there was a God after all, just as you told me, and that because of you He had given me time to earn forgiveness, so that one day, when I finally did tell you, you could take my hand and say: 'Sposa, that was so long ago, and you have made me so happy . . . what you did all those years ago doesn't matter any more.' "

"Cara . . ."

"Because I was going to tell you, Mario . . . someday . . . I swear it. But then I saw Lucy at the station in Philadelphia, and then I knew that there was no miracle, and no forgiveness, and no time for someday to come. Because it *was* Lucy I saw, not the mayor's wife. It was Lucy who sent the box I opened at the opera house. There was a message in it . . . you always knew there was something, didn't you? . . . promising me that very soon she would go to you, and tell you what I should have told you long before . . . "

"Could you not have told me yourself, love? And saved us both the waiting, and the fear?"

She is calm again, still holding his hand between hers. She kisses it, pitying his foolishness. "And looked into your face while I told you? And watched you while you listened?"

He rises quietly from the bed. "Tell me now. It is time, love, for both of us. You must tell me, and I must hear it from you, so both of us can be free of it, once and for all. And I will sit here, where you will not see my face." He chooses a chair beside the window, its back to the room, and waits for her voice behind him, his head silvered by the moonlight.

For a great while there is silence and then, finally, her voice, hardly more than a whisper in the darkness. He closes his eyes, and listens; and so much a part of him has she become, in the four months since he found her, that even in the darkness, even with his back to her and his eyes shut, he can see her face as she begins, at last, to speak . . .

Chapter Twenty-nine

HOME ISN'T A PLACE AT ALL. Did you know that, Mario? I discovered that when I was very small. Home is having someone's face light up when you come into a room. It's knowing that someone waits for you at the end of the day, someone who would be sorry if you never came back. But no one was glad to see me. No one was sorry when I went away.

"I tried hard to be a good child . . . I cleaned my plate, I made my bed. I said the prayers they taught me, knowing that no one was listening. If there was someone who heard, wouldn't He have made them love me? I learned every rule in every house . . . what if I made them angry? Where would I go? And I always thought . . . if I was very, very good . . . better than the others, cleaner, quieter, more obedient . . . someone would want me. Why wouldn't they? There had to be some welcome, somewhere, for one small, quiet child. Someday they would see . . .

"Every July the family had a picnic, all the aunts and uncles and cousins. The July before my eleventh birthday, on the picnic morning, two of my aunts packed up all my things . . . it didn't take long, I hadn't very much. The rest of the family were leaving for the picnic grounds, and I remember one uncle was angry because he had to drive me to the train station, and would be late joining the others. He handed me a ticket, told me to watch the signs and get off at a place called

Rosebank, and then he left, without saying good-bye . . . he was in a great hurry to get back. I didn't know what Rosebank was, or what I was supposed to do once I got there, and he didn't tell me; maybe he thought my aunts had done that, along with the packing.

"The train came and I got on; it was old and slow, and the trip took two hours. I was the only one who got off at Rosebank. The conductor took down my valise and set it on the ground by a little stationhouse, all locked and deserted, then got back on the train without a word, and the train pulled away. There was grass growing between the train tracks, and tall weeds between cracks in the pavement, and the stationhouse windows were all broken out, as if no one ever came there any more. I sat down on my valise to wait. I didn't think anyone would come, not really. They had sent me away, finally. I wasn't surprised. They had sent me to nowhere, to be rid of me . . . to sit and wait for someone who would never come, and I couldn't get back because the station was empty and I didn't know when the next train was due—maybe not for days or weeks—and in any case I had no money to buy a ticket, or even food. And that was when I knew that I would sit there, alone, until I died.

"All I could think of was what one of my cousins had told me . . . that if you die out of doors, the birds come and peck out your eyes, and I pictured someone finding me, maybe in the fall, still sitting on my little traveling bag, with my eyes all pecked away. So I covered my eyes with my hands, and I waited to die."

She draws a long, shuddering sigh. "There wasn't any sound, only the wind in the grass, and once a train whistled, far away. I don't know how long I waited there. Perhaps I fell asleep. Otherwise you would have thought that I would have heard his footsteps on the gravel. But I didn't. I never heard anything at all until a voice said: 'Are you playing hide and seek?' And I opened my eyes and looked up . . . and there was Papa. And he smiled at me. He smiled at me, Mario. At *me*. And then he took my valise in one hand, and my hand with the other, and we drove home together. Home; oh, yes, that was my home . . . *he* was my home, the first home I ever knew . . ."

Only a dome of moon remains, a brilliant arch of silver above the neighboring roof, dwindling swiftly. "You called him that?" Alfieri says, watching it slip away. "You called him 'Papa'?"

"Not at first. That was what Lucy called him; he was married to her mother. After a few days he asked me to call him 'Papa' too, but Lucy wouldn't hear of it, she went wild, screaming that I was nobody, a stranger. She couldn't bear Papa smiling at anyone but her . . . one time she pushed me down the stairs; another time, when she was driving the buggy, she tried to run me down. She said they were accidents but Papa didn't believe her. That's when Papa decided to send her away. He wouldn't let her harm me. And so I didn't call him Papa until she left. I waited."

"Were you afraid when she left?"

"Oh, no. I was afraid before, but not after. There was no reason to be afraid once she was gone."

"You weren't afraid . . . of him?"

"But he loved me. He sent her away to keep me safe. Why would I be afraid of him?"

The last glimmer of moon sinks out of sight. "Wasn't it then that he forced you?"

"Oh." She understands now. "No, Mario."

"Before she left?"

"No."

"When, then?"

"Never." She speaks to the darkness where her husband sits. "He never forced me. We waited until she was gone. He never made me do anything I didn't want to do."

He listens to his wife with the kind of numb agony that is beyond pain. "You loved him."

"Oh, yes. Even though I knew that what we were doing was wrong, and that I was wicked for doing it." He can barely hear her. "For wanting it."

There is blackness beyond the window, so profound that the memory of light seems only a dream. He shuts his eyes and listens to her small voice.

"His wife—Lucy's mother—knew, but she never came out of her

room and Papa wouldn't let me go in there. Lucy knew, but she was thousands of miles away by then; she wrote letters to Papa, begging him to send me away. Tommy found out when he came home for Christmas that first year—Lucy's mother told him—but Tommy didn't believe her. He told Papa what she said, and he was shocked, and said he thought her mind was going.

"And so we were very careful, whenever Tommy came home, never to let him find out. When he was there I would sleep in my own room, and Papa and I would never let ourselves be alone together . . . except sometimes in the deep night, when everyone was fast asleep. And sometimes . . . sometimes in the summer, if Tommy was away, in town— if it was early in the morning, or not too hot a day—we would go to the carriage barn."

"The carriage barn," Alfieri echoes, but she does not hear.

"It was Papa who found the little room. He used to bring Lucy there in the early days, when he was still pretending that he was her mother's husband . . . before Lucy told her the truth, and turned her out of Papa's bedroom so that she could sleep there instead, and then they didn't need the little room any more. With Lucy gone it became our place, Papa's and mine, to use when Tommy was home. Papa hung prisms in the window for me, to make the room prettier. He took them from a chandelier in the parlor that no one ever went into. On a sunny morning it was like lying inside a broken rainbow, with thousands of bits of color everywhere, and sometimes I would keep my eyes open, just to watch the rainbows dance . . ." Alfieri twists in his chair, but she does not see him in the dark and her voice never stops.

"That was what Stafford saw glittering in the box: a prism. I knew what it meant when I saw it. It was Lucy's message to me, telling me that she had found me at last. I thought I had seen her in the crowd at the station. A fat woman, I said, with yellow hair, and you said it was the mayor's wife, and I believed you because I wanted to believe. But when I opened the box, and saw the prism . . . I knew.

"Papa was always afraid of her. He didn't think she was right in her mind—he had a wolf by the ears, he said, and could never let go. He kept her away, the summer after her first year of finishing school. He asked the school to allow her to join a tour of Europe that some of the other students were taking, even though they didn't want her along. Papa wrote and said his wife was very ill, and that it would only disturb her, and frighten Lucy, if Lucy came home.

"And in the second year, instead of sending pocket money to Lucy directly he sent the school a sum for her allowance, instructing the headmistress to give her only a little bit at a time. He was afraid, you see, that she would save it up, and use it to come back, and he didn't want her back until he was ready . . . until he had made plans for me to be sent somewhere safe. He told me that of all the mistakes he had ever made, Lucy had been the worst, and he would pay for it someday.

"But she surprised us. She saved up bits and pieces of her allowance, borrowed some, stole the rest from her schoolmates and teachers, enough to buy her passage home. She left her school the morning after the end of her second year, not waiting for the commencement exercises, and she got to us before the letter from her headmistress did, telling us that she was on her way back.

"Papa and I were doing lessons in the schoolroom when the door opened and Lucy walked in. That was at the beginning of June. And we were never alone again, and we were never happy again, not ever . . . not until the last morning.

"Lucy said she had come to get rid of me, and win Papa back. She said that once I was gone Papa would remember the old days and want her again. He wasn't to touch me ever again, she said, and she swore that if he ever did, even to help me down from a carriage, she would stand up in church the very next Sunday and tell the people what he and I had been doing beneath the same roof as Papa's invalid wife, while Lucy was away at school.

"Papa believed her. He never touched me again. But he kept me with him all the time, every waking hour, because he was afraid of what she would do to me if she had the chance. And that made Lucy wild, because she could never be alone with him, and she made certain that she was always with us, so that Papa and I couldn't be alone either. For a month the three of us were never apart, except when Lucy's mother needed to be fed, or bathed, and then Papa and Lucy would go into her room together. And every night Papa would walk me to my door and wait while I locked myself in, then go to his bedroom and lock himself in too. And Lucy would sleep sitting up in a chair in the doorway of her room—she could see both of our doors from there—to make certain that Papa didn't come to me in the night, and that I didn't go to him.

"We were all nearly mad, by the end of June, from being together all day, every day, every minute. The weather was getting hotter and hotter, and we couldn't escape from one another. Papa had stopped speaking. Some days he hardly even looked at me, from the time we all went down to breakfast together until I locked myself in again at night. I thought he was angry at me, that he had stopped loving me because I was the reason Lucy was tormenting him . . . she would whimper and beg one minute, and the next scream that he had to send me away, that she was sick of the sight of me.

"That was when I became afraid, Mario . . . afraid that she was wearing him down, and that he would give in to her at last, just to stop the sound of her endless whining and screaming. But he wouldn't speak to me and I couldn't ask him if he was angry at me, or had stopped loving me, because Lucy was always there. And I had to know, Mario. I didn't know what I would do if he had stopped, but I had to know."

There is a rustle of the bedclothes as she shifts on the pillows, and a long pause. Alfieri waits in the darkness for her voice. When it comes it is uneven, starting and stopping, as she forces herself to stumble forward in her memory.

"In early July, Tommy came home. He had graduated from college, and after dinner on the night he arrived there was a party in their mother's room, to celebrate. With Tommy there Lucy had to behave more normally, she couldn't crowd us so closely, and Papa excused himself from the party . . . he told Tommy that he would leave the three of them alone to celebrate, since it had been so long since his wife had had both her children with her. I thought Papa meant to speak to me while they were in their mother's room, but Lucy said loudly that they would leave the door open because of the heat, and hoped that the noise wouldn't keep him awake, meaning that she would still

be watching us, even from her mother's room. So Papa just said good-
night to Tommy, then went upstairs and locked himself in his room,
and I did the same.

"It was hot that night, and close—the day had been unbearable—and
there was no air moving. I could barely breathe for the heat. Through
my door I could hear Lucy and Tommy and their mother clearly . . .
they stayed up very late, talking. It was after two when Tommy finally
went to his own room. I heard him say that he had to get to bed because
he needed to go into town early in the morning, and I heard his door
close. A few minutes later I heard Lucy go to her room, but she left
her door open, as she always did. Then it grew very quiet, but still I
couldn't sleep. I could hear the clock downstairs in the parlor. It rang
half past two, then three, then half past three, and there was no sound
anywhere.

"I pulled on my dress and opened my door. I was afraid, but I thought
Lucy couldn't make much of a scene with Tommy in the house—she
wouldn't want Tommy to know the truth about her and Papa—and I
took my pitcher with me so that if she saw me I could say I was going
for some water, that I had used up what I had because of the heat.

"Her door was open but she wasn't in the chair in the doorway, I
couldn't see her at all in the dark. I stepped into the passageway, and
I thought she was awake and had seen me, because I heard her say
something, and I froze there with the pitcher in my hand, waiting and
listening, and then she sighed, said something else, and the springs
squeaked as she turned over . . . she was asleep on her bed. Then I shut
my door behind me and went to Papa's door and scratched on it—so
lightly that I could hardly hear it. But he heard; he hadn't been able to
sleep, either. He opened his door and pulled me inside and then I was
in his arms, and I didn't need to ask if he still loved me . . ."

Alfieri, hearing the little ecstatic laugh, buries his face in his hands.

"It had been so long, a whole month of being together every minute
of every day but not being able to touch, and now we couldn't have
stopped, not if Lucy had broken down the door, but still we were careful
and quiet; we never made a sound. And afterward he held me close and
whispered, with his mouth against my ear, that he had made up his

mind: he was leaving Rosebank and taking me away with him. He hadn't gone before, he said, because there was Lucy's mother to care for, and he felt responsible, but now Lucy was home, and Tommy, too, and the farm was rightfully Tommy's.

"Papa had traveled a great deal as a young man, had collected hundreds of rare and valuable things from all over the world. He had brought them with him from New York, they were there, in the house . . . he would leave them, he said, and Lucy and Tommy could sell them off and keep the money, be comfortable forever. Papa had a little saved besides, just enough to get us to Paris. He could teach in Paris, no one knew him there, I would be his daughter and we would live together always, and be happy . . .

"He was still whispering about Paris when we heard noises in the house. It was Tommy, getting ready to go to town. It had begun to grow light, but we hadn't noticed how late it was getting, and I had to get back to my room before Lucy woke, so I pulled on my dress and waited for Tommy to leave. We heard his door open, heard him go down the stairs, and after a while the sound of the horse as he rode away, and then it was time for me to go.

"But I didn't want to leave him, not yet, not after so long without him, and when Tommy was riding away I remembered where Papa and I had gone the summer before, on mornings when Tommy would go into town. And that was when I said it . . . 'Papa, take me to the carriage barn.' I knew we didn't need to, and it had been safer last year: Tommy didn't know about the room and wouldn't think to go there, but Lucy knew and she was here now, and dangerous.

"But I wanted her to know that Papa still loved me. I wanted to laugh in her face and let her know that I had won after all, that Papa didn't want her, he wanted me, and that soon he would be taking me far away, to live with him forever. I said that Lucy had gone to bed late and she'd probably sleep late, and that if we left now we could finish and be back by the time she woke. I begged him . . . oh, God, I begged him . . . And he laughed, and said wouldn't it be just what she deserved if we did go. He was angry for all the misery she'd put us through . . . he said that, yes, we could go, and be quick, and come back while she was still sleeping, and she would never know until we told her, and he laughed again. We would tell her about it later in the day, he said, and then see how ready she would be to stand up in church and bring scandal on the family, now that her brother, the little minister, was back home . . ."

Alfieri hears her sit up abruptly. She is speaking quickly now, her words jerky and uneven, beyond her power to stop them.

"There was another way out of Papa's room . . . a door that opened onto a sleeping porch, and then stairs from the porch to the backyard. The sky was still dark in the west, and the morning star was shining through the trees . . . after the heat inside, the air was cool and sweet. We held hands on the way, talking about Paris and how lucky it was that I had grown used to calling him Papa, because I would really be his daughter now . . . we talked about what our name should be . . . he said Cenci would be a good choice, and then he laughed, I don't know why . . . but I didn't care what our name would be, I only knew that he loved me, and that soon we would be free."

Beyond the window the void is taking shape once more, the darkness parting. There are houses now, gray and ghostly, where a moment ago there had been nothing, pale against the black sky.

"We never meant to stay there long. Just once, that was all, and then we would go back, and laugh at Lucy later. But it was so cool in the barn, and we were so happy, and so tired afterward, and we fell asleep . . ."

In the gray light Alfieri can see her rocking back and forth in the bed, back and forth, her arms wrapped about herself. "It was the screaming that woke us . . . Lucy, outside, under the window, screaming: 'Papa! Papa! I know what you're doing! Filthy! Don't you dare!' We could hear Tommy too, farther away, running, coming closer. He was screaming too, screaming: 'Lucy, don't! For God's sake, don't!' " Clara's voice has begun to shake.

"It was hot in the room . . . we had slept a long time, the sun was high. Papa got to his feet, looked out the window, and said, 'My God, we're finished,' but I didn't know what he had seen. I looked out the window too . . . I saw Tommy running past, turning the corner for the stairs, still screaming, but there were feet already pounding up the stairs, making the floor shake, and the rainbows were jumping all over the walls . . . there was no time for anything, no place to go . . . Papa took me in his arms, we looked at the door . . ."

She holds herself, rocking back and forth in the growing light. "It burst open and the gun swung up, Papa threw me, there was a flash and a crash—"

She tries to go on, but cannot, and Alfieri is beside her now on the bed, holding her, straining her to him, trying, six years and an eternity too late, to stop the horror.

"Enough," he says, "enough, my God, enough," but there is more and it must be said now, for the first and last time, must be told to pay for what she has done, and the lives she has taken.

"There was smoke in the air, the gun swung up again, and then Tommy was trying to pull it away from her, from Lucy, she was holding the gun . . . but she was bigger, they pulled back and forth, and Papa was in a heap on the floor, and blood was everywhere. I tried to drag him away so they couldn't hurt him any more, and he fell back on me, and I saw him . . . I saw him . . . what was left . . ."—she is sobbing now, great, racking sobs—"I saw . . . and Lucy kept shrieking at Tommy—'Let go! Let go! Let go!'—and then Tommy pulled back hard, and there was another crash . . ."

He does not know how long he rocks her, silently at first, then, as she quiets, singing to her, almost inaudibly as she lies against his breast, a lullaby about the infant Jesus in His blessed mother's arms; rocking and singing until she is still at last. He lays her down, then; she lies with her eyes closed, tears leaking from the corners, slipping into her hair.

"He shouldn't have pushed me away, Mario. He should have held me. I should have died with him."

"Oh, no, my little dear. He loved you. He wanted you to live." His fingers brush her tears. "He wanted you to go on, even if he could not be with you."

"I didn't want to go on. Not without him."

"I know. Love can be very cruel."

She looks up at him, her eyes pleading. "Don't hate him, Mario. Please don't hate him."

He should; he had. Last evening, a hundred years ago, he had hated Edward Fauvell with his whole soul. But in the morning light he cannot find it in him to hate a man who, in the last instant of his own life, had saved the life of the child he loved.

"He never hurt you, *cara?*"

"No, Mario. Never."

"Then why would I hate him? It was his love that gave you to me."

He watches for a while as she sleeps, her hand clutching his, listening to the sounds of the wakening house . . . Margaret's quiet footsteps, Gennarino's stealthy tread, water running in the pipes. Alas for him and his wife: nineteen hundred years after Christ stooped and wrote in the dust, the world will not be kind to the memory of Edward Fauvell, or to the child who had loved him . . . who loves him still. Certain at last that his movement will not wake her, he rises from the bed and passes into the next room, the sitting room he had so carefully furnished to resemble the room at her guardian's—no, her father's—house.

Going to the desk in the corner, he seats himself, pulls out a sheet of paper, dips pen in ink. Four months ago, in the same large, fluid hand, he had written to Thaddeus Chadwick and begun his and Clara's ruin. Now he begins the letter that will conclude it.

My dear Mr. Grau—

I write this with the most profound regret, knowing only too well how it will throw into disarray everything that you, and so many others, have planned for the coming opera season . . .

BOOK III

Chadwick

Chapter Thirty

THE CHIMES OF TRINITY CHURCH ring out six o'clock as the portly
gentleman steps from his office onto the Broadway pavement. There is
a taste of cold rain in the air and the wind blows chill this evening,
more like mid-November than early October. The man pauses to settle
his hat more firmly on his head, button his coat, work his gloves onto
his thick fingers; a cabby calls to him from the curb, sensing a fare, but
the man waves him away and turns uptown, wishing to walk tonight,
despite the inclement weather. He is in the grip of the restiveness that
comes upon him every autumn, after the heavy indolence of summer:
a feeling of urgency, as of great things waiting to happen just ahead,
that must be walked off. Clutching his hat's brim, he joins the army of
black-hatted, black-coated men trudging up Broadway, each with his
right arm holding on to his hat at exactly the same angle, an army in
mufti saluting the wind.

He feels positively buoyant. In the autumn his blood seems to quicken
and his body seems lighter, no longer burdened by the heat and its own
oleaginous heft; and while his home is in Washington Square—far
enough uptown for the village of Greenwich to have served, in the bad
old days, as a refuge from the smallpox and yellow fevers that had
periodically swept New York—the city has long since swallowed up the
little hamlet and its surrounding farms, and on paved and lighted streets

the way from here to there is shorter than it ever was on cow tracks and country lanes.

In any event he wishes to walk tonight, for many reasons, not the least of which is that it will give him time to decide how to break the news to his houseguest . . . a charming young woman, to be sure, but of limited interest and intellect, albeit a mighty constancy of purpose: despite the opportunity she has been given to meet the best people, and form ties which might ensure her future happiness, her single thought still is to know when it is that she will be permitted to do what she has come to New York to do.

Ah, Lucy, doomed to disappointment yet again. It seems, now, that she is to be denied her bliss forever. Mario Alfieri already knows about his wife's dirty past. His lawyer had come to call today, sounding out, with utmost delicacy, the price of silence.

Chadwick smiles into the wind. Priapus, it seems, is wildly in love . . . much too much in love to toss aside the damaged goods he has married and cut his losses, which would be the intelligent thing to do. Of course, he—Chadwick—is not Alfieri's lawyer; if he were, he would make it his business to see that his client did the reasonable thing, just as he had done with Henry Slade and his Jew doxy, twenty years ago . . . not that Alfieri's ridding himself of the girl would save him now. It is too late for that. The Italian must be taught a lesson. Chadwick would have him realize the consequences of having eloped with her—the fool who buys a pig in a poke, after all, must learn to live with the stink he finds once the wrappings are off.

Chadwick had not bothered to ask how the tenor had learned the truth. Despite Lucy's conviction that she would never have the courage, Clara had undoubtedly confessed her misdeeds, either at her husband's urging or the prickings of her own guilty conscience. Chadwick shrugs and keeps on walking. That Alfieri has found out so quickly, and entirely without the benefit of Lucy's ardently awaited denunciation, is a surprise, but it makes no difference at all. It is merely a small, unexpected change in a plan that is still, so far as he can see, having tested all its seams, perfectly sound; and is, if anything, improved. Instead of learning the ugly truth about his bride just before opening night, Alfieri has learned it earlier . . . and so has even more time to feel it.

His end, though, will be precisely the same, and precisely as inevitable as before. There is justice in the world after all, even though men must make it for themselves.

Chadwick is pleased with the way the discussion had gone. He had been noncommittal with the Italian's lawyer. Yes, he has long known of the murder and suicide of which Clara had been the cause . . . how could he not? Mr. Henry Slade was a trustee of the home for delinquent girls to which Clara's family had sent her following the tragedy . . . it was one of Mr. Slade's principal philanthropies. Mr. Slade had been there the day she was brought in—purely by chance, of course—and had watched her being admitted. He had never laid eyes on her before. Philanthropist that he was, Mr. Slade had been deeply moved by the girl's tender age, and the terrible circumstances of her case . . . and when ultimately he decided to make her his ward it was he—Chadwick—who had effected her discharge from the home and brought her to Slade's mansion in Gramercy Park.

But Chadwick could make Buchan no promise of secrecy. Could he justly deny what had happened in Rosebank, if the ugly truth did become known? Surely a fellow attorney would not expect him to dissemble? And as for keeping Lucy Pratt quiet . . . certainly, she is under his roof; but is he his cousin's keeper? Should she be foolish enough to compromise her own reputation, and that of her family, could Chadwick be held responsible? Lucy is, after all, well beyond the age of majority, and answerable for her own actions . . . except that Chadwick would expect her to realize that he could have nothing further to do with her, should the scandal become public knowledge.

"But what makes you suspect, even for a moment, that she—or anyone—would wish to disclose such a story?" Chadwick had asked. "Surely Miss Pratt would not wish to air such stained linen in public, particularly as her family is involved?"

"Perhaps I am being overly prudent," Buchan had replied, "but I must consider my client's welfare . . . and any person, man or woman, who feels gravely ill-used may be less than sensible, if he wishes to harm the one who has harmed him."

The two men had gazed at each other, each perfectly aware of what the other's words meant, and that they understood each other perfectly.

"Do you think . . ." Buchan had asked, with a delicacy that Chadwick had admired, one professional to another. ". . . do you think that Miss Pratt might be persuaded to remain silent? With a . . . well, let us say a gift . . . to help convince her?"

"I would not presume to speak for her, of course," Chadwick had replied, enjoying himself immensely, "but what sort of gift might you consider a proper inducement?"

Buchan, too, had demurred. "That remains to be seen. My client, as you know, is a very wealthy man. He is, of course, not nearly so wealthy as was Mr. Slade—very few men are—but he is prepared to be most generous for an assurance of discretion on Miss Pratt's part."

"Please allow me to take your suggestion under advisement, Mr. Buchan." Chadwick had risen then, ending the meeting. "You must give me some time to consider what you have said, and to think, too, how I might best introduce such a delicate topic to Miss Pratt. Knowing what you do of the tragic episode in Rosebank, I am certain you can appreciate just how very sensitive she is to any mention of your client's wife. I will need to tread very carefully, and it may take me some time. Shall we meet again, say . . . a week from today?"

Which will bring them almost to the middle of October. Time, of course, is on his—Chadwick's—side, and it is most unfortunate that he will be unable, finally—despite his very best efforts—to elicit a promise of silence from Lucy, either now or in the future. But it will be most amusing to hear, in a week's time, just how much the tenor is prepared to pay for the safety he will never attain.

It is the girl's fault, of course; hers and no one else's. Alfieri will come to see that soon. If not for her, he might have gone on singing forever. How like her mother she is, only less so, with not even the trifling musical gifts that had so attracted Henry Slade. No, the only talent Clara shares with her mother lies between her legs, a talent she had no doubt demonstrated to Alfieri the very first time they met. What else could have snared such a man so swiftly and so completely?

Her mother had been the same . . . so eager to please men, so ready to raise her skirts . . . so swift to smell money. She had fluttered and cooed at Henry from the moment they met, looking up at him from under her lashes, her pretty breasts heaving—Chadwick had been there, he had watched her—and Henry, the idiot, the whoremonger, old enough to be her father, had fallen.

She had been certain he would marry her, and Henry had been besotted enough to do it. What did he care that no one would receive her, that they would live like lepers, shunned by the world, trapped within the walls of the Gramercy Park house? They would have each other, Henry had argued, they would travel; he had done well during the war, dealing in shoddy and speculation, and even better in the years since the war, in mines and railroads and shipping. There was money enough to keep them and their children comfortable for many lifetimes . . .

But who had made the money for him? Who had thought for him, worked his deals, fashioned his alliances, butchered his enemies? Had Henry really believed that he—Chadwick—would acquiesce to the marriage? That he would sit quietly by and allow the fortune he had built to be thrown away on a Jew harlot with a bastard in her belly?

That fortune was a lifetime's labor, his labor. He had been twenty-one when he met Henry: Thaddeus Chadwick, from one of the oldest families in New York, with a long pedigree—good English and Knickerbocker blood—and nothing else. His mother had brought a solid fortune to her marriage; by the time Chadwick was ten it was gone. He can remember clearly the shot from the back garden, and his mother's screams. That suicide was the one entirely successful act of his father's worthless life, made perfect by his choice of the outhouse as the place to pull the trigger.

But his mother's people would not permit their own to starve—no, they had succored them . . . with the proverbial widow's mite, forcing his mother to keep up appearances for the family's sake while condemning her and her son to a poverty genteel in name only—and the pride that Chadwick had swallowed over the years had filled his belly far more than the meals of potatoes and butcher's scraps and fried bread that his mother became adept at making ever did. She had died when he was sixteen, and he had gagged down the last of his self-respect applying to her brother for assistance into Columbia College . . . assistance that was only granted when he agreed to take a clerk's position in the office of his uncle's lawyer, as a way of repaying the loan—with interest—while he pursued his studies.

But there is a nourishment in swallowed pride that had served him well: he had graduated summa cum laude in three years, despite working fifty hours a week for his employer, and a year later he had paid off his loan and turned his back on his mother's relations. He has not spoken to a single one of them in forty-three years . . .

His thoughts are interrupted briefly by the crush at the Fulton Street crossing. A draper's wagon has lost a wheel and tipped over into the gutter, spilling huge bolts of cloth onto the wet cobblestones, and the normally impassable intersection is now a jumbled, brawling tangle of streetcars, carriages and drays, all knotted together in an impenetrable mass of rearing horses and cursing, shouting, pushing men. The draper's driver, hatless in the rain, stands staring at the fouled and sodden bolts of cloth, shrieking and pounding his fist against his crippled wagon. Chadwick shoves his way through, indifferent to the commotion.

He had gone to Europe after paying off his loan, he and one of his professors, and the professor's homely daughter, for the Grand Tour. He tries, but he cannot recall the name of the professor, or of the homely daughter, and this hiatus in his memory irritates him vaguely, although there is no reason he should remember after all this time; he has not thought of either of them, until this minute, for a full thirty years and more. He was to have married the young woman—she had been twenty-five, four years older than he—in exchange for her father's patronage and the guarantee of a berth in one of the city's better law firms . . . but three months into their trip, in Venice, Henry Slade had happened along, and Chadwick had wasted no time in quitting his fiancée and her father for a far more alluring opportunity.

He had met Henry in an opulent *postribolo* on the Grand Canal. Henry, traveling with friends, had been alone that night, trying his luck at the gaming tables while his companions were upstairs, enjoying the house's horizontal diversions. Chadwick had watched him drop a small fortune at the roulette wheel, shrug, and drop another on a single hand of cards; he had then introduced himself, American to American, offered to buy Henry a drink, and by the time he helped his sodden compatriot stagger out into a gray Venetian dawn, five hours later, Chadwick had allowed himself to be hired to manage Henry's purse, and prevent more losses like that evening's.

He had returned immediately to his hotel, to commence packing and to announce his defection to the professor and his daughter over breakfast. He may not remember their names, but the desperation on the daughter's face, as he readied himself to go off with Henry Slade and his friends, has stayed with him through the years . . . tears had done nothing to improve her looks. Chadwick smiles inwardly. The state of matrimony she so craved had done nothing for her either. A mutual acquaintance, met by chance in Paris some five years later, had informed him that her father had succeeded at last in securing another of his students for her, and so she had achieved her dream of marriage after all . . . only to die giving birth to a stillborn son ten months after her wedding.

The moral of which is that God has a mordant wit—if one believes in God. And if one does not—as he does not, having seen too many examples in his life of the black void at the heart of the universe—then the moral is that "he travels farthest who travels alone."

Encumbrances kill. One has only to look around. There is the nameless professor's nameless daughter, so eager for encumbrances, dead at twenty-eight, and her child with her.

And he can name so many more. Edward Fauvell, for one, that man of excellent education and distinguished career, who might have used his exile in Rosebank to forge another venture and so risen, Phoenix-like, from the ashes of the first; he had been resourceful enough to begin again. But Fauvell would have his little encumbrances, and the last had been his undoing. Well, she was very like her mother; Chadwick would lay odds that in all the headmaster's years of educating little girls in his own special field of study, he had never found a pupil with more natural ability than Clara. Chadwick's lips twitch, thinking of Fauvell with his brains splattered against a dirty wall and a cloud of flies for a shroud. An abrupt ending, true, but at least he had died satisfied.

And Henry Slade. Henry would have settled down happily with *his* encumbrance, had not Chadwick convinced him of the wretchedness and disrepute such a liaison would inevitably bring. Marriage was utterly inconceivable. But even to set her up as his mistress in some out-of-the-way place to bring up her brat—and surely there would soon be more, for hadn't she proved disgustingly fecund?—would be to invite disaster. There was her hook-nosed family to consider. They could not be kept in ignorance of her whereabouts forever, and once they had found her what would there be to prevent them from descending upon Henry, palms outstretched, seeking compensation for a daughter's ruin?

Worse, what would there be to prevent them, Shylocks that all their kind were, from using their connection with him, however illicit and unofficial, to attempt to obtain loans from reputable bankers, men Henry knew; men whose homes he frequented, whose tables he dined at; men whose wives and daughters set the tone of society?

And how long, then, before Henry was cut from that society, before the name Slade was stricken from the lips of the best people . . . Slade, a name that had resounded in New York since colonial days: an ancestor of Henry's had sat on the council of the royal governor of New York at the time of George the Second. For the sake of a girl who had succumbed to him so quickly that it must be clear, even to him, that her only interest had been to get her hands into his pockets, could Henry risk losing such a name, such a standing in society?

It seems that he could not. Henry had left immediately for a destination that Chadwick had insisted upon not knowing, and he—Chadwick—had been left to call on Henry's harlot, to break the news of her lover's change of heart and the affair's sudden end. And he had been more than fair about it. She had gone to Henry with nothing but the clothes she wore, and he had sent her back that same afternoon in the very same condition—always excepting her swollen belly—but with the promise of enough money each month, as the price of silence, to keep her entire family in comfort . . . and the further promise, which he knew she well believed, that should any of her family ever threaten or disturb Henry, for any reason whatever, he would stop her payments, then sit back and enjoy the spectacle as her family threw her onto the streets.

And what, he had wondered to her, would happen to her then? Of course she might use her looks and her voice—the looks and voice that had almost made her fortune—to support herself and her baby, singing on Bowery corners and in dockside saloons . . . for a little while. But she would soon find that a few drinks, some boozy kisses, and a hand up her petticoats would be needed as well: after all, sailors and laborers were no different from millionaires, except that they rarely bathed and there were so many more of them. Her countless new patrons might itch and stink, but, like Henry, they would require much, much more for their patronage than just some pretty tunes. They would want value for their hard-earned pay.

How long would it be, then, before she stopped bothering to sing at all? She could earn far more money in the good, old-fashioned way that she had already mastered . . . on her back. He gave her six months before she was lifting her skirts in dark alleys to buy enough gin to keep out the cold, or standing with her legs spread and her back braced against a dockside wall to earn the price of a meal.

Of course there was one other alternative for her, beyond either the slime of the streets or being buried alive in her father's house; and he had offered it to her directly, certain that she could not refuse. She was Henry's leavings and a Jew besides, but even big with Henry's bastard she was a pretty thing . . .

The rain is slanting down heavily, now, and the army of northward-marching men is smaller, many having turned off to their homes, others clambering aboard already packed streetcars, or hailing infrequent cabs, to escape the wet. Chadwick walks on, rain whipping beneath the brim of his hat, spattering his spectacles.

She had spit in his face, in his eyes. It had hung on his spectacles, blinding him, and he had had to take them off, fumbling for his handkerchief to mop his brow and cheeks; and while he wiped her contempt from his face she had turned her back upon him and walked from her lover's mansion to the carriage that waited at the curb to carry her back to her family, and to misery. She had not looked at him once during the drive, never uttered another word in his hearing. She even ignored the hand he had offered to help her down at their destination and, overbalanced by her ungainly belly, stumbled and nearly fell. But she had righted herself, and swept into the house, not like a whore, but a duchess, and the door crashed shut behind her, walling her in.

He did not forget. He would not let himself forget. He remembers still, twenty years later. He is very like Lucy Pratt in that way: they are, both of them, exquisite haters, and patient in their vengeance; and the object of that vengeance makes no difference, so long as someone suffers. The woman had been eight years gone, after all, when he gave her little daughter to Fauvell for his pleasure . . . and paid her back, at last, for her arrogance.

And when Fauvell ended as he did, Chadwick had seen at once where his death might lead . . . carpe diem has ever been his credo. The mother had defied him, but if he was clever the daughter could be his instead, and Henry's fortune with her; and thus he—Chadwick—would have victory over both of them in the end. Why not? He held every thread in his hand, like a master puppeteer. Who was there to stop him, after all?

The opera house in Philadelphia suddenly rises in his memory: the stomping, shrieking frenzy of the great, roaring crowd and the lone figure standing onstage before them, smiling while hurled bouquets shower down to fall harmless around his feet, as if nothing that the world contains could harm him . . . and a spasm of rage surges through Chadwick, so strong that he feels it rising in his throat and beating like a pulse in his head. He stops for a moment, steadying himself against a lamppost, raising his face to the sky until the slap of the cold air and the rain have cooled him again, and then he walks on.

At the bottom of his steps he glances up . . . Lucy's silhouette bulks large in the parlor window, blotting out much of the light behind her. It is time to let slip his hound; no one is invincible. Raising his hand in greeting, he slowly mounts the stairs.

Chapter Thirty-one

It is Saturday, October the sixth, and Union Square at noon is an island of golden trees beneath a sky of piercing blue. Two well-dressed men share a bench beneath the leaves, attracting no more than a moment's glance from the passing lunchtime throngs, even though what they discuss seems fraught with sadness: the young, fair one listens to his older, dark companion with his head bowed and his eyes closed, as if in pain. Not once during the narrative does the speaker look into the young man's face; and even after his flow of words has finally halted, the two men merely sit side by side in silence, each lost in his own thoughts. After a while the speaker begins again.

"You have been the best of friends to me, Stafford, and I wanted you, above all, to know the truth. I have seen Buchan already this morning. He went to Chadwick yesterday, pretending that it was Lucy Pratt who needed to be silenced. He offered money, and Chadwick said that he would consult with Lucy and give his answer in a week; but Daniel and I knew, even before they spoke, that there is no chance. Our position is indefensible, and together Daniel and I have worked out a plan—not a good plan, I am afraid, but the only one possible—and I would have you understand why I do what I am going to do.

"And then, too, I wanted to warn you that those close to me will suffer once Clara's story is known—you can see that, of course—which is why I asked you to meet me here, where no one bothers to notice us, rather than at your club or your father's house. You may wish to begin to distance yourself from me. I would understand if you did."

Dyckman raises his head. "Would you? I would not, Mario. If I can help you in any way—in *any* way—you need only ask."

Alfieri's face softens into the merest smile. "*Amico,* I have had my share of grief of late. But knowing you has made it easier to bear."

As always, Stafford blushes, but his troubled eyes quickly return to his friend. Had he heard from anyone else the story that Mario has just told him, Stafford would have struck him and called him a filthy liar. But Mario has said it, and therefore it must be true.

There are two images in Dyckman's mind now, jarring, irreconcilable: Clara as he knows her, with her shy smile and happy laugh, her head on Mario's shoulder and his arm about her; and the child she once had been, lying with her dead lover in a room with bloody walls—dear God, how can Mario bear to know it?—and Dyckman recoils, sick, frightened that he will never be able to look at her again without seeing that horror . . . and if he, who loves them both, cannot free himself of the sight, what will the rest of the world do?

It will crucify them, husband and wife.

"Mario, can't you fight this thing? Stop it from becoming known?"

"How?"

"I don't know . . . there must be some way."

"Must there? Tell me, Stafford, and I will do it. Believe me, we have tried to find a way, Buchan and I. But aside from killing Chadwick outright—which, I freely admit, has been much on my mind—how can he be stopped?"

The young man gropes about for some solution, finds none, nods miserably.

"Then what is your plan?"

Alfieri looks at him calmly. "To run away."

"No!"

"It is all arranged, Stafford, the very best we can do. Clara and I will be on the *Columbia* when she sails on the fifteenth, bound for England. Daniel's clerks are seeing to every detail of the journey for us; Daniel is himself preparing the legal deterrents to buy us more time. A few days in London to transact some final business, then home, to Florence. I will not leave there again."

Dyckman stares at him, saying nothing. Alfieri answers his silence.

"Believe me, there is no other way. I have already written my resignation to Mr. Grau, telling him that Clara's health is too fragile to bear the winter in New York, and that numerous doctors have advised me that I must take her to a warm climate or risk her life. I will not hand it to him until the very last moment, to be certain that he has not the time to take legal action to stop me. During the coming week I will attend rehearsals as if nothing is wrong. And on Monday, October the fifteenth, just before we sail, I will call on Mr. Grau and deliver the letter into his hands. And that will be the end."

Dyckman finds his voice at last. "The end, *sì*. The end of everything."

"You think I do wrong?" Alfieri looks at him, pitying the young man's anguish. "Stafford, if I were alone . . . if what will become known were only about me . . . I would brazen it out and never care, I would let Chadwick do his worst. But my wife, Stafford . . . she has suffered so much already, in one young life. To stay means that she must hear people who are not fit even to touch her shoes calling her the vilest thing a woman can be called. It will not matter how hard I try to shield her . . . such filth has a way of making itself known: a careless word, an unsigned letter . . . a page from a scandal sheet, used to wrap fish, for God's sake.

"Could you do that to someone you love? Keep her here, to learn that her agony has become a filthy joke for all the world to share? Could you bear the shame in her eyes? No. Nor can I. And so we must leave. No opera season in the world is worth such pain." Again that faint smile. "Not even New York's opera season."

"And all the other seasons yet to be? Mario, your career—"

"Is finished." He lays a hand on his friend's arm. "It is over, Stafford, done. If my instructions reach my father in time, and if he can act quickly enough, most of what I now own will soon be no longer mine, but be either divided among my brothers and sisters, or sold and the proceeds distributed among them. If not, we will all be poorer. Either way, I must learn to live on charity." He rises to his feet. "And either way, Chadwick has won."

Dyckman rises with him. "Does Clara know any of this?"

"No! And she will not, I forbid it! Neither the true reason for our departure, nor its consequences to me!" He pauses, lowering his voice. "I will tell her what I will tell Mr. Grau . . . that we go to Italy for her health. And if she asks about my obligations here, I will swear to her that there is no need to worry, because Maurice Grau has so many able tenors, and all of them so eager to take my place, that not a single performance will need to be canceled." He smiles a last, wry smile. "And that, as you know, will be the truth."

Dyckman says: "But none of them will be Alfieri."

The tenor looks at him fondly. "You were always my most devoted believer, Stafford. But you must not be too hard on the rest . . . they, too, must have their chance. Even Alfieri was not always Alfieri."

He might have expected Dyckman to comfort him, but it seems always this way: the older comforting the young, who have not yet learned that what *should be* fails to become what *is* with heartbreaking frequency, and that right does not always triumph in the end.

"Don't be sad," he says. "It had to end sometime. I have had for twenty years what most men only dream of. God knows what He is about, Stafford . . . and it is best to take one's leave while the crowds are still cheering."

He reaches home by one o'clock, climbs the stairs to his front door feeling vastly at peace. He is exhausted, but not yet to the point of collapse. The immense strength, the energy that has always been his: neither has deserted him yet, thank God. He has needed every ounce of them this last month; he needs them still. But the worst, surely, is over now. Fear of his response upon learning the truth, fear of the Pratt woman and her lust for revenge . . . which had been the greater agony for Clara? Well, neither matters any more. She has told him her story and knows, now, that it makes no difference to him, to his love for her. She has laid down the cross of her past, once and for all. And once aboard ship, with Lucy Pratt and the threat of her vengeance dwindling with every mile, Clara can begin to heal at last. Tomorrow the servants will bring up from the cellar the trunks they had emptied only two days ago, and begin packing once again: the week remaining before they sail is ample time to put all in readiness.

As for the rest? He will not miss New York; he has spent so little time in the city—hardly more than a month, in all—that he has formed no very great affection for it, other than as the place in which he found his wife. But he will miss this house, with its simple, married air, its modest feel of other men's reality: of breakfast and the morning paper, and one's wife across the table, pouring coffee; of coming home to dinner at the end of the day, and quiet talk, once the children are asleep, of family news and household expenses, and the prospects for promotion at the firm . . .

It is a life he has never known, will never know. But the brief glimpse he has formed of it here has changed forever the way he thinks of ordinary men and their everyday lives.

And outside of this he has no regrets, none at all. He smiles to himself as he reaches for his keys: much of the world will either think him mad for that lack, or simply refuse to believe it. Many will pity him—chained to the woman who has ruined him—and many more will gloat outright. But only a handful will care to know the truth, or understand what he had long dreamed of, and finally found.

His keys jingle in the lock. Dazzled by the autumn brilliance, he steps blindly into the dim entrance hall, and Gennarino appears as if by magic, to take his hat, gloves, coat. *Sì,* the little signora is awake; she arose around eleven. *Sì,* she has taken her breakfast, although, as usual, she ate almost nothing . . . she was sick again, upon rising, then once more an hour later, after sipping some tea. Now? Now she is taking the sun at the back of the house, in that pocket handkerchief that the people of this city refer to, laughably, as a garden . . .

The small, square patch of grass is enclosed by a high wooden palisade, painted a dark green, which provides a modicum of privacy from eyes in the surrounding houses, and the trellises that line it are thick with late roses, pink and white. A tiny arbor stands in one corner, shaded by still more climbing roses and just big enough to contain a seat for

two. Clara sits in it now, well wrapped against the chill in the October
air, a thick woolen shawl around her shoulders, a lap robe covering the
rest, and a large straw bonnet held in place by a scarf tied under her
chin. Her eyes are shut and her face turned, in a triumph of hope over
reason, to the sun whose rays—doubly checked by hat and leafy can-
opy—never even come near.

Margaret, arranging the shawl more closely around her mistress, steps
back to examine her handiwork, but straightens up as Alfieri emerges
from the house, his finger to his lips. The maid smiles and curtsies, and
crossing paths with her master, vanishes silently inside, leaving the tenor
to draw near and study his wife's small, upturned face in the afternoon
light.

It has changed, somehow, subtly but certainly; and he stares, eyes narrowed, unable for several moments to determine what is different . . .
and then he realizes, with a pang, that she has grown up; that he is
looking, now, at a young woman: ill and deathly tired, but a young
woman nevertheless, her skin almost transparent and stretched tightly
across the bones, her grief visible still in the bruised, swollen lids of her
closed eyes and the thin line of her pretty lips, set tight as if she is
holding back still more grief.

Dear God, she looks so fragile, as if a breath might . . . He touches
her cheek with the back of his fingers; she stiffens, startled, and opens
her eyes.

"I expected you would be still asleep," he says, taking her hands in
his. "If I thought you would wake so soon, *madonna,* I would have
returned earlier. I should have been with you."

She kisses his hands, holds them against her cheek. "You are always
with me," she says, "even when you're not here."

He unties her ridiculous hat and flings it onto the grass so that, seating
himself beside her, he can draw her close and rest her head against his
shoulder.

"Dear love," he says, "I have much to tell you."

"I have much to tell you too," she answers.

"Ah," he says. "But my news is something so big . . . a great change
in our lives."

"Mine too," she says. "Mario, let me tell first."

Something about her voice troubles him . . . he cannot see her face, only the top of her head. He kisses it. "Yes, of course," he says. "If you wish."

But she does not begin at once. She has been trying, since she woke, to find the words, but they will not come. It is strange, but now, when she should need to cry, there are no tears lurking behind her eyes for the first time in years. She has done with tears . . . but the words . . . the words will not come.

Mario waits. This is not the terrified hesitancy of her confession, the reluctance to speak the unspeakable; this is a different silence. He is suddenly afraid.

"Love," he says. "What is it?"

Not finding the right words, she says it simply, plainly, raising her eyes to his. "I've been thinking, since yesterday, about what happened, and what I've allowed to happen since, and what I must do. I betrayed you, I married you without telling you the truth. And there is only one way for me to make amends. I have to leave you."

There is a strange noise in his head, and he wonders if he has suddenly gone deaf, if he has heard her right.

"Why?" he says stupidly, half-surprised that he can hear his own words. "Why?"

"Because I love you," she says. "Better than all the world. So much better than myself. I would die for you."

He hears but cannot comprehend; he must have lost his reason somewhere between the front door and the garden. "And because you love me you would leave me?"

"Not would. Must. And not only for atonement, there are other reasons. I will never bring you anything but disgrace, Mario—"

"Not so!"

"—or worse."

"Worse?" Still he does not understand. "What could be worse for me than losing you?"

"Dying."

He stares at her.

"I'm afraid for you," she says. "For your life. Lucy Pratt is mad. She wants to finish what she tried to do in the carriage barn . . . she wants me dead. And if you try to protect me, if you get in her way, you'll die too, just as Tommy did.

"That's why I have to leave you," she says. "To save you. Help me, Mario, help me to save you . . . let me go away. She won't hurt you if I go away."

He studies her face, his eyes slowly widening. "You want me to send you away to what you believe will be certain death? And you think I will agree to that? That to save my life, I will allow you to lose yours?" He laughs, incredulous. "My God, Clara, I think you are as mad as she! Do you believe that no one has ever threatened me before? What do you think Gennarino is here for? Now that you have told me, you will never be permitted from my sight, or his!"

Ludicrous! Comical! . . . The brainless, impractical mock-heroics of a child! Had he thought her grown? He tries to calm himself. But the last, agonizing month, his impending ruin, all the careful, intricate plans he has made with Buchan to keep her safe . . . the heaped-up mountain of his worries, grown monstrous, has been tottering for days. This is the pebble that trips the landslide . . . this is more than he can bear.

"Do you think me so low as that?" he says, suddenly white with fury. "So helpless that I cannot care for my own wife, and keep her from harm? Or do you believe that only your schoolmaster would sacrifice himself for you?" And she shrinks from his anger.

"But I don't want you to sacrifice yourself for me!" she cries. "I don't want anyone else to die because of me. Especially not you! Don't you understand? Do you think I *want* to leave you? I do this for you, Mario . . . for both of us . . . to keep you from harm and to pay for what I've done—"

"*Enough!*"

In the sudden, shocked silence windows open in some of the neighboring houses; a head pokes from one of them.

"Not here," he says, "where half of New York can hear what we say." Taking her hand, he pulls her to her feet, across the yard, up the stairs and down the long passage to the drawing room, and bangs the doors shut behind him, ignoring the startled face of Peters in the entrance hall.

He turns to her.

"Understand me," he says, his voice barely under control. "For the last month I have been afraid. Yes, afraid! Terrified! As terrified as you, Clara, afraid that I must lose you to some wasting disease that no one can explain, and I am sick of it, sick of being afraid! And just yesterday I learn that the reason for your illness is fear, that perhaps you are not dying after all, and now . . . now you tell me that you must leave me?

"And you expect me to let you go?" He is shaking with anger. "To let you simply walk away? Mario is so patient, he will understand that this is for him, that I do this for his sake. Mario will do anything, so long as I ask it, even allow me to destroy both our lives. No! Mario declines to suffer because you refuse to forgive yourself for a sin you never committed. That is what I said! Enough of your guilt, of blaming yourself! Since our wedding night it has done nothing but make us both wretched. You wish to make amends, Clara? For what? Just what is it you have done, that needs such atonement? No! I will tell you!

"You became a man's mistress, a terrible thing. He was in a position of trust and you were not yet eleven years old. Which of you was guilty of sin? You were lonely and defenseless. He used your years against you, your innocence, your wanting to be loved. What choice did you have, tell me that?"

She stands facing him, unafraid. "I could have refused. He wouldn't have forced me," she says, and Alfieri laughs, mocking her.

"My darling fool, he had no need to force you! He knew that, even if you do not." His eyes glitter with anger. "You are older, now; a woman. Try to understand what he was: a kind and gentle man who took little girls to his bed, masterly at judging which ones were likely to be willing, even eager. God! How he must have licked his lips when he saw you sitting at the station! . . . Like a fox looking at a little bird that has been thrown from its nest."

Clara listens, rigid. Her face is scarlet but she does not turn away.

"He had you all to himself in that wasteland, with no one to interfere, no one to warn you, or protect you. And best of all, he needed never fear your family's interference, not even a letter once a year inquiring after your health, or the progress of your studies. And you still say that you had a choice?"

"It was my decision," she says, stubborn. "I wanted it."

"It was no decision at all. He taught you what to want!" He laughs, maddened, his fists clenched in the air, unable to believe that he cannot make her see. "His was the sin, not yours!"

"He died because of *me*!" she cries, stamping her foot. "He was there because of me—" She claps her hands to her mouth, but the words have been uttered at last.

The anger fades from Alfieri's face, his hands fall tiredly to his sides.

"Is that it?" he says. "You think you caused his death? My poor darling . . . you give yourself too much credit, and take too much blame. You gave him the idea, that was all. He went to the carriage barn for his pride's sake. He was there because he could not control Lucy any more, because she had frightened him, made him look weak and unmanned in his own eyes and yours, and he thought to punish her the only way he could."

He walks to his wife, grips her shoulders, tilts her chin. "That it did not happen before, that he was able to live as long as he did . . . that is the miracle of your story. And if it had not happened when it happened, then it would have happened some other day. He would have grown more careless as he grew older, less sly, less quick with his excuses and his tricks. Someone, someday . . . some crazed father, some brother avenging his sister's honor . . . would have done what Lucy did."

She will not yield, even in her grief. "No! He was taking me away with him, to Paris . . ."

"Even now, *cara*? Do you believe it, even now? That you were the last? He loved you, yes, and he died for you. Not because of you, but *for* you. But if he had lived, if the two of you had escaped to Paris? What would have happened in two or three years, when you were grown, no longer a child? Do you think, however hard he tried, that he could change the tastes of a lifetime, begin to desire what he had never desired before?"

Her eyes close. "No . . . no, I knew," she says. "I knew he would . . . I couldn't let myself think . . ." She leans her forehead against him.

He wraps his arms about her. "No more talk of leaving me," he says.

"No." Then she lifts her head. "But Lucy . . ."

"Lucy Pratt no longer matters."

There is a chair nearby, the same chair he had slept in two nights ago, and awakened in, in such misery. He leads her to it, sits, pulls her into his lap.

"Are you angry with me?" she says, her head on his shoulder.

"Not any more."

"I don't want to make you angry, or unhappy. I love you so much. I meant what I said. I would die for you, the way he did for me."

"I don't want you to die for me. I want you to live for me, I want you with me, always. That is why we are both going away, you and I . . . to leave all the Lucys of the world far behind us, where they can never trouble us again."

"Truly?"

"Truly, love."

"Right after the opera season?"

"No, much sooner. The Monday after next."

She raises her head to look at him, and he presses it back down against his shoulder. "Mario, your debut . . ."

"My debut is canceled. The season will occur without me."

"Mario, please . . . not because of me."

"Hush," he says. "Let me tell you what it's like, where we are going. Our house stands on the side of a hill, shaded by trees. There is a walled garden around it, where figs and peaches and purple grapes ripen in the sun. It is hot there in the afternoon, and still, and the bees make a sleepy music, and then it is good to rest. But the mornings and the evenings are cool, and then the air is like wine, and the birds sing. And beyond the garden walls, in the valley below, lies my city like a jewel in a cup, with her domes and her towers, and all her brave flags flying . . ."

Chapter Thirty-two

Mr. Maurice Grau, general manager of the Metropolitan Opera House, has arranged for an elegant carriage to convey Mario Alfieri from his home to rehearsals and back again. Nevertheless, a singer is a singer; and regardless of how he gets there, the workaday stage door is where he enters and exits the opera house. On Monday, October the eighth, Alfieri steps through that modest entrance to begin rehearsals for the new season, and finds himself greeted by a thunderous welcome from the massed forces of the house—chorus, *comprimari,* musicians, dancers, scenery changers, carpenters, dressers, seamstresses, wigmakers—all gathered to pay homage to the peerless tenor of the age.

He recognizes many, as the cheering goes on, and greets them warmly, but most of the faces are new to him. Still, he speaks to them with no less courtesy, and it is an hour or more before some semblance of order can be restored, and the business of the opera house resume its usual rhythms. But those who have known Alfieri in the past are instantly struck by two particulars worthy of weeks of commentary and debate: first, that his usual shadow, the ubiquitous Gennarino, is absent from his side for the first time in living memory, the tenor being accompanied instead by a new manservant, one Peters, who tries his best to look accustomed to the manic confusion around him, and fails resoundingly; and second, that the great man himself, while as elegant and impeccable as ever, looks, to the eyes of some who had seen him in London only six months ago, to be a full decade older.

An opera house, like any small, self-contained community devoted to a single purpose—such as a school, or a convent or monastery—is the perfect breeding ground for gossip, and especially gossip concerning tragedy; and within the hour the tale is rife, from flies to cellars, from stage door to marble foyer, that Alfieri's young bride, long known to be ill, is worse, and is even now at death's door. That he would leave her side at this critical time to fulfill his obligations is but another example of the dedication that, along with his artistry and the divine beauty of his voice, has made him the greatest of the great.

Alfieri, however, would be the last to argue with the rumormongers, or to call them liars. For one thing, such rumors would play perfectly into the belief he wishes to foster, which is that Clara's health is broken, and that she must be removed to a warm climate to recover. For another, it appears to be true: Clara is still sick, wretched with constant nausea, able to tolerate only weak tea and an occasional mouthful of dry toast, and the tenor's certainty that her illness had been caused by her fear of Lucy Pratt has been shattered. Now he must worry whether an autumn voyage across the North Atlantic, with its prospect of rough weather and seasickness, will increase her misery, or prove too much for her to bear in her already weakened state. He must worry, too, about her wish to atone for her past, and her lunatic idea that leaving him will ensure his safety. Despite her sincere promise that she has dismissed such thoughts, Gennarino is now watchdog to Clara alone; his assignment, until they sail next week, is to protect her not only from Lucy Pratt but from herself and any sudden thoughts she might have of offering herself up as a sacrifice . . . which accounts for Peters's appearance in Gennarino's place.

Add to these worries the stress of dissembling—of pretending to start a season of rehearsals and performances when, in fact, he will be gone in a week, betraying not merely a faceless public but the people who have today given him a hero's welcome—and the surprise is that he looks only ten years older than he did six months ago. He feels as if he has aged twenty.

But what must be done, must be done. He allows himself to be led around the opera house on a thorough tour of his new professional home, and is suitably admiring. The Metropolitan, seating three thousand and larger by far than London's Covent Garden or the Paris Opéra, is but eleven years old, and had been refurbished a mere two years ago, after a fire gutted the auditorium and caused the cancellation of the entire season. Now it is a marvel of magnificence in a city that has raised ostentation to heights previously unimagined: gold leaf gleams on intricately carved pillars and balconies; the enormous central chandelier, like a starburst of diamonds below the carved and gilded grid-work ceiling, lights a vast proscenium arch, and the thick wine velvet of seats and hangings would not be out of place in Windsor Castle or the palace of St. James's.

If Alfieri notices that the builders have concentrated their attention on the front of the house, leaving precious little room at the back for the mundane essentials that the grand patrons in the boxes never see, such as dressing and storage and rehearsal space, or that the scenery for each night's performance must be brought daily from a warehouse and placed, until needed, in an alley behind the opera house, to be rained and snowed upon because there is literally no room for it to be housed within . . . he is properly silent. Such stinting is not new and is hardly unusual. Alfieri takes it all in with the gracious air of an archbishop inspecting a new cathedral: the purpose and appurtenances are the same here as in every other church, and the services will be alike as well; only the decoration varies from one house of worship to the next.

Peters, in the meanwhile, in the private dressing room set aside for the exclusive use of Maestro Alfieri, inspects his immediate surroundings. Signor Gennarino, with an experience of opera houses that covers two decades and the better part of Europe, had told him what he could probably expect. He is not surprised, therefore, either by the room's extremely modest (not to say paltry) size, or by the complete (not to say utter) lack of amenities within. A dressing table, chair, and large mirror constitute the major furnishings; another chair, a tiny table, and a shallow, curtained alcove containing a narrow cot complete the decor . . . a Spartan cell, indeed, for one of the noblest princes of the profession.

Having been given the necessary items by Signor Gennarino, and drilled exhaustively in their proper placement and use, Peters sets them out as he has been told. Then, having nothing more to do until the maestro's return, he pulls a neatly folded newspaper out of one pocket, a slab of cold beef and some bread wrapped in a clean handkerchief out of another, an apple out of a third, and sits down to wait, possessed of all the comforts a man might reasonably need.

Alfieri's tour of the house is comprehensive. By the time he returns, Peters has perused most of the paper and finished his luncheon. He examines Alfieri with concern as the tenor sinks into one of the two chairs once the door has closed behind him. Alfieri looks spent.

"I think we will leave now," the tenor says, leaning back with his eyes closed. "I begin to wonder, Peters, whether we are leaving New York for the sake of my wife's health or mine. I only know that I cannot do more today. I will make my apologies as we go." He stands up slowly.

Peters nods cheerfully, pocketing his newspaper, and is at once ready. "It's just as well that we leave now, sir," he says, holding the coat for Alfieri to don. "It will make people think that the signora is truly ill." He falls back a step as Alfieri turns on him, eyes narrowed.

"Did I hear you right, Peters? Are you saying that she is not? You see what she is like! She has barely eaten in two months . . ."

"Yes, sir, I know. Margaret has told me." Peters, aware of the enormity of his gaffe, looks straight ahead, holding out Alfieri's hat and gloves as if impeccable bearing will somehow remove the foot from his mouth. "But—forgive me, sir—that's not so very unusual." He soldiers on, trying to extricate himself. "Margaret wouldn't know, of course, being the youngest, but her mother—my eldest sister, Catherine, of blessed memory—went through much the same with each of her eleven confinements. She told me straight-out after her eighth was born that she preferred the labor pains, bad as they were . . . at least they were over fairly quick. If there was a way to trade, she said, she'd gladly take twice the pains, just to avoid being so sick the first three months . . ."

Alfieri stares at him, speechless, and sinks back down into his chair. The footman, still holding out hat and gloves, begins to stammer.

"I'm that sorry, maestro . . . I don't mean to compare the signora with my sister, not at all, but their troubles seem so similar . . . I thought it might ease your mind to know that women in the family way can sometimes get taken bad . . ."

"Dear Lord, I never thought . . ." Alfieri's face is a picture of suddenly dawning comprehension. "It never occurred to me, not once. How did I not . . . ? God help me, I should be shot for stupidity." He looks at Peters. "How long since you guessed this?"

"Why, when you returned from Philadelphia, sir. I saw how peaked the little missus looked, and Margaret began describing how she was suffering, and I remembered my sister's words, and what she went through . . ."

"For God's sake, man! Why didn't you speak up, and save me some time in hell? No one has guessed, no one! . . . Not even Daniel Buchan, who has pieced together everything else." Alfieri looks dazed. "Is it possible that we could all of us be so stupid?"

"But Mr. and Mrs. Buchan have no children themselves, do they, sir? I guess it wouldn't spring ready to mind, like."

"But the doctors, Peters? What of the doctors? If I had one examine my wife, I had a dozen. Can they all be incompetent, not to even consider that a young wife might be . . . ?" He holds his hand out before his belly.

"Perhaps they couldn't see the forest for the trees, sir." Peters answers Alfieri's blank look with an apologetic smile. "Perhaps they were all thinking of opening night, when Miss Clara collapsed, and were looking for something more serious than . . . well . . . just a baby."

"Just a baby . . ." Alfieri rises to his feet again, holding the chair back for support. His world is reeling just now; his calculations of his life's losses and gains shifting even as he throws his head back and laughs— truly laughs, for the first time in a month—flushed with sudden joy.

"How many children did your sister have, Peters?"

"Eleven, sir."

"All healthy?"

"Healthy and hardy, sir, God be praised. And my sister back at work within a week of birthing every one."

"What work did she do?"

"She was a laundress, sir, and strong as any man. Used to go up and down stairs with an iron bucket of boiling water in each hand. But the first three months . . ." He shakes his head solemnly.

"You said 'of blessed memory,' " Alfieri says. "She is gone, then, your sister. Nothing to do with . . ."

"Oh, holy Mary, sir, no! Catherine was twenty years senior to me, and was sixty-eight when she passed over, eight years ago. She went very peaceful, with most of her children at her bedside. The rest couldn't fit in the room, God love 'em, or they would have been there too. She was a grandmother thirty-one times, see, and great-grandmother of nine."

Sufficiently reassured, Alfieri takes the hat and gloves that Peters still holds out.

"Alice Buchan has recommended her doctor highly," he says. "We will stop by his office on the way home, Peters, and ask him to pay a call as soon as he may. And if you are right, as I believe you are, I think I can safely promise that the baby will be called Caterina, after your sister of blessed memory."

Peters turns pink with pleasure, but remains logical. "It may be a boy, sir."

"Indeed it may. What is your given name, Peters?

"Gregory, sir."

"Do you like the sound," the tenor smiles, "of the name Gregorio?"

Alfieri stops only long enough to make his excuses and take his leave. To the great astonishment of those they pass as they exit the opera house, he is moving with the step of a young man as he and his servant climb into the waiting carriage and rattle off toward home.

BETWEEN BEDROOM and sitting room is a narrow, doorless corridor: an elegant dressing area for husband and wife, divided in two, each furnished with its own washbasin, hinged triple mirror, cabinets and drawers. The doctor stands at the basin nearest the bedroom, washing his hands while Margaret rearranges the sheet over a red-faced Clara lying in the bed. Alfieri, who had been present during the examination, stands beside his wife, his hand on her shoulder.

"All perfectly normal," the doctor says as he dries his hands. "Everything just as it should be. It's early days, yet. I estimate the baby to be about two months along. Mrs. Alfieri's menses are irregular, and so it is difficult to be more accurate at this stage—but it means that the baby could make its appearance by late April or early May. My congratulations to you both!"

Alice Buchan's doctor is a relatively young man, and has not yet learned to announce such joyous news in an indifferent manner. Rolling down his sleeves, he approaches Alfieri with his hand outstretched, pumps the tenor's arm enthusiastically, and smiles down at Clara, who still has trouble meeting his gaze: the examination—which Mario had had the decency not to watch—is too recent an indignity to permit her to feel entirely comfortable with this stranger, however cheerful he may be.

It was Margaret who had stood at her side during the ordeal, stroking Clara's forehead and allowing her own strong, competent hand to be squeezed tightly by both of Clara's small ones when the doctor pressed too hard or probed too deeply; and it is Margaret whom the doctor addresses now, rightly judging her, at this moment, to be the most reliable person in the room.

"The nausea should abate in another fortnight, more or less. Until then see that your mistress rests a good deal, and that she eats whatever pleases her, so long as she can keep it down . . . but get her to eat. Better toast fingers and custard ten times a day than nothing whatever and the baby deprived of all nourishment. Once the morning sickness has passed your mistress should take regular exercise. Walking is best, weather permitting, at a reasonable pace.

"I am not, by the way, one who thinks that impending motherhood is something to be concealed"—he turns to Clara—"by which I mean, Mrs. Alfieri, that even as your condition becomes more obvious I want you to walk, and if people think you immodest for being out and about . . . well, that is their idiocy. There is nothing shameful about a wife bearing her husband's child . . . on the contrary, it is both natural and beautiful . . . and anyone who thinks it indecent to be seen in public while expecting—that it advertises a wife's engagement in marital relations, and should therefore be kept hidden—is either a fool or a hypocrite.

"And now," he says, addressing husband and wife as he shrugs into his coat, "I will leave you alone . . . you must have a great deal to say to each other. If your maid will accompany me downstairs, I will give her some additional instructions. I'll return in a week, barring any unusual occurrences . . . although I anticipate no trouble of any kind. Again, signore . . . Mrs. Alfieri . . . my heartiest felicitations to you both."

The door closes after him, then opens again almost immediately. "One more thing," he says, poking his head back in. "No tight corsets, please, Mrs. Alfieri. I will allow you to wear them for another month, and for opening night, of course, when you will wish to look as elegant as possible . . . but not laced too tightly and none whatever after opening night. You have a baby inside who needs room to grow. And now goodbye for a week . . ."

There is complete silence in the room for several seconds after the door closes again. They wait, but it remains closed. Mario smiles regretfully. They will not be here in a week for the doctor to visit a second time, and that is a shame.

"Dr. Fisher reminds me of my father," he says. "A great deal younger, but very alike in the art of giving detailed instructions." He looks down at his wife.

Clara lies against the pillows with her eyes closed and both hands pressed to her middle, as if listening for something that she cannot possibly hear. The scarlet embarrassment in her cheeks has softened to rose. She had answered the doctor's questions about her symptoms and her monthly indisposition in a queer, stifled voice, and uttered not a word besides. Alfieri seats himself on the bed beside her, thinking, for a fleeting moment, that they are like two children sharing a secret so delicious that neither wishes to speak.

"Honey love," he says at last. "How do you feel?"

She opens her eyes. "I don't know." But she smiles—her first real smile in months, and to Alfieri like the sun rising after a long, dismal darkness, all the lovelier because their child is the reason—and her little giggle becomes a sob, which she quickly stifles with her hand. "I don't know," she says again, wiping her wet eyes, still laughing. "I don't really believe it, not yet."

She takes his hand in both of hers, plays with his fingers. "But I think I knew it without knowing. Do you remember the other day, in the garden, when you said you should have been with me when I woke? And I said that you are always with me, even when you're not? Well, it's true, Mario, isn't it? It's true, only then I didn't know just how true it is. But here you are," she says, pressing his hand to her belly. "Always with me . . ."

There is a quiet tap at the door a few minutes later . . . Margaret, obeying doctor's orders, back with a tray laden with tea, toast, and, yes, custard for the new mother-to-be. But the first knock goes unanswered, as does the second, and Margaret does not try a third time. Setting the tray down on a table in the hallway, the dishes covered, the teapot well snuggled in its cozy, she disappears back downstairs on silent feet. There are some things that may not be disturbed, even by doctor's orders.

Chapter Thirty-three

LUCY PRATT SITS before her mirror, contemplating her reflection. Ordinarily, at this time of day, Lucy would be dressing for dinner and preparing her toilette as carefully as possible, for the invitations to dine have never stopped coming, and Chadwick is assiduous in accepting on behalf of them both.

But Lucy is not going today. Neither did she go yesterday, nor the day before that, nor even the day before that. Indeed, Lucy has not dined out since last Thursday, pleading an indisposition. Chadwick has gone to dine without her, therefore; and his nightly return in high spirits has done nothing to lessen Lucy's growing resentment, not even when he informs her, as he stops by on his way to his own bed, that her presence had been greatly missed, and that his evening's hostess has asked him to extend her wishes to Miss Pratt for a speedy recovery from the cold that has kept her at home.

It is no cold that has kept her at home.

Last Friday, Chadwick—she has stopped thinking of him as "Uncle" . . . the man's gross insults have robbed her of any urge to think of him in that particularly amicable manner—last Friday, Chadwick had come home from his office with news: Alfieri, it seems, has found out about his wife's lies, her murderous treachery and vile, whorish behavior. In fact, against all probability the little bitch had told him herself, and— even more inconceivable—against all logic and reason Alfieri had not strangled her where she stood. But most staggering of all was the news that the tenor—instead of turning his back on the slut and throwing her into the gutter, to end her days in the misery and filth she so richly deserves—had actually sent his lackey to Chadwick to offer to buy Lucy's silence on the matter of Papa's tragic death.

As if she would ever air that horror in public! As if she would ever admit that her sainted Papa—best and dearest of men!—had succumbed to the vicious wiles of a child whore, and so turned his back on his sickly cripple of a wife and his beautiful, precious daughter. Lucy's desire to tell the harlot's story had been confined to Alfieri alone, in payment of the debt owed to Papa's memory, so that Clara could be properly punished for the unforgivable sin of stealing Papa away.

But declare to the world at large that Papa was fallible? That he could be seduced away from Lucy . . . and her poor, pathetic mother, of course . . . and bring destruction upon his beloved family? Oh, no, it was unthinkable! To admit that Papa could want someone else? Her very being recoils at the thought of it . . .

Gone! In one fell swoop, gone! All of it gone: all of Lucy's joyous anticipation, all her dreams of happy revenge . . . vanished, like a snuffed match! She will have no chance, now, to drive Alfieri mad with the lovingly told details of Clara's seduction and murder of Papa. Certainly the whore had never confessed all her crimes to her husband, but whatever she had imparted had effectively stolen Lucy's thunder.

And that was when Chadwick had made his wicked suggestion. Wreak revenge on them both, he had urged . . . tell all of New York what the little brown mouse did to you, to your mother and brother. Tell everyone how she made you an orphan, left you bereft of every comfort. Your own good name is safe, and will remain so! How can it be otherwise? Were you not in France receiving a lady's education while the shame was taking place? You will never be tarred with that loathsome brush . . .

Never! she had replied. Never! She would never tell, and he was horrid for even suggesting that she do such a thing! How could he want Papa's reputation smirched? Where was the respect for Papa he had shown before, for Papa's great intellect, and Papa's great heart, and the great soul that had animated him? And Chadwick had laughed at her, laughed and called her a sentimental fool, no better than the rest, as if she were supposed to know who the rest were . . .

Lucy stares at her reflection, soothing her bitterness with the pleasurable sight of the bright gleam of her loosened hair, the sparkle of her eyes, the plump pink shoulders and round breasts rising, cloudlike, above the top of her corset.

Chadwick had dared to laugh at her! He had apologized almost immediately—he had seemed unusually jolly that night, as if pleased beyond all measure with himself and the progress of his day—and urged her to go upstairs and dress quickly for dinner, so that they would not keep their hostess waiting, but she had coldly declined to go with him that evening, pleading the onset of an illness that would only be made worse by the wet weather.

And so he had gone off to dinner without her, and has gone without her every night since. Lucy does not mind. It is agreeable, of course, to be immensely popular and loved by everyone, but in the five years since her mother's death she has grown accustomed to her own company, and is quite content to remain here, in the comfort of her own, lovely room, eating her excellent dinner off a heavily laden tray set with linen and crystal and silver, and admiring her image in the glass as she lounges, half-naked, upon the carved rosewood bed with its blue silk coverlet and hangings that just match her eyes.

Alone like this she can do as she pleases . . . try on her many new gowns, one after the other, leaving them in heaps on the floor for the maid to pick up and put away in the morning, or sit at her dressing table, decorating herself with the jewels, mainly diamond and sapphire— to bring out her eyes—that she has purchased with the money Chadwick is realizing on the sale of Papa's things.

Nor has she failed to notice, these last few evenings at home, that just across from her barred windows, past the small back garden with its wooden fence and screen of trees, a handsome, dark-eyed young man, with glorious moustachios, frequently sits and stares boldly at her from one of the little windows of the carriage house across the way. On Sunday night, evidently emboldened by drink, he had leaned toward her from his window, insolent and smiling, with his uniform's tunic half undone, bottle in one hand and cigarette in the other, and blown her a kiss.

Such behavior is shocking, of course, and she should positively find out who his employer is, and complain, and have him fired . . . but he really is very handsome—she giggles, thinking how his moustache would tickle between her thighs—and besides, she has borne with the company of a peevish old man for so horribly long. What a relief it is to see a beautiful young man, and to know that he watches her from the darkness . . . and to be certain that he does, she has taken to keeping her curtains wide and her shades up in her brilliantly lit room, long after dark, and walking back and forth before the window as she dons and discards her gowns, and later prepares for bed.

Tonight, as she sits at her dressing table, the shades are up once more, and the curtains wide, and a sidelong glance tells her that there is a low light in the window across the way. She pushes her dinner tray to one side to give herself more room . . . something clatters to floor, and as she bends to pick it up she laughs, remembering that her mother would say that dropped silverware meant the arrival of a guest: a fork meant a woman, a spoon meant a girl . . . a knife meant a man. She smiles now, looking slantwise from the long blade and ivory handle to the window, then replaces the fallen knife on the tray. Humming to herself, she fastens on a long pair of glittering earrings and a necklace with a brilliant stone that nestles just above the deep valley between her breasts. Next she raises her plump arms high and smooths on a pair of pale blue satin gloves that extend nearly to her shoulders, purchased to be worn with the new ball gown she will wear on the opera's opening night.

The satin corset she wears now is pale blue too, all trimmed in lace, and she rises and moves to the cheval glass that stands between the windows, capering this way and that before the long mirror to enjoy the full effect of her loose hair and opulent figure, her corset and gloves and jewels; always aware, without looking, of the black eyes that watch her from the window across the way.

The sight of her own loveliness excites her. Heated, needing some fresh air, she leaves the mirror and stands at the window, stretching her arms out through the bars into the night, breathing deeply. The light across the way goes out abruptly; all Lucy can see is the dark of the window opening, a black rectangle in a slightly paler wall, and the glowing tip of a cigarette.

Smiling, she grips the iron bars and leans back, arms extended, and sways left and right, allowing her hair to hang far down her back in a yellow curtain. If her admirer wants a show she will gladly oblige him: she is not shy. Papa used to have her walk up and down before him, turn and bend and stretch, clad in nothing at all, her hair swirling about her like a cloak . . .

There is a sound from behind her, and she whirls from the window, nearly falling, gloved arms straining to cover breasts and belly, wholly useless in shielding more than a tiny part of her from view. Chadwick stands just in the doorway, gazing at her with amusement, his eyes traveling deliberately over her, head to toe and back again.

"You failed to hear my knock," he says. "I was just leaving, and wanted to look in and wish you sweet dreams before you retire for the night." His slow gaze lifts over her shoulder, and his eyebrows twitch as he, too, sees the cigarette ember in the darkness.

"In your innocence, my child, you may not realize that there is a mews just beyond the fence, populated by a small army of stablehands and drivers. Your honor is unimpeachable, of course, but a man—and particularly a bachelor—in my position, with a young woman living beneath his roof, must be scrupulously careful. I do not wish the neighbors to think that I am running a bawdy house. In future, please keep your shades drawn and your curtains closed if you wish to disport in a state of undress." He bows, and turns to leave.

Red-faced and furious, Lucy cries: "For decency's sake, you might put a lock on my door that I could turn from the inside. Then you couldn't break in on me unawares!"

Chadwick turns back, smiling. "My apologies, my dear. I was not aware that being broken in upon was something about which you have been overly concerned. Allow me to point out, however, that a lock on your side would not negate the fact that you were cavorting nearly naked before your open window; it would only mean that I would not have had the privilege of stumbling across so exquisite a sight. It is an unforgettable picture that will remain with me always, as I am sure it will with your admirer across the way. Nevertheless"—his smile vanishes—"for decency's sake, do not let me find it happening again with the shades up. I trust that I have made myself clear."

The door swings shut upon the sight of Lucy, eyes wild in her purple face, still clutching herself with her blue-gloved, ineffectual hands.

Chadwick bids good night to his servant at the front door, working his tight calfskin gloves over his fat fingers as his cloak is settled upon his shoulders.

"Don't wait up for me," he says as he takes his hat and walking stick and steps out into the darkness. "I shall probably be very late."

He leans back in the carriage's leather depths as it travels uptown, and someone peering through the window would see no more than a placid, elderly gentleman enjoying a cigar. Only Chadwick's rapid smoking betrays his fury, turning the air in the carriage as thick as fog.

What an extraordinary failure the girl has proved to be! . . . A great, simpering sow of a failure, with an exalted, and entirely baseless, opinion of herself, and a prodigious appetite that is never sated. His one consolation is that he has been able to pocket fully one half of the money received to date from the sale of Fauvell's treasures—he considers it only fair recompense for the cost of feeding her, and for the ordeal of having to spend so many hours with her each day.

Imbecile that she is! Maudlin, revolting trollop! Bringing her beneath his roof had been a cardinal error; she is of no value whatsoever. She was to have been his means of retribution, was she? His implacable Vengeance, who would never rest until her teeth were locked in Clara's throat, and Alfieri was on his knees, never to rise again? Well, the joke is on him—on Chadwick.

Fauvell's good name—the good name of a child corrupter!—means more to her than the revenge for which she had burned so fiercely. Now is the time to strike! Already they have reduced the Adler girl to a wasting invalid, and her husband is distracted, torn between his sickly wife and his obligations to his employers. Now is the time to plant the seeds of the rumors that will crush them both, forever . . . and what had Lucy Pratt done?

She had wept—positively wept!—at his suggestion that she make public the lurid circumstances of the schoolmaster's death, and pay his murderess back once and for all. Having been thwarted in her ability to surprise Alfieri with the tale of his wife's sins, she has determined to do . . . what? Why, nothing at all! . . . Except sulk in her room, deliver him—Chadwick—into penury through her gluttony, and prance before her windows, displaying her wobbling flesh to all the stablehands in the neighborhood.

There is a throbbing behind Chadwick's eyes, and he removes his spectacles to pinch the bridge of his nose. The sight of her before her window, just now, was the final straw. He must rid himself of her. She is only a liability now, a drain on his pocket, on his spirits; a hindrance to his plans . . .

Stepping from the carriage at his destination, he flicks the still-glowing cigar stub into the gutter, oblivious to the arc of its flight. A passing horse shies at the small fountain of sparks that bursts just under its nose, and the driver shouts an obscenity at Chadwick's retreating back that the lawyer, already up the stairs and being welcomed by a liveried servant, does not hear. Still muttering, the irate driver clucks to his horse and moves on, leaving the cigar stub to smolder a while before it winks out on the wet paving stones.

Chapter Thirty-four

Gᴇɴɴᴀʀɪɴᴏ ᴅʀᴀᴡs ᴛʜᴇ cord tight, knots it skillfully, and straightens up, stretching his spine. Looking around at the stacked boxes and trunks, he does a quick mental inventory. *Bene, tutto è pronto.* It is only Saturday, and mid-afternoon, and still he can truly say that all is ready. Well, he cannot abide loose ends, or slipshod work. Tomorrow he and Peters will see it all properly stored aboard ship, then prepare the cabin *per il maestro e la sua sposa.* Nothing will remain to be done, come Monday, but gather up toothbrushes and nightclothes, and leave, neatly and quietly.

Maestro Alfieri will go alone to the opera house that morning. Peters will see to the remaining baggage. Gennarino will accompany the little signora and her maid to the ship, where the maestro will meet them. It has all been worked out, down to the last detail, the last minute; the maestro, too, cannot abide loose ends. It is one of the many things they have in common.

Gennarino has had no qualms, this last week, about staying behind while Peters saw to the maestro at the opera house. Being at the opera house himself would have meant hours of idle time during which to chafe about the progress of the preparations. Here he has been more useful. And with a carriage provided to ferry Maestro Alfieri there and back, Gennarino has had no real fears for his master's safety. Gennarino has known men like lawyer Chadwick before, and even though he has not had the pleasure of meeting this one, he understands well what he will and will not do.

What he will not do is attack out in the open, or hire others to do it. No one will rush up to Maestro Alfieri with a pistol or a knife as he enters or leaves the opera house; no one will aim through the carriage window as it stands immobile, snarled in traffic. Outright assassination is not lawyer Chadwick's style.

Slow death is. Lawyer Chadwick is a serpent, his methods as twisted as his soul. Violence is not for such as he. It accomplishes its ends, yes, but crudely, displaying nothing of the fine mind at work behind the plan. Gennarino is familiar with such men; he is *napoletano,* after all, and such knowledge is in his blood, in his bones. Lawyer Chadwick prefers treachery, chooses to manipulate circumstances to do the work for him; obtains his greatest satisfaction in not merely destroying his enemies, but ensuring that they suffer long.

He regrets that Maestro Alfieri will not allow him to take care of lawyer Chadwick: God Himself is crying out for this man's blood, and nothing could be easier—an elderly man slipping on the Broadway cobblestones, to be crushed beneath the endless, inexorable wheels; or even accosted by a fleet-footed thief on a crowded street and stabbed as he resisted having his pocket picked—but the maestro has forbidden any such accidental death. *Che peccato!* What a shame . . .

He shrugs—orders are orders—then stops, and listens. The front doorbell. Slipping on his coat, he moves swiftly up the stairs to the entrance hall. No one but he may admit anyone to the house. Even the cook has been put on notice: regardless of how well someone may be known at the tradesman's door, no one may be allowed in, no deliveries may be accepted, unless Gennarino is present. Lawyer Chadwick will not stoop to violence, *ma la pazza bionda,* the yellow-haired madwoman . . . according to the maestro, there is no telling what she is capable of. And what had been precious before, and required great care, is beyond price now, and requires supreme vigilance . . . the little signora carries the maestro's child, and the absolute safety of both is now his highest duty.

But no threat stands outside the door this wet afternoon: only Stafford

Dyckman, his face barely visible behind the tall pile of gaily wrapped boxes in his arms.

"*Sono io il primo?*" the young man asks. "Am I the first?"

"*Il primo, signore? No,*" Gennarino answers, taking the packages from him and setting them down, then reaching for his hat and gloves. "*Signora Buchan è qui.*"

Mrs. Buchan has, in fact, been here for some hours already, in the upstairs sitting room with the little signora, for Monday will bring the parting of these two, who have become more like mother and daughter than friends, and particularly now, with a baby on the way, such a leave-taking will be hard. She, too, had come laden with gifts, and the time has been spent opening them and taking tea, which Clara, her nausea abating as the doctor had said it would, is able to enjoy once more.

The gifts, however—the many that Mrs. Buchan had brought with her today, and to which Stafford Dyckman is adding—are neither parting mementos nor are they in honor of the baby. They are birthday presents: Clara Alfieri turns twenty tomorrow. An elegant, formal dinner is planned for tomorrow night to commemorate the last gathering of their little group before the Alfieris sail; but today is set aside solely for the happier celebration of Clara's birthday, to be marked by the opening of gifts.

Clara, seated on the floor amid an island of heaped boxes and torn paper, looks up from her admiration of a pink satin bed jacket as Stafford enters with Gennarino behind him, both with arms laden with yet more parcels.

". . . you should save it," Alice Buchan is saying, "for when all Signor Alfieri's relations come to see the new baby. How elegant you'll look . . ."

Stafford greets the ladies as the two men place their parcels on the carpet around Clara, fencing her in, after which Gennarino whisks the debris from earlier gifts out of sight. Clara stares at the piles of boxes, her expression somewhere between perplexity and wonder.

"I'm afraid we'll have to reserve another stateroom to fit it all," she says. "Poor Gennarino." She watches the valet flattening and folding paper and fitting box into empty box. "He'll never find space for everything."

Gennarino, with the barest of smiles, winds a last bit of torn ribbon around his fingers, drops it into his pocket, and exits silently with the rubbish.

"I think you will find," Dyckman says, as the door shuts behind the valet, "that Gennarino has everything entirely under control." He kisses Alice on the cheek, stoops and drops another on Clara's forehead. "Will Daniel and Mario be joining us?"

"Later," Clara says. "Mario wanted Daniel to go over all the arrangements with him one final time, to make certain that everything is ready for Monday. For the moment you'll have to bear with just the two of us."

She reaches for another box, but the sight of so much treasure is overwhelming. Sighing, she puts her hand to her forehead.

"Are you ill?" Alice says, leaning toward her.

"No," Clara replies. She rubs her temples and smiles wanly. "At least, not in the same way as before. I just feel like a child with too many sweets, that's all. I've opened too many gifts, and it's made me slightly queasy." She looks up at Stafford with a pleading smile. "How ungrateful I must seem! You won't be insulted if I wait a bit and open yours later?"

"Not at all," he says, extending a hand to Clara and helping her to rise from the floor, then moving quickly away. "I've no wish to compete with Alice's selections anyway. Women always have a better sense than men of what someone will want as a gift . . . particularly another woman."

Alice makes room for Clara on the sofa next to her. "You're quite wrong, you know," she replies, arranging her skirts as Clara settles beside her. "Daniel has given me some lovely things over the years. And certainly Signor Alfieri has excellent taste in gifts."

"Oh, but Mario has excellent taste in everything." Stafford laughs a bit too loudly. "Well, it's easy enough for him . . . an emerald bauble here, a ruby trifle there . . . how can he possibly go wrong?"

Alice's eyes light at the implication of his words. "Oh, marvelous!"

she says. "Were you with him? What did he choose this time?" Clara murmurs something and Alice replies: "Well, but a twentieth birthday is not an everyday affair, my dear, nor is news of one's first child! I would be disappointed if he hadn't gotten you something very special."

Clara only shakes her head, refusing to consider what her birthday gift from Mario might be. She is indeed queasy, surfeited with presents and unwilling to contemplate more; rather the way a man might feel when faced with too much food after a lifetime's hunger. In her entire life she has never known a birthday such as this. Before Papa it had been ignored, a day like any other, her birth being no occasion for celebration. And for the two birthdays she had spent with Papa the festivities had been, perforce, very small: just the two of them . . . although that, for Clara, had been indescribable bliss.

But this blizzard of tribute, of gifts and praise . . . she feels giddy today, not herself, just as she had felt in Philadelphia on opening night . . . as if she has been raised high above the common world; and remembering what had happened that night, she is apprehensive . . . foolishly, perhaps, but apprehensive nevertheless. Her life's lesson has been too well learned: too much happiness is a warning. But a warning of what? Mario has sworn to her that all is—and will be—well . . . and yet the feeling persists that something is not right.

And surely there is something strange about Stafford. Alice seems not to notice, but Clara cannot be wrong, she knows him too well . . . he will not look at her today, averts his gaze when their eyes meet, uses every means to avoid addressing her directly. She asks him, once, if anything is the matter, and denying it he laughs again, too loudly, and changes the subject.

Mario and Buchan arrive at four, just as the lamps are being lit. The day is raw, and the two men are ruddy from the chill air and drizzle. Clara, as always, sees Mario enter with a quick catch of breath. Reason tells her that she must, in time, grow used to him; that someday her heart will not jump at the sight of him, nor her palms grow damp, but that day has not yet come. She looks up at him, her face so alight as he bends to kiss her, that the others turn away, smiling, almost blinded by its brightness.

Alice rises from the sofa, to allow Alfieri to sit beside his wife, and Clara nestles against his side, wholly safe at last, as she only ever is when she is with him. Still, even with his arm about her, the uneasiness persists. She listens, with only half her attention, to the talk and the laughter.

". . . Will you not stay to dinner?" she hears Mario saying. "Why leave at all? We have so little time left together . . . *Madonna*," he says, looking down at her, "don't you agree that our friends should stay?"

Yes, of course she agrees. Dinner tonight will be informal: no need to change into evening clothes, or stand on ceremony . . . just the five of them, enjoying one another's company . . .

Clara closes her eyes, willing the anxiety gone, barely following the others' conversation—Daniel Buchan has booked passage for them on the *Columbia* under his own name, so that it is unlikely that they will be disturbed by celebrity seekers, and Mario replies how content he will be to remain in their stateroom and sleep for the length of the voyage home, and indeed, Alice says, he looks tired—and why then can she not shake off this underlying current of dread when the voices around her are so familiar and dear, and Mario's shoulder is so warm and her eyes are so very heavy . . . ?

She hears his voice coming from very far away. "I think," he says, "that my wife needs to sleep for a while . . ."

He ignores her murmured protest, and their guests exit quietly while he lifts her feet, places a pillow beneath her head, and covers her with a soft shawl. He bends over her.

"If you sleep long, *piccola,* I will wake you in time for dinner. If not, we will be in the drawing room, should you wish to join us. No, love, you cannot keep your eyes open . . ."

He lowers the lamps; the room is dim gold, full of shadows and soft sounds . . . the clock ticking on the mantel, and flames sparking in the grate . . . and it is so good to sink into the warm darkness . . .

SHE OPENS her eyes: the room is the same, the fire lower. She does not move at first, enjoying the warm silence, then sits up and looks at the clock . . . less than an hour since Mario left her to rest. Such a brief nap, and yet she feels so rested. Yawning, she puts the pillow back in its place, folds the shawl and drapes it over the back of the sofa.

How calm she feels, how full of well-being . . . it must have been pure fatigue that made her so fearful before. Or perhaps—she smiles a small, contented cat-smile and touches her belly, caressing the baby within—perhaps being with child makes one fanciful and timid. She yawns again—a vast yawn that makes her eyes water—and shakes her head. It is time she joined the others in the drawing room . . . first she had rudely refused to open Stafford's presents, and then she had fallen asleep in the middle of their conversation . . . what they must think of her manners!

Shutting the door behind her, she slips quietly down the stairs—her lightly shod feet make no sound on the carpet—and approaches the drawing room. The entrance hall is dim, lit only by the lamp in the little vestibule between the inner and outer door that shines through the fanlight; and by the narrow bar of golden light that streams from the drawing room, the doors of which are not quite shut. Stafford's voice, tight and strident, is audible halfway up the stairs.

Approaching the drawing room door, she hesitates, her hand on the pull. Through the narrow opening she can see Daniel Buchan, sitting with his back to the door, and Alice in a chair closer to the fire, looking up at Stafford, who stands by the mantelpiece, his face white and strained. Mario is nowhere to be seen. Alice is leaning forward to make a point, saying something that Clara cannot hear, and Stafford explodes in reply, his voice sharp and very clear.

"I don't care what you or Daniel say, and I care less for the law! He's getting away with it . . . and no one and nothing can touch him . . . that's what's so maddening!"

She hears Alice's voice then, soothing, and Stafford's angry reply. "Forgive me, Alice, but no, I cannot be calm! A great artist is being cut off in his prime, his career smashed . . . it goes against everything just and decent!"

Daniel Buchan says something then, but his back is to her and again Clara cannot hear, and then Mario appears, crossing from the window, where he must have been standing all this time. He stands facing Stafford, his face dark with anger.

"Amico," he says, "the career is mine, not yours! If I have made my peace with what has happened, why cannot you do the same?"

"But you haven't heard him!" Dyckman's open hands stretch toward Mario, his face turns from one to the other, trying to make them understand. "He's started already . . . I was at Mrs. Paran Stevens's last night, and Chadwick was there. He had a group of the men around him, and they were all very intent, their heads close together . . . I passed by and heard one of them laugh and say 'The Pratt girl told you that? Oh, surely not,' and Chadwick said something and they all laughed." His voice trembles and threatens to break. "And then Chadwick saw me, and he smiled . . . he smiled, the insolent . . . dear God, how I wanted to smash his face, how I wanted to . . . It's begun, Mario. I had no idea how horrible . . ." He buries his face in his hands.

Mario steers him to a chair and forces him to sit. Daniel Buchan rises and disappears from sight, reappearing again with a filled glass which he carries to the young man. Stafford reaches for it eagerly but cannot raise the glass to his mouth: his hand shakes and the liquid slops over the sides. Mario, still close beside him with a hand on his shoulder, reaches down with the other and holds the glass for him, his hand steadying Stafford's, and the young man drinks at last. Across the room Alice sits motionless in her chair, head bowed as if in prayer.

After a moment Stafford coughs, pushes the glass away. When he speaks his voice is calmer; Clara must strain to hear him.

"Lucy Pratt hasn't been with Chadwick all week. Supposedly she's indisposed, hasn't left his house. I can't believe that she knows what he's doing, using her as the source of his stories . . . even she couldn't be as shameless as that. Oh, Mario, if you could have seen their expressions!" And twisting free of his friend's grasp he buries his face in the crook of his arm, as if his own features must have absorbed the look of those others, and be unfit to be seen.

Mario looks at Daniel over Stafford's huddled form. "How does it feel," he says, "to be so right?"

"Not entirely right," Daniel answers, crossing to his wife and touching her cheek with the backs of his fingers. Alice raises her head and takes his hand in her own.

"He has begun early," Buchan continues, addressing Alfieri but looking at his wife. "I was certain he would wait until just before opening night. But it seems that you are leaving not a moment too soon . . ."

Clara, wide-eyed, backs away from the door, sits down abruptly on the hall seat among the coats swinging from their hooks. So Lucy Pratt is in the city, as she thought . . . well, who else could have told Mario about Rosebank? But living with Chadwick? Clara had no idea that they knew each other . . . the thought of their combined malignancy is appalling, terrifying.

And she understands this much from what she has heard: everyone in the drawing room—Alice, Stafford, Mr. Buchan—knows what had happened in Rosebank. They have sat with her, talked to her, looked her in the face, all the while knowing—for how long?—picturing her . . . and for a moment such a wave of shame envelops her that she cannot breathe . . . and then the other realization overwhelms the first, filling her mind like a great blackness: Mario is ruined. What does it matter if Alice and Daniel know of her shame? If Stafford is right, if Chadwick is telling her story, then the whole world knows, or soon will know, what she has done. Mario is taking her from New York the day after tomorrow, not for her health, but to escape the dishonor she has brought him.

His career smashed, Stafford had said. Cut off in his prime. Of course . . . Mario has broken his contract with the opera house to run from the scandal . . . what else can it mean? But she had not been the ward of a consummate businessman for four years without learning what such a violation sets in motion. They will come after him with every weapon they possess; his life will be a nightmare of lawsuits, legal fees, humiliations . . . and in the end they will win because he is in the wrong. The reason does not matter; he has broken his contract.

Because of her. Because of what she had done, and what she had failed to do. Because of her cowardice, her refusal to tell him the truth when it would have made a difference, when he was still free to take back his offer of marriage.

It is another, the latest, in a long list of disasters she has caused. Everyone she touches . . . everyone she has ever loved . . . is destroyed, or dies too soon. Her mother . . . Papa . . . her guardian. And now Mario, whom she loves better . . .

Than herself. Oh, far better. If she can, she will salvage his career, save him from the consequences of having loved her. She thinks she knows how . . . something that Stafford said gives her a tiny hope that it might be possible . . . he said that Lucy cannot know what Chadwick is doing, and that must be true . . . mad as she is, Lucy may have killed Papa, but she would never, ever allow his name to be sullied. And if she learns of what Chadwick is doing . . . would she not stop him? At least there might be a chance. Lucy must be told.

And if Lucy will not listen . . . if, instead, she turns on Clara . . .

A shadow falls across the band of light on the hall floor. From the drawing room comes the sound of the rustle of skirts approaching the door . . . Alice. Clara shrinks back among the coats, but it is no use; if the door opens, she must be seen. But a voice is raised within the room.

"Yes?" Alice says. Her hand is on the door; Clara can see her fingers curled against the wood, ready to slide it back. Alice pauses, listens to the voice behind her, says: "Oh, Daniel . . ." and turns away. The light flows once more through the narrow gap in the door.

There is no more time. Clara searches among the hanging coats for her own, seizes it, pulls down a hat from its hook. Silently, she opens the glass-paneled door to the vestibule and shuts it behind her, then steps through the front door and out onto the broad top step of the stairs to the sidewalk. With this door shut behind her she feels safer . . . it is solid wood; even if Alice should step from the drawing room this instant, she could not see who stands just outside, slipping on her coat and tying on her hat.

The drizzle is light but steady, and the wind is cold. Clara pulls her gloves from her coat pockets . . . her card case is here, thank God, and there should be some coins . . . yes! More than enough for a cab. Fitting on her gloves, she carefully descends the stairs, peering up over her shoulder. The drawing room is there, but no one stands at the window, looking out at the street, and she turns right, at the bottom of the stairs, to Twenty-sixth Street, and is soon out of sight of the windows. She moves quickly, realizing with dismay that she has made one serious error; her thin-soled slippers are meant for the house, not for rain-slicked streets, and her feet are soaked through by the time she reaches the end of the block and turns the corner.

No matter. There is no turning back now. She will simply walk as quickly as possible. She is lucky, of course: Fifth Avenue, only one block to the west, is the quickest way to Washington Square . . .

Chapter Thirty-five

He must light an extra candle in church tomorrow. Had he blinked, he would have missed her. In the moment between seeing her small figure hurrying past the servants' hall window, snatching his coat from the hook by the door, and reaching the pavement to follow her, he has time only to scribble a nearly illegible note with a pencil stub on a scrap of butcher's paper and thrust it at the astonished cook, pointing upstairs as he does so.

Emerging from the servants' entrance, Gennarino turns right, following Clara's lead; Madison Avenue is quiet tonight, its usually heavy traffic reduced by the cold rain to a trickle of closed carriages, hansoms, and tarpaulin-covered carts. He dashes to the corner of Twenty-sixth Street, quickly scans east and west. To the east, toward Third Avenue, there is no one on foot; directly across from him, the bench-lined verge of Madison Square, overhung by sodden trees with near-naked branches, is empty. To the right, halfway down the block, a hansom cab stands beneath a street lamp. Gennarino catches a glimpse of skirts and a small foot disappearing into it before the driver closes the door and the horse clatters off toward Fifth Avenue.

He dashes after it, silent, hoping not to catch it so much as to keep it in sight. No sense calling out for her to stop . . . to know that she is being followed will only cause her to order the driver to go faster. And it would be madness to try and follow her in another cab, too easy to lose her, to become separated from her as other vehicles cut in and out. He can maneuver far more easily on foot . . .

The cab turns left onto Fifth Avenue. Good and bad. The traffic is heavier here, and slower, but there is the Fifth Avenue Hotel, where he and the maestro had stayed after first arriving in New York: brilliantly lit, lobbies and sidewalks crowded, its curb is lined with hansoms and four-wheelers continually pulling out into the great, sweeping current of the grand boulevard—how does he keep from losing her cab amid a thousand others, all identical, as it threads its way downtown, passing and being passed?—and where Broadway crosses Fifth Avenue the confusion becomes lunacy, and the cacophony of bellowing drivers and horses' hooves and iron-bound wheels on paving stones is like something from the pit of hell . . .

There! That one! Racing across the wide angle of intersecting streets, deaf to the shouts and curses of cabbies and the startled screams of horses, dodging vehicles from a dozen different directions, he slips twice on the slick cobblestones, once beneath the nose of a horse that rears and plunges, nearly crushing him, but he is up in a second and onto the opposite pavement . . . A vast wagon loaded with barrels, drawn by a team of six, lumbers across his line of sight, and he shrieks in frustration.

O Dio m'assisti! Where is she now? Which one? Clambering high onto the slow-moving wagon to the fury of its driver, he cranes his head back and forth, eyes sweeping the streets, almost weeping with frenzy. He is a dead man! . . . He may as well throw himself beneath the wheels around him, for the maestro will surely kill him if he returns without her . . . *O Dio! Dio e la Santa Vergine,* is it . . . ? The hansom with the scrape on its side? *Sì! Ecco! Eccola là!* . . . heading down Fifth Avenue . . .

Leaping down from the wagon, he lands wrong, his foot twisting under him, but he gains the pavement and begins to run once more, leaving the swearing driver still swinging his whip at empty air.

South down Fifth Avenue, ducking and weaving among the slower walkers and their umbrellas, keeping her always in sight. But where is she going? To what end? Still south, past Fourteenth Street. The horse moves at a slow trot, treading carefully on the slippery stones, lifting its feet high, enabling Gennarino to keep it in sight, but now he is tiring, and his twisted ankle throbbing badly. Twelfth Street . . . Tenth Street . . . elegant older houses and quieter streets, and the driver flicks his whip. The horse picks up speed, pulling away. A graceful arch fills the end of Fifth Avenue, and behind it a large, lamp-lit green. The hansom cab, two full blocks ahead of him, turns right at the arch, disappearing from view.

Oh, God, to lose her after all this! Sobbing with the effort, Gennarino puts on a final burst of speed, causing two men with umbrellas to flatten themselves against an iron fence as he dashes by. Swinging around the corner, he stops, doubled over, chest heaving. The cab is just pulling away from the curb, but Signora Alfieri, clear in the light of the lamps that flank the door, already stands at the top of the stairs of a wide red brick house. As he watches, clinging to a railing for support, the door opens, pouring more light onto her upturned face, and she steps inside and disappears from view.

Miss Pratt?" The footman will ascertain if she is in. "Who shall I say . . . ?"

That question, at least, is answered. Lucy *is* living here. Please, God, Clara thinks; don't let me die tonight. Mario would be so angry . . . She hands the footman her card.

But the drawing-room doors are open to the entrance hall and a jovial voice booms out. "A visitor for Miss Pratt? And on such a filthy night? We mustn't stand on ceremony, John. Show our guest in to me."

No! Impossible! He dines out every night . . . he cannot possibly be here! She turns to run, down the stairs and away, anywhere, anywhere but here . . . but if she runs it will be to Mario's ruin, and her everlasting shame, and neither of them will rise again. No, she is here, she has come with a purpose; she cannot falter now. Let her ask him directly if he will stop, if he will spare them . . . she will beg him on her knees, if she must. But there is no need for her to remove her bonnet and coat, she can get down on her knees in her coat. And there is no need to let him come too near . . .

Chadwick's eyes gleam as the servant ushers her into the well-lit drawing room, or perhaps it is just the lamplight on his spectacles. He is the picture of comfort, reclining in a large chair by the fire, a pile of books and legal journals on the table close at hand, along with his cigars and a decanter. He rises and comes forward, hand outstretched, as she enters.

"John, this is Mrs. Alfieri; the very same Miss Adler who was to have come here to live. You remember her, don't you? She would dine here from time to time, with her guardian, Mr. Slade."

John acknowledges recalling the very same Miss Adler.

"But take off your things, my dear. Now that you are here you must stay a while . . . no, I insist!" Stepping close to her, ignoring her stammered protests, he removes her hat and coat as one would those of a five-year-old, and she shrinks back, trying to maintain her composure.

"Thank you, John, that will be all. And, oh . . . I think we should perhaps *not* inform Miss Lucy of our guest's presence. Very good, John, thank you . . . and close the doors behind you as you go. There! And so we are alone together once more, my dear. How delightful of you to visit . . . and after such a long time too. Here am I, captive to the inclement weather and cursing my fate for having to stay at home, and what happens? A lovely young woman calls upon me! No, no, my dear, not that chair . . . it's entirely too far away. After all this time I want you near me. This one . . . yes, that's right, I want the firelight on your pretty face, so I can see you better.

"How fortunate for me that I am at home tonight . . . I had expected to be dining with Mrs. Grenville and a few friends, but sadly, I had to send my apologies; it would have been such a charming evening too, but I have been feeling a cold coming on, and at my age one can never be too careful . . ." He smiles, shrugging away his affliction.

She stares up at Chadwick from the depths of the large wing chair. The lawyer watches as her eyes dart from side to side, for all the world like those of any small, suddenly trapped animal. She is as tiny as ever, he notes, and despite the thinness of her face, she has grown prettier . . . prettier, even, than her mother had been. He reflects, too, upon the fact that her figure has grown fuller and more womanly . . .

the natural effect, Chadwick supposes, of the nightly gallops her Italian puts her through. He is pleased to see that she still bites her fingernails.

"Let me think," he says genially, seating himself opposite her and smiling to see the flicker of relief in her eyes as the distance between them increases. "How long is it since we've seen each other? Why . . . is it possible? . . . four months? Our last meeting is so clear in my mind."

In hers too. She looks away briefly, then meets his eyes again, blushing at the memory. Their last meeting had taken place the day before her wedding. Chadwick had come to the Gramercy Park house for his usual Tuesday luncheon, full of bonhomie and high spirits, talking of nothing but his eagerness to have her beneath his roof. He had been excited by the thought of Friday, when he would be claiming her at last, and he had touched her constantly . . . her face, her arm, her neck and hair . . . and after the dishes were cleared and Margaret had left them alone, he had kissed her, not waiting until he was leaving this time, pulling her against him. When she fought him he slapped her face, knocking her to the floor, but the blow had brought him to himself. He had stood over her, breathing heavily, straightening his clothes.

"Understand me," he had said. "In my house certain things will be expected."

She had never told Mario, afraid of what he might do to Chadwick, but also knowing that her own past had made such advances inevitable. And, then, how to tell Mario, only to have him find on their wedding night that what she had resisted with Chadwick was something she had long ago—and often—done with someone else?

"I am sorry if I disappointed you." It is as much as she can bring herself to say.

"Disappointed me? By running off with a debauchee rather than accepting my hospitality?" His smile widens at the tightening of her lips. "I suppose that I must lay the fault at the feet of Eros. I fear that unbridled passion is responsible for so many of the world's miseries. Naturally, dear girl, I hope that your future with your singer will be a happy one; but I fear that old philandering habits, such as he has cultivated, die hard . . ." He lets his words trail off.

"At least," he says, "you seem relatively well. I have heard terrifying stories about the state of your health . . . opening night in Philadelphia, for instance . . ." He clucks his tongue. "But your appearance tonight puts paid to that tale. Your singer does seem to care for you, after all. I will take great pleasure in strangling that particular rumor."

Clara lifts her chin. "He is my husband," she says. "Not my singer. And speaking of rumors, is Lucy in? I would like a few words with her."

"Why, my dear, can it be possible that I've angered you by sharing common gossip? You must forgive me; you know how I love good gossip." Chadwick cocks his head. "And as far as Lucy goes, you must know that she is not . . . overly fond of you."

"But I would still speak with her."

"Are you certain of that? She is rather . . . well, let us simply say that she seems to have developed an extraordinary animus toward you. I do not think an interview with her would be wise."

"Perhaps. But I wish to speak with her. Alone, please."

"Foolish, my dear."

"Yes. But that is why I came. Not to see you. I am sorry if that hurts your feelings."

He sits back in his chair with a smile. "Clara, my dear . . ."

"I am not your dear. You are trying to . . . Stafford Dyckman says that you have been saying things . . . telling people . . ." Faced with his mocking gaze, she suddenly cannot go on. But why else is she here, exposing herself to this humiliation? "He said that you were telling people about . . ."

"About . . . ?"

"About Dr. Fauvell . . ." Her face is white, now, her hands beginning to twist.

Chadwick nods. "Certainly I am." he says. "His story makes most edifying conversation over port and cigars. I knew him, you see, long before you did. I knew his wife and stepdaughter . . . that is how Lucy Pratt comes to be staying with me now. The man was quite a character . . . but of course, you know that far better than I . . . perhaps better than anyone, except Lucy. And your husband, of course. I'm certain he has a special appreciation for Dr. Fauvell's . . . singularity."

Clara forces herself to look at him. "Do you hate Mario so much?"

"Well, you see, my dear, it is a combination of forces. By going off with him, you had the ill luck to shatter plans in which I had invested a great deal of time and effort. Your . . . singer, on the other hand, annoys me with his arrogance. He needs to be taken down a peg or two. And I am scrupulous in making people who have injured me pay for that mistake. Your mother, for instance . . . your mother insulted me, and through you I have been—and continue to be—able to pay her back."

Clara blinks, feeling the blood rushing to her face. "You knew . . . you knew my mother? You never told me."

"There was no reason for me to tell you before," Chadwick says. "Yes, I knew her, although not nearly so well as I should have liked. And only for a few months. She was very like you, my dear . . . or, rather, you are very much as she was when I knew her . . . only much prettier."

"What was she like?" Wide-eyed as a child at Christmas, Clara stares up at him, all thoughts of anything else gone. For the first time in her life she will hear about the mother she has never known. "Please . . . what was she like?"

"Very blithe and charming. Quite a little bird, with a bewitching smile and a sunny disposition. She, too, had chestnut hair. And she had lovely eyes, my dear; certainly you have your mother's eyes." His smile fades. "But she had her faults too, and one in particular. Can you guess what it was? She was proud. I imagine it came of being a Jew . . . but whatever the reason, she was too proud for her own good. The Good Book says, after all, that 'pride goeth before destruction, and a haughty spirit before a fall.' Your mother tried to fly too high—poor little bird!— and her pretty feathers were singed for her trouble."

"You said she insulted you. Perhaps you misunderstood; perhaps she never intended—"

"Oh, no, my dear," he says. "There was no mistaking what she did. But she paid for her insolence . . . or rather, you did. I had Edward Fauvell take you in, and very soon the debt was paid."

He watches her as his words sink in, leans forward and touches her frozen face, running his fingers down her cheek. "Little Clara," he says. "I had almost forgiven you for being her child. And then you had to spoil everything by running off with your singer. Pity." He leans back in his chair.

She is staring at him now with a look of uncomprehending horror. "You? You sent me to Papa?"

"So you call him Papa too." He laughs and shrugs. "I knew a family who needed schooling for a child. I knew a man who was eminently qualified to teach her. I had a debt to settle. It all made so very much sense . . . and it was so very convenient."

She is trying to piece the enormity together. "My family were your clients? How? And where did my mother go?"

"As to your last question, I do not know, and my wishes for her destination will not make it so. Her own behavior will do that. As to how . . . no, your family were not my clients. But I was under an obligation to assist them with anything to do with you."

"Why?"

He answers with another question. "Why," he says, "do you never ask about your father?"

She has a sudden vision of herself as a marionette, her strings pulled from above. Beyond the hand that holds the strings, dim and gigantic in the sky, is the face of Thaddeus Chadwick, and nothing that happens in her life happens without his fingers guiding the threads . . . "I don't want to know any more," she whispers. "Please let me leave. I want to go home."

"So soon? Why you've barely just arrived. We have so much to say."

"No . . . no more. I shouldn't have come."

"Now there I agree with you. Fortunately, Lucy and I are not on speaking terms any longer—a situation welcomed by both of us, I assure you—otherwise your visit might have ended quite differently. But she stays largely in her own room—the room that would have been yours, my dear—when I am at home.

"Besides, you needn't speak to her. You are here to try and stop my happy tale-telling. Stafford Dyckman has overheard me at someone's house, and is shocked that I would impart such information about a lady of his acquaintance. But you are no lady, my child—you never will be; your sins are written for all time, along with Papa Fauvell's and Lucy Pratt's—and your husband is no gentleman. Both he and you owe me a debt."

"Please," she says. "Please don't."

He gazes at her with a small, contemptuous smile. "Your happiness means nothing to me. Why should it? Give me a tangible reason not to make your sins public."

She hesitates, unsure of telling. "I'm having a child," she says finally. "We've just found out. It's due in May, we think." She raises her eyes to him. "Don't ruin us, Uncle Chadwick."

He nods. How perfect. Her mother's daughter, to the life. So disgustingly fecund. He pictures her in six months' time, distorted and gross, swollen to bursting with the Italian's child, looking as her mother had looked. A shame, for the daughter is prettier . . .

"I have a proposition."

She looks up, not daring to hope. If she can come to some sort of understanding with him . . . if she can save Mario's career . . .

"I made your mother an offer. She spat in my face. The consequence of that was three years' imprisonment in her parents' house—with you, my dear—before she climbed down a drainpipe and disappeared forever. I make you a similar offer. The stakes, I think, are rather higher . . . not three years' internment, but the swift and absolute end, forever, of an illustrious career, and the permanent expulsion—for both of you—from every form of polite society. The situation, too, is quite different, of course: you are married, and that fact may sway you against my little offer. But I presume you love your husband. Knowing, then, what the price of refusal is, I am certain that love will find a way.

"Think for a moment before you refuse! You are so much like her, my child . . . although, as I said, even prettier. It should be possible to meet somewhere . . . twice a week, I think, is sufficient for my needs . . . until you become too big to be attractive, and I am no longer interested . . . say perhaps three months from now?

She looks sick and white. "No," she whispers. "Oh, no. Not ever."

His eyebrows shoot skyward. "Really, my dear? Such a flat refusal, and so quickly? But what am I asking, after all? Nothing that you have not done before, and it will all be over in three months. A small price to pay for silence, I would have thought, especially to one who started so young."

Clara stumbles to the door, her hand over her mouth.

"Your husband has you to blame for this. Do you think he will thank you for your scruples when he is nothing? When he is remembered only as a dirty joke? Good night, then, my dear," he says as she reaches for the handle. "I quite enjoyed our visit . . . I only regret that our parting must be so final. I dine on Monday night with Mrs. Hamilton Fish. My, but doesn't she have a sharp tongue! She and her other guests will love the story of Dr. Edward Fauvell and his last pupil."

She sags against the door, eyes closed. "I can't," she whispers. "Please don't make me."

"I'm not making you do anything, child. The decision is entirely yours. You are free to go if you wish."

A wrench at the door and she is out in the entrance hall . . . and standing just ahead of her, halfway down the stairs, is Lucy Pratt. The two women stare at each other for a long moment . . . Lucy blinks and smiles, incredulous, and begins to descend, almost creeping from step to step, amazingly quiet for one so large, never taking her eyes from Clara.

Clara hears Chadwick's voice calling: "My compliments to your husband, my dear!"

She must pass the bottom of the stairs to reach the front door, and in another instant Lucy will be between her and escape. She flings herself forward, praying as she hits the door that the servants have not locked it . . . tears at it, sobbing, and suddenly is outside, half falling down the front steps and running, lifting her skirts and running, down the black night streets in a cold and steady rain, with the sound of Lucy's shriek rising behind her . . .

Chapter Thirty-six

H<small>E HAS FOUND</small> himself a bench, a little way into the park, from which he can watch the house. The view is unobstructed. If she comes out—or if she does not—he will know. One advantage of the rain is that not many are clamoring to sit beside him . . . he can raise his injured leg and stretch it out on the bench. The ankle is already so swollen that the top of his leather boot bulges; he cannot tell if it is broken or merely twisted, but whichever makes no difference; the result is the same: he can no longer put any weight on the foot.

Settling into the corner of the bench, he folds his arms and tries to retreat as far as he can into his coat, which is already wet through; the rain runs in little rivers down his neck, plastering his hair to his scalp. The signora has been in the house perhaps ten minutes already. If she does not emerge within the next ten minutes he will go in and get her . . . the question is how, considering that he will find it almost impossible to walk up the stairs to ring the doorbell, much less climb up the back of the building to slip through a window. Still, something must be done. If the house is lawyer Chadwick's, as he suspects, he cannot let her stay there any length of time. The thought of what could happen, particularly if the crazy Pratt woman is within, makes him sweat beneath the cold rain.

Gesù Maria, but they must be wild at home. By now the cook must have given his note to the maestro, but that will tell him only that

Gennarino has followed the signora from the house, not where he had
followed her to. And who in his right mind would think that she would
come here? He fastens his eyes to the front of the house and lets his
mind roam, trying to solve the problem of how to reach her . . . and
does not sense the presence behind him until the stick jams into his ribs.

"An' what might you be doin' here, mister?"

Gennarino raises his head. His appearance is against him . . . soaking
wet and hatless on a bench in the rain. His answer does nothing to help
either. At the sound of his broken English, the policeman nods.

"An Eye-tie," he says. "Move on. No vagrants allowed on these
benches. Try Mulberry Street . . . they're less particular there."

He gestures toward the next street over, and stands tapping his club
in his other hand, waiting and watching as Gennarino gets to his feet—
one foot, really, the other being only a lump of agony—and hobbles
away east along Waverly Place, using railings as crutches, having no idea
of either what or where Mulberry Street is, and even less interest. He
turns the corner back onto Fifth Avenue. Just past the houses is a mews
that must run behind the Chadwick house; he had missed it before, in
his haste to follow the hansom. Now he limps quietly into it.

The lights are on in several of the carriage houses; one or two men
move in and out of the rain carrying harnesses and bridles. They eye
him briefly, but make no attempt to question him, or bar his way.
Counting the correct number of houses, Gennarino limps along slowly
until he stands by a six-foot-high wooden fence that effectively separates
the mews from the little garden behind Chadwick's house. No gate. No
entrance of any kind. No way to gain access to the grounds, other than
climbing over the fence and dropping down on the other side, which is
precisely what he is incapable of doing. Defeated, he looks up at the
windows of the house itself.

The parlor floor is invisible, hidden by the fence. But the windows of
the floor above blaze with light; and framed in one of them is the figure of
a vastly fat woman who bends and sways in place, her arms raised, as if
dancing to the strains of music only she can hear. She dips and turns, and
as the light strikes her hair Gennarino can see that she is blond.

He watches for several minutes, fascinated and appalled, the agony of his swollen foot almost forgotten . . . certain that he is seeing Lucy Pratt for the first time, and relieved at the sight: this woman wears her corset and little else, and unless she had invited the little signora to her bedroom to watch her prance about, it is probable that *la pazza* does not even know of the presence of such a guest within the house.

This time he hears the footsteps coming slowly up behind him, and turns warily, fearing the return of the policeman . . . but it is a stranger. In the dim light of the mews, Gennarino can see that he is young, dark, and well built, with an impressive black *mustacchio* like a *brigante* from the hills, dressed in tunic, jodhpurs, high boots—no doubt one of the drivers who lives above the carriages. The rain has slowed to a drizzle now, and he stands a few feet away, saying nothing, only looking Gennarino up and down; then, still silent, he lights a cigarette—the rasp of the match is surprisingly loud—and blows a cloud of smoke in Gennarino's direction.

Gennarino nods. It will be wise to be polite . . . he is trespassing, and in no condition to defend himself. *"Buona sera, signore,"* he says.

The young man answers in Italian. "Looking for something?"

Gennarino's heart jumps. A *compatriota!* "For someone, not something. My master's lady is visiting there." He gestures with his head to the house behind him. "I'm waiting for her to come out."

"She won't be coming this way." The young man sweeps his hand toward the fence. "No way out."

Gennarino nods. *"Sì,* I realize. I would have gone in a minute. But I couldn't help stopping to watch . . ." He looks up at the window. Lucy Pratt still spins and sways, her bulk silhouetted against the light. The young man stares at the twirling apparition, his head to one side, a small lewd smile on his face.

"Not your master's lady, is she? No, I didn't think so, but it's best to ask . . . I wouldn't want to insult your *padrone.*" He takes a long drag of his cigarette, still staring up at Lucy. "A lot of woman, that," he says, his voice thick. "A man could drown in all that flesh. He could suffocate." He shakes his hand while sucking in his breath. "Imagine burying your face between those two melons . . . a man could fall right in and never be heard from again."

They both laugh.

"Does she do this often?" Gennarino says. The dance recital is apparently over: Lucy is pinning up her hair, still standing before the window.

"She started about a week ago. I certainly never noticed it before that—and believe me, I would have—although I know she's been living here for a month or two. I'd seen her at the window, but not shaking her . . ." He wiggles his buttocks and laughs, then extends his cigarette case; Gennarino accepts with thanks.

"You like them big?" Gennarino says, leaning into the match the young man offers.

"I like them any way I can get them . . . big, small, young, old, blond, brown, red-haired. But the fat ones . . . the fat ones are juicy. They squeal a lot when you push it in, and they jiggle like pudding . . ." He drops his own cigarette on the ground, crushes it with the toe of his boot, then runs his hands over his face.

"The bitch knows I see her, and she knows she's safe because I can't get at her. Even if I got over the fence and could climb up there, I could never get in her windows. Iron bars." He nods toward Lucy's windows. "You see?"

Lucy is dressing slowly, fastening the buttons of her bodice, working from the bottom up, bending forward as she encloses her breasts behind the fabric.

"Yes," says Gennarino. "I see." He looks at the young man, holding out his hand. "I am Salvatore Gennarino."

"Ferruccio Cirri," the young man says, taking it. He gestures at Gennarino's foot. "You seem to be in some trouble. Can I be of any help?"

"Signor Cirri," Gennarino says. "I think the good God has brought us together. We have known each other a very short time . . . but I wonder if I might ask you a great favor?"

THE RAIN has stopped. Alfieri stands by the drawing-room window, staring out, waiting for something to appear . . . willing it with every fragment of his being. Every carriage that looms into view is followed by his eyes, only to leave him looking empty and defeated as it passes by without stopping.

A scrap of brown paper lies between his fingers; he turns it over and over, folding it, worrying it, rubbing it like a charm, making the original illegible scrawl on it quite unreadable. By the time they board ship on Monday he will be grateful for a lifetime of nothingness; he wonders if he will even live that long. God knows he cannot bear much more . . . every time he thinks it is finally over, another blow falls . . .

I have nothing left to give, he thinks. I have given it all, there is nothing left. Father, don't let this happen. Bring her back to me . . . safe, with our child unharmed. I ask for nothing else, only that. Bring her back to me. I have nothing to give You now but my heart's blood, and that is Yours, too, if You will only bring her back . . .

Alice enters the room with a rustle of skirts. Alfieri turns to her and she stares at his anguished face, her heart aching for him.

"Did you know," he says, as if they have been talking all the while, "that she offered to leave me? To keep me safe from Lucy Pratt . . . to keep *me* safe . . ."

Daniel Buchan enters, stands beside his wife. He, too, looks at Alfieri, and instinctively his hand gropes for that of his wife. Mario looks at the two of them, at their clasped hands, and turns away, back to the window.

An elegant private carriage turns onto Madison Avenue from the direction of Twenty-sixth Street, a shiny burgundy brougham with lanterns gleaming. Alfieri raises his head, more from force of habit than any expectation, and watches it with dull eyes. The uniformed driver, young and dark, with a fine black moustache, turns the horse neatly and brings the carriage to a halt directly in front of the house; and Alfieri, his face bloodless, is out of the house and down the stairs in the time the driver takes to jump down and open the carriage door . . .

Gennarino smiles tiredly from the wine-leather cushions, looking drowned, holding a sleeping Clara in his arms.

Chapter Thirty-seven

THE ALFIERIS' LAST full day in New York dawns silvery wet, the sun hidden behind high clouds that seem always about to break, and never do. It is Sunday, October the fourteenth, and on this day of rest there is still much for some to do.

Gennarino, for instance, supervises the departure from the Madison Avenue house despite having one useless leg. Dr. Fisher, coming promptly when summoned last night, had examined the injured ankle—so swollen that the boot had to be cut from the foot—and pronounced it sprained but not broken; which news did nothing to cheer the patient, as the resulting period of enforced inactivity is the same: one full month, at least. But this morning Gennarino has Peters strategically place two chairs in the servants' hall, one for his posterior and another for his bandaged foot; and sitting with his arms crossed before him, every inch the Bonaparte, he oversees the loading of trunks and boxes onto the carts that will transport them to the dock . . . and onto the ship for England.

It is all being done so efficiently that the master and mistress of the household have very little to do, except remain out of the way, until the time comes to prepare for the little farewell dinner party and birthday celebration, the final festivity to be held by them beneath that roof.

At ten in the morning, therefore, Alfieri enters the sitting room looking for his wife. The pretty room looks sad now, abandoned, like the half-bare autumn trees outside, all its little amenities stripped away. Clara, sitting in the midst of the barrenness, lost in her thoughts, looks the same. Watching her from the doorway, Alfieri has a sudden glimpse of a child sitting alone at a deserted railway station . . .

He has not spoken to her, yet, of yesterday's adventure; there has been no time. She had been too exhausted, when Gennarino brought her home, to do more than bathe, be examined by the doctor—who found that neither she nor the baby had taken any harm from the experience—and let herself be put to bed. And this morning, for the first time since shortly before his marriage, Alfieri has gone to Mass, and lit candles to the Blessed Virgin in thanks for the safe return of his wife and child.

And now, at last, it is time to speak . . . but not here, in this sadness.

"Madonna," he says. "Will you walk with me? The sun is coming out, the day will be pretty. If you're tired we needn't go far."

Together they go downstairs to the entrance hall . . . where their plans are halted for half of an hour, while the trunk containing Clara's cloaks and wrappers is located and unloaded from the cart, and a coat retrieved from it; and the proper hatbox found amid a dozen others; and the whereabouts of her gloves tracked down: for she had fled from Chadwick last night leaving those things behind, and substitutes must be provided.

The delay only sinks her into greater melancholy. She sits in the drawing room, waiting, head down, her eyes fixed absently on nothing, and her fingers, which fidget incessantly, pull at her already ragged nails and torn cuticles. Alfieri reaches over once, and puts his hand on hers to stop them, and she does stop, mortified . . . but when he takes his hand away again, hers slowly return to their self-mutilation, their owner unaware of what they do.

She is not even aware when her husband leaves the room for a few moments. He returns with something in his hands that he holds behind his back, but she is no more aware of his return than she was of his leaving, and he bends and kisses the top of her head to get her attention. Startled, she looks up.

"I was saving this to give you before our guests arrive tonight, *diletta.*

But perhaps, while we wait, you'd like to open it now? I thought that it might cheer you. It is my special gift to you for your special day, the first of many we will spend together, God willing."

She keeps her head down, unable to look at him. After she has terrified him as she has, after she has failed . . . She slides the ribbon from the flat velvet box and lifts the lid . . .

Green . . . she has never seen such green . . . she looks up, incredulous, her mouth an open O of wonder, and then down again at the circle of perfect emeralds nestled in white satin.

"To match your eyes," he says. "Your lovely eyes. Happy birthday, my dearest love."

She lifts her head again. Her eyes brim with tears. After she has failed, he would give her these. After she has ruined his life . . .

"I can save you," she says. "I can. I can save your career."

His smile is gone. "*Cara* . . . what are you saying?"

"I can save you. No! No, don't ask how! Only know that I can." Her face is white again, and sick. "That was when I ran away . . . that was why . . . Mario, tell me I did right." She wipes her eyes with the backs of her hands. "If you want me to," she whispers, "I will. To save you, I will . . . if you want me to." She is shaking now. "Mario, tell me not to . . . tell me I did right . . . Mario, tell me . . ."

And all the while he is kissing her hands and face, telling her, oh! that she did right a thousand times, she did right!—dear God, could she think otherwise for one moment?—she did right! . . . He cannot breathe with wanting to kill, with the rage filling his lungs, clogging his throat, choking him. He sobs, once, writhing inside, wild that he cannot close his hands around Chadwick's throat and crush the life from it, but Clara thinks he is angry with her, and he says again into her hair: "No, no . . . never with you, never with you . . . you did right, you did right . . ."

Through the window Alfieri can see the huge cart drawn up to the curb, and watch the men wrestling the trunks into place. Tomorrow he and Clara will be gone, by evening they will be well out to sea and on their way home . . . home for good and all, home forever and ever. He regrets nothing he has done, only what he leaves undone: Chadwick still lives—the man who had sent Clara to Fauvell's bed still lives, to blacken her name, to denounce her to the world for the shame to which he had sent her; to laugh at the misery he has shaped. "Vengeance is mine," God said; "I will repay." But Chadwick still lives: esteemed, successful, free to spread his filth into the ears of the world.

He almost thinks it, almost prays: God, let me be the instrument of your vengeance; let me be the one . . . But last night, in this room, he had offered his heart's blood for his wife's safe return. And she is here; frightened and ashamed but here, and unharmed, and their child with her; and he has no right to ask for more, and nothing more to give. He will sail away with her, and raise his family quietly, if God will allow; and they will shut their ears to what the world may say, and live for each other.

"Father," he says. "Amen."

Margaret brings Clara's hat, coat, and gloves at last. Husband and wife walk slowly through Madison Square in the watery sunshine, kicking through the soggy leaves, nodding to other couples promenading along the paths on this Sabbath morning. They stop, after a while, to sit on a damp bench, and Clara tells him the entire tale, ending with her panicked flight into the dark streets, running anywhere, anywhere . . .

"I don't know where Gennarino came from. I stopped, finally, at what I thought was a church—I saw a bell tower in the distance and I ran toward it thinking I would be safe there—but when I got there it wasn't a church at all, and I couldn't run any more, and didn't know where I was . . . a wide street with trains thundering by overhead. I ran up the steps of the building—wide steps, like a church—and squeezed into the doorway as far as I could, to get out of the rain, and hide. All I could think of then was you, Mario, and how much I wanted to live so the baby could be born.

"And then a carriage stopped in front of the steps. The driver got down, opened the door, and helped a man out . . . the man seemed injured, or crippled, he couldn't walk, and the driver had to help him. They started toward the steps and I stood up, ready to run down the other side . . . and then"—she laughs with tears in her throat—"then I heard Gennarino's voice coming from the crippled man, calling: *"Signora!*

Signora, rimani, rimani! Non fuggire!" Still laughing, she takes the handkerchief Alfieri hands her and wipes her eyes.

"Gennarino told me," Alfieri says, "that God was watching, from beginning to end. The driver of the carriage is employed by the neighbor next door to Chadwick, and we owe him a great debt. He was gallant to come to our aid . . . if his use of the carriage is discovered he could lose his job. He had it ready in a moment, helped Gennarino in, and drove to the front of Chadwick's house just in time to see you fly down the stairs as if all the hounds of hell were after you . . . and they followed while you ran. Even with God looking down, Gennarino said, he recited the Ave Maria all the time they followed you. Twice you were nearly run down by cabs."

"I don't remember."

"No," he says, and raises her hand to his lips. "It was all very brave, and very, very stupid."

She searches his face. "You're not angry?"

"As a mother is when her child runs into the road." He touches her cheek. "And when the fright is over, grateful that all is well."

The answer gives her the strength to go on. "The night I told you my story . . . you already knew it. Who told you?"

"Daniel Buchan."

"How did he know?"

"Chadwick made threats against us when he discovered we had eloped. Because no one knew anything of your past, *piccola,* Daniel thought it wise to look into it. I agreed that he should."

"Does he know all about me?"

"All, *madonna?"*

"Everything. Where I come from, who I am. What happened."

"Sì."

"And you know too?"

"I know what he knows."

"Do you know who my father is?"

"Yes."

"Tell me."

He takes both her hands in his. *"Cara,* your father was Henry Slade."

"Thank you," she whispers, "thank you, thank you, thank you." And she buries her face against her husband's arm and weeps a little for what might have been, had she only known. After a while she lifts her head again.

"I never knew why he took me in. I thought I was just someone he found at his charity school, and adopted out of pity." She rests her head on Alfieri's shoulder. "I lived with him all those years and never guessed. Isn't it funny? . . . The one I called Papa wasn't, and I loved him. And the one who was my father I didn't love, not really."

"Didn't you? You became so ill, *madonna,* when he died."

"I was so frightened. It seemed that everyone who protected me or cared for me vanished from my life, or died. He was the latest, after Papa and my mother. And to be alone again . . . and to have no one standing between me and . . ." She draws a deep breath. "I didn't love him, but he had been kind to me, and I couldn't bear that he was gone. And afterward . . . he knew I was afraid, he had promised to leave me enough to make me independent, so that I wouldn't have to rely on anyone . . . and then there was nothing at all . . . only Mr. Chadwick. And I knew what he wanted. I always knew." Her voice is almost inaudible. "I would have died. I would have died very soon if you hadn't found me, if you hadn't taken me away. I couldn't bear it, to have him touch me, to have to . . ."

"Hush, dear heart." Alfieri raises her hands to his lips. "You're free of him, now, free of him forever. He doesn't matter any more."

"But he does matter. He's the reason we're running away, the reason you're losing everything."

"*Cara,* why can't I make you understand? The only thing I fear losing is you. That, I think, would stop my heart. The rest . . ." He shakes his head, then presses his lips to her bare wrist, just above her glove, and she curves her fingers to his cheek before laying her head against his shoulder once more.

They fall silent, sitting with their fingers intertwined, watching other couples pass them by, yet not watching at all. After a while he stands, holds out his hand to her, and they walk slowly back. At the edge of the square she stops, and he looks down into her face.

"At the beginning," she says, "when you found me . . . why did you love me?"

"Because you loved me."

She almost laughs at the pure foolishness of his words. "But everyone loves you. They always have."

"No . . . they love Mario Alfieri."

She does not understand. "You *are* Mario Alfieri."

"Not to you. Not then. To you I was only a stranger with a strange name, come to make you homeless. And still you loved me. I could see it in your eyes. You loved *me* . . . not what I had become to the world."

The cart is gone from in front of the house; their belongings are on their way to the ship, with Margaret and Peters following close behind, to prepare the cabins for tomorrow's sailing. Clara stops at the top of the stairs, before the front door. One final thing has been on her mind.

"Mario," she says, contritely, "about my birthday gift . . . I think that emeralds are an extravagance we can't afford, not now. We haven't time, but Daniel could take them back and send you the money . . ." Alfieri throws his head back and shouts with laughter, so that several people on the street below turn and look, smiling.

"Now you sound like a real wife, *una moglie genuina*! I knew this day would come! Well, first let me say," he says, holding the door for her, "that I can still buy emeralds for my wife if I choose. Secondly, emeralds are an excellent investment. We can always pawn them to buy coal for the fire, just before we send the children out to sell matches in the snow . . ."

Chapter Thirty-eight

CHADWICK STARES UP at the ceiling of his drawing room. The same lumbering tread, back and forth, back and forth, back and forth. He sets his book down in his lap, unhooks his spectacles from behind his ears, and pinches the bridge of his nose. It is a gesture he has been repeating often, of late, designed to relieve the pressure he feels just behind his eyes, whenever reminded of Lucy's presence beneath his roof.

His campaign is going well without her. He has seen the look in the eyes of the many men who gather around to listen over their glasses of port after dinner. They puff at their cigars a little too fast, while he speaks; roll them in their mouths a little too roughly; their eyes are a little too bright. They remember the Adler girl, of course they do; all of them had dealings with Slade, visited the house at Gramercy Park. A pretty child. Chadwick can watch them picturing her as he speaks— sweet and smooth, with her rosy red mouth, and her limpid eyes looking up shyly from under long lashes—picturing her, aged thirteen, rutting with Edward Fauvell on the carriage barn floor as the door bursts open . . . an irresistible sight, even in the mind's eye.

Yes, it is going very well. By opening night, a month away, everyone in the two horseshoe tiers of balconies—Diamond and Golden—should see the horns springing from the fabulous tenor's head the moment he steps onstage, and any of the audience still in ignorance will see them too, by the end of the first interval.

Let him come out a second night! Let him walk out into the lights before that cavernous house, before an audience of three thousand, each of whom knows that the tenor's wife is no better than the slut who struts her wares on the Bowery . . . that their virile, invincible star, devourer of women, has been duped and degraded, has taken a harlot as the bride of his heart . . .

He pinches his nose again, breathing hard. He'd had the bitch's coat and hat thrown onto the fire; he wishes she had been in them. Did she ever get home last night? She had disappeared into the rain heading west, toward the river and the slaughterhouses, Lucy snatching at her skirts and screeching like a train whistle. He envisions her wandering the labyrinth of streets, lost in the sodden darkness, accosted by some stinking tanner, or a butcher in his cups with a bloody apron and a meat hook. More convincing than a simple proposition, a meat hook . . . let her say no to a meat hook . . . let her find herself bent backwards over a barrel in a loading dock beneath the slabs of meat, with her skirts up around her waist and a crowd gathering to watch and cheer and take their turns . . .

He staggers to his feet, trembling and short of breath, his book tumbling from his lap. Lurching to the sideboard, he fills a glass with whiskey, neat, and gulps it down, the liquor spilling from the corners of his mouth, and stands half bent over, hearing Lucy's tread, endlessly marching back and forth, back and forth, back and forth . . .

Her mother had spit at him, but she . . . she had looked at him with the kind of disgust with which you wipe the dung from your shoe! She had looked at him—Chadwick!—as if he were filth, had fled from him, sick and shaking. Her mother had been offended by the idea . . . but she—the daughter—had been revolted by *him* . . . he had felt it like a blow across the face. That whore's spawn! Who was she, that she should look at him that way!

Another glass . . . his hand shakes, and he splashes the whiskey onto the polished surface of the sideboard. Never mind! He squeezes the bridge of his nose again, bent over and breathing loudly. If he were not the rational, balanced person he is he would have snatched up the poker . . . he could have reached her before she reached the door . . .

he has visions of his arm rising and falling, rising and falling, feels the sweet, sweet sensation of fury flowing out, flowing down his arm and away with each thud . . .

It takes a few minutes, but the whiskey is effective. In a few minutes the shaking stops and his breathing slows, and he combs his sparse hair back with not quite steady fingers, and sponges the front of his coat and shirt with his handkerchief.

He passes Lucy's door a few minutes later, on his way to change for dinner. Her residence here is finished; he wants her gone, as soon as possible. Her unspeakable scene last night, after the Adler girl had fled, has made it impossible for him to keep her any longer.

She had lunged for Clara as the girl fled down the steps, while Chadwick danced with delight, urging her on, and missed her by mere inches, her fat hands closing on air, snapping open and shut, like crab claws, in wild frustration. Had Lucy only caught her and held on . . . she would have dragged Clara back and snapped her neck, or strangled her where she stood . . . and Chadwick would then have summoned the police with the greatest pleasure, and exerted himself on her behalf just sufficiently to appear genuinely distressed when she was sentenced to hang for murder . . .

Dear God, to be rid of both of them so neatly! But it had not happened. To chase a light-footed young thing who is racing for her life is something of which Lucy is not capable. Stupid, worthless cow! She had stood at the top of the steps and screamed after Clara as the girl disappeared into the darkness. "Whore!" she had shrieked. "Whore! You're not fit to live!" . . . And it had taken John and himself, assisted by the cook and the parlor maid, to drag her back inside, where she had screamed for another hour, calling him every vile name she had learned in her fancy French finishing school, for letting the little bitch go. He had spent most of this morning visiting houses on either side, quietly apologizing for the unhinged young woman he has taken beneath his roof, and assuring them that she would soon be gone.

Now he stands before his mirror, silver-backed brush in each hand, smoothing his hair into place. Serenity, always serenity . . . he must take better care of himself going forward . . . he must remember that serenity is his watchword. He has ignored it, of late, to his detriment; but he seems less able to keep his emotions under check than he had been before . . . a sign of age, perhaps; an increasing amount of bile. He takes a few deep breaths. No matter. Once Lucy is gone he can settle back into the sweet routine of his life, and there will be little to disturb him, or break the smooth flow of planned and orderly hours, falling as gently as petals into the well of time . . .

As he passes by on his way downstairs, John arrives at Lucy's door with her dinner tray. A big man, the servant can barely handle the load of covered dishes and cutlery, and is raising an encumbered hand to knock when the door is wrenched open from the inside. Chadwick and Lucy stare at each other for a moment; then she pointedly turns her back on him and flounces off into her room, and he proceeds downstairs to his own dinner. He is coldly amused to see that she is clad in a dressing gown like a lavishly frilled circus tent; he will wager any amount that beneath it she wears only her corset, and that she has been pirou-etting before her window again, displaying her charms to the grooms.

Dinner is excellent, and uneventful, and Chadwick follows it with a quiet glass of port, and a cigar, in the drawing room. Tonight will be an early night . . . yesterday's excitement has left him fatigued. Perhaps he is getting old, after all. He must be on the qui vive tomorrow; dinner with Mrs. Fish means quick repartee . . . her contempt for the rest of the world is easily the equal of his, and she enjoys an acid give-and-take—mainly give, since it is her table—with him as her guest. And then, after dinner, there will be many who have not yet heard the remarkable tale of the former headmaster of St. Justin Martyr and the little girl who has become the wife of Mario Alfieri . . .

Lucy's door is ajar, when he climbs the stairs to return to his room. He taps, and hears the stiff rustle of her frills as she approaches. The door swings open; she stands there, unblinking.

"May I come in?" he says, and she steps back wordlessly.

He walks to the center of the room. The shades are up once more, and the curtains flung wide, but at least she is covered for the moment . . . the sight of that mountain of flesh directly after dinner would make him vomit. The room itself resembles a pigsty . . . clothing, jewelry, jars of cream, books, hairpins, scent bottles, papers; open boxes of candy, their half-eaten contents spilling out . . . all jumbled together, lying everywhere, over every surface . . . a nightmare simulacrum, in miniature, of her rooms in Rosebank. On her dressing table lies the dinner tray, dish covers scattered, damask napkin lying in a pool of congealed gravy, glasses overturned, gnawed bones heaped on plates. A greasy knife sticks straight up from a half-eaten pork chop, its ivory handle jutting obscenely into the air. Chadwick's fastidious soul revolts at the sight.

"The neighbors were less than pleased with your shrieking obscenities down the street last night." Chadwick does not believe in wasting time, whether for good news or bad. "I must ask you to leave my house."

"Gladly. I can't wait to get away from you." Lucy's face is splotchy and swollen, as if she has been crying; she is not at her most attractive.

Chadwick bows and smiles. "Then it appears that, for once at least, in recent weeks, we are in complete agreement." He turns to go.

"Why didn't you call me downstairs?" she demands. "Why didn't you tell me she was here?"

He swings back. "You were brought here for a reason, my dear. That reason was to tell Maestro Alfieri about his wife's little peccadilloes. When it became clear that he had found out in some other way, your reason for being here ceased to exist. I very fairly laid another opportunity before you . . . to tell the rest of the world what Alfieri already knew about his wife, and destroy her that way. You would hear none of it, however. You would not have your precious Papa's name sullied. Very well. But considering that you are somewhat overexcitable, my dear—which you proved so brilliantly last evening—I was loath to have you face-to-face with her. Brains and blood are messy, which I am certain you know . . . it was you, was it not, who tried to sponge the muck off the wall in the carriage barn? . . . and I prefer not to have my house look like an abattoir if I can possibly prevent it."

"You brought me here to get justice!" Lucy's eyes suddenly narrow. "Just why were you so interested in justice for me, after all these years? I've never asked you before. You were as eager to have me speak to Alfieri as I was to speak to him. Why?"

Chadwick smiles. "I think you remember what you want to, my dear. You were the one who said that the Adler girl's husband should be told of her misdeeds."

"Yes," Lucy answers, "but you were the one who said you could introduce me to her husband, that you knew him . . . 'in a small way,' you said. And you offered to bring me to New York. And then you did even more . . . you suggested we go to Philadelphia, to see them when they arrived. It was you who placed me in the crowd by the platform, on the chance that she might see me. It was your idea that we return for opening night, your idea that we send her the prism." Lucy cocks her head to one side. "You've been every bit as interested in my revenge as I have. And so I ask again . . . why?"

Chadwick says: "Why? Because my sole concern was to assist you in your distress."

She shakes her head. "That won't do . . . Uncle. It was your visit to Rosebank to tell me of her marriage that began my 'distress.' I would never have known of it, but for you. Last night I began to pick it all apart. For instance, just how did her people know to send her to Papa? I never thought to ask that before. Papa never asked for students in Rosebank, never sought them out. So how would a family of Jew shop-keepers know of him or where he was? And then I remembered . . . you knew Papa from St. Justin's, didn't you? And you knew where he had gone. And when Papa was dead the little bitch wound up in a charity school supported by your client, and then in your client's house. It suddenly occurred to me . . . Uncle Chadwick . . . that all of the threads lead back to you."

Chadwick smiles and, raising his hands, begins to applaud slowly. "*Brava*, my dear! You have proven me wrong, after all this time. I had supposed that you were far too stupid ever to piece my little plan together . . . and yes, you are quite right . . . it was I who sent the little brown mouse to your dear Papa. The why needn't concern you. Suffice it to say that his—predilection—gave me the revenge I wanted."

A smile spreads across Lucy's swollen face. "But not enough revenge, Uncle, clearly. Oh, no . . . nowhere near enough. Because you came to me wanting the slut crushed, or better yet, dead. But you wouldn't dirty your hands, so I was to have the honor of doing it for you. Why? What had she done to you? What reason could you have for hating her so much, for hating her as much as I did? And then I remembered her face. I was coming down the stairs when she ran from the drawing room, I saw it clearly. She was in a panic, Uncle . . . running from you. Oh, no! Don't try to put the blame on me! She was terrified before she saw me. *You* frightened her."

She tilts her head, grotesquely coquettish, her smile ghastly. "I lay awake all last night, thinking, and there is only one explanation that covers everything. You wanted her, Uncle, but you couldn't have her. Your client died and you wanted her for your own, but she ran away, she eloped with the tenor, and that drove you mad. And you still want her, don't you? What happened, Uncle, to frighten her so? Because something you said or did last night sent her flying out the door." She pauses, as if reliving the scene in her memory.

"No . . . no, I misspoke. It wasn't fear that made her run. I remember the look on her face, as clear as day. Not fear . . . disgust. Something you did disgusted her—I can only imagine what that was—and she ran away." Lucy's face is flushed, her swollen eyes wide. "You disgust her, Uncle Chadwick. You want her, but you disgust her, and she'll never be yours."

The blood is beating like a pulse in his head; his eyes throb. "Disgust? That, my girl, is a word you should scrupulously avoid. Disgust? What do you think he thought of you . . . your precious Papa? Do you think, once he caught sight of *her*, that you ever stood a chance? God, how long I've laughed at you, with your sniveling self-pity, and your pious, moronic nonsense about what a good man he was. A good man? He married to save his neck, but he chose your mother so that he could continue bedding you . . . did you think I didn't know? You're not clever enough to keep secrets from me!

"But you were getting older, weren't you? You could take your mother's place in his bed and laugh at her heartache, but you couldn't stop yourself from becoming a woman and losing him anyway. Look at yourself . . . udders like a cow, acres of flesh, and you thought you'd be able to keep him?" He watches the color deepen in her face, the tears of rage well in her eyes. "If we're to talk about disgust, my dear, let's talk about you. And then let's talk about our little Clara. What was she like when she first arrived? Small? Elfin? Enchanting?"

He smiles indulgently. "Why, you must have known the moment you saw her that it was over for you, that he'd never look at you again! How long did it take before he sent you away? Weeks? Days? You went and she stayed. Did you picture them together while you sat in your French classroom, becoming a lady?"

"Stop it!"

"And at night, when you lay in your chaste French bed, did you dream of them together, rolling around in the sheets, laughing at you?"

Her voice rises to a shriek. "Stop it!"

"She was perfect for him, of course . . . not a great cow, all teats and buttocks, but a dainty brown mouse . . . just the proper little fairy for that good man, your Papa. That good, kind man, that saint!" He laughs, his head thrown back, the pain in his head suddenly gone. "Saint Edward the Depraved, who suffered little children to come unto him! I knew he couldn't resist her, I knew it, I knew it!"

Chadwick stares into Lucy's wet eyes, his spectacles winking in the light.

"Frankly, my dear, you should be grateful to me. You'd lost him in any case; this way you got an elegant French education for your pains. You won't admit it, I know, but I did you a favor, after all, by tucking little Clara into your Papa's bed. You might have been walled up in Rosebank forever, and never seen the world." He turns to go, stops, and turns back. "And speaking of Rosebank," he says, "I want you gone as quickly as possible. You can return to your farm, of course, or you can stay in the city, whichever you please. I'm certain you can afford a fine place, with all the money you've realized from the sale of Fauvell's things. But either way, I want you out of my house, and soon. I'll have nothing more to do with women. You're all more trouble than you're worth."

He bows to her. "And now, my dear, I must bid you good night. I have had an exhausting day, apologizing to the neighbors for your crudeness."

He walks to the door. Lucy stares after him. If there are any thoughts at all behind her eyes, they do not register on her face; she moves toward him swiftly, silent, snatching up the ivory-handled knife from her dirty plate as she goes. His hand is on the doorknob; he does not hear her come up behind him, to wrap one strong arm around his throat, and with the other drive the knife low into his side with all her strength, ripping upward as she thrusts.

He shrieks, eyes bulging, clutching at the arm squeezing his throat, staggering and thrashing, shrieks and shrieks again as she wrenches up and up, the knife buried to the hilt in his side, until the blade snaps and she flings away the ivory haft. Still screaming, he lurches wildly about the room dragging Lucy with him, smashing into walls and furniture, frantic to dislodge the demon on his back, but she clings to him, panting, wordless; her free hand—the one that had wielded the knife—bloody and groping for his eyes beneath his spectacles.

The door bursts open—the servants, brought on the run by the noise of the struggle—and five pairs of hands drag the murderess from her victim's back; three hold her down while two servants lug their master out and drag him to his room. She fights them all, still silent, too intent on killing to waste her breath on words, legs and fists swinging, flailing—now the dressing table crashes to the floor, scattering chaos everywhere, the cheval glass bursts into a rain of glittering shards—and the servants tumble out the door, battered and torn, thrusting her back into the cage of her room like a wounded animal, turning the lock, imprisoning her inside.

Chadwick lies on his bed, dying, his face shiny with sweat from the agony of the blade still buried in his side. His eyes, unfocused, stare up at the ceiling; he breathes heavily, chest laboring, a thin line of blood trickling from the corner of his mouth. One servant has rushed to summon the doctor; the rest stand or kneel around his bed, praying, weeping, or both; the cook wipes his face with a cloth dipped in cool water.

From Lucy's room comes the sound of crashing, ripping and tearing, and fearsome screams. The door shudders as she pounds at it with her fists, and kicks at it, but the wood is solid, and the lock holds firm. The servants pay her no mind . . . she is a madwoman, and roars and shrieks are what one expects in an asylum. They close the door to Chadwick's room, muffling the sound of Lucy's cries.

The deathwatch continues. Twice Chadwick stirs on his bed and tries to reach behind, to pull the knife from his body; but any movement is agony, and his shrieks drown out Lucy's before he subsides once more, wet with sweat, his mouth filled with blood. The hammering from the madwoman's room is louder now, her shrieks frantic. The servants stop their ears, ignoring her cries. Let her rage and howl! Look at what she has done! Let her tear herself to pieces in her frenzy!

It is no wonder that they do not hear the pounding on the front door. It is not until the shouts from outside the house mingle with the pounding and the sound of firebells coming closer that they look up and stir themselves. John, the footman, throws open the window and thrusts his head out . . .

A large crowd has gathered below, frantic faces turned up, arms raised, pointing, and as he appears a great roar goes up. "Get out!" rises from a hundred throats. "Get out! Fire! Fire!" The footman pulls back, appalled, rushes to the door, flings it open.

The hallway, landing, and staircase are filled with smoke that seeps and curls from around Lucy's door. A quick foray onto the stairs proves the ground floor relatively clear, and the panicked servants form a makeshift litter of blankets, transfer Chadwick to it—his shrieks, as they lift him, can be heard in the street below—and carry him, as tenderly as can be, out of the burning house to the safety of the pavement across the street, to wait for the doctor who will come too late.

Chadwick's lips move. John lowers his head—it is almost impossible to hear in that incredible din—and puts his ear to the dying man's mouth.

"Safe," Chadwick whispers, looking up at his house—clouds of red-lit smoke roll above it, pouring from the back. "Safe, safe . . ."

"Yes, sir," the servant starts to say, unabashed tears running down his face. "You are safe." And he looks down at Chadwick, just in time to see his eyes glaze over.

THE BLAZE, it seems, is confined to the back of the house. Even now the fire engines are crowding into the mews that run behind, and

Ferruccio Cirri sits at his window, the best box in the house, and watches the last act of the tragedy with unabashed tears running down his face.

He had been there when the curtain rose . . . had watched the pantomime confrontation between the fat one and the old man, had seen her rush after him, to attack him from behind—he had applauded at first, thinking he watched a farce—then seen the room wrecked as they struggled, and the servants poured in to rescue one and lock the other in. But as they shoved her back inside he had seen what no one else had: the small cloud of smoke that burst into bright flame as some torn hanging, fallen too near the grate, had ignited . . . and the swift blaze had spread from wall to wall across the jumbled, littered floor, engulfing the bed, roaring up the curtains.

He had raced downstairs, rung the fire alarm, summoning help. She had been at her door . . . he had seen her, through the flames, flinging herself against it, kicking, pounding, before he ran down to sound the alarm. He had run to the front of the house, then, hammered at the door, alerted those in the neighboring houses before returning to his room, certain that someone would have heard her by that time, would have freed her from the inferno . . .

But she was still there—oh! God!, she was there!—at the window, now, eyes mad with terror, shrieking out into the night, stretching out her arms to him, and he had to watch her die because he could not get at her, because even if he could get over the fence, could climb up there, he could never get in her windows, past the bars, the iron bars . . .

Chapter Thirty-nine

MAURICE GRAU'S ASSISTANT flushes slightly as he rises from behind his desk in the outer office. He is a young man of both competence and quick intelligence, both of which are critical when one must deal daily with a vast assortment of conductors, agents, board members and their wives, managers, salesmen, music critics, and singers, male and female, of assorted amounts of temperament and at various stages of renown, either growing or fading . . . but he nevertheless wipes his hand on his trousers before extending it to the man who has just entered.

He recognizes Alfieri, of course—Mr. Grau would hardly have hired him were he not a fervent devotee of the opera—but he has never met the great man before, and he stammers slightly as he greets him, his little prepared speech forgotten in the suddenness of the moment.

Alfieri smiles at him—the youngster reminds him of Stafford, only more grave by virtue of having greater responsibilities—and obligingly takes a seat while the assistant disappears into the inner sanctum, to let Mr. Grau know that his ten o'clock appointment has arrived, prompt to the minute.

While he waits Alfieri reaches into his coat and touches the envelope that rests above his heart. They had had their party last night, celebrated Clara's birthday, said their official good-byes, toasted their friendships with champagne. He feels strange today, oddly detached from anything having to do with his reason for being here; his thoughts are with Clara, already waiting for him aboard the ship. He will make his interview with Grau as short as courtesy will allow.

The impresario emerges from his office, all smiles and *bel rispetto,* to thank Maestro Alfieri for calling upon him so soon after commencing rehearsals—"by rights, of course, maestro, I should be calling upon you."

"Ah," says Alfieri, looking around him appreciatively, "but my dressing room is a poor place to entertain." The office of the general manager is large and its appointments wonderfully tasteful, as befits the steward of New York's premier cultural establishment, but without being ostentatious . . . as befits the office of a man whose responsibility it is, above all, to run a profitable organization.

Yes, Alfieri would love coffee—he knows that here, at least, he will be served true Italian coffee, not the poor, weak brew wrongly called by that name in America—and the two men discuss their mutual passion, opera, as they wait, and particularly the fortunes of the Metropolitan Opera House.

"You had a great triumph in Philadelphia," Grau says. "I am glad for you, maestro, but sad for the poor Metropolitan."

"It is a triumph I could easily have done without," Alfieri replies. "My time there . . ." He shakes his head.

"But the *Manon Lescaut* . . . so wonderfully received!"

"That was gratifying, yes. But my wife's illness robbed it of much of its joy."

Grau's face grows solemn. "Yes, of course," he says. "I was so caught up in the success of the work itself that I did not think . . . please forgive me. How is she now? Better, I sincerely trust."

"That's just what I've come to you to speak of, Mr. Grau—"

There is a knock at the door; the coffee is brought in, poured, served, and conversation ceases for the duration. The door closes again behind the departing waiter. Grau takes a sip of his coffee—true Italian coffee—puts down his cup and folds his hands before him, waiting for Alfieri to begin.

"You and I have been busy on different continents, Mr. Grau, although we are players in the same game. One of the reasons I agreed to come to New York was because of your reputation. It would be foolish for me to pretend that mine was not known to you as well." He hesitates and smiles. "And not just for singing. But so much has changed since my arrival here. I will be grateful to you always for that alone . . . I would never have met my wife had you not invited me here."

Grau listens silently, unable to fathom where the tenor is leading him.

"And now that I am a married man, my life can never be the same. That is what I am here to tell you, and you are the first to know it, as is only right—"

There is a rapid knocking at the door, loud and impatient. Both men look toward the interruption. The knocking begins again.

"Excuse me, please, Maestro Alfieri," Grau says, clearly annoyed, "while I see what the matter is. I gave strict instructions that we were not to be disturbed."

But the door opens before he reaches it, revealing Grau's assistant, with Stafford Dyckman hovering over his shoulder, an indescribable look upon his face.

At the sight of him Alfieri is at the door, pale, fearing some new horror, some unforeseen disaster. "What is it? What's happened?"

"I must speak with you," Dyckman says, gripping his wrist. His hand is trembling. "Mr. Grau, forgive my intrusion, but I must have five minutes alone with Maestro Alfieri. Is there somewhere?"

Grau, who knows Dyckman vaguely, nods in amazement at this sudden disturbance and shows them into a small office adjacent to his own. As the door closes behind them Alfieri grabs Dyckman's arm. "For God's sake, what's happened? Tell me!"

"Mario, have you given him the resignation? *Have you?*"

"No, why? What—"

"Daniel sent me." Dyckman is shaking visibly. "We were on the way to the ship, to stay with Clara until you came, when he got the news. He is finding out as much as he can; Alice has gone to tell Clara. He sent me to tell you, to stop you if I could."

"Heard *what*? Tell me *what*? Stafford, as God is my witness—"

"Mario, he's dead." The young man laughs shrilly; there are tears in his eyes. "Chadwick is dead."

The words are only sounds in a dream; they carry no meaning. "Dead . . ."

"Yes, dead! Thaddeus Chadwick is dead. Lucy Pratt killed him. She's dead too; there was a fire . . ."

Alfieri says nothing, merely shuts his eyes.

"Mario, did you hear what I said? Chadwick—"

"Yes . . . yes, I heard . . . yes." He gropes for a chair and sits, trying to make sense of what he has just heard. They are empty words still. If Alfieri feels anything at all it is shock, and even pain: he has readied himself for oblivion and started toward it, gaining momentum every day, and his downward rush into the void has suddenly been halted, like colliding with a wall. To stagger to his feet now requires more strength than he has left.

"Aren't you happy?" Dyckman stares at him, frantic at his indifference.

"Happy?" He raises his head. A man who has stood looking into his open grave must have time, must step back from the edge before he can understand that he has been allowed to live. "I must be, mustn't I? Yes . . . I am sure I am." He sees the expression on Dyckman's face. "Am I disappointing you again? Dear Stafford . . . you have picked a poor idol, I'm afraid. First I run away, and now I cannot even cheer my enemy's death."

"Mario, I never . . ."

But little by little he is beginning to feel again . . . like regaining one's senses after a blow to the head. And he is still alive—breathing, and lighter now, the stone that he had not even known was there rolled away from his chest. *"Ragazzo,"* he says gently, "how is it that, after all these years, you never know when I tease you?" He rises to his feet.

"I must get back to Mr. Grau . . . he is a busy man, Stafford, and I would not take up too much of his time. You are going now to the boat? You will see Clara?"

Dyckman nods.

"Good. Then give her this for me, with all my love. Tell her it is a present for our child." He takes the envelope from his breast pocket, tears it in half, then in half again, places the pieces in Dyckman's hand and closes his fingers over them. "I'll come to her as soon as I can."

Dyckman rises to leave, his eyes shining. Alfieri stops him at the door.

"Stafford?" The young man turns around. *"Mille grazie, caro amico. Per tutti."*

"Is everything well?" Grau asks when the two of them are face-to-face in his office once more. His concern is very real, considering what the opera house has riding on this man. "Nothing serious, I hope? No problem with your wife's health?"

"No," Alfieri says, "thank God. Nothing serious. Stafford sometimes is overly excitable." Alfieri shrugs and smiles. "The drama of youth. But as for my wife's health . . ." He laughs suddenly, a deep, exultant laugh, and leans back in his chair with the air of a man who owns the whole world.

"My wife's health . . . that was what I was about to speak of when we were so suddenly interrupted. Oh, no! . . . Did you think my news was going to be bad? My apologies, certainly! No, only the gladdest of glad tidings, today. Clara is well. And I? I think, Mr. Grau, that I may truly be the happiest man in the world. You would think that no one had ever been a father before. We are expecting, you see, and the baby will arrive, or so we believe, just at the end of the season . . . well, of course we wanted you to be the first to know . . ."

Epilogue

As a topic of conversation, nothing bests death. And for sheer, unadulterated enthrallment, nothing surpasses the violent endings of people one knows. Thaddeus Chadwick's murder at the hands of Lucy Pratt, and her death in the flames of his house, were the only subjects discussed in New York for at least a fortnight following the horrible events.

Such a bright, open, cheerful countenance Lucy had had! Such rare charm she had showed! Neither Chadwick's servants, closely questioned by their master's friends and acquaintances, nor the authorities investigating the tragedies were able to determine any clear reason for her murderous attack, or for the insane rage that had ignited the fatal blaze. Why she had turned upon the man to whom she had seemed so devoted would remain a mystery: a gruesomely delectable itch in society's side, to be happily scratched for years to come.

But there was more, and better, still to be discovered.

On the morning of Tuesday, November the sixth, a little more than three weeks after the deaths in Washington Square, workmen had broken into a locked iron safe that had been discovered within the charred walls of the room in which Lucy Pratt had died. Present at the opening, in addition to the workmen, were a veritable skulk of lawyers, all of whom expected, in one way or another, to profit from the Chadwick estate, and for whom the contents of the safe were, therefore, of the most crucial interest.

The safe itself was located in what had been the very back of a very small cupboard. It had undoubtedly been there a long while, as no one— outside of Mr. Chadwick—seemed to have known of its existence . . . except for a workman who, during the renovations that had transformed the room from a bachelor's chamber into a young lady's boudoir, had built a false front for it and papered it over, so that during Lucy Pratt's residence it had been entirely undetectable.

But however long the safe had been there, it had served its purpose well. Having gone through fire and emerged unscathed, it had preserved its contents for the eager eyes of the men gathered around, to wit: twenty thousand dollars of ready money in bills of small denomination and gold coin; a carefully preserved and wonderfully detailed daguerre-otype of a young matron to whom those who had known the late Mr. Chadwick noted a marked resemblance . . .

And—to the incredulity of the attorneys who gaped as it was pulled from the safe as if it were an exotic relic from some long-lost pharaoh's tomb—an innocuous looking long parchment envelope, bearing the words "The Last Will and Testament of Henry Ogden Slade."

With more than a dozen lawyers to witness its emergence into the light, there was no chance of the document disappearing. It was shortly delivered over to probate, where it was closely examined and found to be properly signed and witnessed . . . and to be more recent by some twenty-five years than the will Thaddeus Chadwick had opened and read in the library of Slade's own mansion only seven months before.

Less than a week later, on Monday, November the twelfth, a small deputation from New York's legal establishment, including two of its most illustrious judges and a quietly triumphant Daniel Buchan, called upon Clara Adler Alfieri. Her husband, understandably, was not at home to help her receive her unexpected guests, his presence being required at the Metropolitan Opera House, where in one week to the day he would be opening the season. And so Mario Alfieri did not officially learn, until he returned for dinner that evening, that in the space of a single afternoon his wife had come into possession of thirty-five million dollars and a forty-two room mansion on Gramercy Park, and was now the richest woman, in her own right, in New York City.

The only, and charmingly modest, reaction of Mrs. Alfieri to her stunning turn of fortune was the purchase of a carriage and horses, and the addition to her household of a lavishly moustachioed young driver, from Maestro Alfieri's homeland, who winked shamelessly at pretty women as he went past. The only, and inevitable, reaction of the beau monde to the emergence of this new millionairess—whom Slade, in his will, had acknowledged as his only, and dearly loved, child—was to rally around . . . as solid in their support of her as they would be of any newly discovered Cinderella upon whom the glass slipper of immense wealth had suddenly, and miraculously, been fitted.

There was no doubt but that it would suit her little foot. From Mrs. Astor on down, everyone was of the opinion that they had always liked the girl and never seen enough of her. Many remembered that they had told her father—although they had thought him only her guardian then—that such a delightful young woman should not be kept hidden away, but should be brought more into society. Still others discussed in great detail the remarkable resemblance between father and daughter that they had always claimed to see—hadn't Mrs. Bradley Martin been saying just that to Mrs. Paran Stevens mere days before dear Mr. Slade's death?—and could not understand why so few others had had either the acuity or the wisdom to see the same.

How pleased they were that she had come into her own at last, and was to be recognized by all the world for the bright and charming creature that she was! As for her marriage to her Prince Charming of a husband, why, that was quite something out of a fairy tale. The "happily ever after" to this particular story, needless to say, was the news of Mrs. Alfieri's interesting condition, which Maurice Grau, first recipient of the information, and well aware of its potential effect on an already deluged ticket office, had immediately announced to the public.

Now, birth is *not* a comfortable topic. While clearly indispensable for the continuation of life, it is, nevertheless, awkward to discuss. Babies themselves are joyous innocents, of course; small cherubs who are as close as we shall ever get, here below, to the bright tenants of heaven. But the means by which babies come to be is best left alone, a subject scrupulously to be avoided in polite conversation . . . to the extent that anyone not already familiar with the provenance of infants might actually believe that parents in refined society have absolutely nothing to do with the creation of their own progeny, but merely wake one morning to find babies in their nurseries, fully formed, as though ordered to specification from some great, celestial emporium.

Clara's new well-wishers discussed her condition with the usual indirection reserved for such occasions: conversations about it focused entirely upon the coming blessed event, which a reliable source— namely the proud father-to-be—predicted would take place about May, and not at all upon the father-to-be's previously much-discussed skill at doing precisely what is necessary to bring such an event about.

It was universally agreed that all this felicity could only be attributed to New York's first-rate standing in the Almighty's sight. The city now had the hand that trumped all others, the thumb of thumbs to stick right in the eye of Philadelphia's pretensions. Mrs. Mario Alfieri might have collapsed twice in the City of Brotherly Love, but the probable reason for those occasions was her impending motherhood . . . and anyone who could count to nine would know that the breathlessly awaited child of the world's most exalted tenor, and of his wife, the daughter of one of New York's oldest and wealthiest families, would be born *here*.

They had known it all along, of course; New York had known it all along. Mrs. Astor and all her court, skilled at assessing the true worth of a lady or a gentleman, had known all along just how it would be. No fools, they. The Adler girl was a princess raised among the ashes. As for the informality of her parents' ties . . . well, who among the elite did not have a skeleton or two rattling around in an ancestral closet? But quality will always out, and justice always wins in the end . . . if it did not, would any of them be where they were now? How grand life is for the deserving few!

Little remains to be said, except that some particularly obscene rumors about Clara Adler that Thaddeus Chadwick had tried to purvey shortly before his death—shocking, but no more so than the discovery of his utterly unsuspected wickedness—were promptly banished from New York's collective mind and forgotten. That the rumors had to be connected, in some way, with the concealment of Slade's will was clearly understood; but what the lawyer's intentions had been, and just how he had hoped to benefit from his crimes, were never ascertained. Those who had done business with his firm promptly took their affairs—all of which proved to be in perfect order—elsewhere; and those who had not, congratulated themselves on their amazing perspicacity in avoiding him in the first place; and in a perfect example of the good that an ill wind can blow, Daniel Buchan came in for a significant share of the transferred business, particularly once it became known that his firm handled all the affairs of that golden couple, Maestro and Madama Alfieri.

Of the Alfieris' happiness it is impossible to write. There were those who resented it, of course, wondering how some have all the luck in the world and never suffer or know pain—whose money makes money, whose good fortune breeds more good fortune; whose skies are always blue and whose lives are always sweet—but there will always be those who begrudge the bliss of others, and it is best to simply ignore them.

The Metropolitan Opera House opened its season, on the night of November the nineteenth, with a performance by Mario Alfieri that will surely rank among the century's greatest. And at the ball afterward, Mrs. Clara Adler Alfieri, gleaming in emeralds, clad in a froth of pearls and moonlight—the shining magnet of all eyes—waltzed up the dawn in her husband's arms.

About the Author

Paula Cohen is a native, and a lifelong resident, of Brooklyn, New York. A passionate Victorian for as long as she can remember, she has always known that she was born in the wrong century. Her other love, as readers can guess, is the opera. She lives in the Park Slope section of Brooklyn with her husband and their cat, Mouche. This is her first novel.